SIXTH COLUMN

Also by James Long

Hard News
Collateral Damage
Game Ten

SIXTH COLUMN

JAMES LONG

New York London Toronto Sydney Tokyo Singapore

First published in Great Britain by Simon & Schuster, 1995
First published by Pocket Books, 1996
An imprint of Simon & Schuster Ltd
A Viacom Company

Simon & Schuster Ltd
West Garden Place
Kendal Street
London W2 2AQ

Simon & Schuster of Australia Pty Ltd
Sydney

A CIP catalogue record for this book is available from the British Library.

ISBN 0-671-85105-5

Printed and bound in Great Britain by Caledonian International Book Manufacturing, Glasgow

For Sharne who stopped too early
and for Rodney who carries on.

CHAPTER ONE

Sweat was starting to run down the inside of Johnny's neck from his soaked hair. The balaclava he'd brought with him was intended for the Arctic, not a Mayfair mews house with the central heating up full blast. He looked at Clicker, bent over the safe, then rolled the wool up over his forehead and opened another drawer. There was a short crackle from the radio and his heart jumped. Clicker turned his head sharply, eyes and mouth rimmed clownlike in white against his black mask, listening, but nothing else came.

He couldn't see anything interesting in the last drawer. He cast around for something else and saw the end of the briefcase sticking out from behind an armchair. He moved towards it, opened it. Inside was a passport and a fat envelope. Pulling out the envelope, he flicked up the flap and saw inside a wad of currency, large denominations wrapped up in some sort of list.

'Yeah!' he said softly. Clicker turned, and he put a thumb up, tossed him the envelope which he pushed into his bag. At that moment there was a noise outside. Somewhere below and downstairs – and with a rattle of sliding locks that was the overture to disaster, the front door opened.

Clicker recoiled from the safe door, rocking back on his heels, then stayed crouching, poised with one hand steadying himself on the ground, ready to leap. Johnny's brain turned to mush. He looked towards the door, heard the sound of two voices, one male, American, one female, English, moving up the stairs. They should both be American, he thought, and anyway, they shouldn't be there at all. He looked helplessly at the radio. Why hadn't Mac warned them? Clicker was gesturing violently at him, at his face, desperately miming something. He got it, pulled the balaclava down again. Clicker picked his tools up silently, put them in the bag. Johnny reached for the radio then it was too late for anything else.

The door opened and a light went on revealing a fat man in evening dress, pulling a giggling blonde girl by the hand. The pair stopped abruptly, the man's expression changing from drunken lust to frightened anger in a moment, then Clicker was moving, charging at the door, his shoulder taking the man in the chest throwing him backwards, his legs getting caught up with Clicker's so that they both somersaulted back across the landing. The top banister rail caught Clicker a blow across the neck, dropping him, while the fat man flipped over Clicker's flailing legs and careered on his back, head-first down the stairs. His yell was cut off by a cracking thump as his head reached the bottom and he lay still, chin forced hard into his chest by the weight of his body pressing down.

The girl's screams were stopping Johnny thinking.

'Out,' yelled Clicker, picking himself up. He took the stairs three at a time, hurdled the fat man's body and was gone. Johnny looked back at the girl for a moment, wishing she'd stop, and could think of no other course but to follow. Out of the door, he turned left for the street corner where Mac and the car were waiting. He was a second too slow at taking in the van parked outboard of the car, blocking it in and the profile of the uniform caps on the heads of the two men standing by Mac's door in the darkness. They were looking in his direction hearing the screams and as he turned they shouted and started to run.

Fear came over him, not disabling him but lending him speed he'd forgotten he had. This wasn't in the script. It should have been a doddle. Down Park Street, the pavement empty, he was holding them off. Over the pounding shock of his feet on the stones and the rising thud of his blood in his ears he heard a whistle and a vague feeling of surprise came over him that they still used such things.

It was the personal radio that got him, though. The second

policeman dropped back to call in some help and halfway down Culross Street, his breath starting to go, they seemed to come at him from all directions. He was slowing down to give up when an over-zealous PC with a lot of club rugby behind him tackled him hard.

Three of them piled him into the van, rough despite his lack of resistance. The police radio was crackling with messages.

'What's your name, then?' shouted a sergeant in his ear. Johnny kept his silence. That was the thing to do, keep quiet. Say nothing. Don't let them hear the sound of your voice.

'We're bringing him in,' said the driver into the mike. 'No sign of the other one. Over.'

The speaker squawked, 'All units. Upper Brook Street area, blue Cavalier, number starts G Golf four niner three. Stop and apprehend with care.'

That's Mac, thought Johnny. The bastard must have got clear when they were chasing me. Lot of use he was. Then he realized the police must have stopped in the first place to check Mac out, must have been standing there right by him so he couldn't pass on the warning. What about Clicker, he wondered, and more to the point, what about me?

They were taking it oh so seriously at the police station. He was surrounded by men on the way in, bundled into an interview-room, cautioned and then confronted by a burly plain clothes man who set the tapes rolling.

'Detective Sergeant Frankland interviewing suspect. No name given. 10.20 p.m., June 18th,' the man said and looked hard at him. 'All right, let's start with your name.'

Johnny didn't meet his gaze, just sat staring down at the table wondering how everything had got quite so messy.

'Listen to me,' said Frankland. 'The man you pushed down the stairs. He's snuffed it. Skull and neck. So that puts you in major trouble, right? If you want any kind of break, you'd better start talking, and we'll begin by you telling me who you are and who your mate in the car might be.'

It was all new to Johnny. He'd imagined scenes like this before, even come close on a couple of occasions when jobs had gone wrong, but this was the first time it had ever been for real. Clicker and Mac, he thought. Give them time. Mouth shut, he kept saying to himself, keep your mouth shut.

Half an hour passed in one-way pointless interrogation before the door opened. The detective looked round as a man in chief inspector's uniform came in looking extremely angry.

'Jim, a word outside,' the man said.

The detective turned the tape off. A uniformed constable came in and stood by the door. Johnny avoided his gaze. Ten minutes went by then the Chief Inspector came back in.

He jerked his head and the PC left. He paced up and down the room, swung sharply on his heel and stared at Johnny. 'Look,' he said, 'I don't like this one little bit. If it was down to me, I'd teach you a bloody good lesson. You're just like anyone else, whoever the hell you are. You break the law, it stays broken.' His voice and his colour were both rising. 'Unfortunately, it's not bloody well down to me, is it? I don't have a choice, so that means you get to go.'

A vast sense of relief swept over Johnny. The Chief Inspector stared at him with a face like the prelude to a punch. 'There's a car down in the garage. Just get the fuck out of here before I forget myself.'

John Aubrey de Hane Kay, junior officer in the Counter-Proliferation Directorate of Her Majesty's Security Service, more colloquially known as MI5, walked out, still without saying a word.

CHAPTER TWO

The relief didn't last long. The car waiting for him had one of the older drivers at the wheel, an ex-Met squad-car man who occasionally forgot that in this job discretion usually came before speed. For once he drove the car as if it were a hearse and he wasn't heading for Thames House. Both factors, Johnny realized, were bad signs.

'Bit of trouble then, Sir?' was all he said when Johnny got in and they settled in to their separate silences. They took the Mall to Horse Guards and then cut through to the back of Tothill Street, to a grimy, ancient office block in a courtyard. That spoke volumes. Johnny had sometimes used it for interviews during the interminable year he'd spent in the vetting section. It's the isolation ward, he thought glumly. They don't want me anywhere near Millbank.

He was shown down peeling corridors to a back room with cream paint and dusty venetian blinds, guarded by an old soldier at a desk in the ante-room. It made a disconcerting contrast to the modern smart-card protected electronic monitoring of Thames House. There were three of them already there, sitting in silence at the table, staring as he walked through the door. His director, the legal man and, as if to confirm that this was as bad as it could get, the Deputy DG Operations.

'Sit down, Kay,' said the Deputy DG, 'we've got a lot of damage to deal with, so no bullshit, right?'

'No. Of course not. What about the other two?'

His director looked harassed and cross. '*They* got clear,' she said, 'McDonald was able to drive off when the police ran after you, though he had to do a bit of pushing and shoving past their van. Tarling had the sense to keep his eyes open and go the other way when he saw them. What we want to know from you is how we wound up with a dead American on our hands. Maybe you would be kind enough just to run over the facts.'

Johnny took a deep breath. 'It should have been completely routine. We knew this man Clymer had made an approach to a Marconi development engineer. We knew from monitoring the cash transfers that he must have several more people on his shopping list. We got proper authorization to have a look when information from Monitoring told us he and his wife would be at Glyndebourne.' He saw his director flinch slightly at *proper*.

'Not him and his wife,' she said quickly, 'his wife and her sister. If you'd been a bit more thorough you would have known he was having an affair and you might just have guessed he'd use every excuse he could to get a few hours for his own ends. You might also have followed proper procedure and made sure your surveillance car was parked in a position where it wouldn't attract the attention of the police, instead of right outside the house of a rather important Saudi.'

Thanks a lot, Mac, thought Johnny bitterly. So much for delegation. Everybody did it, but he knew where the buck stopped officially and there was no way out of that one.

The Deputy DG was scribbling on his pad. He stopped and stared at Johnny from under lowered brows. 'A complete foul-up, I'd say,' he said with terrifying calmness. 'Leaving us with six policemen to sort out – for whom we'll have to concoct a rather unconvincing story – plus some unpleasantly hot phone calls already coming in from Grosvenor Square.'

Johnny wondered whether to say it and decided he had nothing to lose. 'I would like to stress it was an accident, sir. It was unfortunate that Clicker Tarling happened to collide—'

The Deputy DG stopped him in his tracks, 'Well planned operations don't have accidents, Kay, and field officers in charge of operations do not try to shift the blame to others on their team.'

Johnny left, to be driven home under suspension, followed

by the legal man with a long list of urgent actions to set in motion. The Deputy DG turned his attention to the Director. 'You should have been looking over his shoulder. I know he came out of the Wineglass incident well enough in the end but this rather points up the old theory that Wineglass was more luck than judgement.'

'Look, George,' said the Director, chancing the familiarity to try to get back to firm ground, 'you know we wouldn't have the little sod if it wasn't for his mother. I think it's time for a radical change.'

Lady Viola Kay was a legend in the office, on the hunting field, in the corridors of government and wherever else she impacted on her less forceful fellows. A brief marriage to a career diplomat had ended when passion was chased away by irreconcilable views of the world. 'The man turned into a bloody Communist' was her habitual way of describing her first husband's sympathetic approach to the final dismantling of Empire. The marriage left her with a son, John, an increasingly violent disregard of weak compromise and an entrée to the realms of the Secret State. The Cold War had been her private seventh heaven. Margaret Thatcher had been her ideal prime minister. The only politics were conviction politics. The protection of the State from external and internal dangers was the avowed purpose of the Security Service and she rose through its ranks propelled by a willingness to see those dangers where others might pause to wonder.

Her second husband, Sir Greville Kay, was as near a soul mate as she was likely to get while firmly maintaining the upper hand. He was the founder of a rapidly expanding chemicals empire, a man who (like his wife) was quite sure he knew what was best for others. She saw all kinds of benefits from a husband-and-wife team that straddled the border between the overt and covert means of government. Encouraged by her, he'd gone into politics, calling in his major gifts to successive election campaigns to be granted one of the safest seats in the Tory heartland. The two of them had watched the political assassination of Margaret Thatcher with outraged horror and hitched their wagon firmly to the New Right movement that expanded into her vacuum.

Lady Viola had eventually left the Service as part of her contribution to her husband's political career, to start off instead a small think-tank which provided him and his political circle with well-sourced information – and well-sourced it certainly was, because her contacts inside remained excellent. Hers was one of a number of organizations to profit from the general fear of redundancy which afflicted both the MIs, 5 and 6, in the first flush of post-Cold War relaxation. Jobs awaited those who were 'one of us' and they'd do well to remember that long before they switched employer.

It took very little time for her to learn exactly what had happened to her only child and Johnny was woken by loud knocking on his door just after seven thirty the next morning. He immediately knew who it was. The porter down in the lobby was meant to ring before he let anyone up the stairs to the flats. Johnny paid a large service charge for that privilege, but his mother had sorted the porters out to her satisfaction in the first week after he'd moved in and none of them dared stop her. He put on a dressing gown and let her in.

'You silly little shit.'

'Good morning, Mother.'

'Put the bloody kettle on. This is no time to be sulking in bed.'

She made him feel, as she always did, about thirteen years old. He looked at her and realized age was at last starting to catch up with her, too much make-up and exposure to expensive foreign sunshine. For all that, she could have passed for no more than fifty – tall, thin to the point of boniness, any extra flesh burnt off by the constant restless furies she directed against the threats she perceived to her England.

She turned a kitchen chair round and sat astride it like a horse. 'You've had it, Johnno, you do know that?'

'I'm suspended, Mother. They'll investigate it then we'll see.'

She raised her eyes to the ceiling. 'God Almighty. You're so bloody naïve. They've already decided. It's Support Services for you. Bloody paper-clips job. Early retirement if you make it that far without taking to the bottle.'

He felt sick. If she said it, then that was the way it was. He could just imagine the phone call. She always knew far more about what was going on in the office than he did. He sat down heavily at the table.

'You could get out,' she said.

'Join your think-tank?'

She laughed cruelly. 'No, of course not. You haven't got the brains.'

'Well thank you,' he said.

'Use what you've got,' she said, 'look for something that fits.'

'What, then?' he said, trying to keep a dignified note in his voice. 'The City? It's not easy with a great big gap in your CV, you know.'

She looked at him hard. 'I have some friends. I'll get them to call you. One condition, though.'

'What?'

'Don't screw it up, and get rid of that ghastly little girl Marge or whatever she's called. She'll do you no good at all.'

That's two conditions, he thought, not one, and it was Marsha not Marge. Anyway Marsha had gone, taking her CDs and her fluffy animals with her, transferred to another part of the office so they wouldn't have to meet, but he didn't want to admit that.

'That's my business, Mother,' he said levelly, but she was already going, not even bothering to contradict the self-evident fallacy.

The phone call came after twenty-four hours spent in the gloom of take-aways, videos and frequently discarded books.

'Johnny Kay?'

'Yes.'

'Ivor Sibley. I know your mother. She suggested I call.'

'Oh right.' Sibley, he thought, I remember that name. Surely he was a director? Left the office soon after I joined. Is that the right one?

'Would you care to meet?'
'Well . . . I suppose so.'
'I heard the office is giving you a hard time.'
'Really?'
The other man chuckled. 'I've got something that would interest you far more. What about Browns Hotel, half past twelve.'
'Fine.'
'Ask at the desk.'
Filling the time, Johnny turned on Radio Four and got *Any Questions*. Someone with what his mother always called a proper accent was halfway through an answer.
'. . . nothing to do with them at all. If a landowner doesn't want people on his land, he has a perfect right to have that enforced. These hunt saboteurs don't give a hang about foxes. They just want to stop a traditional country spectacle. It's high time trespass was completely criminalized. No use going halfway. Should have happened years ago.'
There was a small burst of applause and a few voices from the audience were raised in dissent. Jonathan Dimbleby moved it on to the next speaker. 'Sir Michael?'
The well known voice of one of the country's favourite moderates eased into action. 'Well, I have to say I'm very worried by this. It may not suit every landowner but there's a long tradition in this country, stretching back centuries, that people are free to walk through our countryside so long as they don't do any damage and that, I think, is a right we should very much miss . . .' A burst of loud clapping interrupted whatever he had been going to say next, but Johnny's finger, propelled by years of loathing inspired by violent matriarchal conditioning, was already on the off button. Sir Michael Parry, former British Ambassador in Paris, Bonn and Washington, scholar, aesthete, liberal supporter of just causes, Johnny's father, was a voice that was not to be heard.

Browns Hotel is well suited for the rich and private. Cheapskates might meet over coffee in the lobby but Ivor Sibley had a suite. Johnny was shown up to it and there was an array of smoked salmon sandwiches waiting on the table. He recognized Sibley. The only things that had changed were his girth and the quality of his suit, both of which had increased considerably.

'Viola's told me all about it,' said Sibley when they'd shaken hands. 'Bloody annoying from your point of view. Sounds to me as though you were in the right.'

Johnny, as ever with someone who was clearly in his mother's confidence but outside the office circle, didn't know quite how much to say so he played it safe. 'These things happen.'

Sibley wasn't to be deflected. 'It's no damn good playing the game the Yanks' way over proliferation. You weren't to know this Clymer feller had their blessing, were you?'

Good God, thought Johnny, he really does know the whole thing.

Sibley gave a slight smile, seeing his reaction, and went on. 'It's like this, Johnny. There's people like you, doing your level best to stop weapons systems spreading into the wrong hands, lumps of bloody weapons-grade plutonium being traded round the world as if they were Red Army cap badges, and then there's other people who should be on the same side doing their level best to nobble you all the bloody way.' He looked enquiringly at him. 'D'you know what anti-proliferation means to the Yanks?'

There was no danger that Sibley wasn't about to tell him so Johnny kept silent.

'Commercial advantage, that's what. Commercial advantage, backed up with a very big stick. It means if anyone's going to sell big weapons system it's going to be the good old US of A. The wars of the future are going to be commercial wars, Johnny, and you fell foul of a preliminary skirmish. You thought friend Clymer was in it for himself. Easy mistake to make.'

'Very interesting.'

'Very discreet reaction, young Johnny. No need. Your friends are my friends.'

'You left the office a few years ago, didn't you?'

'Does one ever really leave? Did your mother?'

'Well, yes. She did actually.'

'Doesn't she still know what's going on, maybe before you do?'

Johnny chose not to answer that one.

Sibley took a sandwich, poured Muscadet into their glasses and chewed for a while, smiling.

'Look,' he said, just as Johnny was about to take a mouthful of his own sandwich, 'would you like a job?'

'I've already got one.'

Sibley just took another bite and raised his eyebrows. Johnny, untouched sandwich still in his hand, took a little step towards the bait.

'What sort of job?'

'Not that different from the one you've got now. Private sector, though.'

'You mean a security firm?'

Sibley laughed loudly, 'Group Four, you mean? Certainly not. Serious stuff. Your mother knows us well.' He lowered his voice and leaned forward confidingly. 'We have a *lot* of support. You wouldn't notice much difference in the resources we can call on except maybe that there are fewer constraints. Private sector salaries too. I could give you a list of a dozen people you'd remember from the office who've come our way, plus another dozen from SIS.'

Johnny felt only deep uncertainty. 'I'm not sure I'm in quite the hole you think I am, Mr Sibley.'

'Make it Ivor, for Heaven's sake. We're not stuffy. And you are, you know – in the hole I mean. Even if you weren't, you're in a shrinking industry. I mean it was very clever of Stella to get the anti-Irish role or Five would have lost half its staff now you don't have to snoop on every Russki in London. Couldn't last. Noble efforts to screw up the Anglo-Irish peace talks, but you—'

'Oh come on,' Johnny interjected, 'you can't believe that the office—'

Sibley cut him off with a laugh. 'You're not that wet behind the ears, surely, laddie? Preserving jobs comes first. Where's Five going to find a new role if the Micks really stop killing each other? Redundancies, that's what that means, and if you're pushing paper-clips in admin, you'll be the first.'

Johnny finally took a bite of smoked salmon and chewed, thinking, knowing he was under careful scrutiny. 'Who owns this outfit of yours?'

Sibley gave him a knowing look. 'People you'd approve of.'

'Who?'

'I suppose you'll only check at Companies House if I don't tell you. Lord Crane's a director. So's Ethan Margrave.'

Crane was a former defence minister. Ethan Margrave was a Tory grandee, on the board of a group of key defence companies.

'Sir Max Calstock is the chairman. I expect you know him,' Sibley added with the air of one administering the *coup de grâce*.

'My mother does,' said Johnny, remembering a man with a quiet voice and visionary eyes. Calstock was a man who'd dropped out of the public gaze. He'd served in some Conservative government of long ago. Which one? Heath's? He couldn't remember. Then he'd gone quiet, moved into the background, where his name just surfaced from time to time in the occasional bubble rising from activity down there on the seabed.

'What's your organization called?' he said in the end.

'Well, on the brass plate it's Baron, Hockley Associates, but we have our own pet name. You've probably heard it. It's becoming pretty universal now.'

'And that is?'

Sibley smiled. 'MI7,' he said.

CHAPTER THREE

In Johnny Kay's circle of acquaintances, and that is all they tended to be, a lot of the conversations that took place behind his back would start 'The trouble with Johnny is . . .' although very few of them ever came to the same conclusion. There was something about him that didn't quite add up for others occupying the establishment world of traditional values in which he had always lived.

On one level it seemed to be about timing. Johnny was usually a heartbeat behind his peers in his expressions of opinion. The *certainties* which propelled them seemed less *certain* for him. It wasn't that he didn't come to the same conclusion. Whether the subject was Socialism, the perfidy of Brussels, the absolute need to end capital taxation completely or the unfairness of forcing those with private health insurance to contribute to the NHS, he was always eventually on the same side but not without a brief internal hiccup each time. There was generally no other conclusion within his range of experience he could come to, but he was left feeling there was somehow a whole range of data he was ignoring. He kept all that very much to himself and those around him saw this apparent slowness to concur simply as a sign of slight stupidity.

There was even a physical side to Johnny's inability to fit precisely into the ready-made background constructed so firmly for him by his mother. Johnny's demeanour, language and leisure activities were robust and privileged, Henley, Goodwood and Twickenham. He could fly and had bought a share in a light plane but saw it mostly as an easy means of getting to

French or Irish racecourses in congenial company. He had always pushed himself, testing himself in competitive sport, preferably with a hard physical side. His face however was at odds with that. Under wavy dark hair it was almost elfin, finely sculptured with a feminine touch, miraculously undamaged by the potential ravages of weekend rugger.

There were things he should have liked, indeed strived to like, about that life which, try as he might, he simply couldn't – so, as he approached thirty, he seemed unable to get beyond superficialities with the Sloane girls in the office and in his social circle. The only girls for whom he felt genuine attraction were somehow unsuitable and had to be kept apart from the rest of his life. None of them lasted long. He took to reading in depth for the first time since school, but kept that a secret too. Poetry and esoteric religions accounted for a growing part of the untidy pile beside his bed.

Even to himself, Johnny didn't quite add up. To find himself transplanted so abruptly from something he had seen as an inevitable and quite exciting career into the complete unknown of Ivor Sibley's private enterprise kept a small froth of disquiet foaming away just under his ribcage.

The cab dropped Johnny at the side of the Tate Gallery and he walked through to John Islip Street. He had to ring the bell twice but then the lock buzzed open without any of the expected metallic interrogation via the little speaker. The first day of his new job – the first stake-out and the first major moment of unease. That wasn't the way it was done in the office. Inside, the hall was furnished in discount store repro. Out of habit, he glanced at the names on the mail stacked on the cabriole legged occasional table without seeing any that he recognized then he climbed the stairs to the second floor past a Renoir print no longer completely laminated to its supporting chipboard. He tapped at the door of the flat and it was opened by a burly blond man who looked too young for his blazer and Guards tie. He remembered the face. 'Johnny Kay,' he said.

'Glad you're with us, Johnny. Adam Finberg. We were on that Coleraine thing together.'

Shush, he thought, not here on the landing. 'Yes, of course,' he said.

Finberg stepped back to let him in and closed the door. It was a sitting-room with big sash-windows looking out over the street to the houses opposite, cluttered with all the usual paraphernalia of a stake-out. Tables, chairs and a sofa had been pushed to the walls to clear space for the tripod in the middle of the field of vision. Johnny was still worrying about the unguarded response to the doorbell. He glanced down at the street to reassure himself that perhaps Finberg had been on the alert but the pavement just below was obscured by the projections of the architecture.

'Did you see me coming?' he asked casually, reviewing his movements to be certain he had been on this side of the road.

'No, why?' said Finberg, then laughed dismissively. 'Relax, Johnny. You're marching to the beat of a different drum now. Who else could you have been?' The voice went with the clothes, clubland.

'So, tell me the story,' said Johnny.

'Should be quite fun. The flat's one floor down, diagonal right. Green curtains. You see it?'

He peered across the road. 'Got it.'

'There's no one there at the moment. Chummy's due in about an hour. Fifi L'Amour's gone out shopping. Probably run out of baby oil or instant whip or something. You can see the bed from here and I went in and jinxed the curtain rail, bent the runner a bit when she went out so either they take the risk or chummy has to take a cold shower.'

'Or they don't do it on the bed.'

'Oh, but that wouldn't be the same, Johnny boy. The bed's got the leather straps and the handcuffs on it.'

'Who is he?'

'Ansell? Thought you'd know. Member for somewhere unpronounceable on the Welsh border.'

'Oh, yes, that one. Why are we doing it?'

Finberg looked at him in surprise. 'Because we're getting bloody well paid. Why else?'

'No, I meant, who for? I mean it's not just routine, is it?

The office does those all the time. Members' members, we called it.'

Finberg shrugged. 'So, what's the difference?'

'Well, it's pretty obvious, isn't it? That's protective surveillance. Makes sure we know if they're getting into hot water. In case they open themselves up to blackmail.'

Finberg laughed rudely. 'Come on. It's information, that's all. Information to be used to swing things. You're not a Boy Scout and you never were.'

That stung him a bit. He didn't want to sound naïve. A lot of his energy had always been expended on trying not to sound naive. 'I just wondered who wants to know.'

'If it makes you feel any better, for all I know we might be subcontracting for the office. You do know you're working for Calstock, don't you?'

'Of course I do.'

'So what's the problem? He's just the unelected part of the government. That means he's always in power, right? By the way, did Ivor tell you about the brown envelopes?'

'What brown envelopes?'

'Thought not. Silly bugger always leaves out the best bits. Came as a surprise to me too. Thing is, old boy, only two thirds of your pay goes into the bank. You get the rest in cash. Brown envelope job, marked "Unquantified Expenses". Pretty sound practice that, I reckon.'

'I haven't really heard much about anything yet. He told me to come straight here this morning, so I haven't even seen the place.'

'Asked, I'm sure, not told. Ivor likes to preserve a gentlemanly feeling. It's not a bad pad. Lots of space. Good area. Harrods is just round the corner. Nice bit of crumpet on the front desk instead of those wall-eyed human Rottweilers at Thames House. Secure car park down below, space for one and all. Bloody sight more relaxed than life at the old place, I can tell you.'

Johnny, looking sideways down the street, said, 'Is that her?'

It couldn't really be anyone else, he thought, unless John Islip Street was a secret centre for startlingly exotic Brazilian hookers with a taste for bouffant hair and low-cut Lycra tops.

'That's Fifi,' said Adam, and he crossed over to the table to flick switches on the equipment.

'What's she really called?'

'God knows. Sybil something, I think. It's written down in the log.'

They heard, clearly through their speaker, the sound of her key in the front door then her feet climbing the stairs and the door opening so loudly that Adam had to turn the volume down. It was only then that Johnny looked at the equipment closely for the first time and realized both that he knew it well and that it was odd that he should do so. It was state of the art surveillance hardware, the very same gear he'd used in the office, a product of the government scientific centre at Hanslope. The familiarity was disconcerting.

'I heard the story,' said Adam, attaching the Nikon to the big reflector telephoto.

'What story?' There was a touch of arrogance about him that went with the expensive clothes and it was already irritating Johnny.

'The Yank. Your wet job.'

'It wasn't a wet job. It was an accident and it wasn't me that knocked him down the stairs.'

Adam looked at him, weighing him up. 'Have it your own way. I wasn't complaining. The other one was you, though, Wineglass, wasn't it?'

Did everybody know about Wineglass?

'That was me.'

'Bloody good show. Everyone thought so.'

'Not everyone. There was a lot of trouble,' said Johnny, remembering the endless inquiry.

'Everyone worth asking. Sort of thing we should do more often, not leave it to the Hereford lads. Bloody brave, what you did. Not many would have grabbed the chance.'

Another little decision down the long trail of deception. It was no contest, really, so much easier to take the accolade and not try to insist on the less glamorous truth. Johnny just nodded and added another layer to the heavily varnished image of his past. Wineglass. Everyone knew the story but no one knew the story and for sure he wasn't going to tell this man what had *really* happened. Not now.

Finberg looked down to screw the lens to the tripod and the conversation was over.

The appointed time came and there was no sign of the man they expected. The girl appeared in the bedroom from time to time slipping clothes on and off with complete disregard for the open curtains. Johnny was just admiring her bronze breasts when his companion said, 'She's a bloke really, of course.'

'What?'

'Brazilian. Typical Rio number. Had the operation. Looks like it went well. I hope the bugger comes. I've got the day off tomorrow. Ivor said I'd have to stay on if this lot goes over. Pain in the bloody arse that would be.'

'Something important?'

'Invitation to hunt with the Quorn. Can't miss that.'

Johnny was silent and Finberg looked at him, trying to read his face. 'D'you hunt?'

'No.'

'Ride?'

'Oh yes. Sometimes.'

'Surprised you haven't ridden to hounds. Only riding worth a damn. Bloody boring just sitting on a horse. Never tried it?'

'Only once, when I was a lad. Didn't catch on.'

The phone rang in the girl's flat and they heard her answer it, could even hear the sound – though not the detail – of the other side of the conversation. Their target.

'Baby . . . Why not?' she asked plaintively. There was a buzzing rattle of explanation.

'Two then, OK, huwwy honeybun. I wai'. I have no clo' on.'

It wasn't quite true. They watched her as she sat on the bed and rolled a joint, then lay back, smoking with one hand and stroking herself with the other, which merited three quick frames of motor-driven Nikon.

Their own doorbell buzzed. 'Ah, good-oh,' said Finberg, 'lunch.'

Johnny stood back, watching, feeling his capacity for surprise being tested once again as the other man went downstairs and came back carrying a small wicker hamper.

Finberg undid it, taking out foil packets and plastic plates. 'God, Greek again,' he said, 'I wish Ivor wouldn't go for Greek. It's the only one I don't like.'

It was expensive Greek, a beautifully prepared meze with a half bottle of cold retsina.

Johnny gave up waiting for an explanation and explored the subject cautiously. 'Does this go with the job?'

'London stake-outs, yes, whenever possible. If it's a really long boring one you get a hamper from Fortnum's.' Finberg looked at him questioningly. 'You haven't really got the hang of this yet, have you? You're in the private sector now, Kay. Money no object and all that, at least for the sort of things we do.' He chewed, made a face, spat out an olive stone. 'Your mother hunts, I've seen her.'

'Yes.' Johnny froze, then put down the food in his hand. It came winging back to him, across the years, a clear, cutting memory of a cold day in the muddy edge of a field, a crumpled fox corpse, partly savaged, and the dogs being whipped off it. His mother with a fierce look of satisfaction, leading him closer by the hand and then the foul, acrid smell as the bleeding stumpy tail was pushed at him, into his face. Wet blood smearing on his face and the smooth, white powder of her face, red lipstick, bright eyes framed by the netted hair and the riding hat. 'Hold your bloody head still, Johnny. Oh, for God's sake, don't puke. It's the blooding, you stupid little boy. It's an honour. Take it like a man.' As so often, he'd embarrassed her in front of her friends.

His head began to ache as it usually did when the subject of his mother came up.

The target arrived at two sharp, just as they finished lunch. Ansell was almost running with pent-up sexual desire. Johnny recognized him, wondered vaguely why his peccadilloes mattered and to whom. He wasn't a minister, wasn't even likely to be one. Maybe he featured on some committee or other. Used as he was to not questioning the motives behind his instructions, he suppressed the doubts. The girl, back in her clothes now, made a token effort at closing the curtains but the bent rail prevented her and they could hear through the mike that it was an uneven struggle.

'Leave it, for God's sake. No one can see us up here. I want you now.'

'All righ'. Don' panic. I here,' she said. 'What you wan' do?'

'Same as before. You know.' He sounded unwilling to say the words.

Finberg clicked away with the camera, chortling as Ansell stripped and lay on the bed without touching her once. She bent to each corner in turn, pulling straps tight, then stood just on the edge of their line of vision, slowly peeling off her clothes to reveal herself in some kind of dark underwear.

'Leather,' said Finberg, 'love it.'

Without the telephoto to help, Johnny could only see vaguely what happened next but he soon had no regrets about that. She straddled the man on the bed, on her knees above him. Liquid splashing noises came through the mike and Ansell's groans of pleasure.

'You mucky little bugger,' said Finberg, keeping the camera going on its motor drive, film winding out of the big bulk magazine clipped to its back. 'Yuck. Must have huge laundry bills.'

Later, a van came to collect the equipment. Johnny took the film and the tapes to the office, in a square between Knightsbridge and the Brompton Road. A camera looked at him and the barrier into the car park lifted. He slotted his little Mazda sports car into a row of expensive toys, two Mercedes coupés, a hot BMW and a whole line of Discoveries. In the far corner were a couple of black taxi cabs and an LEB electricity van. A trick borrowed from the office for when surveillance transport really had to be invisible. A lift took him up to front reception where the girl was indeed just as pretty as Finberg had said.

'Mr Kay,' she said, giving him a big inviting smile, 'I'm Sam. Mr Sibley's expecting you. Second floor, straight opposite the lift.'

'It's Johnny,' he said, returning the smile.

Sibley's office had a bank of TV monitors on one wall, all showing horse-racing. The opposite wall was dominated by a huge and gloomy oil painting of red-clad British soldiers in close quarters combat with tribesmen, desert in the foreground, sombre rocky crags behind.

'Did it go all right, Johnny?' asked Sibley.

'Fine. Ansell's got some strange tastes.'

'Get on all right with Adam?'

'Yes.'

'Good. I've got something for you tomorrow. Bit different. A spot of B-and-E. Have to be late in the day. Nothing for you before that. It's all set up, so take the day off and come in for a briefing at five p.m.'

'Breaking and entering? Where do we stand?'

'If you get caught, you mean? Same place you would have stood in the office. In it up to your neck, I'd say. But you won't get caught, will you, Johnny?'

They walked through the college grounds holding hands and laughing and the few passers-by who took any notice must have thought how happy they were together. Maggie was quoting a long nonsense poem by Edward Lear at him because you always had something harmless going on, but he was genuinely enjoying it. For two people who had been introduced just an hour and a half earlier, they were doing pretty well. Maggie had been the only surprise at the briefing. Johnny was quite sure he'd never seen her before so she'd probably come from Century, not Thames House. She had a certain extra touch of colour and urbanity about her that went with MI6.

She came to the end of the poem and there was no one near by. 'Pasteur House,' she said as they passed a sign, 'it's the brick building at the end. See the double door?'

'I see it,' he said, remembering the briefing. 'Inside, straight through the little kitchen and turn left. That way you miss the front desk.'

'Ten out of ten. Got the keys?'

'Of course.'

Johnny had arrived at the briefing room next to Sibley's office on the dot of five after a day which started with squash, swimming and breakfast at the Lansdowne and then took in a quick dash down to Bisley for a session on the pistol range. This was his second day and apart from Sibley, Sam and Adam Finberg, he had still seen no one else there. He wondered if he was being kept out of the way of the others while he earned his spurs and showed he was there to stay. Two other people came into the room with Sibley. The first was a short black-bearded man with heavy eyebrows and a fixed, cross expression. Immediately behind him came a slender, elegant young woman with a deep tan and long shining black hair.

'Johnny,' said Sibley, 'this is Maggie and this gentleman represents our client.' He didn't give a name.

The man looked hard at him and went to the podium. He pressed a button and the projector spread a map across the screen.

'Queen Victoria College, Barnes,' he said. 'The medical research centre occupies three buildings at the south-east corner.' He threw an arrow on to the map with a light wand. 'Pasteur House is the one we're interested in.' He looked morosely at Johnny and Maggie. 'There's a man trying to make a reputation working in there. His name's Matthew Quill. Officially, he's doing research on behavioral effects of food additives. He's been trying to prove some of the fast-food chains use special sugars to give their products a mildly addictive quality. Unofficially, we believe that's led him into trespassing into an area with defence implications which overlaps with certain important work we're doing.'

He handed a sheet of paper each to Maggie and Johnny and replaced the map on the screen with a list of names.

'There is a dark green filing cabinet beside his desk in room 102P. In the top drawer there should be a file marked "Combination Effects". We want copies of documents from that file which mention any of the ten compounds on this list.'

Ivor broke in, looking at Johnny. 'Don't worry. You'll be able to take that list with you.'

'Well,' said the other man sharply, 'it's not that difficult to learn, surely?'

The first compound ran to thirteen syllables and started with *propylparahydroxy* . . .

'We would also like to see any paperwork in the file which mentions any of the following – and this one is certainly *not* a list you can take with you.'

The screen showed a short list, divided up into four groups. The first looked like place names: Maxton Heath, Westrop Manor and Flaxmore. The second was a list of names: J. Davies, G. Bacon, W. Collishaw. The third consisted of companies: PBD Biosystems, Chempropa International and Murray, Sinclair Hatton. The last had just two constituents, CN512 and Rage.

'Take as long as you want,' said Ivor, which was the wrong thing to say because for Johnny, it immediately became a matter of pride and when, three minutes later, Maggie said, 'OK,' he had to nod, even though he wasn't yet completely sure.

'Looking for those is just the first part,' said the bearded man. 'The trickier bit comes next. Three doors down from Quill's office, in 108P, is a lab. Just inside the door on the wall to the right is a glass cabinet. Inside it, Quill has an experiment in progress which will end some time tomorrow and which, if he's done it right, may confirm some ideas he has which we do not want confirmed. The cabinet is temperature controlled and if you simply open it, that will show up on the monitor graph.' A photograph of the cabinet flashed up on the screen. 'You have to note the temperature on the big dial, stop the monitor with the orange button here and *then* open it.'

He lifted the lid of a black leather case and brought out a small metal box with a battery pack attached. 'In this box are four glass containers marked identically to the ones you will find in Quill's cabinet and labelled consecutively starting with number sixteen. You will substitute these, leaving them exactly as the others are positioned, and bring back the four you find there.'

He turned and flashed the light pointer at the temperature dial. 'This is very important. You must not take longer than one minute to make the switch. You must then close the cabinet and wait for the dial to get back exactly to the original temperature reading before you press the blue button to start the monitor roll moving again. That way there will be no visible discontinuity. If you do that wrong, Quill will know the cabinet has been opened and then he will know why his experiment has failed to give him the result he hoped.'

The double doors into Pasteur House weren't locked. So far they were still in the clear, within the excuse envelope of two people looking for a friend who'd gone slightly the wrong way. The little kitchen was empty, a place of thin institutional hospitality judging by the open boxes of tea bags, a catering tin of coffee powder and a wooden rack of mugs. They went through it to a corridor, walking confidently, smiles on their faces to set the tone for any chance encounter. Room 102P had a Yale lock and this was the moment of crossing the Rubicon. They knocked quietly and there was no answer. The keys for the office and the lab were almost identical, but had the figures 2 and 8 scratched on the grips to show which was which. Johnny slipped 2 into the lock but it wouldn't turn. He fiddled with it while Maggie looked at him, alarmed. It wouldn't go. He tried the other one. The door opened. He let out a snort of irritation but she was past him, into the office, pulling him behind her. He closed the door quietly.

The filing cabinet was exactly as described and this time the key they'd been given worked straight off. The file wasn't thick but the papers it contained were close-typed and filled with the long names of complex compounds. Maggie divided the pile roughly into two, pulled the slim black document copier out of her shoulder bag, plugged it in and they set to work. Two of the compounds featured frequently in Johnny's pile though he could make no sense of the context and didn't waste time trying to. He copied six A4 pages. There was just one more document, a short handwritten letter.

Dear Matthew,

I really hope you're wrong. I'm not going to agree to meet until I've had some time to think about what you've said but I promise this. If I find any evidence here that your suggestion has any basis in fact, I will certainly help you with your investigation. I don't think anything we are doing here has the sort of application you describe but hope to find out more about the parallel Chempropa team at Westrop.

I'd love to be able to say that GKC International doesn't do that sort of thing but you would think that simplistic. Don't contact me again. I will get in touch if I find grounds to take this further.

Yours
Jean Davies.

He read it, then read it again, his mind suddenly racing. There wasn't time now for all the questions it raised so he pushed them aside for consideration later and copied it. He waited while Maggie copied two more pages then they carefully put them all back exactly as they had found them and moved on to the lab.

It was there that the entire operation nearly came unravelled and it was caused by such a basic little hitch. There were four buttons on the front of the cabinet, not two as on the version they had been shown in the photo. There was a blue button, certainly, but the other three were yellow, red and green. Of an orange button, there was no sign. They argued in whispers.

'Yellow's pretty much like orange,' Maggie urged.

Johnny objected. 'So's red. Anyway you might as well say green's pretty much like blue.'

They spent a precious two or three minutes looking over it, peering in through a small gap in the side, trying to follow the tangle of wiring from the switches to the monitor, which was quietly tracing its inked line on to the slowly revolving paper roll.

'I think we should try it. See if we can switch it on and off without opening it. That way, it won't show if we screw it up,' Johnny suggested.

'Which colours?'

'I'll pick the first one. You pick the second.'

His finger wavered between orange and red. Orange for caution or red for stop? He settled on red, pushed it firmly and a buzzer filled the lab with startling sound. Thinking quickly, he stabbed green and the buzzer stopped but at that same moment they heard footsteps in the corridor, footsteps that halted and retraced their path. A key rattled in the lock and Maggie was suddenly on him, leaping up, wrapping her arms round his neck and her legs around his waist, rocking hard against him so that he staggered off balance. As the door opened behind Johnny, she broke into unstoppable rising moans. There was a startled mutter from the doorway and it banged abruptly shut again. She kept up the moans until they heard the footsteps retreating, then she stopped abruptly and disentangled herself leaving Johnny in a state of unexpected arousal, with only the memory of her pelvis pounding against his.

She turned to the cabinet, pressed the yellow button and the monitor roll stopped.

'Eighty-three point six,' she said, looking up at the dial. 'Mark that.'

They went smoothly through the procedure for the swap. The blue button did its job and they left much more cautiously than they had arrived. Outside it was hand in hand again, which despite Johnny's attempt at professionalism, brought back disturbing memories of what had just happened.

'That was very quick thinking in there,' he said, 'I couldn't believe the way you moved.'

The *double entendre* wasn't intentional but she squashed it fast. 'All in the line of business,' she said, considering him. 'Anyway, just in case you were thinking of following up, I should probably tell you now to save you the trouble, I swing the other way.'

'Oh . . . fine.'

They parted when they were safely outside. She was taking the documents and samples back to a rendezvous with the bearded man. Johnny wasn't invited, but he didn't mind that. He needed to spend a little time by himself, to speculate on why this routine job for an anonymous client had suddenly become personal and he wasn't thinking of Maggie's simulated sex. He was wondering why Jean Davies' letter should refer to GKC International. Greville Kay Chemicals International, his stepfather's company.

CHAPTER FOUR

'You were the natural choice, Johnny,' said Sibley, undisturbed at his challenge. 'We've had a lot to do with Sir Greville and your mother. If it doesn't bother us that they're the client, I don't see why it need bother you.'

Johnny had spent an uneasy night and decided in the end to confront Sibley as soon as he could. He wasn't sure he'd get very far, but 'need to know' rules didn't seem to apply so strictly here. Sibley confessed readily that GKC was indeed behind the previous day's operation.

'I would have told you anyway,' he said. 'We've got a meeting here in an hour and a half. I need you in on it. Sir Greville's coming.'

The schoolboy feeling. An hour and a half to do nothing much in a largely empty office, where the studied business of the few other inhabitants simply made his inactivity more acutely noticeable – and Sir Greville at the end of it. He felt uneasy, as if at any moment someone might call to say he was late for First XV rugger practice or that the Latin master wanted to see him about his grammar test. When a call did come on the intercom summoning him, he took the lift to the basement trying to feel grown-up, professional, expert. Walking into a room containing his stepfather ensured the attempt would end in failure.

The meeting was held in the safe room, which Johnny suspected was as much a product of Sibley's marketing skills as a solution to a real eavesdropping risk. It was ostentatiously being swept for bugs as he came in through the electrically operated double doors. The low hum of an electronic disrupter moved up and down in a narrow range of frequencies as they began to talk. Sibley, Maggie and a man Johnny recognized but couldn't name from past years in the office were standing talking to two visitors. One was the bearded man from the previous day's briefing, who was nodding with little lip movements of impatient petulance at something Maggie was saying to him. The other was Sir Greville. Sibley was standing too close to him, talking animatedly, and he was leaning away from the contact, aloof as ever, his top lip lifted slightly in that look of mild disdain which was his habitual expression. One eyelid drooped slightly, a recent affliction which added to the effect, and the suit was country tweed, very, very expensive. Johnny, trying to fix his mind on neutral ground to avoid his step-father smelling his fear, guessed the afternoon was earmarked for one of his mother's rural bloodlettings, involving some combination of guns, hounds and horses.

To Johnny's hyper-sensitive ears, Sir Greville welcomed him, as always, as if he was still in short trousers. 'Johnny. Good to see you, boy. Glad to see we've got a real lion on the job, eh, Ivor?'

The gaze stayed on him for barely a moment, flicking back to Sibley before the sentence was finished to make it quite clear there was little meaning behind the words.

Sibley gestured around the chairs, sat down and passed folders around.

He looked round to see they were all settled and ready and cleared his throat. 'Matthew Quill,' he said. 'Yesterday's substitution went exactly to plan. We now have to consider the next phase, which is why we are here today. He's a persistent young man and we must make sure he sees a good reason to look elsewhere. Maggie.'

'Thank you, Ivor,' said Maggie, opening her folder. 'In the past two months, we have put into play a successful vulnerability programme against the subject. This has taken three main directions, financial, psychological and professional. If I could start with the financial side? You'll find it at Appendix 2A.'

Appendix 2A was a list. Johnny and the others all around the table scanned down it.

'Just to run through,' said Maggie. 'Quinn's an easy one for the treatment. He's been living on a shoestring and we've managed to fray the string to breaking point with very little trouble. Cash withdrawals first. This month we have made unauthorized cash machine withdrawals of a hundred and fifty pounds from his account, removing the surplus balance. We have used machines he normally uses himself and we have satisfied ourselves from inspection of his flat that he keeps few records and is unlikely to be able to make a convincing case to the bank even if he does pin down the individual transactions. We did in fact put receipts covering the transactions in his briefcase, where he stores unsorted paperwork, so if he does try to check back he will be very confused.'

She looked down at the list. 'Uninsured property. For recreation at weekends he had a bicycle, a fairly expensive Rockhopper mountain bike. That was removed last week. He lacks funds to replace it. Then there's domestic bills. Let's see.' She glanced further down. 'We gained entry to his flat a few days ago and substituted a defective motor and a worn pump for components in his washing-machine. It's a German one and the bill's going to be at least one hundred and seventy pounds. Carwise, he runs an old Fiesta. He parked it last Saturday morning in Knightsbridge on a meter. We were able to move it on to double yellow lines while he was gone and it was subsequently towed away. All told he's down about seven hundred and fifty pounds in unforeseen expenses in the month and that's much more than he can afford. He's now seeking loan facilities but we've arranged entries on the credit registers which should ensure no one will be prepared to lend him money.'

Sir Greville interrupted her. 'All well and good, but does it stop him working?'

Sibley answered. 'His research grant's ending this week, Sir Greville. He has to show sufficient progress on the project to get it renewed. As of yesterday' – he paused, and smiled –

'thanks to Maggie and Johnny, he has virtually nothing to show. The samples they substituted will provide him with no evidence whatsoever.'

'So that's it? We just hope he packs his bags and leaves us alone? After spending a year of his life chasing it?' Sir Greville's tone was mild but no one mistook his meaning.

'No, of course not. What we do next is offer him an alternative research job as outlined in the proposal of which there is a copy in your file.'

Sir Greville waved his hand in a dismissive gesture. 'I've seen it. So, maybe he'll agree. Maybe he'll go to New Zealand. But it's still food additives, isn't it? I mean that's his field, after all. It might be a different direction but it does raise the danger he might start experimenting again in a direction we don't want, doesn't it?'

'He'll be kept busy and we'll keep an eye on him. It buys you time, Sir Greville.'

'All right,' he said, 'do it. Now, what about this bloody woman, Jean Davies?'

'The letter would indicate that you have a big potential problem there.'

Sir Greville nodded. 'Severe discipline, I think.'

Most of what had just happened had passed over Johnny. He'd heard of vulnerability enhancement as a theoretical technique – in the office, they'd called it wallet-hitting – but he'd never been directly involved and he still didn't know exactly what Quill had done to make himself a target. In a sudden hush he became aware that Ivor Sibley and Maggie were looking at him.

'This is where Johnny comes in,' said Sibley. 'You said you'd like to be involved in his briefing so I thought we'd kill two birds with one stone.'

Sir Greville nodded at the bearded man who had never been introduced. 'Gordon?'

The man looked at him morosely, then back at Johnny. 'Have you been following the Hurst Inquiry?'

'On and off,' said Johnny, who hadn't really. He thought hard of what he knew. A spin-off from the revelations of the

Scott Inquiry and the Pergau Dam affair. Once the rumours of arms-deal brokers who were a little too close to Tory grandees for comfort proved unstoppable, a series of fresh inquiries had become inevitable. Sir Roger Hurst's task was to look into arms sales to less developed countries.

'A little while back,' said the man called Gordon, glancing with heavy import back at his boss, 'the Hurst Inquiry was sent a transcript of a proposal we were making to a . . . let's just say a foreign group, concerning the sale of a trial quantity of a new product, CN512. The Inquiry had it within a week or two of our transmitting it and they've given us notice that they're calling Sir Greville for questioning.'

He looked expectantly at Johnny.

'So you want us to find out who gave it to the inquiry?' Johnny asked, thinking it sounded like an internal security job. Routine. Find out who had access, who had an axe to grind, and start whittling them down.

'Oh no,' said the man, 'we know that. The person who sent it' – he paused for effect – 'was a twenty-nine year old youth worker from Yorkshire called Heather Weston. What we want to know is how the hell did *she* get it?'

Sibley held up a six-by-four black and white. 'That's her, Johnny. You'll find all we've got on her in the file. We can talk tactics afterwards.'

He looked at the picture – a bit grainy, taken on a long lens as she was coming out through what looked like a shop door, hair blowing across her forehead. It was hard to make much of it except that she looked happy and friendly and about as unlikely a person as you could find to be sending defence secrets to a government inquiry.

There was a silence, broken by Sir Greville who leaned forward and in a dangerous tone of voice that Johnny had known since childhood said: 'Isn't there anything else you'd like to know, young Johnny?'

It meant, as it had always meant, that he'd missed something obvious and was in imminent danger of being shown up. He racked his brains and fell back on the safest ground he could find. 'I'll read the file. If there is, I'll be in touch.' He was rather proud of the level way he said it, but his stepfather's eyes lifted in a tiny but deadly expression of impatience.

'Wouldn't it help you to know what this is all about? What CN512 is?'

'If this is a suitable moment,' said Johnny trying very hard to sound incisive and determined and immediately aware that he had failed.

Gordon took his cue. 'Quill is engaged on dietary analysis of effects in combination of food additives,' he said. 'He was prompted into this research by observed correlations of the rise in consumption of some types of fast food and aggressive and antisocial behaviour among the age-group consuming them.'

'In other words,' said Sir Greville, 'young thugs eat burgers and beat up old ladies.'

Gordon was clearly used to such interruptions from his boss. 'It is well established that some additives produce hyperactivity which can involve aggression in a proportion of people,' he went on, 'but there are some complex sugars which are known to have a dual effect. They provide very rapid bursts of energy, which bring the kids back for more, and Quill seems to believe that they are used in fast food to give an addictive effect: but they also, in some surprising cases, produce a psychological effect. They appear to inhibit understanding of the consequences of actions.'

Sir Greville was enjoying this. He interrupted again. 'Aggression magnifiers. They get rid of the natural control mechanisms, you see? Stop your brain warning you what might happen next.'

'By themselves,' said Gordon, 'they are unpredictable in effect and seem to depend on the metabolism of the consumer. However our research has shown that in combination with two other groups of additives, one a preservative and the other an emulsifier, they take on a new range of powers and predictability.'

'That's where we came in,' said Sir Greville. 'Packaged as a drink and given to troops involved in close-quarters combat at the right time, they can give the winning edge.'

'What exactly happens?' asked Johnny.

CHAPTER FIVE

The phone had woken Peter Hansen at four in the morning and what he had been told made no sense at all, not even to someone used to the bizarre turns of Central European politics. There was nothing for it but to go up and see for himself. The UNPROROM duty officer sounded half asleep when he answered the call and dropped the phone twice but he promised an escort ready to go within half an hour, Irish troops freshly arrived in Western Romania and not yet used to the peace-keeping role. Hansen had the usual breakfast out of the usual cans, augmented by some fresh tomatoes bought the previous day in the market.

The remains of the towers and battlements ringing the steep summit of the town showed very faintly in the light of the half moon as they set out for the hard drive north to Tirgu Mures. Forty miles of bumps with the speed set by the tracked escort so that even Peter's hardened Land Rover, with its abused springs and tendency to be knocked off course by every pothole, was well below its comfortable cruising speed.

Another day as a UN observer in the never-ending unravelling of the Balkans. Oh, to be back drinking good Norwegian beer in Stavanger. He missed his cabin in the mountains and the wholesome certainty of knowing there would be no mass exterminations to spoil his day.

The white-painted convoy snaked out of the town towards – well, what exactly? The man on the phone had been far from clear. Another massacre involving the miners, that was quite obvious. Another foul and probably untraceable atrocity in the growing swell of such incidents. Another crime in the name of ethnic cleansing against a minority population. Hansen sighed as he changed up into top and caught a glimpse of an old farmhouse in its walled enclosure as his headlights swung across it. The incursion of the totalitarian Ceaucescu years was less marked here than in the country to the east, towards the capital. The road got worse as they reached the river and the sun was just starting to glint on the peaks of the wild Transylvanian Alps to the north and the east, the highest point the Carpathians would achieve for many, many miles, their lower slopes still covered with forests that softened the stark edges of the canyons.

Hansen was a historian which helped him understand as far as it could be understood. This should never have been Romania. There had been no perfect solution for Transylvania, a mass of Magyars – Hungarians cut off from their own country and surrounded by an even greater mass of Romanians – but the solution after the First World War of simply handing them over to Romania had been very far from perfect and now, nearly eighty years on, it was trying its best to come unravelled.

Bloody hard to deal with it, he thought, when half the time you're not even up against soldiers. The simmering violence directed at the Magyars from the east was often instigated by the Romanian miners, the brutal but conveniently amateur shock troops used from Ceaucescu's time onwards against those who became targets of the State. They seemed always ready to leave their pits and career into town in commandeered trucks and buses, always ready with their crowbars and axe handles to split the skulls of the protestors. First it was to put right what they saw as the dangerous tide of reformism after Ceaucescu's expedient death lanced the boil of revolution. Now it was the Magyars, though on the side, they were usually prepared to have a go at the gypsies, every other Romanian's favourite target.

The UN convoy's passing disturbed a heron on the last straight before Tirgu Mures and Hansen watched it flap heavily away in the first light of dawn. He followed it with his eyes for as long as possible to grab what he was sure would be the last peaceful moment of the day until, in the end, he had to turn back to look at the road. Marosvasarhely was the town's Hungarian name and on the outskirts they were flagged down by the local man, standing, waiting anxiously next to his car with its oversize UN stickers down both sides and a UN flag flying from the radio aerial.

'Istvan!' Hansen hailed, climbing stiffly down.

'Mr Hansen. I am glad you have come. You must follow me.'

Hansen asked no questions. He thought he knew what they were going to see. Istvan could only have misunderstood the situation in the darkness. It was inconceivable that his account could be correct. They would find a tragedy that would fit into a now familiar pattern, a small hamlet of wrecked, burnt houses. The bodies of the villagers would be sprawled where they had been killed, their heads usually shattered by the miners' hammer blows. If there were any survivors, they would tell, as far as they were able, a stomach-turning tale of brutal rape and murder then they would slump back into a blank, bewildered stupor in which the future held nothing.

He was wrong and Istvan, against the odds, was right. The hamlet was eight miles from the town, hard to get to, the far side of the river which was called either Mures or Maros depending on whether you were giving or receiving the miners' blows. The first inkling he had that the man in the car leading the way had told it the way it was came when he noticed the lack of smoke. The houses still had their roofs on. All looked normal – normal, that is, until he took in the objects on top of the poles that lined the road past the church. He braked hard and there was a chain reaction through the rest of the convoy. Unable to take his eyes off them, he got slowly down from the driver's seat, leaving the door swinging open behind him, and walked towards them with reluctant, necessary steps. The young lieutenant, O'Driscoll or something like that, got there before he did and stopped in bewilderment, looking up. The poles were thin, perhaps eight or nine feet tall, bending and bobbing slightly with the weight.

Impaled on top of them were heads, human heads, sawn

roughly through the necks so that ragged flesh, yellowing gristle and hideous tubes hung from the cuts.

'God in heaven,' said the lieutenant. 'Who has done this? Miners?'

'Look again, Lieutenant,' said Hansen, 'look at their faces. They're not Magyars. These *are* the miners.'

'On poles, though,' the younger man said, and Hansen knew he had to keep talking to keep it all at bay, 'why on poles?'

'Local custom maybe,' said Hansen, trying to keep his own voice steady – the responsibility of the older man. 'Haven't you heard of Vlad Tsepesh, son of Vlad Dracul?'

'Dracul? Like Dracula?'

'Only in fiction. In history, he was Vlad the Impaler. He did this to the Turks. Came from just down the road.' He dragged his eyes away from poles as a small gust of wind set them swaying and bobbing again. 'I think someone must have a misplaced sense of tradition.'

The villagers were everywhere, wandering around like people in a dream, sitting only to jump up again. They had clearly been up all night. Many had blood-soaked clothing and they all looked grey in the face, entirely exhausted. Despite that they were talking, talking, talking – to each other, to themselves, to anybody who would stop to listen.

Istvan joined Hansen and the lieutenant as they walked cautiously into the midst of a surreal scene. Sprawled on the ground wherever they looked were bodies, bodies that had come to the most violent of ends. Three that they could see were clearly villagers: a teenage girl, an old woman and a brawny man with one arm. All the rest were dressed in miners' gear, drab overalls, belts and helmets. Some were headless. Most were not but that was almost worse, because their faces were set into snarling masks of terror.

'Whoever did this is well clear by now. Must have got clean away,' said the lieutenant. 'What do you think? Some kind of Hungarian commando unit?'

'They don't have anything like that,' Hansen replied, 'a few local militias is all. We have never seen anything that could do this. Usually the miners come and do what they want.'

'Well, no one here could have stopped them.'

Hansen looked at the villagers still pacing and mumbling around them, showing very little interest in the ranks of corpses. He could see the truth of it. There were perhaps no more than forty villagers, which judging by the size of the hamlet was probably the entire population. He could only count nine of them who could be described as men in the prime of life. But despite that, they were all wearing clothes which were soaked in blood and some of them, not all men, were completely drenched in it, stiffening now so that their shirts and jackets were hardening into a dark crust. And they still went on and on talking.

'What are they saying, Istvan?' he asked, puzzled once more by their strange behaviour.

The Romanian shook his head. 'Nothing of good sense.' He tried to talk to a very old woman who was gesticulating violently with a rusty scythe. He spoke sharply to her and she dropped the scythe, looked up at him like a trusting child as he talked, then burst into voluble speech herself.

He came back shaking his head. 'Bad choice. She try to tell me how she cheated someone. Gave them bad eggs for good money. She wrong in the head.'

'Try someone else.'

He was soon back again, 'This crazy place, Mr Hansen. Stupid people. All the same. The man there, he just talk and talk 'bout how he sleep with wife of baker. That one there, he crying. Say he not good man. Steal something when he was in school. No sense. I tell you. They all think I'm priest or what? They think is time for confession. Ah, piss.' He spat.

Behind him, the Irish squaddies were lifting the bodies and piling them in an empty shed.

'Mr Hansen!' He looked round. One was waving at him. 'Come here. There's one alive.'

He ran, Istvan behind him. The miner had been covered by two other bodies and he was in a bad way. His shirt was soaked in blood from stab wounds all across his torso and a slash from some ragged blade had laid one cheek open from the eyeball to the side of his mouth so that half his face was a congealing mass of blood. He was breathing in short gasps and looking at them.

The lieutenant was with them. 'Bring the kit!' he shouted, but his sergeant was ahead of him, already opening the box and unwrapping field dressings.

'Fuck me,' the sergeant said, looking at the miner's chest, 'where do you start?'

'Morphine,' said the lieutenant, 'morphine and as many pads as we've got. We'll call for a chopper from Brasov.'

'Wait,' said Hansen, 'before the morphine. Just give me a moment. Istvan, ask him what happened.'

The Romanian bent down to the desperately injured miner and asked the question. The man's mouth fought to frame words in a whisper. It was awful to watch, each slow word seeming to suck out some of his ebbing vitality. After what seemed an age, Hansen was on the verge of stopping it when the miner broke off and Istvan turned to him, looking incredulous.

'He hurt bad, maybe raving. He say it was them. These people.' In case Hansen missed the point he waved a hand around at the villagers. 'They waiting. The miners came at evening. Just to scare, to break windows maybe – well, that's what he say. Start some fires. All these people waiting. All mad. They come running with knives, lots of blades. Hack, hack, hack. Even the old women, he say. Can not stop them. Like a storm wave, he says. All mad.'

An ancient man with a wide grin showing just a scatter of dark teeth in a lopsided mouth pushed in between them, seeming to notice the mortally injured miner for the first time. The sergeant was strapping pads around the man's chest while a squaddie gently lifted him. The old man said something in a conversational tone to Istvan, punctuated by giggles, pointing at the man's chest.

'He did that cut, he say.'

'Him? Ask him how he—'

That was as far as Hansen got because, still giggling, the old man dropped awkwardly on one knee, pulled a small knife from his pocket and before anyone could move to prevent him, plunged it into the miner's neck, sending bright arterial blood squirting across them.

It was chaos for two or three more minutes, an unsuccessful fight to save the miner's life in parallel with a brief mêlée in which the old man, still talking volubly, was disarmed and led away.

When it was over Hansen stood looking at the scene. If there was any tiny hint of satisfaction at seeing the tables turned on the brutal miners by their usually helpless victims it was suppressed under many layers of concern, centred on the knowledge that something very disturbing had happened here and he was going to have a hard time writing a report that made sense.

'Let's have another look round,' he said to the lieutenant. 'I'll take the houses beyond the church, you take the ones this side.'

'What are we looking for?'

'Anything that might explain this.'

It was bad luck, that was all. If he'd just done it the other way round he would probably have noticed what the lieutenant missed. Someone had done a clearing up job but they'd failed to spot a couple of containers. The lieutenant did see them, crumpled under a chair in the corner of a room, but he'd only been in Romania for a few days. The screwed-up foil packets had drinking straws built into them, drinking straws with threaded ends where they had been sealed by a plastic cap. A bright, badly glued label showed juice dripping from sliced oranges and blue letters spelt the words *Citrus Sun*.

Hansen, who knew the local shops and markets well, would have known at once these did not belong, but to O'Driscoll, used to the modern packaging on sale in his native Dublin, they were nothing extraordinary. The drips still inside them might have given up their secret to careful analysis, although much of it was indeed orange juice and the other ingredients were uncommon only in their proportions, not their nature.

In any case, by that time the man who had brought them to the village and stayed long enough to observe their effect was long gone.

CHAPTER SIX

It had started two months earlier.

Pacman Gerow was hacked off. A rear screen for the Buick was going to be three hundred at least, maybe more. Plus the wait, which meant plastic and sticky tape and not being able to park anyplace that wasn't secure. He should have traded the Buick for that Volvo in Silver Spring. Everyone told him but Lanie wouldn't listen – just said she liked the Buick. Then she'd given him all kinds of shit when he told the kid how he felt about it. There's a place for baseball, that was all he'd been trying to say. There's goddam grass out there. There's even a sports field. Why did you have to play right by the house, for God's sake? Lanie shouldn't have taken Billy's side like that. Sure the grass was kind of muddy. That wasn't any kind of excuse. So the kid was bored, was that his fault?

Lanie hated it, said it was just a shitty foreign posting despite all the crap they fed you back in Fort Meade, Maryland. Glamour? Shit.

The bottom line was he was late arriving at his desk in the bunker and there were looks that told him you didn't do things like that on a posting. Not in the NSA, not if you were trick trash, working the shifts. Maybe the day ladies could get away with it but if you were late for your trick someone else was late getting off because the ears couldn't be left alone.

Trouble with the NSA, glamour just didn't come into it. Not like being CIA. OK, so ninety per cent of the CIA were backroom, non-active. The ten per cent who weren't kept the options going for the rest, left it an open question what sort of guy you were when you dropped the hint. NSA, shit, that ten per cent came right down to one per cent max, dropped the glamour right out of it. Square eyed techno-freaks with underground complexions and beeps in their brains.

Wasn't always that way. Pacman's dad Walter E. Gerow died of the glamour, tumbling down to earth in the burning fragments of an EC130 ferret plane to burst apart in the mountains of Soviet Armenia. Seventeen of them, killed by five MiGs scrambled from Yerevan. Pacman, three months short of being born then, knew the bloody history of those years by heart as some kind of substitute for knowing his father. NSA ferret planes, bristling with electronics, prowled the limits of the Iron Curtain hunting for radar, plotting the Soviet defences for the day when US planes might need to know where they could get through.

Its four propellers had pulled this one into the air from Incirlik, Turkey, climbing up to circle over Trabzon to calibrate with the US Air Force Security Service listening post there, then heading for the fence, playing fox and hounds right along the Russian border all the way to Iran. Pacman lost his chance of knowing his father on the way back. The ferret tested the Soviet defences once too often and once too far. It was around Leninakan when the MiGs bounced it, five jet fighters against one unarmed, four engined freight car. The ferret's tail section fell off first, then turning over and over as it burned, the rest of it plummeting into the mountains.

The US public didn't get to hear about it all for a long time. The air force put out the agreed story: one of their planes on a peaceful mission, studying radio-wave propagation, had been brutally attacked. The US public didn't know about the NSA – not then and barely now. Pacman's mother Molly knew, and as Pacman grew up she made sure he knew too. It was the worst loss of the signals intelligence war and it stayed that way for just over ten years until an EC-121 carrying six tons of listening gear, one marine and thirty navy SigInt specialists was blown from the skies south of Chongjin by North Korean jets.

They weren't strictly NSA, so Pacman knew only the numbers on that one. The *Liberty* was different. He could recite the names of every one of the thirty-four dead. It was the worst punch the secret ear ever took and it came not from the Soviets but from the Israelis.

June 7th, 1967 in the eastern Mediterranean: the Israelis, pushing their borders out into Sinai and the West Bank, didn't want the superpowers to stop them too soon. The *Liberty* was in the way, monitoring their signals from international waters, fourteen miles out to sea. Mirage jets and Israeli Navy torpedo boats took care of the *Liberty*, conveniently mistaking her for an Egyptian coastal steamer a quarter of her size in an act of butchery that the American government promptly swept under the rug and classified secret.

Some NSA history buffs still believed they knew the real reason for the attack - that the *Liberty* had on board the intercepts that would have showed it was Israeli forces and not the Egyptians who started the war.

Pacman joined the Agency for all the wrong reasons in the mistaken belief he could prove himself his father's son, ride the boundaries of the sky a hair's breadth from missile-born obliteration. The Agency, short on Vets and dynasties, took him on for those same wrong reasons.

Times had changed. He looked across to the new consoles at position eight and tried to lift his mood by visualizing the power that lay behind them, hoping that way maybe just a little bit of glamour would start to creep back in. Saddlebush Three. Biggest project yet. Megabucks. Civilians crawling all over it for two years but now it was up and running, in commission, and he was on hand to see it. Signals Collection Officer Gerow was good at what he did, graded GG12 with a rare parallel aptitude for both cryptanalysis and track pattern monitoring.

The NSA spotted and nurtured those skills, saw the intuition in him and gave him a long rein, adding back in the human element that the computers just couldn't match, the hunch that sometimes got far more out of the processed data than the very best software.

Way, way up there, right out in the cold darkness on the road to the moon hung their latest weapon in the listening war, Saddlebush SV, punched into orbit by a Titan rocket, the biggest ear there had ever been, listening to everything there was to hear. Down here at the bottom of the chain of information pouring back was the bunker and outside the bunker stood the dome farm, lines of giant geodesic-framed golf balls hiding the dishes from casual inspection so no smart-ass with a score to settle could make mileage out of which way they were pointing.

'Hey, Pacman?' He looked up from the screen to see his section leader coming up behind with a young guy in tow, maybe Mexican. 'Pacman, meet Al Menendez. He's going through indoctrination. Gonna be working Gapfish. I've got you a half-hour backup so you can show him some of what the Bush will do.'

'Fine by me.'

Menendez settled in to the chair beside him. Acoustics muted the electronic hums right through the bunker so that each desk position in the long row seemed to live in its own bubble of silence. The world's most expensive lighting system made sure no one misread a screen through eye fatigue. Everything was backed up, interlocked, failsafed.

'OK, Al, you just arrived? I guess you know the basics. Saddlebush is geostationary, northern hemisphere, pulling in everything that's bouncing off all the other birds it can see. Figure a max of a hundred thousand simultaneous phone calls on every bird, that's a big heap of international traffic. We downleg everything in this hemisphere, right in here. You're on Gapfish?'

Menendez was red hot, couldn't wait to show what he knew. 'We sort it, right? Goes through the sieve.'

When Pacman joined they'd called it the dictionary. Now the bank of Crays were so much faster than anything they'd had back then the name had got faster too. The sieve lay at the heart of everything, a Band-aid on human frailty. The machines could do so much more than the men. A million calls, ten million calls? There was no effective limit that dollars couldn't fix. They could hoover it all up. Recording wasn't the problem, listening was. Time just didn't stretch far enough and that was where the sieve came in. You fed in the key words, the ears listened for them and out came the goodies, straight into the massive printout known as SOLIS – the SigInt On-Line Intelligence System. That's if you'd picked the right key words.

'OK,' said Pacman, 'so you'll be resetting parameters all the time. That's the bitch. Back home, they change their mind every five seconds. New numbers, new words, new names, all the goddam time. Always got to be looking for something else. So the sieve weeds out the shit, looks for the good bits and you pull the data, feed the tapes back home to Maryland. What you starting on?'

'MidEast.'

'Israel. The friendly eye.'

'What are you doing on this desk?'

'This desk, we're the wild cards,' said Pacman, and he pushed his baseball cap back on his head. 'Here's the way it is. Normally we just strip the data, right? Strip all that raw data right outta the sky. Sieve it for anything with the right buzzwords, then we bird it back home. That's where the clever guys get to listen to it. That works if they know who and what they want to listen to. Other times, maybe they have a suspicion, yeah? Maybe they have half an idea but no hard facts. So then they hand it to us and we go snooping, just dipping in and out. The world is my oyster and I'm telling you it's one hell of a big, juicy oyster.'

He punched buttons. Scrolling numbers filled the screen. 'Every international call going out right now.' He punched more buttons. 'You tell me a town, I got it. Tell me a company, a street, a house, I got it. Mobiles too, no problem.'

'Every call?'

'Anywhere this side of the world.'

'You mean like national calls too? Inside the country?'

Pacman just looked at him. 'How long you been here, kid? Five minutes here should be long enough to learn there are some questions you don't ask.'

Menendez had that streetwise look that said he'd been a cheeky kid. 'So, like if I was gonna take a stroll around the neighbourhood, I wouldn't kinda happen to fall over any telecoms microwave towers close by or anything like that?'

Pacman was deadpan, or maybe mock deadpan. Even he wasn't sure he knew which he was trying to be. 'Towers? Yeah, sure. There's one five miles away. Coincidence.'

'Yeah. Weird – huh?' There was a short silence. 'Hey, Pacman?'

He knew what was coming. It was the question they always asked. 'Yeah?'

'All that stuff they give you. Like, about the people here? Is that all straight up?'

'Listen, Al, you got your wife over here?'

'Not yet awhile. She's coming in a few weeks.'

'Well, boy, you just keep your horny little dick locked away out of trouble. It's no joke. What does it say? "No fraternization with foreign nationals." You meet them out there, it's a friendly hi howya doing, end of story.'

'I seen that poster on the way in, the intruder one?'

'"Beware Intruders. If you see these women hit the panic button", that stuff?'

'Yeah. One of those women looks kinda neat.'

Pacman just shook his head.

Menendez sighed. 'Bum posting, huh?'

'Hey, come on. It's a plum. You just think – could have been Alaska.' Then Pacman thought about the bleak, tiny houses staggered across the compound out there behind the wire in cramped blocks of four. Damp, cold, small rooms. He thought about the wind that howled down off the hills blowing over the barbecues and the kids' slides. He thought about the rain that never seemed to stop, so that the short grass between the curves of houses was a bright green sponge. He thought about the boredom of the families on the base, the growing complaints of his wife that they never went anywhere and that there was nowhere to go. National Security Agency Field Station N82 was the pits. He hadn't imagined England being like this.

'Yeah,' he said, 'bum posting.'

There was a muted beep from the screen and a message box flashed. One of his watch list numbers was up.

'OK,' he said, 'listen in on this,' and he tossed Menendez the second pair of cans. It was brief and disappointing, a plummy English voice calling some garage to get his transmission fixed.

'So what's that all about?'

'Piggyback. British security asked us to tape that number. We kind of like to know why so we listen out when it comes up. Load of crap so far.'

Menendez looked genuinely puzzled. 'Why don't they do it themselves?'

'Hey, hold on there, buddy. You had the talk yet?'

'Shoulda been this morning. Got cancelled. Rescheduled tomorrow.'

Pacman laughed. 'Now I got it. Why don't I give it you straight then you just might understand all the crap they hand out later.'

Menendez laughed. 'Sounds good to me.'

Pacman took a look round and lowered his voice. 'British security, people here say MI5. Ivy-league accents and nicely pressed shirts. We got this place with them, GCHQ Cheltenham?' He put the stress on the 'ham'.

'Right.'

'OK now, Cheltenham does a lotta the same things we do here, only not so well. *But*, if the Brits want to listen in on all those miles of tapes they record, then they got the same problem we got back home. They gotta get a warrant from their government, answer all kinds of questions. Very sensitive. So there's an easy way.'

'They ask us?'

'You got it. Cuts both ways. Law says we want to listen in on a US citizen from US turf, we can't do it. From here, no problem, or we can always ask the Brits if we need really clean hands. So it's live and let live. They leave us alone.'

'While we listen in on them from right here. Neat.'

'That sort you out?'

'Yeah. One thing. This place. Ramsgill Stray. That's the code-name, right? Like Comfy Cobalt?'

Pacman grinned widely. 'Shit, no. That's the kinda dumb

name they use round here. This is NSA Field Station N82, Ramsgill Stray, Blubberhouses Moor. I mean, Blubberhouses? Like you'd never sell a condo development with a name like that. Comfy Cobalt, that's Edzell up in Scotland.'

'Scotland's like a separate country?'

Pacman thought. 'Yeah, sort of.' He really ought to take the time to find out one day.

'Gotta go,' said Menendez. 'Appreciate the help.'

'Come by at noon. I'm expecting a real fun call 'bout then.'

Left to himself, he went back to thinking about the bill for the Buick and whether Lanie would back him if he stopped Billy's allowance. Then the pace of work speeded up and midday came quickly. He heard footsteps coming up behind him and began to turn to welcome Menendez back but the screen beeped. The call was two minutes early and it caught him halfway through changing parameters. He flipped the spare cans sideways for the man and scrambled to save the work on the screen before cutting in to the call.

Yeah. The familiar voice. 'Get this,' he hissed, 'it's the Prince,' then he gave it his full concentration.

'. . . after the weekend,' said the voice in his cans. 'Can't wait, old girl. Just got to get shot of this bloody boring thing of Mummy's. Tickets booked, I think the fellow said he's put them under Dixon. I'll tell you . . .'

Pacman was distracted by Menendez's arm, which came into the corner of his field of vision, putting a Styrofoam cup of coffee down on the desk next to the keyboard.

'No, no,' he said, 'didn't they tell you? No drinks by the consoles. Spill it, you're dead. A million bucks of damage. Only in the . . .'

He turned and stopped in his tracks. The face he was looking into wasn't Mexican. The cans were clamped to the ears of a woman of maybe thirty, dressed in a faded cotton jacket, woollen leggings and muddy walking boots. She had a broad grin on her face as she looked at him.

The poster. He yanked the cord, tore the headset from her,

turning to the squawk box as he did so to punch out security's number.

'Intruder!' he yelled so that heads turned right down the row of desks, his heart pumping faster, 'intruder alert. Help me, someone.'

There were fresh faces to meet on Monday morning. Johnny got a warm welcome from Sam at the front desk and went up to the open-plan area of the office to find a positive gaggle of people there. It was a relief to see evidence of activity. In the old place, life had been structured and that had suited him. People had told you what to do, a bit like being in the services. It wasn't that he had no initiative, it was just that whenever he was forced to exercise it, he would suddenly find the range of options rather terrifying and, as often as not, would settle on a course of action that everyone else would find somehow inappropriate.

The lack of such a structure at MI7 unnerved him and the prospect of a silent day waiting for some obscure instruction from the more or less invisible Sibley had not appealed. He had, it was true, the photo and address of this woman in Yorkshire to chase up but no one had yet told him what resources there were on hand to help. It wasn't going to be like the old office; there terminals keyed you directly into the Social Security computer and anyone who'd ever registered with a doctor, paid National Insurance contributions or been issued with a birth certificate was on it and you could find them just like that. Then you'd start teasing out the usual trails, police and vehicle records, tax, bank and credit card data. The paper trail usually gave a pretty good picture and it was all on tap, but that was there and this was here and no one had told him where to start.

He was hailed by Adam Finberg as soon as he entered the room.

'Johnny, come and say hello! You must know these guys?'

'Some of them,' Johnny said, seeing a few faces in the group round Finberg that stirred old office memories.

'OK,' said Finberg, 'this reprobate here is Den Bramfield, the one hiding behind him is Sir James Brodie, Bart., don't forget the Bart., and this is Erica who more than makes up for both of them. I give you Johnny Kay, ex-Five, now Seven.'

Erica had the sort of face you see in *Country Life* engagement photos, soft focus all the way, puppy fat blown into shape by the wind of gymkhanas but not quite set into its final form. Belying that, there was a hard pair of eyes fixed on him when he met her gaze. Bramfield and Brodie both had an expensive, tough, travelled look. Six, he thought, all three of them.

Brodie was looking at him. 'I say,' he said, and the tone was a touch affected, 'of course. Wineglass. That was you, wasn't it? Frightfully good show, that one.'

Johnny gave a quick, tight smile but Brodie didn't follow it up. A story was being told and everybody wanted to hear the end.

'Go on, Den,' said Finberg. 'They're just back from a job, Johnny. Good yarn.'

'Well, that was about it. Hardest part was finding out where the bloody miners were going next. We followed this bunch around for a week, couldn't get ahead of them. Bunch of thugs they were, all right. I've never seen so many broken heads in my life. Erica did it in the end, cosied up to this out-of-work actor in some dive who'd do anything for a few lei. He went and bleated to the local lads about this village where his mother, who was of course a good Romanian, you know, pause for sliced onion and harp music or whatever they play, had been thrown out of her house by the brutal Magyars. Right, said the miners, where is it? They were just about to steam straight off there, which would have screwed it up all over again 'cos we wouldn't have had enough time, so this little darling here,' he gave Erica a somewhat intimate squeeze and she grinned, 'told them the village was having a feast next evening and wouldn't it be fun to break it up? Thinking on her feet, you see. Worked a treat. They got all steamed up and bombed off all ready to break heads but Sir Jimmy here got in there with the stuff. Told everyone it was market research, free samples and they'd get paid to drink it, handed out a few banknotes and that was that.'

'What stuff?' asked Johnny. There was a sudden pause and they all looked at him.

'Jungle Juice,' said Den. 'Hasn't Ivor filled you in?' and Johnny, ever the outsider trying to be inside, didn't choose to answer.

They dispersed to their desks and he looked at his terminal, wondering where to start. Just like the ones back at the office. Finberg came over and leaned on the partition.

'Getting on all right?'

'I think so. No one's told me about data access, though. I've got a target to follow up and I don't know what we've got.'

'Bloody Ivor,' said Finberg. 'Same when I joined. He expects you to guess.'

'So what do I do?'

'Pretend you never left.'

'What do you mean?'

'Just what I say. Go on, give it a try,' said Finberg, smiling broadly, and wandered off.

The woman would keep talking at him, and security were slow so she had plenty of time. She looked at his dog-tag. 'Hello Mr Gerow. How do you say that? Is that Gerow with a *ger* or Jerow with a *jer*?'

Like all the rest, whenever she confronted them, he didn't seem able to talk, overcome by the awfulness of her proximity. She stepped sharply back as he reached out to grab her arm.

'No, don't do that, I bruise very easily. That's actual bodily harm. Let's see where our wonderful police force's got to. The modplods take their time, don't they?' She gave him another broad smile. 'I'd just like you to know while we're waiting that I have every right to be here. This is my country. I don't agree with what this place is doing and I really don't think you should be doing it.'

He was trying to herd her into a corner of the wall, away from the desk. There was a little knot of technicians behind him and the supervisor was coming up fast from the far end but it seemed like no one wanted to get too close, as if she might bite.

She was talking again. 'What do you think, Mr Gerow? How would you like it if we built a base in Texas or somewhere and started listening to *your* phones? Would you think that was fair? By the way that sounded like a very interesting call you picked up there. Was that who I think—'

At last. The Ministry of Defence police were there, three of them, surrounding her with arms outstretched, not touching, herding her towards the door.

'Heather Weston, you are trespassing on private property. I am asking you to leave immediately,' said one in a Yorkshire accent. He was in shirtsleeves, very red in the face, the man who should have been at the desk in the entrance to the bunker.

'Come on. You're doing it all wrong,' she said. Her voice was musical, southern, full of memories of an expensive education. She turned to the third and youngest policeman, worried, thin faced, in his twenties. 'You're new, aren't you? Don't listen to them. They don't know the law like real plods. When you're a modplod the old MOD doesn't bother to teach you the finer points, does it? What you have to say is that you're acting on behalf of the occupier and then you can only take action if you ask me three times and I still don't agree to go.'

'Just button it,' said the oldest of them, curtly, every inch the ex-Sergeant major. 'On behalf of the occupier, we're asking you to leave.'

'Actually, I've come to talk to the occupier, so I'm not trespassing, am I? Can you just tell me who the occupier is and where I can find him . . . or her?' She had a big, irritating smile on her face again.

'The occupier does not wish to talk to you. The occupier wishes us to ask you to leave. This is a final warning.'

She knew when it was time to bend. 'I'm leaving now,' she said. 'Do you want me to go back the same way I came in, because I sort of wandered all over the place and it might take quite a long time, or are you going to give me a lift in your nice big van?'

She was escorted out.

Pacman went some of the way down the corridor after them,

watching her as she just went on and on talking at them. The shirtsleeved PC went behind his desk again.

'How did she get past you?' Pacman asked him.

He got a look of fury back. 'I don't have a clue, chum. Maybe she didn't come in this way.'

Pacman was going to say there wasn't any other way but thought better of it. Something on the wall caught his eye. The intruder poster was still there, but over the photo of Heather Weston someone had neatly stuck a picture of the Base Commander.

Johnny looked at his keyboard and tapped in the old MI5 entry code. The screen went into a short electronic fussing fit and cleared to the familiar display, exactly as Finberg had said. It asked for his ID and he tapped in the well-used letters.

The options menu came up. This was the test. Was this just some clever-clever bit of software copying or was it what it appeared to be, a direct extension of the system? He went into the search, tapped in *Heather Weston* and the machine went all the way with him. Inside five seconds, there it was on the screen, the first, familiar listing. He went on, just as he would have done at the office, and the screen jumped neatly through all the hoops for him, coughed up all the traces without a murmur. He wanted to ask how? How is this possible? But that felt like a very big question. Half of him was relieved that life here wouldn't be so different, wouldn't be more demanding on investigative talents he wasn't quite sure he had. The other half squirmed awkwardly further down his consciousness. He'd never been a natural letter opener, lens peeper, mike snooper but the simple justification of being a sanctioned part of the machinery of state had kept him happy. Everyone else on his course, the class of '89, had smiled their way through the obligatory session on the new Security Service Act. He had read it right through, word for word, and even if it hadn't done all that much to help, it was still there like a crutch propped in a corner of his mind.

It took an hour to be sure he had got everything he could get, to pull out into the light of day the usual desiccated story. Miss

Heather Weston. Twenty-nine years and two months old. Only daughter of Gareth and Gabrielle Weston who had both given their occupations on her birth certificate as 'writer'. Family moved from Hampshire to Yorkshire when she was eight. Both parents now dead. Healthy. Well educated. Once well off but now poor. Scraping a living working at some sort of home for tearaway kids. Owner of an old Citroën 2CV. Often in debt, despite her apparently simple way of life, but there was a reason for that and it came flying out of the screen. Heather Weston, normal, middle-class Heather Weston, had quite recently turned into some sort of persistent, unrepentant criminal. The list was extraordinary. He'd encountered plenty of villains around the fringe of the intelligence world, but for sheer intensity he had never seen a criminal record that was anything like this.

The bottom end of Heather Weston's scale of wrongdoing had started with obstructing the police in the execution of their duty. After that came criminal damage, breaking and entering and theft, followed by a group of associated offences, two breaches of bail conditions and three short spells inside for contempt of court. They were all in the last three years. The brief entries gave Johnny no real clue about the full nature of the offences but he copied the dates and details across to his own file for future checking.

The latest one, two months ago, was just a charge so far. A court date was looming. Grievous bodily harm: assault on a police officer.

He spent some more time simply gazing at her photo. Of course the picture couldn't tell tales but that face sat oddly with her record. It was the face of someone who, he felt, would always think the best of anybody and by doing so would perhaps bring out that best. Irritated with himself, he dismissed that as fanciful. A microsecond after the shutter had clicked her face would have relaxed back to a more familiar expression and she would have looked every inch the violent slag she undoubtedly was.

But there was much more to it than that. Attached to the details of her little Citroën on the Swansea DVLC computer was a cross-referencing code that was very familiar. Special Branch had an interest in her. Any routine check by an ordinary police patrol on her vehicle would ring bells. Locations and dates would then be passed along the chain and that chain, he knew well, would end at MI5. He searched through again and spotted some of the same fingerprints elsewhere in her files. Someone was already trying to keep loose tabs on Miss Heather Weston and that gave her string of offences a political rather than a criminal hue. It had the smell of animal rights about it or something like that. The papers she had sent to the inquiry, the criminal damage charges, it would all tie in neatly with CN512. Someone having a go at research laboratories.

He was pleased with himself for that little bit of deduction but unsure where he could go next. At Thames House he would simply have gone down and checked out the physical file. Here he wasn't sure how to proceed. He buzzed Sibley on the intercom.

'It's Johnny Kay, Ivor. I've got a lot on this Weston woman. Um, I don't suppose we have access to files from Registry, do we?'

'Sometimes.' Sibley sounded distracted, only half concentrating. 'But let's not get into that yet. You've only got to get alongside her. Might not pay to know too much at this stage. Just find out where she goes, how you can meet her, that sort of thing. OK? If you can't get anywhere and you want a phone tap, call Mo Wigley. Number's in the directory. Tell him he can spend up to five hundred pounds but no more. He's been billing a bit too high lately. I'd rather keep the cost down if you can.'

In the van, the older man got in the back with her. 'Donny,' he said to the new recruit as he went to get in the driving seat, 'just go and check Gate Eighteen, will you?'

'I checked it already, Sarge.'

'Go and do it again, then.'

Heather felt a small twinge of alarm. 'Please stay here,' she called out, 'I think your sergeant's planning to assault me.'

Donny walked off, looking back unhappily.

'I want you to tell me, right now, how you got in here.' The Sergeant's voice was thick with anger.

She pulled a notebook and a biro out of her pocket. 'I'm going to write down our conversation verbatim,' she said.

He reached over and pulled the biro from her hand. 'Prisoner's property,' he said. He snapped it in half. 'Whoops,' he said, 'broken prisoner's property. Now, answer the question.'

'You should get some counselling, you know,' she said. 'Deal with all that aggression. You'd be a much happier person. I simply exercised my right to walk down a public right of way.' She kept her voice as level as possible, aware that this man could flip into irrational aggression as easily as a dog sniffing fear.

'You know that's bullshit. The path is closed.'

'Not legally.'

His voice went up a little both in pitch and in volume. 'Are you going to tell me how you got in?'

'I have told you.'

'Right,' he said with a note of triumph, bringing a padlock out of his pocket, 'I have to warn you in that case that this morning, while inspecting the gates, I found this padlock, clearly sawn through, and I am therefore arresting you on suspicion of causing criminal damage to Her Majesty's property. Anything you say will be taken down in evidence and may be used against you in a court of law . . .'

'Take this down, then,' she said.

He made no move to take out his own notebook.

'Two people witnessed me gain access to the public right of way. They will testify that I did not damage any locks. I very much doubt that lock is Her Majesty's property anyway. It's got a very American look to me and I strongly suspect it's one you prepared earlier, in which case you—'

The attack was sudden. He lunged forward, got two hands round her neck and jerked her head back so sharply it struck the metalwork between the side windows with a crack. She cried out. His face was close to hers, his mouth working, uncontrolled anger preventing him from framing his words. The front door of the van opened and the pressure on her neck eased as he let go quickly and lurched back.

'I've checked the gate, Sarge,' said the younger man's voice as she blinked away tears of pain. He sounded very uncertain, worried. 'What do you want me to do. Shall I start up?'

'Yeah.'

'I could make a complaint,' she said, angry that her wavering voice betrayed her.

'I told you to be careful, throwing yourself around like that,' the sergeant said.

They took her through the gate, past the twin flagpoles where the Stars and Stripes flew next to the Union Jack.

'Does it make you proud,' she asked, 'having our very own flag up there just for you. I mean, twelve hundred Americans and twenty five English policemen and they give you a flag just the same size.'

There was a stony silence. A little Renault drew up and parked on the verge of the country road outside.

The sergeant opened the van's back door, got out and stood there as she followed. 'That your friend Margo, then?' he said. 'Just tell her from me to watch herself. She knows her bail provisions. One foot inside the boundary and I'll have her, then I can promise you it'll be straight in the slammer.'

Heather felt fully back in control now and her voice was once again full of sweet reason. 'Well, perhaps you can tell us, Sergeant Hayter, just what exactly is the boundary?' She pointed. 'Is it the grass verge, or the hedge, or the ditch, or the second hedge or the wire fence? No one seems to know.'

He got back in the van, pretending he hadn't heard. She walked over to the car. 'What happened to your head?' said the driver. She was older but very much in Heather's mould.

'Hayter,' said Heather, 'he lost his cool.'

'Are you all right?'

'Just a headache. They're digging foundations for another block the other side of the Bannerfish building. I got the site drawings. The foreman left them on the table in the office.'

'You were chancing it. Suppose they'd searched you? That would have been another theft charge.'

'Something you of course never did,' Heather said and laughed. 'To quote you – what was it? "A woman's got to do what a man wouldn't do"? Anyway there were six copies there. I thought they probably wouldn't miss one. It's got all the wiring and everything. Should give us a pretty good clue about what they're going to do in there.'

Johnny punched up the back door into the British Telecom billing computer. Heather Weston had made a lot of calls recently, mostly local. There was no immediate pattern. Tapping the buttons turned the list of numbers into a list of addresses. Ripon, Harrogate, Pateley Bridge, Otley. Initials, names, roads, postcodes. No pattern yet, the odd garage, a cinema, the rest just houses in streets that sounded Victorian, terraced, named while the Empire still stood. He ran down the list and found two, very recent, that were different and seemed linked. Applewick Guesthouse, Malham, and the Morray Arms, Horton in Ribblesdale.

Those place names immediately suggested something. He put a map disk into the CD-ROM and prowled through the index that appeared on his screen. Malham and Horton were both on the same map, the Ordnance Survey Outdoor Leisure map of Upper Wharfedale. As he expected, a dotted green line wound its way between them, north past Malham Tarn, up over Fountains Fell then west in a zigzag via the summit of Pen-y-ghent to Horton. He knew what it was – the Pennine Way, an easy one-day section of the great three-hundred-mile route that boot-slogged up the spine of Britain from the Peak peatbogs of Derbyshire to beyond the Scottish border. He knew most of the route, knew it through the soles of his boots, but not this bit. This section of the Way was in a part of Britain that he'd shunned for years. Even looking at the map induced a sense of guilt. Now though duty called, and duty always came first. He called the Malham number.

An elderly woman with a far from Yorkshire accent said, 'Applewick Guesthouse?' in a questioning tremolo. An immigrant from the Home Counties.

'Hello,' he said, 'I wonder if you can help me? My sister's booked in somewhere in the Malham area and she's asked me to change the booking but I've lost the piece of paper.'

He succeeded in sounding dithery, flustered, older and she responded just as he'd hoped.

'Oh, yes, of course, dear, what name was it?'

'Thank you so much. Weston.'

'Oh yes, I remember, she's been before. Just hold on a sec, dear.'

She came back sounding triumphant. 'Yes, I thought so. This Friday, her and her friend Miss Cowley. Just for one night. Now what did you want to change because I should warn you I'm already full for Saturday?'

'Oh no,' he said, 'thank you. I don't think that's her, not with a friend. Is that Mrs Anna Weston?'

'Oh no dear, it's Heather Weston. I am sorry. I bet you thought you'd got it first time, didn't you?'

'Thanks for trying,' he said and hung up.

The Morray Arms confirmed the rest of the picture. Two single rooms booked for Miss Weston and Miss Cowley. He left it an hour, called back in a much gruffer, down-to-earth voice and booked himself a room at both places, then he started to think about where he'd last seen his walking boots.

Hayter was on the spot. Chief Inspector Reed was already in the Base Commander's office when he was summoned but it was the Commander, a thin-lipped, austere man, who did the talking, leaving no doubt where the real power lay in the room.

'Sergeant Hayter,' he said, and his voice was Alabama soft, Alabama brutal, though to Hayter it was just another drawl, 'can you explain how this woman Weston managed to gain access to the command desk of the Saddlebush bunker without your man on the door even noticing?'

'I believe Hoskin may have had to leave his post for a very short time, sir, and I suspect she may have been waiting for the opportunity.'

'Hoskin needed to take a leak and you weren't prepared to spell him. Isn't that right, Sergeant?'

'I wouldn't say that, sir. What happened was—'

'Here's what happened, Sergeant,' said the commander and

he pressed a button. There was a bleep and a crackle from a speaker, then perfect quality, straight off the police radio link, Hoskin's voice first.

'I need a jimmy riddle, Sarge. Are you near by?'

'What's the matter, Chris? Got a weak bladder or what? That's the second time today.'

'Knock it off, Sarge, I'm bursting.'

'Stiff upper lip son, show the fucking Yanks what a Brit's made of. I've only just started my smoke break.'

Bloody hell, thought Hayter. I didn't know they were recording *us*. He made a mental note to put the word round and never, ever to let his guard slip like that again.

'Sorry, sir,' he said.

'Sorry, Sergeant? Sorry. You're a sorry joke,' said the Commander. 'I've gotten used to you not being able to stop foreign nationals walking round our base like it was open day. When they start getting open access to Saddlebush because you're taking time out for a smoke, I start to get very angry. I've been telling the Chief Inspector here that if this carries on we're going to have to insist on taking a more direct role in base security. This has gotta stop. Am I making myself clear?' He was looking at both of them, ignoring the conventions of Reed's position and their differing ranks, and so far, Reed hadn't said a thing.

Hayter left the room at a dismissive nod from Reed. The American commander glared at the English chief inspector. 'You got a problem Friday. You across it?'

Reed's mouth went dry. He disliked the Commander intensely and hated every second of the humiliation he had been put through.

'What problem would that be?'

'You don't know?'

'How can I be sure unless you tell me what you're talking about, Commander?'

'You tell me first, Chief Inspector. Do you know of any potential problem affecting us, here, this Friday? Is that plain enough?'

The policeman squirmed. 'No,' he said curtly.

The Commander had extracted his pound of flesh. He reached into his top drawer, pulled out a large sheaf of papers clipped together and passed it over.

'Mass trespass. Midday. The biggest yet. Goddam peace groups from all over the north coming through our wire.'

The words felt like drips of freezing water down the policeman's back. He leafed through the papers.

'These are phone intercepts? I need to read them.'

'I didn't say what they were. Read them here and read them fast. Outside this room you don't know they exist. Get on it, Chief Inspector. See if just maybe, just for once, you can stop them walking right through my base.'

It took Reed ten minutes to go through the papers under the Commander's sardonic gaze, ten minutes in which he kept wondering how domestic phone intercepts had sidetracked him so embarrassingly without coming down the usual pipeline from Cheltenham.

Bob and Dolly did a lot of business that Friday morning. Margo, Heather and the other peace women had given them plenty of warning and they turned up in the lay-by bright and early, laden down with supplies. Four times the usual stock of bacon, sausages, beefburgers and rolls, a hundred of Dolly's juicy cottage pies and two hundred portions of the thick crusted apple pie that always went well when there was a special occasion at the Stray. They were raking in the money from the moment they raised the caravan shutters. The police were rotated through their refreshment breaks and being civilian coppers, not the MOD, they were excluded from going into the base unless it became operationally necessary. The local Harrogate and Otley lads knew Dolly's reputation for good food and weren't slow to spread the word, so the queue at the caravan's open flap stretched away into the distance all morning.

Bob and Dolly usually saw quite a lot of the modplods, as they patrolled the base perimeter and stopped off for a mug of tea and a chat. Today though, there was no sign of them. They were all inside the base, called in whether they were on shift or not, feverishly checking the wire, eyes glued to the monitor console in the Operations Room for any sign of trouble. Bob and Dolly's customers today were regulars called in from as far away as Northallerton and York, deserting their usual duties to line the lanes all round the outside of the base, riot shields and helmets piled up in the backs of the vans. They didn't take it too seriously. Previous demonstrations around the base had usually been good-tempered affairs, with most of the spleen coming from their MOD opposite numbers, who seemed to take it all very personally. The civilian bobbies didn't think much of their MOD colleagues and weren't slow in saying so. 'They just don't know the law' was the usual verdict; 'arrogant sods too. They're going to go too far one day, kick someone's head in, I shouldn't wonder.'

By midday the visiting police were, to a man, pissed off.

'Bloody mass trespass? Like bloody hell,' said a dour sergeant. 'I'll have a burger, please, love.'

'Sorry. You're a bit too late for that. Do you a nice sausage in a roll with a bit of extra bacon on it?' She was sorry there were no more burgers. It was her private joke, when they asked for ketchup, to paint a CND badge on to the burger with the spout of the plastic ketchup squeezer before putting the bun on top. She did it in full view and they never noticed.

'All right, then, and a mug of coffee and maybe a bit of that apple pie with it.'

'So there's nothing happening? Do you want custard?'

'Got a bit of cream? I'll say there's nothing bloody happening. Bloody fools in there don't know what the bloody hell they're talking about. It's going to cost someone a flaming fortune in overtime, this lot.'

His radio crackled. 'Sarge. Ops Room have been on. They say they can see two people coming your way on the monitor, down the sideroad. Can you check them out?'

He looked round. Two old women, one with a stick, walked slowly up the lane from the south and stopped by the main road. A small bus ground into view over the hill, slowed to a halt and picked them up.

The sergeant balanced his plates in one hand and keyed the

transmit switch. 'Yeah. Tell the Ops Room it's Che Guevara and Chairman Mao and I'm pretty sure they've got the Red Army in their shopping bags.'

A dribble of cream slid off the apple pie and down the sleeve of his uniform. 'Bugger!' he said with feeling.

Inside Ramsgill Stray, Chief Inspector Reed was starting to feel quite pleased with himself. He was in the Operations Room with the Commander standing beside him and the Commander was showing signs of tension as the clock ticked on. The Commander's pal, the old spook with the cropped hair, was standing there impassively. Noon was only seconds away, and the cameras covering the roads around the base told their story all too clearly. By now, on a peace group day of action, there should have been a mass of activity, cars, minibuses, even coaches disgorging hundreds of protesters unwrapping their banners and getting ready for a bit of sitting down or fence rattling. Usually it was a colourful scene. Instead the screens were dominated by white and blue police vans lined up along the verges as far as the camera could see, bored policemen strolling up and down or sitting inside reading their newspapers.

As the hands of the clock hit noon, he turned to the Commander. He'd chosen the words carefully, rehearsed them for maximum impact.

'What would you like me to do with all these people?' he said mildly.

Before the Commander could answer all six of the phones on the desk chose the same moment to start ringing. They jumped, looked quickly at the monitors. Nothing. The Chief Inspector picked up the nearest phone. 'Reed here.'

It was an unfamiliar man's voice and it sounded surprised for a moment. 'Ah! Chief Inspector Reed. How nice to have the chance to talk to you. My name's Maurice Cannon and I'm just ringing to ask you to consider whether as an upholder of British law you really should be helping to preserve a foreign operation on our soil which is probably illegal and certainly interfering with the . . .'

He put the phone down, looked around and saw others in the room who'd also picked up phones and were now staring, hypnotized by what was being said to them. He picked the receiver up again. But the man at the other end hadn't stopped. His voice went relentlessly on. '. . . things they couldn't do in America. If we had a proper constitution in this country you would probably be facing charges of . . .' He put it back down and looked at the Commander.

'There's your mass trespass,' he said, 'mass trespass by telephone. I don't think your people could have done quite enough work on their transcripts, do you?'

The Commander looked round at all the phones. 'How did they get the numbers?' he said, and he sounded suddenly less hard, less confident.

They heard running footsteps and a young man in a blue suit came into the room fast. Olly Gandrell, the Commander's gopher.

'Sir,' he said, 'I couldn't call you. The phone system's all backed up. Every phone in the place seems to be going.'

'Everywhere? Not just the Ops Room?'

'Right through the main block.'

'Goddam it.' Until then he'd been hoping this was some kind of police problem. The Ops Room was a British operation, just the MOD police. If their numbers had leaked into the world outside that was one thing, but the direct dials into the main block? Those were NSA numbers and that bothered him a lot. 'Gandrell. I'll want a complete log of all incoming calls, who they are, what they said. Everything.'

'Sir.'

It wasn't just in the offices within the base – it was in the club, the restaurant, the bank, the workshops and even, most worryingly for the security staff, down in the depths of the Saddlebush bunker. After the first five minutes the word went round, spread by the separate intercom system, that no one was to pick up any phone until further notice. Normal work ground gradually to a halt. But the Commander was slow to absorb the fact that this was only part of it. In the houses clustered in the northern end of the base compound the phones were also ringing, and wives of base personnel were being exposed to an outside world they didn't often encounter. Even those who had chosen to live outside the base, in the surrounding villages, weren't immune.

The local peace groups had worked long and hard. Their first source was the pile of internal phone directories which they had collected on various illicit trips into the base, copied and passed around among themselves. Then there was another file, put together slowly and laboriously by a dedicated group. It had meant going through each successive issue of the local phone book, collecting new names, looking at where they lived and whether they sounded American, then ringing them under some pretext to see if they were base workers living in the surrounding area. They'd been astonishingly successful.

When the word reached the group around the Base Commander that the families were all being called, it elicited a series of very contradictory responses. The Commander was shocked and furious. The impassive older man next to him began to think, as he always did, about whether there was anything in this set-back that could be turned to advantage. There was a problem he was dealing with and in these unexpected events, he began to discern a possible solution. He moved rapidly in search of a suitable helper.

Since noon, Heather had made six calls to offices inside the base. Alone in the quiet, cluttered room she used as a study in her small stone cottage, she wished they could all be doing this together. It would be much more fun if she could break off and tell some of the others the funnier moments along the way, but she knew they didn't have access to any one place with enough phones to make it work, knew also that the electronic trespass had to be organized with care, by post and word of mouth, lest the electronic ears they were trying to block should get to hear of what they were planning and take steps to frustrate it.

It had been Margo who had the idea of deliberately misleading the other side while at the same time checking out once and for all what they believed to be true, that their own phones were targets of the buggers on the Stray; so they'd made carefully orchestrated phone calls discussing the timetable and the arrangements for the trespass, phone calls that had been designed to suggest the trespass would be a physical event. Then they'd sent a car past to take a look a couple of hours before noon and had a good laugh at the fuss they seemed to have caused. So someone out there was listening. It came as no surprise.

Heather moved on to the seventh number on her list. Of the first four, two had allowed her to say her piece, without comment except a polite, 'Thank you ma'am,' one had slammed the phone down straight away and the fourth had broken into a tirade of foul-mouthed abuse until someone at his own end of the line had interrupted him. The last two calls had just rung and rung so she had switched to the list of house numbers.

This one rang twice and was answered by a very American female voice, high pitched, weary, nasal. 'Lanie Gerow.'

'Oh, hello,' she said, 'I just thought I'd call you for a chat.'

'Who is this, please?,

'You don't know me. My name's Heather. I live near by. We're just a group of people anxious to extend the hand of friendship to newcomers to our community.'

The woman's voice brightened a bit. 'Gee, that's nice. I haven't met too many British people since we moved in. My old man says British people don't like us too much.'

'Oh, that's a shame. It's not your fault that your husband works for the NSA. I'm sure you didn't ask him to.'

'Well, that's right,' Lanie said with enthusiasm, and then a little note of caution crept in to her voice. 'How do you mean, not my fault?'

Heather kept her voice breezy. 'Well, I thought that was what you meant about your old man. I mean if the British don't like what the NSA is doing here that's no reason to be nasty to families like yours, now is it?'

'Well, I guess that's right,' said Lanie, 'but Pacman, he ain't doing nothing wrong here, just keeping the world safe for democracy.'

'There's a lot of good men who believe that, Lanie. Like I say, it's not their fault the NSA's doing things it shouldn't really be doing, listening in on our phones for example. Probably even listening in to this call.'

'Well, I'll tell you, Heather. I don't hold with that either. Not back home and not here. If my Pacman's doing that, it ain't right.'

'I'm glad to hear you say that, Lanie.'

'I been feelin' it. Just haven't found the opportunity to say it before.'

Heather knew she mustn't let this one slip away. 'Lanie, I'll give you my number. If you want to talk more, give me a call.'

In the normal way of things, Pacman didn't go inside the dish buildings. That was for engineers. The message came from Olly Gandrell in person, springing him from his shift. That made it unusual and it made it interesting. He expected Gandrell to come with him but he waved a goodbye as Pacman got in the Buick. He wondered about it as he drove down the road into the dish farm and bumped left on to the unfinished new track which led to the latest addition to the Stray's battery of giant dishes.

There was a Nissan coupé parked outside but no one was in it. The door in the base of the golf ball opened as he came to it. He'd seen the man who stood there around the base but only fleetingly, a wizened man in late middle age whose creased leathery skin fitted closely round the bones of his face under a brush of close cropped vertical hair. His eyes gave nothing away.

'Mr Gerow,' he said in a rasping voice, 'I apologize for any inconvenience or disruption I might be causing to your work.'

'No need,' said Pacman, wondering. The man's eyes looked yellow but that could have been the light filtering through the translucent plastic of the soaring dome above their heads. The gantry loomed above them, the dish installed on its pivots ready to swing up to receive the beam from the bird. For now though it was standing vertical, focused uselessly on the horizon, waiting for the infinite minutiae of connections for its commissioning.

'The name's Ray,' said the man putting out his hand, 'from OS/M5.'

Office of Security, thought Pacman with a sudden tingle, the spooks' spooks.

'You want to check me out,' said the man nodding at the phone on the wall, 'Gandrell's on the other end.'

Pacman shook his head. 'I buy it.'

'We got a little problem you can help with. Detach you from duty from time to time. Intensive monitoring of a few targets. Personal for me and my mob. Could just include one or two unorthodox operations.'

Unorthodox operations. Pacman thought about it. 'Do I get paperwork?'

The older man looked at him coolly. 'No, I guess not.'

The four words hung between them and the meaning was quite clear. Even by the NSA's unaccountable standards this was an unaccountable assignment. If anything misfired no one but Pacman himself would be in the firing line. Private snooping would be the explanation, a regrettable departure from this officer's impeccable record, a lapse of judgement with implications for his future career. End of story.

As if Ray knew what he was thinking, the other man said, 'Been reading your life story. Get stuck or something? You're only a GG12, Pacman. GG12 with a great record and a double load of talent. That the limit of your ambition, son? Gonna stay a technician all your life?'

To go higher in the NSA, you had to professionalize, cross the line to the back room. Somewhere in Pacman's image of his future self was a man who would always be at the sharp end, ready for the days when they'd take to the air again to ride their electronic chariots against some other evil empire.

'Why not?' he said.

'Just wondered. File says you're too smart for it.'

'I like it.'

'Your choice. Thing is, on the back of this one, say you

happen to want promotion, then I guess I could help.' The man looked at him, summing him up. 'Your old man would have wanted you to move up the ladder.'

'My dad? What do you know about my dad?'

'Walt? We were pals at Incirlik. I flew with him. Shoulda been on that flight myself but I went sick with some kinda stomach bug. Saved my life, that bug.'

'You were on the ferret flights?' Pacman reassessed the man's age. Had to be late fifties – older than he looked, old for the NSA.

'And some. I was on the *Liberty* too.'

'Ray . . .' Pacman reviewed the ship's survivor list in his head and got it. 'You're Ray Mackeson?'

'Yeah.' The man nodded and knew that Pacman was his, hook, line and sinker. 'Tell you 'bout your old man later,' he said, 'we gotta move. See, the way it is, we got a little problem with your wife and I aim to see you ain't compromised. This phone trespass thing? She took a call. Guess she was a bit indiscreet. She said some things she shouldn't have.'

Pacman looked shocked and then angry. 'Goddam. OK, I'll talk to her. I'll see she don't talk to them again.'

'No, no, son,' said Mackeson, 'you got it all wrong. You and I need to go have a friendly chat with Lanie. Calling them again is just exactly what we *do* want.'

Heather was amazed when the phone call came so quickly.

'Heather. It's Lanie Gerow? I was thinking about what you said? I'd really like to meet.'

'Fine. Where did you have in mind?'

At the end of the call, Lanie – her eyes still red – put the phone down. Pacman squeezed her shoulder.

'That's my girl.'

The scary old man with the funny skin just gave her a big wolfish grin.

CHAPTER SEVEN

They were still reminiscing about the day of the telephone trespass on the drive to Malham.

'Getting Lanie on board was a real coup,' said Margo. 'It was very brave of her to give you the documents. Have you talked to her lately?'

'Three times in eight weeks. I don't want to push her too hard. She has to be very careful which phones she uses. I told her we sent the stuff to the Hurst Inquiry but I'm not at all sure she knew what it was. She's totally unpolitical.'

'Could she get in trouble?'

'She says it can't be traced back.'

They made good time to Skipton in the Friday evening traffic, though the little Citroën was slow up anything resembling a hill. Beyond Gargrave a new lightness crept into the countryside, small fields now divided by pale stone walls of gleaming limestone. Beside the splashing course of the River Aire black-faced sheep cropped bright grass, their spindly legs looking inadequate for the thick woolly mass they had to support. Up to Malham the road wound through fields and small hamlets with the river running beside them from time to time, then veering away again. The roof of the 2CV was rolled back and they could smell the summer evening warmth releasing a rich mixture from the fields as they passed.

'We haven't done this for a while,' said Margo, looking at the view.

'We shouldn't be doing it now,' Heather replied. 'It's very extravagant of you but I do appreciate it.'

'I can't think of a better use for a hundred pounds which I wasn't even expecting. I think you need the fresh air, not to mention a break from the evil presence of Ramsgill Stray.'

'I don't know what I'd do without you.'

Heather first met Margo her first week at the Hall. Tinderley Hall was a last resort for incorrigible boys, sent there from all over the country when all else failed. Margo was a legend there. She was a visiting psychologist who possessed a rare ability to break through the age gap, and the even bigger attitude gap, to the boys in the Hall. Heather tried to follow her lead and found it hard. Then Margo disappeared and it was only by persistent questioning that Heather found out where she was. It was a shock to learn she was in prison. She went to visit to find out what it was that meant so much to this sane, stable mother-figure, twenty years older than her, that she was prepared to hazard everything. A month for criminal damage was one thing but worse was the threat of professional censure that followed, a threat that Margo fought off by insisting that her ultimate professional commitment was to preserve life and if her personal belief was that active involvement in the peace movement was the logical final flowering of that, then she was only doing what she ought to. It took little time to radicalize Heather and when Margo was finally banned from entering the base by bail conditions and an onerous injunction, she took up the challenge to the full.

For the last few miles past Airton and Kirkby Malham there was a sports car behind them, a little green Mazda MX5 with the top down. Heather expected it to whizz past at the first straight but the driver seemed content to loaf along behind them in the evening sun. She could see in the mirror he had dark glasses and a flying jacket on and but for his slow pace she would have dismissed him as another macho jerk. He was still behind them as they drove into the village of Malham, still behind them when they turned down the lane to the guest-house, still behind them when she turned into the gate and as she stopped he pulled up alongside.

'Hmm,' said Margo, 'fellow guest, do you think? Or is he just a closet Citroën fancier?'

'I haven't a clue.'

'Well, don't let me cramp your style, Heather. He's rather gorgeous.'

'Oh come on, Margo. Not my type, I like wholemeal, not sliced white.'

Matthew Quill had come to the end of a very surprising week. In the last month, he had come to dread the postman. The pile of letters on the mat when he got back home from the labs each evening seemed to make his predicament worse and worse. So many petty things, all conspiring to empty his bank account. Now the bloody washing machine too. There quite simply wasn't any money left and it wasn't as if he'd been extravagant. He was absolutely certain he hadn't take out the cash his statement said he had. The receipts made no sense. What had he been doing, sleepwalking? He had the receipts. He couldn't argue with that and therefore he couldn't argue with the bank. Was he going mad? Then his bank manager refused him a loan and that was very, very nearly the final straw. The call from the head hunters had come out of the blue. He knew such things happened but somehow not to him. What he had going for him was a very slender body of research and it needed more time. It wasn't as if he had results he could publish yet, so why did they want him?

The man he went to see near St Pauls was smooth, enthusiastic and vague on details.

'Good pay. Very good, even. Bloody good lifestyle in Auckland. Excellent move for a man at your stage of career development. Five year contract.'

'Why me?'

'Can't really tell you that. Someone somewhere likes you. Your name was on a very short list by the time it got to me.'

'It's not even my line.'

The head hunter peered doubtfully at the file in front of him. 'They seem to think so.'

'I've been concentrating on psychoactive effects.'

'Look, old boy, they're offering you a flight out for a look-see. Think of it as a free holiday. I'd bite their hand off if I were you. It's a hell of a lot of money.'

New Zealand. He'd felt a bit depressed going back to his office, back to the painstaking re-analysis which might tell him where his experiment had screwed up, back to find a Post-it note that his bank manager wanted a call back as soon as possible please. Two days to think about it.

And then that night, unlocking the front door and bending with a shudder to pick up the pile of bad news – that was when the real surprise had come. One of the envelopes was thick and white and had 'Palmer and Hunt' neatly imprinted across the top of the back flap.

They sounded like lawyers and his first chill thought was of a summons but it was nothing like that. His aunt, Bernice Hodges, had, said Mr Hunt of Palmer and Hunt, passed away on the twenty eighth of the previous month and had bequeathed to him her house near Petworth in Sussex and the residue of her estate which Mr Hunt estimated to be of the order of £83,000 net. Probate would take some time to grant, he said, but in the meantime he was sure Mr Quill would wish to visit his inheritance and a key would be available on demand from his office and so on.

It changed everything. He hadn't seen Aunt Bernice since childhood although there were no other members to his family. She just hadn't felt like a relation. He tried to feel sorry for her, summoned up only a twinge of guilt that he could put no face to her name and could only think instead that now he could, for a time, forget research grants. Now he could carry on by himself. He rang the head hunter and turned down the New Zealand job.

'Look, no need to be in a rush,' the man said, 'take a few days.'

'I thought you said I had to make up my mind quickly.'

'Just think about it, that's all I'm saying. It's a chance in a million.'

'I have thought, thanks. Goodbye.'

The head hunter put the phone down, frowned and picked

it up again. Matthew Quill did the same, without the frown, and called Mr Hunt.

'I'm coming down tomorrow. I'll stay the night at the house. How do I get the key?'

'My secretary lives in the next street. She can take it home with her. Do you want me to ask her to get anything ready for you?'

'No thanks.'

He drove to Sussex on Saturday morning in his Fiesta, reclaimed from the car pound, to investigate. The Maples was large and gloomy, built in Victorian times of red brick interspersed with sections of knapped flint. He knew within seconds that he would never live there but that wasn't important. Selling the house would buy him time to carry on. Aunt Bernice, he thought, had saved him.

Had he but known, she had really put him in direct and dreadful danger.

The house was set back behind a high brick wall, among lawns dotted with overgrown and gloomy trees. Aunt Bernice had lived an old-fashioned, simple life. Someone would have a lot of work to do. It was a house of sculleries and pantries, passages and box rooms on which nothing in the way of a design trend had had any effect since some time in the Fifties. He wanted to stay the night just so that waking up in the morning he might start to feel and understand his good fortune and spend a little time thanking this distant aunt for her final kind thought.

He put the radio on in the evening – there was no television. The house, unlived in for some time, the lawyer had said, while his aunt spent her last weeks in hospital, grew sharply colder when it got dark. There was no central heating but he'd seen a pile of coal in the sheds at the back. He went outside. The yard light didn't work and there was no moon, so he groped his way across the uneven paving stones to the long row of outbuildings. In daylight he'd seen the evidence of what had probably been loose boxes to each side of the wide central doorway, but the spaces were now filled up with rubbish – rusted bicycles, piles of broken furniture, ladders and the like.

In the dark, his hand closed on the light switch set high up on the wall inside.

He turned it on and for a moment nothing happened then a rusty neon light glowed dull orange and began to flicker cold white light. The darknesses in between its clicks and flutters were too long, it couldn't catch. Then he glanced to his left and his blood froze. There was movement in the flashes. From the far end of the stables, a figure was strobing horribly towards him, terrifyingly closer with each flash, arms rising to threaten – a man's figure, swathed in darkness from head to toe, darkness that defied the neon. A flickering, violent nightmare, disappearing in the black between the flashes and reappearing ever larger, ever nearer. A man with darkness for a face in a scene from a 3D horror film.

He started to scream but nothing came out, then tried to get his legs to turn and run. The man reached him – no ghost this – hurled him to the ground, spraying something in his face which made his throat burn and his stomach's acid contents come heaving galvanically up his throat. He doubled up on the rough concrete outside, vomiting and shrieking through his vomit, trying to see though watering eyes where the threat had gone. The light's brief bursts lent fresh terror to the darkness as the man reappeared, framed in the doorway.

He tried to organize his jellied legs, tried to get away from the shape that now had in its hand a blade, bouncing neon back at him in lethal, flashing reflection. He got as far as his knees but the man had him by the collar, pulling him off balance as he tried to protect himself with arms that offered their feeble defensive sacrifice of skin, bone and sinew.

He was pulled back against the doorpost and released. He lifted his head, saw the arm drawn back with the knife in it and closed his eyes, powerless to avoid sharp, shocking death.

There was a thud, just a thud, right next to his ear and the sound of running feet.

He opened his eyes again and away in the lane heard a car door slam, an engine start and tyres scatter gravel. Heart beating so fast that the other senses seemed to have no space in his head, he turned, trying to control his retching. The knife wasn't a knife, it was a wood chisel. It was embedded in the doorpost an inch from his eyes skewering a piece of newspaper to the woodwork. With shaking hands, he pulled it out, trying to make sense of it as the chemical spray dripped down his face mixing with the vomit on his chin. The light chose that moment, far too late, to come on fully. TOP SCIENTIST FOUND DEAD, the headline said.

Mrs Marsh was used to walkers, dependent on them even. A painted sign, impossible to ignore, said *Dirty feet this way please!* with a peremptory arrow to back up the exclamation mark. It led to a large lean-to out of sight around the side of the house where boots could be levered from tired feet and scraped clean in a big Belfast sink. There were racks to stack them in and ranged in an inner lobby which served as a second line of defence an array of old slippers lay waiting as the passport to final entry. Heather and Margo knew this from their last trip the year before and they knew why. Mrs Marsh kept not just a clean house but an immaculate, obsessively, surgically clean house – a perverse ambition for the owner of a guest-house whose main appeal was its location in the middle of the most spectacular, wild – and frequently wet – walking country in the north.

'Do we dare go straight in?' asked Margo.

'We're clean and dry and we have nothing to fear but fear itself – and Mrs Marsh,' said Heather. She took her backpack and headed firmly for the front door. It opened before she got to it and Mrs Marsh, all five foot two inches of her below a frizzy halo of white hair, came out, preceded by her bosom, with a broad smile of welcome on her face.

'Miss Weston, welcome back, and Miss Cowley. How very nice to see you again. Your rooms are all ready.' Heather didn't miss the surreptitious glance she shot at their feet. 'And that must be Mr Kennedy. Have you all come together?'

'No,' said Heather, looking round. The man in the flying jacket was a few yards away putting the hood up on his sports car. He fastened the clips, took off his sun glasses and smiled at all of them. It was a nice smile, Heather thought to herself, impish perhaps. It made her think that if he had sisters they would certainly be beautiful. He took a bag out of the boot and strolled over.

'Hello,' he said to Mrs Marsh, 'I'm Johnny Kennedy. I booked a room for tonight?'

'You did indeed, and this is Miss Weston and Miss Cowley. Do come in and I'll show you to your rooms.' She looked somewhat more obviously at *his* feet but they passed the test because she led the way to the front door. They reached the door almost together and the man stood aside and bowed Heather and Margo through. How old fashioned, Heather thought. Inside it was just as she remembered, an over-upholstered fluffy fantasy, frills and cushions everywhere and the cats . . . not real cats of course, they would rapidly have disrupted the fragile equilibrium of Mrs Marsh's little heaven. These were porcelain, plaster, wood, stone, plastic, anything that could be carved into a cat shape and painted. They were in the form of teapots, biscuit boxes, pin cushions, on every flat surface, on special shelf units and display cabinets, on the floor as doorstops – everywhere you looked.

Heather saw the expression on the man's face for just a second as he took it in. This was clearly someone who would have been much more at ease staying in the local pub. He caught her looking at him and got his expression back under control.

'I've put you two in the same rooms as last time, Tabitha for you Miss Weston and Duchess for Miss Cowley.' She handed them keys and then turned to the man.

'It's Macavity for you, Mr Kennedy. I hope you don't mind being up another flight. It's a very cosy room with a dormer.'

'That's no problem, Mrs Marsh,' he said. 'Tell me, will it be all right to leave the car out there until Sunday? I'm walking, you see.'

'I've three more coming tomorrow but if you move it right over by the hedge there should be space. That's what Miss Weston and Miss Cowley are doing too. What time would you all like your breakfast?'

The man paused and looked questioningly at Heather for her to answer first.

'Eight o'clock?' she suggested and Margo nodded.

'Could I have mine around seven thirty?' he asked.

Heather and Margo had half an hour to shower, stretch and take temporary possession of their rooms by laying out a few of the markers of occupancy: tomorrow's clothes, hairbrushes, books. After that they strolled together down through the village to the pub where they bought shandies at the bar and studied the menu on the blackboard. Margo caught Heather scanning the crowded room.

'Looking for Mr Kennedy?' she enquired mischievously.

Heather snorted. 'Well, I suppose I was, if you must know. Only because I can't see him spending an evening at Mrs Marsh's.'

'He looked so funny, didn't he? Really out of place. Sort of the wrong size. I could see Mrs Marsh worrying in case he swept one of her precious cats to the floor.'

'I know. I supposed he just picked it at random. It's not the sort of place you expect to find beautiful single men. No sign of a woolly hat or an anorak either. He just doesn't seem the type to be out for a weekend by himself.'

'OK, let's guess,' suggested Margo. 'I think he's a male model who's on the rebound from discovering his partner has run off with a top politician.'

'What sex is the partner?'

'What party is the politician?'

'No, anyway I think you're wrong. I think he's a top Olympic bob-sleigh rider who crashed terribly badly last time out and now he's come to the hills to wrestle with his overwhelming fear of downhill slopes.'

'Oh dear,' said Margo, 'and Mrs Marsh has gone and put him in the top room. Do you think we'd better ask her to move him in with one of us in case he has nightmares?

'He's all yours if you want him,' said Heather. 'You're right, though, he's very good looking, but he's still not my type.'

'Don't be cruel. He's the sort who would leap up and offer

me his chair because I'm old enough to be his mother's younger sister.'

They didn't see him in the morning. Mrs Marsh said he'd gone off straight after his breakfast but he'd remembered to park his car very neatly out of the way first and wasn't he a nice young man? They swung up the lane northwards out of the village, the Pennines beckoning through clear refreshing air that was full of birdsong. The footpath branched right beside a stream into woodland. Malham Cove came into sudden view through the trees, a curved rampart of limestone one hundred yards high, the skeleton below the long departed foaming skin of a giant waterfall.

They climbed up and around the edge of the cliff and paused at the top, standing on the petrified river bed, eroded into blocks with waving edges. Deep in the damp cracks between the blocks, green ferns softened the darkness. They gazed past the wooded valley at their feet to the wide stretch of open ground to the south. Margo looked round and pointed suddenly. Away to their left on the shoulder of the hill, a far-off figure sat in the sunlight.

'There's your bob-sleigh champion,' she said, 'facing up to his fear.'

'He's off course if he's trying to follow the Way,' Heather observed, studying him in the distance. 'Do you think he knows?'

'I think he's old enough to look after himself,' said Margo, and they set off again.

They were hot and thirsty by the time they came to the great still lake at Malham Tarn and they went down to the water's edge to drink from their bottles and splash the peaty lake water on their faces.

'I could live somewhere like this,' said Heather, 'find me a farmer or something and stop worrying about the world.'

'You wouldn't though, would you?' said Margo calmly. 'You couldn't take your eye off it all, not with what you know. That's the trouble. It's too late for you.'

'Do you wish you hadn't started?'

She pulled off her boots and socks and splashed her feet in the water. 'What's the point of wishing? I suppose everyone starts off trusting the State. Then maybe a few scandals crop up or they hear a few things that make them sit up and think. Most people go on thinking: well, OK, maybe the State sometimes cocks it up, maybe it has to do something a bit murky every now and then, but its heart's in the right place. I mean, the State is us, right? It's only when you realize the state isn't us, that somehow, somewhere along the way our great-grandfathers passed over control of all the important things to a bunch of faceless, nameless custodians who think *we* can't be trusted with them. That's when you just have to get stuck in and say you're not going to take it.'

Heather nodded. 'When did that moment come for you?'

Margo considered silently for a while. 'Put it down to one of the lessons of a failed marriage.'

Heather waited, but nothing else came. 'Just that?'

'Believe it or not, I was married to a policeman,' Margo said as if that explained everything.

They sat there for a few more minutes, content to look out across the surface of the tarn to the hills rising beyond, neither of them noticing that Johnny had passed them and strode on ahead. In a while they heaved their packs on to their backs again, left the lake behind and started climbing the long hillside.

They weren't in any particular hurry. The day was theirs and the mileage wasn't great. They stopped often to soak up the view, struck by the grim determination of most of the other walkers they frequently met on the well-worn path. They went off the track on the side of Fountains Fell, climbing up to the little tarn below the stone worm casts that marked the old mine workings on the bleak summit. There they ate Mrs Marsh's lunch then stretched out with their packs as pillows and went to sleep for an hour. The sunshine balanced the fresh breeze which blew across their faces with the soft scent of miles of heathery moor. When they woke they set off round the far shoulder of the Fell, bearing to the west and there ahead, an hour's walk away, loomed the last obstacle of the day: the great rounded sphinx that was Pen-y-ghent, crouched across the valley, a double step in its edge showing where it wore its millstone grit cap on top of the limestone.

Margo sighed. 'The Hill of the Winds. That's what it means. Celtic. It's quite reassuring,' she said, 'it gives you back a sense of scale – makes you realize we're just ants.'

'Dangerous ants,' said Heather. 'I'd back the mountain against us ants long term, but we'll probably manage to do something pretty horrible to it along the way.'

'Well, forget that for now. Just breathe in the air and listen to the peaceful sound of the—'

She was cut short by the sudden arrival of a phenomenon. A grey needle-nosed shape rushed silently into view from around the side of the hill, almost on their level, slanting round the contour with immense speed just over their heads. They had a microsecond to recognize the RAF roundels on its swept-back wings before they were assaulted by a battering crescendo of pure noise that seemed to shake the whole hillside, dwindling only gradually as the fighter ducked even lower to the ground behind them, leaving in its wake a paraffin-lamp smell of hydrocarbons being burnt at a fantastic rate.

'Christ Al-bloody-mighty!' Margo shouted. 'What the hell do they think they're doing? Why do they have to come and ruin everything?'

Heather couldn't repress a grin. 'The peaceful sound of *what* were you about to say?'

Margo snorted.

'Have you heard what they do in America?' she went on. 'Sometimes, when you get an airbase near a town they put up signs saying "Don't complain. The sound you hear is the sound of freedom." Honest!'

'More like the sound of someone setting fire to my tax contributions.'

'You know what we just saw, don't you?'

'What?'

'An ant on stilts with a megaphone.'

It was getting late in the afternoon when they finally struggled up the steep path of slippery earth and loose rock to the rounded top of Pen-y-ghent. Heather's pack, its straps stiffened by a year of disuse, had started to chafe her shoulders and it made for heavy going up the gradient. She looked down at her feet as she climbed doggedly, taking it one step at a time. It was a relief when the slope abruptly slackened and an instant later she heard Margo say, 'Well, look who we have here.'

Sitting on the stile that led over the stone wall ahead was Mr Johnny Kennedy, studying a map intently. He looked up at Margo's voice.

'Hello,' he said with enthusiasm, 'this is a nice surprise. Have you had a good day?'

'I have,' said Margo. 'Poor Heather's suffering a bit. She's been having a bit of trouble with her pack.'

'It's nothing,' said Heather, 'it's not far now anyway.'

'Are you heading for Horton?' he said, jumping down from the stile.

'Yes.'

'Me too. I'll take your pack.'

'What about yours?' she said.

'No problem. It's very light. I can strap it on to yours.'

'There's no need really,' she said.

'It's easy. My bergen's got nothing much in it, I'd enjoy the extra bit of weight – helps the balance.'

She noticed the use of what sounded like an army term. 'Well . . . it's kind of you. If you don't mind.'

'Not a bit.'

It was downhill steeply for a while to the valley west of Pen-y-ghent, past the gaping mouth of Hunt Pot. They couldn't easily walk together until they were down on the flat, which gave Heather plenty of time to study the man walking in front of her and wonder about him. Very athletic, clearly. Expensive gear and clothing.

They stopped to look at the pothole entrance.

'Have you ever been down one?' he asked.

'No. Have you?'

'Absolutely not. I can't imagine anything worse. I could just about cope with crawling along through rock tunnels, it's the idea of going through U-bends full of water and hoping you get to the other side before your breath runs out that gets me. Give me the clear blue sky any day – the sky and a few clouds to tear around.'

'You fly?'

'I'm a pilot. That's what I do.'

Margo had been listening. 'Not RAF, are you?'

He laughed. 'Oh no. Commercial.'

'Just as well. We nearly got blown off our feet by some cowboy practising flying below ground level.'

'That Tornado? I saw it. No, I fly quiet little things, Cessnas, Pipers and stuff like that.'

'Where are you from?' Heather asked.

'Nowhere much lately. I've been out in Australia for a few years. Just come back. I've borrowed a flat in London but I'm looking around for something to do.'

'We'd better get on,' said Margo, 'we don't want the Morray to give our rooms away.'

'The Morray Arms? Are you staying there too?' he said with pleasure in his voice. 'So am I.'

'Twice in two nights. Well, there's a surprise,' said Heather.

'One thing though . . .' he dropped his voice and put on a look of acute worry.

'What?'

'Do they go in for . . . you know . . .'

'No, I don't. What?'

'Cats.'

Heather and Margo burst out laughing and the gap between them and their new companion shrank.

'No,' Heather said, 'no cats.'

'Not even pictures of cats?'

'No.'

'Cat decorations on the plates?'

'Absolutely not. I think there might be a real cat though.'

'A real cat? Oh, that's all right.'

The pub welcomed them with comfortable rooms and hot baths. Heather and Margo opened the interconnecting door between their rooms and found they could talk while lying in their baths.

'Have you changed your mind?' Margo called.

'About?'

'About him not being your type.'

'Oh, do stop it. No, I haven't. He's a posh pilot with a sports car. I shouldn't think we've got any common ground at all. Probably votes Conservative, eats red meat twice a day, plays polo and has loads of girlfriends who go to flower-arranging classes.'

'So why's he out on the Pennines all by himself?'

'I told you. Bobsleigh accident.'

'In Australia?'

'Well, a surfboard, then.'

'I think you're wrong. Why don't we ask him if he wants to eat with us?'

'Why?'

'Well, we're all going to be walking back the same way tomorrow and he did carry your backpack.'

'Him Tarzan, we Jane?'

'I think he might be just a little bit lonely. Maybe he's not a fascist. There's something quite romantic about him.'

'Margo. I'm starting to think you've got it bad.'

She had her way, though. They knocked on his door and soon they were sitting round an old oak table in the dining-room of the bar, looking at menus.

'The vegetarian bit's on page three,' Heather said to Margo.

Johnny flipped over to it. 'Oh good,' he said, 'I was wondering. Broccoli and mushroom mornay sounds about right.'

One preconception gone, thought Heather.

'I did a bit of work for the Flying Doctor Service, out around Alice Springs,' said Johnny. 'One of them was a dietitian. He put me off meat for life.'

'I should think that's an uphill struggle out there,' said Heather. 'I thought they liked their meat raw.'

'Some of them,' he said vaguely. 'This guy was big on additives too. Scary stuff.'

Margo and Heather exchanged a look.

'Are you going to go on flying now you're back?' asked Margo.

'I hope so. Plane deliveries, air-taxi work, that sort of stuff. If I have to, I'll train as an instructor.'

Heather was studying him. 'Why did you come back?' she said suddenly.

'Well,' he said, 'I suppose I missed it.'

'Your family?'

'I don't have any real family.'

'What then?'

'All this' – he indicated the room, or maybe the hills outside – 'Shared experience.'

'Has it changed much?'

'Yes,' he said, 'a lot. It's got much more repressive in many ways. People don't seem nearly so free. I'm surprised more of them don't complain at what's being done to them. I think you have to be prepared to stand up and be counted.'

'What are you prepared to stand up and be counted for?' said Heather.

'No,' he said, 'you first. You've asked me lots of questions.'

The waitress arrived and took their order. They waited until she'd gone.

'That's fair,' said Margo. 'Go on, Heather, you tell him what you're prepared to stand up against.'

Heather looked at him thoughtfully. 'Have you ever heard of a place called Ramsgill Stray?' she said.

'You've been in there?' Johnny asked incredulously when she finished.

'Of course I have,' said Heather in surprise. Margo laughed. 'Heather's spent more time in the Stray than some of the people who work there,' she said. 'I have too in the past. There's an injunction says I can't now.'

Johnny was having the utmost difficulty covering up his emotions. It had all fallen into place with a thud. Heather's list of offences suddenly made complete sense. Honest answers weren't on the agenda at the moment but when she asked him if he'd ever heard of Ramsgill Stray the completely honest answer would have been: "Yes, of course, but only as an enigma." In the office he'd had plenty to do with GCHQ, but that was only two or three stops along the secrecy line. Everyone out there in the civilian world knew about Cheltenham even if they didn't know the full extent of what happened there. Ramsgill Stray was different. If Cheltenham was the tip of the iceberg, Ramsgill Stray was somewhere down in the frozen Arctic depths below its base. In the business you couldn't help knowing about it but that was like saying you couldn't help knowing about the abominable snowman. It was an enormous mystery, a prompt for silent speculation, something you just didn't try and probe too far – because you knew you'd get nowhere. Now here was this healthy fresh faced attractive girl telling him that she'd spent much of the last three years wandering in and out of the place at will.

Sitting here in the companionable fug of the pub, relaxing after an ideal day, an extraordinary thought rose in him, quickly suppressed. It would have been nice to be honest.

He looked at her with new eyes. Back at Thames House, no one at his level was ever told anything that mattered about US SigInt operations in Britain. Whatever the NSA was up to, MI5 would rather not know officially if it was likely to prove embarrassing. You picked up the subcurrent, though, and you met NSA staffers, so you learned to read between the lines. What you heard if you listened hard to the silences was that the Stray was there whether the Brits liked it or not, that if you were a good boy you might just get some intelligence crumb allowed to fall from its groaning table. If Cheltenham couldn't get you what you wanted, maybe some wire-tap the Home Secretary wouldn't sign the warrant for, then your last resort was to hope the Yanks might play ball and slip you a transcript like it came out of thin air.

It was what they were doing the rest of the time that used to worry some. Heather's quick description chimed in with that worry. 'It's just sitting there on our land,' she'd said, 'listening in on our phones just so some fat-cat Americans can get richer.

I mean, I don't give a damn about the British defence industry, but what we hear is it's not just defence – they'll bug anything or anyone if they think it might give one of their own companies a leg up at our expense and we just sit back and let them.'

'Isn't it guarded?' he said, feeling idiotic. Of course it was.

'Yes, but there's lots of ways in.'

'That's brilliant,' he said, 'you're very brave. What do you do when you're in there?'

'Grab anything I can get my hands on. Look round to see what new installations they're building. Talk to people.'

'Talk?'

'I'm trying to change attitudes, Johnny. Some people just need it explained to them, that's all. It's amazing what you can do with a bit of rational conversation. One or two of them even get quite sympathetic. You have to talk to these people. If you let things go on without trying to change them, you lose your right to complain.'

It was only then, as they moved into the lounge for coffee, that CN512 came back. The implications hit him hard. This woman arranging herself gracefully in the chair in front of him had sent a document on CN512 to the inquiry. It must have come from inside Ramsgill Stray. That meant it had either been given to her by a sympathizer or she had stolen it. Its presence there in the first place had to mean the NSA was bugging GKC's communications and was presumably taking a close interest in their mysterious product.

'I think it's terrible,' he said, 'I had no idea. I'd like to come and look at it. Would you show me?'

'It's not hard to find,' she said.

Margo was sitting back in her armchair, reading a paper from the pile on the table. Johnny looked at Heather, studying her face while she was pouring out more coffee. One of the foundations on which he had constructed his world began to crumble a little at the edges.

It was not Johnny's fault that he was as he was. Whatever genetic inheritance it might have brought to the party, no impressionable infant mind could have survived Lady Viola's assault: the early years of autocratic female domination ploughed deep furrows in a mental landscape surrounded and isolated by the acres of blinkered privilege. Johnny's first images of womanhood were of his mother and battalions of like minded nannies, the domestic shock-troops lined up to take him on in her frequent absences. Then came a single-sex public school education. Grappling with the furtive stirrings of sexuality, those around him took their various vague directions. Many veered towards other boys for a while or for ever. Some locked themselves inside a shell which in the long-term they would only ever open fully to expensive S&M experts in leather catsuits. A larger group sought refuge instead in a fluffy romantic dream of dehumanized girls, submissive, sexy, socially acceptable and domestically skilled, who would never threaten or challenge or vie for personal space. In Johnny's mother's world of house parties, shooting parties and hunt balls, there were such girls, or at least girls who until experience broke their shackles lived the same dream – a dream in which the most thrilling word they knew was 'fiancé'.

To Johnny and to the circle of his professional colleagues who had been pressed through a similar mould, 'peace women' came straight from hell, dangerously individualistic, impossible to neutralize by romance – the rocky outcrops above the ground that connected straight to their most deeply buried prejudice. They stereotyped them and derided them and so had he.

Until now.

These two didn't fit the preconception. They were both funny, smart and well informed. He enjoyed talking to them, Margo with her slightly cynical wisdom and Heather with her flashes of burning conviction. Heather in particular, he would have to admit. He found, in a reverse of the usual process, that he was dressing her mentally in some expensive high-fashion silk creation with an extravagant hat for Ascot or Cheltenham, decorating her face in Knightsbridge make-up, creating a more familiar illusion and then snapping back to reality to find he preferred her as she was in jeans and a floppy sweater.

'Jesus Christ! Have you read this?' Margo said savagely, sitting up and holding out the paper. 'Criminal trespass. They're bloody well talking about tightening it up all over again, so anyone who trespasses on anyone else's land at any time runs the risk of being arrested. Forget all that cant about "disrupting legal activity", they want to make it into a blanket ban. Can you believe it?'

She held it out to Heather who read rapidly through it, exclaimed in indignation and passed it to Johnny. He looked at it with suitable expressions of outrage, was starting to hold it out to give back when a name jumped out at him from the article under it and he looked at it again.

TOP SCIENTIST FOUND DEAD the headline read, then underneath followed a story which drew his eyes to it, hypnotizing him and seeming to suck the surrounding noise out of the air so that he and the paper existed in a tiny cold vacuum.

> The body of top chemist Jean Davies, 45, was found in her car yesterday at a well-known Lancashire beauty spot. A hose led in through the car window from the exhaust pipe. Miss Davies, who was employed by PBD Biosystems of Flaxmore, a subsidiary of GKC International, was one of Britain's leading specialists in food technology. Police said there were no suspicious circumstances.

Johnny saw again in his head a letter – a letter he had taken from Matthew Quill's files at Queen Victoria College, a letter that started 'Dear Matthew' and went on to say: 'If I find any evidence here that your suggestion has any basis in fact, I will certainly help you with your investigation.'

'What did you see?' said Heather, curiously, as he gave the paper back to Margo.

'Oh . . . I thought I saw a name I knew, but it wasn't.'

It was another fine day and they left the pub after a good breakfast, Heather looked longingly at the track leading north.

'It's almost irresistible,' she said, 'Wensleydale and all that. I wish we had a week.'

'Come on,' said Margo, 'you're on duty tonight.'

'Don't remind me.'

'Is it hard work?' said Johnny.

'At the Hall? You could say that. These are kids who've been in more trouble than you'd believe. They only get sent to us if everyone else has given up. You have to have your wits about you.'

'Sounds like they need a good thrashing,' he said and he was aware as soon as the words were out of his mouth that this was just the sort of thing he shouldn't be saying.

'Nooo,' said Heather, putting at least two syllables into the word and looking puzzled. 'That's certainly not what they need.'

It was the same look she'd given him the previous evening when they'd sat down at the table and he had ushered them both into their seats just as he would have done with some vapid Honourable at Simpsons.

'Only joking,' he said.

Margo was slightly ahead, swinging along, retracing yesterday's footsteps. Heather wondered if she was leaving them together on purpose. 'It's the thrashings that probably started it. We have to break the cycle.' She studied him and he looked eager, ignorant, trying to understand. 'Why are you here?' she said. 'Why are you bothering with us?'

He looked startled and suddenly vulnerable and she thought: Perhaps Margo's right. Perhaps he is just lonely.

'Sorry,' she said, 'that wasn't called for. Don't start getting at my boys, though.'

They walked in silence for a while.

'They come from families which were never families the way you know them,' she said in the end when he made no move to change the subject. 'All their roads are closed. There's no reality outside crime and the dole and if it's OK for your dad to thrash you, it's OK for you to do some thrashing too. So don't try to tell me there's no link between crime and unemployment.'

It jarred with everything he'd ever been given to believe. As soon as he had been old enough to read long words, Lady Viola had made him read her *Telegraph* front page stories – questioning him to ensure he drew the proper inferences, seeking to graft its opinions directly into what she regarded as his inadequate brain. What Heather had just said was anathema to that version of him, but her sincerity carried him along and somewhere inside him a suppressed person opened long closed ears and gave a small cheer. That surprised and disconcerted him and, dealing with that, he didn't answer.

They stopped for a breather back on the top of Pen-y-ghent and Margo sat next to Heather. 'I forgot to tell you. Dorrie and Mo both said they'd seen new footings being dug the other side of the Saddlebush bunker,' she said.

'What sort of size?'

'They couldn't tell, there's no easy way through there because there's three cameras looking at it and they've got vibration alarms all over that middle fence.'

'So we can't see,' Heather mused. 'That's a shame.'

Johnny said, 'What is?' without putting too much interest into his voice.

'Nothing much. Just Ramsgill Stray business.'

'I'd really like to see it,' he said, and Heather almost giggled, trying to imagine what the other women would think of this correct, polite, expensive intruder in their midst. A sports car, Ray-Bans and a flying jacket. Still, she supposed, the last two were things he maybe actually needed, being a pilot.

'Hey,' she said, 'how badly do you want to see it?'

'You've got me interested. I could come up next weekend maybe. Perhaps during the week even. I haven't got much on right now.'

'Tell me, Johnny. What happens if you try and fly over a place like the Stray?'

CHAPTER EIGHT

Two cars and three people backtracked out of Malham, winding down the valley back into a lower and more complicated world. In the Citroën, as soon as they were out on the road, seeing Johnny accelerating away with a wave, Margo said: 'Well? What do you think of him?'

Staring ahead at the diminishing Mazda, she spoke hesitantly. 'I don't know who he is. Jet-setter, rambler or what? And his attitude – I mean one minute he'd be agreeing with everything we said and the next he'd let something slip through that sounded really right wing. I kept swinging from thinking there's a really sweet guy inside here to wondering why on earth he wanted to have anything to do with the likes of us.'

'That's not too hard. I told you. One: he fancies you, two: he's a bit of a lost soul. I think he needs rescue.'

'Rescue him yourself, then.'

'Give him a chance, Heather. You're the one who's always saying you have to go on talking to people, telling them why you disagree however stubborn or set in their ways they might be. Here's the perfect object for your reforming skills and I happen to think he might be worth it. Seems to me he's been saddled with the wrong background and whatever he's been in the past I think there's something deeper down you could really appeal to.'

'So we go for the flight?'

'We? No way. You're going, not me. I hate planes. I'm sure I'd get airsick in one of those little jobs.' She gave Heather a shrewd look. 'You do like him though, don't you?'

Heather reached up and unclipped the fabric roof so that it flipped open in the slipstream and a sudden rush of air sent her hair streaming backwards.

'I like him. I just smell something very fishy.'

They didn't smell a thing, thought Johnny, hammering his car around the bends back towards Gargrave. Mission accomplished. I'm alongside them, just as ordered, and what's more the office is going to be paying for some flying. Brilliant. He said it out loud to himself, 'Brilliant,' because just thinking it wasn't quite enough to quell the clamour of self doubt caused by the lurking fear that he'd just betrayed his own moral standards. Above all the image of Jean Davies, a faceless body – blue with asphyxiation – slumped over a steering-wheel, kept hovering in his mind's eye whenever he gave it space. 'Brilliant,' he said again but it didn't convince him at all. He put a tape in the cassette, turned it up loud and drove hard. Long after the 2CV had disappeared from his rear-view mirror he kept glancing back, subconsciously hoping for a sight of it.

He was in London at midnight and in the office at nine the next morning and he could tell from Sibley's response that the news he brought with him came as a complete surprise.

'Bloody well done, young Johnny,' said Sibley, leaning back in his chair, 'on the job ten minutes and you're ahead of the game already. Raises a few questions though, doesn't it? If the NSA's in there with an interest, Sir Greville had better watch his step. I think you've probably done your bit for now.'

'Oh no, I don't agree,' said Johnny quickly. 'We don't know nearly enough yet, surely. We don't know for absolutely certain that stuff came out of Ramsgill Stray and it was only part of a document anyway. Won't GKC want to know what else there is?' He avoided using his stepfather's name.

'I don't know. I don't see where else it could have come from. I'll be briefing him later on. Don't make any plans yet and I'll tell you as soon as I speak to him.'

Johnny turned to go, then plucked up his courage. 'Ivor?'

'Mmm?'

'Jean Davies.'

'Yes?'

'I was wondering what happened.'

'Who's Jean Davies?' said Ivor with a completely blank look on his face.

Sir Greville was quite clear what he wanted. He read the briefing delivered by Ivor Sibley's messenger, didn't bother with the cautionary note at the end and got straight on the phone.

'Put that bloody f— put my stepson across this one, Sibley. Get him on this call, I want no bloody misunderstandings.' He was paying the bills so he got his way. Ivor Sibley buzzed Johnny and switched him into the conference circuit.

'Is he on?' barked Sir Greville.

'I'm listening,' said Johnny.

'Right. I'm up in front of this bloody inquiry in a week or two about this bloody Rage business and I—'

'Sir G. wait a second,' said Sibley urgently, 'did you read my note?'

'What damned note and what's this bloody Sir G. business? Who the hell do you think—'

'No, no, read the note. On the end of the report? Please? Telephone procedures are very important bearing in mind the nature of the information we've provided to you. You must avoid specific names and products.'

There was a pause at the other end of the line and Johnny distinctly heard his mother's voice in the background, reading something out loud. He knew what it was. Sibley had pointed out that NSA interest meant any communications were likely to be intercepted and anything containing sensitive trigger words on the watch list would be transcribed and read.

'This is bloody absurd!' bellowed his stepfather in a few seconds. 'Are you saying these bloody Yanks could be listening on this phone?'

'It's possible, yes.'

'God Almighty.' He paused for thought. 'Get round here, then. Both of you.' He put the phone down.

They were taken in Sibley's Mercedes, driven by Sibley's driver for the short ride to Grosvenor Square.

'Bit of a character, your stepfather,' said Sibley with fake joviality as they moved off.

'He certainly can be a little abrupt.'

'Your mother's quite a forceful woman too.'

'Yes. I think I heard her there. I expect we'll be seeing both of them,' said Johnny and saw Ivor blanch.

They were shown straight up to the Beckenden Room. On his election, Sir Greville and Lady Viola had bought Beckenden Manor in his Leicestershire constituency for their weekends, mostly for the hunting that went with it, and Johnny's mother had decided that what GKC's head office needed was a private retreat within it. To that end she had duplicated Beckenden's drawing room to the last touch, even having the Whistlers and the Dutch landscapes copied. Ceiling heights, doors, everything had been adjusted to match the prototype. Only the view towards the Post Office Tower lacked the appearance of the Leicestershire original. For Johnny it worked perfectly. He felt just as uncomfortable here as he did at Beckenden.

There were no niceties. As soon as the door had closed behind them, Lady Viola turned from the window, nodded curtly at them and launched into full flood before her husband could open his mouth.

'This is outrageous,' she said, 'the idea that our allies should be eavesdropping on our commercial activities from within our own country. The question is what are we going to do about it? The very first thing we need to know is exactly what else these ghastly women have got their hands on.'

Johnny's head started to ache. Sibley spoke too soon, 'Of course, Lady Viola, we don't know anything really about what they *have* given the Hurst Inquiry.'

'Speak for yourself,' she said scathingly, and she stabbed a finger at some papers on the table. 'I've got an idea. No bloody point in spending half your life doing favours for Civil Service morons if you can't get a favour out of *them* when you need it. I know what they've got is only part of a document.'

Sir Greville waved a languid hand and she let him speak.

'It sounds as though it could be part of a sales document

we have sent out to a few potential customers for this product so far,' said Sir Greville. 'We don't know which document it is and so we don't know which of our secure communications routes has been compromised – but it is certainly about our product known until now as CN512 which we are marketing under the brand name "Rage" which of course we've briefed you on.'

Ivor Sibley said, 'It's not exactly a new concept – the idea of a performance enhancer for troops in field conditions. Something that gets them through high-stress combat situations. You know they gave them rum in the First World War before they went over the top? Well, this is the same without the alcohol.'

Johnny remembered Den Bramfield's words in the office and light began to dawn. 'Jungle Juice. So it was field-tested in Romania?'

Ivor looked a little embarrassed and Lady Viola, who had been cruising restlessly around them, her face looking more than ever sprayed with some brown, glossy chemical hardener, snapped, 'Damn stupid name.' She glared at Johnny as if it was all his fault. 'Look,' she said, 'it's very simple,' in exactly the tones she'd used when he was ten and she'd tried to tell him how to get his pony to jump the huge fence at the end of the paddock. 'What we need to know is which lines these bloody Americans are listening to, exactly what Hurst's got and what else these dreadful peace women know. Shouldn't be beyond you Johnny, I don't think?' but her inflection made it clear she wasn't sure.

'I can go back up there and—'

'You do that,' she said, 'and Sibley, do keep your people under control. Now we've got to get on so off you both go.'

In the car going back there was tattered pride to paper over on both parts. Johnny felt as he always felt when leaving his mother's presence, as if he was a cartoon character inflating back into shape after being run down by a steamroller. Sibley needed to move matters on. 'What exactly did you have in mind next with these women?'

'I said I'd take them for a flight round this Ramsgill Stray place. 'I've got a share in a Cessna, but it's down in Hampshire. It would make more sense to rent one up there.'

'What would that cost?'

'Maybe a hundred and fifty pounds for a couple of hours.'

'Peanuts. Do it.'

Lanie had a *big* fight with Pacman that morning. 'You shouldn't go at Billy like that,' she said after the boy left, eyes still tear stained, to go to school.

'You should be backing me up. Ain't right he goes round wrecking things.'

'He's got nothing else to do, Pacman. I ain't either. This place gives me the goddam creeps. I wanna be back in Maryland.'

'Well, why don't you go and do that. You take Billy with you, you hear? I'll go right in and fix it with Welfare. You say the word!' He was shouting. 'My mam didn't do that to pop. She *knew* he was doin' what he had to do. She stood by him.'

Not that again, Lanie thought. 'It ain't the same now, Pacman. You go talk to Welfare. Right now. I want out.'

He suddenly caved in. 'I'm sorry, honey.' He sighed and seemed to curve down shorter. 'Yeah, I know. Look, when I get off shift, I'll take you and Billy down the Commissary, get some of that Key Lime pie inside us.'

She nodded slowly.

'Shee-it,' he said, 'I can't. Not today.'

'Oh, why not, Pacman?'

'Big meeting. I forgot.'

'Tell them you can't go.'

'I have to. Site meeting in the new bunker. Induction. They've got it all ready, the plans, everything. Starts at five.'

He went. Lanie, fuming, rang Heather. 'Want to meet?' she said.

An hour later, the two of them were sitting on the edge of Fewston Reservoir, talking. It was where they had first met, when Lanie – as a gesture, she said, of goodwill – handed over the Rage transcript, saying she'd found it in Pacman's pocket. Mackeson had told Lanie to go on seeing Heather, to keep the contact going just in case it should be useful again. What he hadn't allowed for was the effect on her. Here she was, actually *talking* to someone who actually *listened*, who didn't steer the conversation away when she talked of how hard it was with the boy, with Pacman giving himself heart and soul to a goddam job.

She liked Heather. Heather was not some goddam automaton lobotomized *Stepford Wife* creation of the NSA. They met this time because Lanie wanted to meet, needed to meet. She told the story of their fight, of their ruined evening, of where Pacman was going to be instead: and Heather listened with sympathy and deep interest.

It had been Johnny's intention to get there and get the paperwork done early, before Heather arrived, but he was frustrated by endless road works on the M1. The light plane hangars faced the Leeds/Bradford passenger terminal across the runway. He saw the Citroën waiting and she got out as he pulled up.

'Hello. I'm sorry to keep you,' he said.

'That's OK. It's interesting. I've been watching the planes.' She smiled. 'I keep feeling someone ought to come up and arrest me. I think it must be the effect of the wire fences.'

'It's a nice day for it,' he said, and a terrible thought struck him. Inside, they were going to want to see his pilot's licence, the licence which said in it *Johnny Kay* not *Johnny Kennedy*. He cursed the road works silently.

'I'll just pop inside and sort out the papers,' he said nonchalantly. 'I'll give you a shout when we're ready.'

He didn't give her time to consider and was in through the door while she was still looking mildly surprised. 'Morning,' said a dark haired man wearing an airline pilot's uniform jacket.

'Hello,' he said, looking round; the coast was clear. 'I'm Johnny Kay. You've got a Cessna 172 for me.'

'Tony Milburn. Come and have a seat.'

The formalities seemed to take an age. Through the window he could see her watching the planes. She kept glancing across at the hangar and then, finally, she turned and walked briskly towards it. He heard the door open just as he signed the form and pushed it across the other man.

'OK,' said the man, glancing down at it, then up over his shoulder as the door opened. 'Just a quick check-flight, then, Mr Kay.'

He looked round and there was Heather. 'I came to see how you were doing,' she said.

Check flight. Mr Kay. His mind went numb then cleared again as he realized she hadn't batted an eyelid at "Kay", that she must be taking it as a matey alternative to Kennedy. Check-flight. Of course there'd be a check-flight.

'Just one quick circuit to check you out on the avionics pack. I expect it's different to what you're used to,' said Milburn.

You're not fooling me a bit, thought Johnny. One quick circuit to check I'm competent and I'm not going to spread your Cessna halfway across Yorkshire is more like it.

'I'll take you through to the hangar,' the man said, 'Gavin will go up with you.'

He did the pre-flight under their watchful eyes, understanding perfectly well this wasn't just the standard check on the plane but a further test of his own competence. He did the routine walk-round, checking the panel fastenings and peering into the mechanism as he waggled all the control surfaces in turn, then gave the undercarriage a hard stare. He pulled a step-ladder into place and climbed up to check the petrol tanks. Never, ever trust a gauge, his instructor had drilled into him. Gauges go wrong. Look in the tanks. See for yourself. He undid the fuel cap in the top wing section, peered in, struggling to see much in the gloom. He dragged the ladder round to the other wing and checked that side too. Finally, he looked in the cockpit for the fuel tester, a clear plastic cylinder with a tube sticking out of it, and used it to drain a sample of fuel from each tank. It was as it should be, light blue and clear with no dirt and no trace of the globules of water at the base which could spell sudden trouble.

'OK,' he said, 'check over. Thanks.'

Milburn pushed down on the fuselage just ahead of the

tail and they pivoted the plane round then pulled it out of the hangar by a long handle clipped to the front undercarriage leg.

Milburn, seemed to have taken a shine to Heather. Would the name thing come up again? Probably not. There was nothing he could do about it.

From the moment the engine coughed into life Heather was out of his hearing and the Cessna was already two hundred feet up in the air when Milburn turned to her. 'He looks pretty good. Very confident.'

'Well, he should be, shouldn't he? I mean, he's a professional pilot.'

'Come again?' said Milburn, amused. 'Professional pilot? With a PPL? Has he been spinning you a line or what? He's no professional.' Heather looked at him blankly. If he hadn't been feeling a bit jealous of Johnny he might have let it ride. 'PPL,' he said, 'private pilot's licence. You're not allowed to fly anyone or anything whose paying for it. Professional pilots need a CPL. Commercial pilot's licence.'

'Can't you have both?'

He suddenly felt he'd gone a bit too far. He just shrugged expressively and they stood in awkward silence as they watched the plane bank around in a circuit and settle in for an impeccable landing. It disappeared behind the hangars for a while then taxied round the corner into view with a sudden crescendo of exhaust, weaving on to the apron in front of them before the engine cut and the propeller rocked to a sudden halt. Gavin got out and beckoned to her.

'He'll do,' he said, 'have fun.'

She clambered in on to a utilitarian seat of pale blue plastic and Johnny showed her how the straps worked. He gave her a headset, fiddled with the switches, then the engine started with a blast of noise which made her glad of the muffling headphones.

'Are you ready?' His voice was tinny in her ears.

She nodded. He looked all around, pushed the throttle open and swung the plane around. They taxied out past the hangars and paused short of the runway. A voice came in her ears and she realized it was Johnny, talking in a flat, experienced tone to someone else.

'172 Golf Kilo Uniform, ready for departure. Outward to Blubberhouses Moor, for local practice flying.'

Another voice came on. 'Roger Kilo Uniform. You're clear for take-off. Wind eight knots two five oh degrees. Not above two thousand feet until you clear the area.'

She expected to be scared but was instead simply surprised at the full throttle crescendo of noise and vibration. She lost sight of the runway ahead and it wasn't until she looked out of the side window and down at the dwindling ground that she realized how little time the plane had taken to leap back into its element.

'Look straight ahead,' Johnny's voice said in her ear and there, already – dragged close as height pushed back the horizon – the sun showed bright on the ranks of huge white golf balls standing out from the dun moorland around them.

'Can we just fly over them?'

'Apparently we can. There's no restriction zone. The man says he thinks the Americans have asked for one but the Home Office wouldn't agree. It's not like radar. They aren't beaming out any microwaves to fry low flying planes, they're only receiving signals. Anyway they're an important landmark for pilots coming in to the Leeds Bradford control area.'

'How low can we go?'

'As soon as we're out of the airport control area, we can go down to five hundred feet.'

He flew in slow circles, low down over the base, banked over so she could see straight down out of the side window. She knew it so well but this was the first time she had ever had the luxury of seeing the entirety of it, laid out like a map, seeing it without the constant expectation of shouts, screeching tyres, heavy hands on her shoulder. They went round and round and round until she had taken in every inch, sketching plans in her notebook of exactly where the new construction was, where a diagonal track was being bulldozed the other side of the Saddlebush bunker, where an interesting door she had never seen before opened into the back of the new Frogwood bunker behind it.

'Seen enough?' Johnny asked in the end.

Reluctantly she nodded.

'Let's go back the pretty way,' he said.

She took him in, relaxed, expert, scanning the sky around ceaselessly.

'What are you looking for?'

'Other traffic,' he said, 'I had a near miss with a Tornado once. He wasn't looking where he was going. One minute there was a tiny little speck high up on the left. The next he was right on top of me. When he came by I could hear the engines and that's saying something in one of these. Gives you a healthy respect.'

'You're obviously an expert,' she said.

He grinned. 'Kind of you to say so.'

'Well, after all, you are a professional pilot.'

'That's right.'

'I must have misunderstood,' she said. 'The man back there said you couldn't be because you've only got a private licence.'

The plane wobbled. It definitely wobbled and it wasn't turbulence. Johnny took a deep breath and tried to force his hand back into the proper relaxed touch on the yoke. The hand, coupled to the world's biggest lie-detector, still threatened to betray him.

'I'm sorry?' he said. 'What do you mean?'

'The man back there when you hired the plane. When you took off the first time, I told him you flew for a living and he said you have to have a different sort of licence for that.'

Johnny put on a surprised face and took a moment to search the horizon. 'I've got both,' he said as casually as he could. 'The thing is, I got my commercial licence in Australia so until I do the paperwork here it's easier to show them my PPL.'

'Oh, I see.'

He glanced at her, wondering whether to force the issue by asking a 'Don't you trust me?' question but she looked quite happy and he decided he'd only be pushing his luck. Distraction seemed a better idea.

'Right,' he said, 'it's your turn.'

'My turn to what?'

'Fly it.'

'Oh come on,' she said, 'I can't fly.'

'It's not so difficult once you're up in the air – at least until you have to come down again. Go on. Just rest your hand on the yoke. Put your feet on the pedals and follow my movements.'

He showed her the basics for a few minutes while they flew in lazy circles over the moors and gradually saw her relax.

'OK,' he said, 'it's all yours. Just keep the wings level and the horizon about where it is now.'

She didn't stiffen up like most people do. There was just a trace of tension in her face but that quickly softened into a delighted smile as she felt the plane responding. He coached her through some turns and she got the idea of co-ordinating her hands and feet in no time at all. 'Hey, this is fun,' she said.

He glanced out of the side window, looking for a reference point, and saw a microwave tower almost below them. 'OK, try a full three-sixty-degree circle. See if you can make that tower the centre of it. Just concentrate on keeping a steady rate of turn and bank.'

'What tower?' she said and he pointed. 'That must be Raven Stones,' she said, 'The BT tower.'

They started the circle. She was concentrating, glancing sideways to check where the tower was, then ahead at the horizon again. She looked sideways again and this time she stayed looking sideways so that the nose began to dip and the bank steepened.

'Straighten out,' said Johnny calmly as the air speed rose and the altimeter began to unwind.

'Sorry,' she said, and he helped her with a light finger on his control yoke as she got the nose up.

'You stopped looking at the horizon,' he said, 'that's what happened.'

'I was . . .' She started to make an excuse then stopped herself. 'No. You're right.' She looked out of the window again. 'Just let me do one more turn?' She did a careful wide circle to the left, then straightened up. 'Can you take it back over the Stray while I have one last look?' she asked.

'OK.' Johnny looked ahead. The Raven Stones microwave tower was dead ahead, and beyond it, almost in line, was the white gleam of the Stray's golf balls. He concentrated on those, saw her looking down to the side but concerned himself with checking the rest of the sky and didn't see what it was that held her interest down on the moor below. A small tracked digger, working on a short trench in the middle of nowhere. It was an unusual sight in the middle of a moor – just a digger, a pick-up truck and half a dozen men, standing stock-still, waiting for the plane to go away.

'Can you do one last circle over the Stray?' she asked and when they got there, she concentrated hard on the new bunker, Frogwood – the bunker where, Lanie had said, they were all ready for a big induction meeting this evening. It wasn't a new door, the place she had seen. It was some sort of small, ragged hole. She marked it and its surroundings carefully.

'OK,' she said, 'can I have another go?'

Under his coaching, she flew it all the way back until they could see the airport ahead. He called in on the radio and took over as they waited for a small airliner to clear the runway and then they began to angle down to the ground on final approach. 'It's a funny one,' he said, 'Whatsisname showed me on the check-flight. You have to come in on the high side when the wind's like this, because you can get a sudden down-draught at the last minute.'

No sooner had he said it than the Cessna abruptly began to sink sickeningly but he was ready with more throttle and the touchdown was almost perfect.

'Sorry about that last bit,' he said as they taxied in.

'It was fine,' she said, 'I really, really enjoyed that. Thank you, Johnny.'

There was a warm feeling in his chest as he looked at the expression on her face. 'You're a pretty calm customer,' he said, 'I've known passengers scream on approaches like that.'

'I can't think why.'

Back in the office, he did the paperwork, paying cash so she didn't see any credit cards in his real name.

'Thanks a lot, Mr Kay. Hope you enjoyed it,' said Milburn as they left, but, the name once again seemed to slip naturally past her.

What now? he thought. This was an opportunity to grab with both hands, to move their relationship on a few notches. That was the whole point and he had to have something to take back to Sibley. He didn't even begin to admit to himself that there were other, equally powerful reasons for wanting to spend more time with her.

'What about a walk somewhere?' he said as they got in the car.

'Why not?' she said. 'A walk was just what I had in mind. Well, a sort of walk, anyway. You've shown me a bit of your world. I'd like to show you a bit of mine.'

He didn't tumble to it for a while, following the Citroën up the road, through Otley and beyond, turning off to thread their way through lanes and small hamlets. He thought they would be heading towards open moorland, to some favourite spot of Heather's, and was therefore surprised when she pulled off the lane and stopped on a wide verge barely on the edge of the moor with fields stretching back down the slope behind them, dotted by farm buildings. He looked around, surprised and a little disappointed, unable to see over the rising ground immediately ahead where rough bracken promised the end of cultivation.

'Where are we?' He asked but she shook her head, laughing.

'Follow me.'

There was a farm track heading uphill on the other side of the lane but it wasn't until they were a few hundred yards up it that the convex slope of the hill revealed the first disconcerting hint of what lay ahead and he kicked himself for not guessing earlier.

With every step they took, more and more was revealed of the stark, startling white bulk of the Ramsgill Stray radome array.

Heather, slightly ahead of him, stopped and turned.

'There you are. I thought you ought to see it from the ground; see the whole foul extent of the place. Somehow it doesn't look quite so bad from the air.'

The base was now in full view, stretching out to the east and far to the south of them. The golf balls were not quite circular, but had been constructed of small flat panels round geodesic frames. There were trees in between them screening parts of it.

'It's huge,' he said, 'huge and horrible. I take your point. Now can we go somewhere nice?'

'Nice? No, I want to take you inside.'

Just like my first dive, he thought, when my mother conned me all the way to the top of the high diving board saying she wanted to show me something then wouldn't let me go back down the ladder. He remembered clearly the balance of ridicule against paralysing fear as he looked down at the far off surface of the water and knew he was being allowed no other way out. Heather was calling his bluff, though she didn't know it, making him one of them. Ivor would probably be very pleased, he thought. He squared his shoulders and headed into the unknown.

The track came to a small road at the edge of the base. Beyond a narrow belt of trees, bushes and scrub there was a high wire fence and beyond that he could see a sweep of brick-built houses set round a perimeter road. The golf balls rose into the sky on the far side of the houses. Johnny saw a remote camera on a spidery metal tower, scanning the fence.

'Stop looking at the camera,' Heather said, 'stick close to me, and when we're inside just look confident. Like we're going somewhere. Talk to me as we go.'

Ironic, he thought, she's teaching her grandfather to suck eggs. I've been through school on this one. She's found out the hard way.

Out of the corner of his eye he saw the camera swivel slowly away from them.

'There's at least fifty monitor screens inside,' she said, 'they can't watch them all at once. As soon as it's facing the other way, we have to go quickly.'

'Go where?' he said, looking at the fence, but she glanced up at the camera and was off, straight into the bushes. He followed, pushing between the branches and found himself up against the wire mesh, next to her.

'Damn,' she said, 'they've fixed it. There was a gap here last time. We'll just have to climb.'

Climb? He looked up at ten feet of mesh. 'Won't someone see us?'

'Maybe. Maybe not.' He was talking to her feet. She was up the fence like a cat and he had to go after her. His feet were bigger than hers and the toes of his shoes were blunter so it was hard to get much purchase in the diamond gaps of the mesh. His fingers took the strain, making him wish for gloves. He felt as vulnerable as it was possible to be as they climbed higher, certain that at any moment someone would look out of a window or glance at a monitor. He pushed the thought out of his mind and went on climbing, aware that Heather had already reached the top and swung quickly down the far side.

The top was the worst bit, something he hadn't been good at even on the assault courses of his extension training, a knife-edge frontier, defying balance. Heather's voice reached him.

'Roll over it. Reach down for a handhold, head first, and swing your body down.'

That hurt. His fingers, hooked into the narrow wire, took the full momentum of his thirteen stones swinging downwards. When they could take no more, he let go and fell the remaining distance, rolling as he hit the ground and coming up panting, but unhurt.

'Right,' she said, 'I'll tell you about it as we walk, but don't look round like a tourist – only if I point things out. You've got to be so engrossed in me that no one expects us say anything to them as we pass. Talk very quietly though in case they hear your accent.'

They'd crossed a strange national border into a mongrel land where the worst of British council house architecture was surrounded by a sedimentary layer of Americanization. Some of the cars parked at the kerb seemed to rival the houses in size. Bright red and yellow plastic was everywhere, slides, sandpits, climbing frames; their colours, designed to battle Texan sunshine, undimmed by the Yorkshire sky's feeble challenge.

There were houses both sides of the curving road, brick houses built in ugly little terraces, four to each terrace with open grass around them. Beyond the houses they came to a school with a red roof, bright pictures taped to the windows surrounded by a playground full of more climbing frames, ladders, scrambling nets though the plastic was here replaced by wood, soaked in red ranch-paint. After that was a bank with an unfamiliar cash machine in the wall, then a big building with a glass conservatory built on one side in which they could see people eating.

'That's the commissary, the restaurant,' said Heather, 'the food's quite good.'

'You've eaten in there?'

'Not since they got to know my face and tightened up security.'

Not since they got to know my face – and here he was walking beside that face. Oh God, he thought, this could be the final test of Ivor's pulling power. In the office you knew they'd get you out of trouble somewhere down the line. Was it really the same at MI7? He wondered.

'Where are we going?'

So far no one had taken any notice of them but there hadn't been many people around by the houses. Now though, they were approaching a crossroads. Ahead lay a series of more industrial-looking buildings; stores and workshops, it seemed. There were things going on there, trucks moving around them, people walking in and out of the doorways. To their right the road led past a series of low office buildings straight to the main gate and the police post a couple of hundred yards away. Heather swung left.

'Down the yellow brick road,' she said.

The road led straight down a gentle slope into a wide open

landscape of grassland dominated by the giant puffball shapes of the radomes scattered across it. There were a few low roofed buildings grouped among them but Johnny's eyes were drawn to the bunkers, grass growing on their ramped sides, each flat top large enough for a pair of football pitches. The radomes and the other installations were protected by double or triple wire fences. This wasn't a road for walking down and he knew they were conspicuous. Vans and cars drove past them and now it was quite obvious they were attracting some curious looks. Heather started pointing things out.

'That's Saddlebush over there,' she said, 'the big bunker on the right. That's the real state of the art bit. They're very proud of it. The one on the left where they're building is the Frogwood— Uh-oh.'

'What's the matter?'

'That camera just swivelled. It's looking straight at us. They've picked us up.'

A feeling of stepping still further into the unknown swept through Johnny. 'So what do we do, go back?'

'Come on, Mr Intrepid Pilot, where's your sense of adventure? Remember that entrance we saw from the plane? Follow me.'

She sprinted off the road across the grass and he followed, finding he had to run hard to keep up, taking a quick look back over his shoulder and seeing there was no sign yet of any pursuit. The Frogwood bunker loomed out of the earth closest to them, cranes and parked dump trucks showing it was still under construction. A tarmac driveway led to a big entrance on the side facing them but Heather veered left, hurdled a pile of concrete blocks and ran round the corner. There was a shout from somewhere behind them. At ground level, the place they had seen from the Cessna was hidden by a heaped-up bank of earth, but she found it straight away. It was small and dark and it gave access to a low tunnel running downhill into the heart of the bunker. It looked like a duct or temporary access of some sort, due to serve its purpose during construction and then be closed up. They had to bend down and go slowly but it went all the way through and as the tunnel came to an end, lights showed ahead. The inside of the bunker was one enormous open space, maybe twenty feet high and at least two hundred feet along each of its walls. It was still being built but work had clearly finished for the day. Floors were being laid at one end and great bunches of cabling were sticking out of ducts on all sides, just waiting to be connected up. A temporary office had been set up directly opposite them, a square box with big windows in its plywood walls. Crescent rows of folding chairs were set out on a new section of floor in front. An easel with a flip-chart board stood there.

Heather ran up the wooden steps to its door, went inside and was back out before he could follow. She was grinning and she had a piece of paper in her hand.

'All ready for their meeting,' she said. 'There's a whole pile. Can you believe it? They just left them there!'

She held it out to him. 'Can you take it? Stuff it down your pants or something, then they might not find it.'

Might not? He took it as though it might burn him, four photocopied A4 sheets stapled together. He got out his penknife, slit the stitching for an inch inside one jacket pocket, rolled the pages, pushed them through and let them unroll into the space inside the lining.

There was the sound of running feet. They both turned and four men burst in through the main entrance, They were all in police uniform and all out of breath. The oldest of the three, wearing sergeant's stripes, was red in the face and looking very angry.

'Oh, Sergeant Hayter,' said Heather grimly, 'this is a surprise. I was just showing a friend around.'

'Check the place, Davis,' said Hayter, 'you and Ferrall. Any damage, I want to know about it sharpish.' He turned to Johnny. 'Right, what's your name then? I know who this cow is, but I never seen you before.'

'John Kennedy,' said Johnny.

'Address?'

I should have worked this out before, he thought. They'll check it, it'll have to be a real one. Johnny could never remember postal districts except his own, so pressured by a silence that was already too long, he broke all the rules and gave his own. 'Three, Cadogan Mansions, Oakley Street,' he said.

'Oakley Street where?'

'London SW3,' said Johnny, as though it was obvious.

'Right, Miss Weston and Mr Kennedy, I have to tell you on behalf of the occupier that you are trespassing and you are required to leave at once. I have to tell you on behalf of—'

'OK, Sergeant, we're going,' said Heather, 'forget that three in a row nonsense. By the way, you're meant to give us time to do what you ask. We're going. Is the van outside? I do hope it's clean. I don't mind walking if you'd rather save petrol.' She turned to Johnny. 'Sergeant Hayter's inclined to forget himself. We have to be very polite to him.'

Davis and Ferrall came back, reporting no signs of damage, and – shepherded by the three constables – they were led outside to where a white police van sat with its engine running and a driver waiting at the wheel. All the policemen were looking at Johnny with interest. He was clearly right out of the usual run of intruders. Sergeant Hayter came along behind, speaking quietly into his radio.

Heather talked all the way. 'Now, Mr Davis, tell me. Do you have any idea what they're going to do in there when it's finished, when they've got Frogwood working?'

Davis made the mistake of replying. 'Course I don't.'

'You don't know what they're going to do. But you're prepared to protect them regardless?'

'It's none of my business.'

'None of your business? It's your business to uphold the law of this country. They're foreign nationals doing illegal phone tapping and you say that it's none of your business. How can you say that?'

Davis didn't answer. Hayter, standing outside, stopped talking into his radio and opened the back door. 'You button your fucking lip, you fucking bitch. What I want to know is—'

Johnny swung round in instant anger, astonished by the man's words. 'Don't you use that sort of language to a woman, Sergeant. I won't have it.'

'It's all right, Johnny,' said Heather quickly, 'they're just modplods. They don't behave like real police.'

The sergeant gave a mocking laugh, looking at Johnny. 'You won't have it? I want to know a bit more about you, Mister er—' he made a big show of looking at his notebook. 'Kennedy or whatever your name might be.' He got in. 'Back to the office, Gary. I want a word with these two.'

Johnny and Heather were sitting opposite each other, flanked by the policemen. Johnny looked at Heather and she gave him a troubled look in reply, clearly worried by the Sergeant's words. Unusually, she was silent for the short journey back to the police post.

They were hustled into an interview-room and searched. The jacket lining escaped their scrutiny. It surprised Johnny that they were kept together.

'Now,' said Sergeant Hayter again, 'let's have that name and address again, shall we?'

'I told you, Kennedy, Three, Cadogan Mansions, Oakley Street.'

'Yes, but you see the owner of that address is given as Mr John Kay, not Kennedy, and we've found a Mazda car parked next to a Citroën belonging to Miss Weston up the road that's registered to that same Mr Kay.'

Heather and the sergeant were staring at him with equal intensity.

'All right,' he said, 'so what? Technically my name's still legally Kay. I can't stand it for . . . for personal family reasons. I'm changing it to Kennedy, OK?'

'Well that may be, sunshine, but legally speaking what you just did there was to give me a false name and I've got a perfect right to take action against you for wasting police time. You'd better show me some I.D. Mr Kay or whatever it is.'

Johnny tossed over a driving licence.

'Got anything else?'

'What's wrong with that?'

The sergeant's voice took on a harder, bullying note. 'Empty your pockets. Right now. On the table.'

As Johnny did so, his pilot's licence was conspicuous in the small pile. The Sergeant picked it up and looked at it and comprehension dawned across his face.

'A flier boy,' he said, 'right. That was you, then, doing circles, was it?'

'Yes,' said Johnny shortly.

'Very unsafe, what you were doing, round here. Low flying. I think we might have to report that.'

'Sergeant, I was above five hundred feet and I wasn't breaking any regulations. Go ahead and report me.'

Hayter gave up on that one, took some notes and put the licence back on the table. Johnny stood up to get it back and Hayter stood up too.

'I don't want to see you on my patch again, right?' His voice started rising. 'I've told your friend here a million times and so far I've been very, very patient. She knows what can happen. She's going to be put away for what she did and she fucking deserves it so—'

'You mind your language, Sergeant,' said Johnny, 'I've told you before.'

Hayter stepped up to him, chin thrust forward towards him and shoved him aggressively backwards with both hands, using a stiff jab to the chest which spoke of more to come if his control snapped. Johnny's head banged sharply against the wall behind and a red rage started to well up in him. He fought it back. This is a policeman, he thought, I'll really blow it if I hit him. He clenched his fists at his sides.

They were marched out of the gate and watched by Hayter and his band as they set off down the road back towards the cars.

'I don't bloody believe it,' said Johnny, 'how can that man get away with it?'

'He's done far worse things than that,' said Heather soberly. 'Remind me to tell you what he did to my friend Jo. That was nothing, believe me.' She glanced at him, noting the obvious anger in his face. 'But what of you? You're a man of mystery, aren't you, Mr Kay?'

CHAPTER NINE

It was a day whose ripples were already spreading in many surprising directions. Before Johnny and Heather even had time to reach their cars, Hayter had made his report to Chief Inspector Reed. The Chief Inspector, mulling it all over, decided to refer it down the line to London at once, to his section head at the Ministry of Defence. He didn't get the chance. Before he could take any action, the phone summoned him to an urgent meeting with the Base Commander.

Here we bloody go again, he thought wearily. Forget chains of command and division of responsibilities. Bloody Yanks know what's going on quicker than we do. I wish someone would tell me who I work for.

There were two people already with the Base Commander when he went in, Olly Gandrell, as ever at the Commander's elbow, and the other man, the one with the leathery skin whom no one ever introduced.

'Now tell me, Reed,' said the Base Commander instead of a greeting, 'this man you picked up, Kay. What have you got on him?'

'I'll put his name through channels and as soon as I know anything, you'll get the report.'

'I didn't ask what you're gonna do, I said what have you got?'

Reed sighed. 'He gave us a different version of his name. When we pressed him he claimed he prefers to call himself Kennedy. That was him flying the Cessna earlier. Drives a Mazda MX5 sports car, wears expensive clothes and lives in a smart part of London.'

'What does he do?'
'I don't know yet.'
'Why was he here?'
'He came in with Heather Weston.'
The leather-faced man butted in. His voice was husky, damaged. 'He's not your usual peace protester. Give us your best guess, Mr Reed.'
'He's got money. He didn't look like a journalist. If you really want a guess, my sergeant reckons he fancies Weston. Hayter said he kept leaping to her defence.'
'Not the cleverest of men, your Mr Hayter,' said the man.
The Chief Inspector didn't disagree but he wasn't going to say so.
Olly Gandrell seemed to think the conversation had moved far enough down the pecking order for him to be allowed a turn.
'Did they see anything?'
'They were inside the new bunker. There's not a lot to see.'
'You're meant to have a guard on the gate.'
'We did. Your contractors dug an access duct into the bunker, left it wide open and didn't tell us. We found their footprints inside it. You also left a stack of briefing notes in the bunker.'
'Did they see them.'
'They weren't there long enough to read them and when they were searched, they didn't have a copy.'
He saw Leatherface making a note and his temper showed for a moment in his voice. 'I can tell you, it's no joke having to push our luck with the trespass laws. You think we'd miss a chance to do them for something real like theft or criminal damage? If I had my way we'd leave them a whole lot longer after we picked them up on the cameras. We'd let them do something they'd regret, something that would really stick, like the charge Weston's facing for attacking Hayter.'
The Base Commander just looked at him. 'Camera thirty-nine? That was the camera that picked them up?'
'Yes.'

'That's pretty far in, Mr Reed. You seem to have plenty of trouble just finding them. Don't make it any easier. They're getting out of this base with enough sensitive material as it is.'

He was shown out by Gandrell.

Left alone, the man with the leather face looked at the Base Commander, gave a slow smile and winked. The Base Commander took it as a shared moment with an equal. 'Running as hard as he can and a million miles behind,' he said.

'I gotta go see SUSLO tonight,' said Mackeson.

'Give my best regards to Grosvenor Square.'

Johnny thought he was telling Heather a clever but necessary lie, sitting next to her on a rock, but who knows what will come out when a soul is trawled under pressure for a quick excuse . . .

'Kay's my stepfather's name,' he explained. 'I can't stand him. He's a smooth, rich shit. Completely unscrupulous. My mother was always pretty narrowminded and she's got worse and worse since she married him. I stay away as much as I can. I can't remember ever seeing my real father. They split up when I was tiny and my mother goes completely off her trolley if anyone even mentions him but I decided I'd rather use his name.'

He was pleased with that. It sounded convincing even to him.

'Poor Johnny,' she said.

'What's the story with you and that foul sergeant?'

'Hayter? He loathes me. It's getting worse and worse. A few weeks ago, he attacked me in the back of one of their vans – banged my head against the side, then next time I saw him he went the whole hog, knocked me out and put me in hospital.'

'You've got him, then, surely. Were there witnesses?'

She sighed. 'Quite the reverse. He thinks *he's* got *me*. He knew he was in serious trouble as soon as the ambulance came so while I was out of it, he disappeared and got one of his mates to hit him in the face. The end result is I'm up for

GBH and he's saying what happened to me was self-defence on his part.'

'They'll never believe that, surely? A woman?'

'Oh, Johnny. Yes, they will. We're peace protesters. We don't qualify as women to a York jury.'

'So what will happen?'

'I'm probably going to lose. I could get as much as two years.'

'Two years?' he said, horrified. 'In prison?'

'That's right.' She looked around. 'So . . . time is short. Let's breathe in the fresh air while I still can.'

He looked at the eyesore in front. Raven Stones tower, festooned with the horns, dishes and antennae of BT's microwave links. This had been her idea of a walk but it wasn't his. The thing was hideous, industrial and so were the tracks they'd walked along, where some bulldozer had been ripping up the peaty turf. It wasn't there now, that was one good thing.

'That was quick thinking – the way you hid those papers. Can I have a look at them?'

With difficulty and at the expense of a lot more of his pocket's stitching, he got them out again. They were baffling to him – two sheets of tables, technical specifications and one that was some kind of wiring diagram or cabling plan. She let out a sudden whoop.

'Fantastic! Wait till Maurice sees these. He's our electronics expert.'

She studied the diagram in silence for a while and he looked at her profile and the fall of her long hair, then she suddenly looked up at the tower in front of them.

'Look at this,' she said with excitement in her voice, pointing at the diagram. The cables, if cables they were, had arrows at their ends presumably meant to identify their destinations. The one she was indicating said BTRS next to it. 'How about that?' she said.

'What is it?'

'I'd give you ten to one it means British Telecom Raven Stones.'

'What if it did?'

'Oh, Johnny! No, sorry, why should you know? The thing we've always suspected, always wanted to prove, is that the base is tapping into the British domestic phone system.'

'BTRS . . .' he objected. 'It might mean anything.'

'No,' she said with total certainty, 'I think what you smuggled out of there in your jacket, Johnny Kennedy, was the smoking gun.'

They walked for a while then until she stopped and looked at her watch.

'Shall we go and get some food somewhere?' He imagined them sitting in a quiet corner of some cosy moorland pub.

'I've got a meeting,' she said, 'I really can't.'

'You could miss it,' he said, and knew he'd hit a sour note.

'No I couldn't. It's important.'

'Is it about Ramsgill Stray?'

'Of course it is. It's a public meeting about planning permission.'

'How come?'

'They have to put in planning permission. It's only a formality. They always get it. Now they want a few more of their repulsive domes. The point is, it's on the edge of an Area of Outstanding Natural Beauty and they've bent the boundary so they can get away with it. There's this outfit called the CPRE, I think it's the Council for the Protection of Rural England. Anyway, they've called a meeting so I want to go and listen.'

Johnny thought about where he was, who he was with and who he might meet and threw caution to the winds. 'Can I come too?'

'Do you really want to?' She looked at him searchingly.

'Yes.'

'Look, Johnny. I think I have to say something.' She hesitated for a long second. 'If you're interested in the issue, that's one thing. If you're interested in . . . me, then I think I should tell you that my life's pretty much taken up by all this stuff. That and my job. Anyway, I'm a pretty bad bet with this case coming up.'

Her directness disconcerted him.

'OK,' he said and his voice sounded all wrong to his ears, over-formal, 'that's fine. I would like to come to the meeting. I didn't like the way that policeman behaved.'

She shook her head. 'You're not getting it. I don't need a knight-errant either. We're all big girls now. We've been doing this for a long time. Part of the reason Hayter was worse than usual today was directly because you were there so that forced him to get all macho.'

Johnny was stung. He could feel his role slipping away, accused of some responsibility for the scene.

'But you said he's done dreadful things before.'

'Yes. We have to find ways of coping with it. You should talk to my friend Jo.'

'What happened to him.'

'Her. She can tell you herself. She'll be there this evening, in a wheelchair.'

'Can I come?'

'I can't stop you. It's a public meeting. It's just . . . well, my friends don't drive sports cars, they don't fly planes, they don't wear fancy jackets.'

'I've got an old anorak in the boot.'

She laughed. 'You haven't a clue what I'm talking about, have you?'

'Have we got time for a drink beforehand?'

'Oh . . . come on, then.'

The meeting was in a village hall and they saw Jo as soon as they walked in, a woman with cropped hair and a big smile sitting in a wheelchair talking animatedly to the group around her. Margo was one of them and she hailed Heather. The rows of chairs were half full and more and more people were trickling in all the time. Johnny followed Heather over to the group around Jo and tried unsuccessfully to hang on to all their names in a volley of introductions. They were mostly women but there were two middle-aged men sharing a common studious look and another in his twenties who blinked a great deal and said little.

Heather drew Margo out of the circle, 'We flew over the Stray,' she said. 'We circled right round it. You could see everything. It was fantastic. I even flew the plane.'

'They didn't shoot you down, then.'

Heather laughed. 'I took Johnny in over the wire afterwards. We got all the way in to the new bunker before Hayter caught us. We came out with something pretty good. I'll show you later.'

'Got it on you?'

'Yes.'

'Don't take it home. They might come with a warrant again.'

'No, I'm sure . . . our usual friend will look after it.'

'Did Hayter behave himself?'

'Yes, he did.' 'No he didn't,' said Heather and Johnny simultaneously.

'Johnny's very well brought up. He didn't like Hayter's manners,' Heather explained with just a trace of irony in her voice.

'If you wind up without bruises, we reckon he behaved himself,' said Margo.

'I've got bruises,' said Johnny, with feeling, 'the back of my head met a wall thanks to him.'

Margo didn't look impressed. 'You should ask Jo about Sergeant Hayter.'

'That's what Heather said.'

'Why don't you talk to her now. There's five minutes before it starts.'

By this time the hall was three-quarters full but the platform was empty, waiting for the panel. They made a space at one end of a row for Jo's wheelchair and Johnny sat down beside her.

'You want to know about my little shindig, do you?' she said. Her voice was gravelly but amusement bubbled in it and behind her heavy-framed glasses her eyes were friendly, shining.

'What happened?'

'Last year,' she said, 'Thanksgiving. We heard they were having some speeches at the base so we thought we'd go and join them. Share a bit of turkey. Make a few points maybe. See what the Base Commander reckoned there was to give thanks for. Anyway, the modplods had instructions not to let us spoil their fun. We gave them the run-around. Some of us got over all three of the triple fences round the Sieve building.' She laughed. 'It's good fun that, because the modplods don't have the keys and they can't climb like we can so they just had to stand there until someone came and opened the gates for them. You know Binny?'

'Er, let's see. I think so.'

'She's the tall one over there talking to Heather. She was with me while Margo and Elsa took the rest of them over to the housing area, singing songs and sort of holding up proceedings. Now usually they would have hustled us right off the base but they knew we'd be straight back in and they didn't want that, not with the speeches coming up so instead they grabbed us all and they bunged us in a kind of storeroom place. There were fourteen of us all squashed against each other and it was tiny and bloody hot in there because there was a radiator going full blast.'

She fell silent for a moment, remembering, brooding suddenly, then gave a little shrug.

'It was like the black hole of Calcutta. Anyway, after a few minutes, I started having an asthma attack. Well, it shouldn't really have been a problem, but my inhaler ran out and I'd left the spare outside the gate in my car. The others all started shouting and banging on the door until Hayter came. They told him what was going on and he just laughed and walked off.'

'And?'

'And no one came near us for an hour so I never got the inhaler. At least not until the speeches were over. By that time I'd nearly croaked. Roger Mitchell came by then. He's one of the more decent plods, and he whistled up an ambulance. I was in hospital three weeks and now I start wheezing soon as I try walking.'

Johnny was shocked to his core. 'I suppose Hayter didn't realize how bad it was?'

'You reckon?'

There was a silence between them for a few moments.

'Can't you sue him?' he said.

'I'm trying, believe me, I'm trying, but that's another story. It was hard enough just serving the writ.'

He wanted to know more but just then the audience fell silent as an elderly man in a grey suit stepped on to the platform and raised a hand for silence.

Two hundred miles south in Mayfair another meeting was in progress. Normally, NSA business was conducted in the heart of the American Embassy in Grosvenor Square, on the fourth floor, just above the CIA office. This time, SUSLO had decided to do business at home, in the comfortable Bryanston Square flat just to the north of Marble Arch, an easy ten minutes from the Embassy. SUSLO, the Senior US Liaison Officer, was Curtis Walsh and Curtis Walsh ran NSA affairs in Britain. There was a secure room in the flat, regularly swept for bugs and out of reach of focused laser window-pane snooping devices.

He was lounging back in his chair with his feet on his desk, trying the owlish look he was cultivating, peering with a wrinkled brow over the top of his bifocals at Miriam and Ray Mackeson.

'So that's what happened,' he said, looking down at his notes again. 'Four circuits of the Stray then they took a guided tour of the moors. No reason to call in the marines, surely? They didn't drop bombs or anything?'

Mackeson grinned. 'Maybe if I told you that this is the son of Sir Greville Kay?'

He took his feet off the desk. Slowly, it's true, but nevertheless off the desk and Miriam, watching carefully, knew Mackeson had scored a hit.

She chimed in. 'Maybe if I added that he was an MI5 staffer until last month and he's now believed to be working for Calstock's organization.'

Walsh grunted the grunt of someone caught out by a good practical joke. 'And Calstock's organization is working for GKC?'

'You got it.'

Curtis Walsh liked Miriam. She reminded him just a little of his own daughter-in-law and his son had inherited his father's taste in women. She was sharp as a knife – new here, straight from SigInt City, the huge NSA headquarters halfway between Washington and Baltimore at Fort Meade, Maryland, after spending two years shuttling between Fort Meade and nearby Langley on CIA liaison. She was used to operating in the clear air of the leafy fringe of Washington, where the political rules were still fairly straightforward. He didn't want to see her tripping over herself in the byzantine coils of the special relationship.

'Look, Miriam,' he began cautiously, 'I just want to know something.'

'Yes?'

'UKUSA,' he said, 'give me the quick version. I'm sure Ray won't mind.' He pronounced it 'Yookooza'.

'UK-USA Signals Intelligence Pact 1946. The deal by which we're here at all. We share SigInt with the Brits. Everything they get through GCHQ, we see too.'

'And vice versa?'

She just laughed.

'And bases?'

'Pretty much the same. We can put listening posts on their turf. They can put theirs on ours.'

'Right. We've got eight bases in Britain. How many do they have in the US?'

'Like none.'

Curtis tried looking over his glasses again. He was getting it right now, building in a bit of extra subtlety with the eyebrows. '1946 is a long time ago. What did they tell you in Fort Meade 'bout how we stand now?'

'"The wars of the future are commercial wars,"' she quoted. '"The NSA's role in Eastern-bloc surveillance may have been scaled down but it has been more than replaced by the need to keep a close watch on undesirable commercial developments in the distribution of advanced technological and defence products where full information may not be provided by the vendor." Meaning, we don't like other people selling whizz-bangs to the spics, wops, towel-heads and slant-eyes instead of us. Brackets, if those other people are our old Cold War allies, tough shit, business comes first, close brackets.'

'Cynical.'

'True.'

Mackeson nodded. 'Look, Miriam,' he said, 'it's like this. When I first came over, I was teamed up with this Brit called Nigel. GCHQ liaison. MI5 from birth. Positively vetted on the way out before they'd let the midwife cut the cord. Now you couldn't ever have called him smart but he was steady, very steady. He was a one-joke man, Nigel. Every time we met, "Hello, Ray, we're a pair of buggers, aren't we?" Never missed it. He knew we were on the same side, fighting off the Red hordes. He's been put out to grass. He's Sir Nigel now, off in some country bog-hole walking his dogs all day long. The Cold War warriors are drawing their pensions. MI5 spend as much time talking to the French and the Germans as they do to us.'

'So we keep the good bits to ourselves.'

'Yeah, course we do. Since the Gulf War anyway. The point is, UKUSA's a handy piece of fiction to have around on account of we need those bases here and we need access to their telecoms but we have to walk on eggshells sometimes.'

'You're saying Kay is an eggshell?'

Curtis Walsh answered that. 'Looks like one to me. Go over it. Tell me I'm wrong.' He ticked off the points on his fingers. 'One, influential hard-right British MP has a chemicals group. Two, his group develops a product that interests us a lot, CN512. Three, he's starting to sell it to people we just don't want him to be selling it to. Four, we do a little clever leaking and I hand it to you, Ray, getting that intercept out to those women without them knowing was pretty damned close to genius. So far so good, then *boiing*, five, Sir Greville's stepson pops up like Aladdin's genie, snooping inside the Stray. Crunch of egg-shells. Sounds to me like there's the potential for the biggest omelette you ever saw.'

She nodded calmly as if he hadn't said anything new. 'Put like that, I take the point. So what's the answer?'

'Keep the fat hot and have the herbs ready.'

* * *

In the village hall, the master of ceremonies was trying to kindle some enthusiasm amongst the audience.

'Ladies and Gentlemen,' he said in a reedy voice with only the faintest of Yorkshire accents, 'thank you all for coming tonight. As you know, the CPRE has called this meeting to discuss the exclusion from the Area of Outstanding Natural Beauty of the Ramsgill Stray base and the subsequent submission of major expansion plans for the base. I'd like to introduce our first platform member.'

He turned to the side of the stage with a stiff one-armed flourish that looked like someone trying to ease the cramp in their shoulder. The organizers had clearly thought it a good idea that he should bring on the speakers one at a time in an attempt to drum up a sense of expectation. As an idea it might have passed muster but in execution it was destined to failure. His voice rose to a painful falsetto.

'First of all, I would like you to welcome Mrs Jean Havergale, our local representative of the Council for the Protection of Rural England.'

There was a sporadic scatter of clapping as a large woman dressed in brown upholstery material clumped on to the stage, sat down in the wrong chair and had to be moved with maximum confusion to the one next to it.

'From the Planning Department, I ask you to put your hands together for Mr Tony Ramsay.'

A furtive man, tall and stooped, joined her, putting down a pile of papers which promptly spilled off the desk.

'From the Chamber of Commerce and also representing the views of a large section of the community, our very own Councillor Derek Percival.'

To Johnny's slight discomfiture there was a scatter of catcalls and whistles from the women around him as a short man strode confidently on to the platform. His projecting stomach was barely restrained by a valiant waistcoat and from there upwards his profile receded all the way past a massive chin to a small swept-back forehead.

'And finally, we're very pleased indeed to welcome a well-respected member of our local community for some years, with quite a few things to say on this issue.' It seemed suddenly that he'd forgotten the last name. Either that or it was another ham attempt at building up the suspense because he stood there with his mouth open as a tall dignified man in a tweed suit, leonine mane of white hair waving above a fine and sensitive face, strode on the stage to a great burst of applause.

Jo nudged Johnny without looking round at him. 'Great bloke,' she said, 'he's been a real help to us.'

Johnny said nothing. In that moment he knew he shouldn't have come, knew that this barred part of Yorkshire should have stayed that way. Pure panic welled up in him at the presence of the Devil incarnate as the chairman belatedly found his words.

'Our former ambassador, Sir Michael Parry.'

Johnny stared in appalled fascination at his father.

CHAPTER TEN

Don't ever be fooled, his mother had said as soon as he was old enough to be aware of his father's background presence on the television, the radio, in newspaper quotes. He's the most dangerous sort, Johnny. He can sound so reasonable and he gets people on his side but it can suck the backbone out of you. He can persuade you that black is white but his sort lack any kind of vision, Johnny. They just boil everyone's opinion down into a disgusting soggy mess of agreement.

He could remember her so well, bending over his bed. He was twelve years old and he'd fallen asleep with the radio on, listening to some comedy show. She'd come in. God knows why, she didn't usually. She was drawn perhaps by the faint sound of that hated voice. The jokes were over. Something serious had followed it and he was one of the speakers.

It hadn't been enough for her just to switch it off. Anger had wiped out logic in her brain. She'd had to wake him up to make sure he hadn't been listening to it, confusing him as the swirls of fresh sleep fled. Shouting at him, then calming down into mere lecturing. You mustn't listen to him, ever. Never let that voice into your ears because it will stop you believing in things, she'd said. You'll never be certain of anything again and then you will achieve *nothing*. If this country takes his route it will never be great again. It will dissipate its strength. It doesn't help anyone to hobble your achievers, to drag down the doers. Better that the rest realize they've just got to damn well get up and get going. He talks about liberty, she'd said, but he doesn't mean my liberty or your liberty. We're the people who've shown we deserve it. He'd hand over our liberty to a bunch of spongers and freeloaders.

For as long as he could remember, Johnny had dutifully switched off the radio, turned off the TV, averted his eyes from the newspaper articles. Sir Michael Parry, the doyen of international diplomacy, had been someone he merely glimpsed, a subliminal, threatening idea, the Lorelei waiting to lure him to his doom in a swirling pool of compromise.

Now, sitting in plain view, not thirty feet away, he could not avoid the reality. He could not even get up and leave without attracting attention. There was no choice but to sit there, looking and listening.

The woman from the CPRE went first. She lauded the beauties of Kex Gill and Blubberhouses Moor. She said the domes of Ramsgill Stray were already an eyesore and should not have been put there. She had a map projected on to a screen, inevitably back to front to start with, then crooked, then out of focus. In the end they could see the bent outlines of the Area of Outstanding Natural Beauty where it hiccupped to accommodate the American base.

It was bad enough, she explained, having it there at all, but at least it was in a hollow. Now, she said, they planned to put in some real monster dishes, covered by domes which would poke over the skyline and spoil the view for many miles to the north and west.

She sat down to a little polite applause.

Ramsay the furtive planner came next, hesitant in his wording but deploring any suggestion in Mrs Havergale's speech that proper procedures had not been followed and wishing to underline that at no time had the outline of the AONB been modified with any criteria in mind except the proper ones set down by statute. There was no reason for anyone not directly related to him to applaud his effort and no one did.

Councillor Derek Percival, waistcoat bulging, was third and the women around Johnny stirred restlessly when he stood up.

'What does a bump in a line matter,' he said and his

speech was pure Yorkshire, 'what does a little bump in a line matter against our national security and the wealth of our community?' There was a burst of clapping then from seats at the back and Johnny realized the Councillor had a powerful group of supporters with him.

'We've done well out of the base,' he said, 'and speaking for the Chamber of Commerce I have no hesitation in welcoming the proposed expansion because it will bring more trade to our community. We're pleased to see our American comrades in our shops, in our pubs, in our restaurants.'

'And in our telephones,' called Margo. Heads turned to look at her, mostly with frosty expressions on them.

'They're doing a service for all of us,' the Councillor went on, ignoring her. 'Protecting our freedom with their ceaseless vigil, scanning the skies over our heads for any threats that may face us.'

'Spare us,' said Jo in a loud whisper, 'he thinks it's a bloody radar station.'

The Councillor rambled on in this vein for some time, unable to come to any closing crescendo of argument, but nevertheless sat down to prolonged applause from well over half the people in the hall. It washed over Johnny. He was sitting with his eyes fixed on Sir Michael as Eve might have looked at the serpent.

'Thank you, Councillor Percival,' said the Chairman, 'always one to speak your mind. Now Sir Michael Parry, who needs no introduction from me other than to say that when there's a local issue to be addressed he's always been one to make everyone see a bit of sense.'

Sir Michael got to his feet slowly as if still thinking what he should say and this time the anticipatory applause was general. All round Johnny, the women were clapping as hard as they could and, as far as he could see, that was the reception throughout the rest of the hall too.

'Thank you for inviting me to speak,' he began, looking around. 'As many of you know, my family have lived here for over a hundred years, so I think I can very nearly say I belong.' A few people laughed. 'I myself have lived here on and off for more than thirty years now. It was a place I always looked forward to coming back to from my postings in the diplomatic service and since I retired, it has been the centre of my life.'

There was a general approving murmur.

'I can well understand Councillor Percival's concern with the wealth of the community,' he said, looking down in slightly absent benevolence at Percival whose chair was pushed far back from the table to accommodate his stomach, 'but should that be the only consideration?'

He had a habit of starting to speak while still looking down as if plumbing the great depths of his brain for the right words, then lifting his head sharply so that he seemed to cast them out across the audience.

'Most of you are dales people. You know what it means to breathe the moorland air, to stride out to the horizon without anyone stopping you. In all the hurly-burly of our modern life that is still the great free delight this county of ours can offer us and it has been kept that way by a system of rules and regulations which are designed to protect our heritage.'

Don't be fooled, don't be fooled was going through Johnny's head like a mantra. *Don't let him into your head.* But who? The man in front of him seemed to mean every word he said. It didn't fit the image of the professional word-twister he had carried around with him since childhood, the silver-tongued compromiser who left behind him a trail of betrayed causes.

'Now you may say,' went on Sir Michael, passing his gaze across them, 'that the special relationship between Britain and the United States of America should transcend such rules and regulations – that if our American friends feel it is necessary for our mutual safety for them to enlarge their base then we should simply say, "Let it be so." Ten years ago I think I would possibly have agreed with that approach. Now, I have to say, I am not so sure. There are allegations about the activities carried on inside this establishment which I find frankly disturbing. Whatever the truth of them, it is no longer enough to say in this period of changing political balance in the world that there should be *carte blanche*.' There were some restless whisperings in the audience as they absorbed his message.

'Above all,' he said, 'I am a firm believer in the rule of law. It has been a cause of some sadness to me that laws have been misused in an attempt to prevent protests at Ramsgill Stray. Without necessarily sharing the protestors' objectives, I do not think that is acceptable, just as I do not think any special exceptions should be made in the planning process for those trying to expand the activities of the base.'

He sat down abruptly to a round of applause that was only a little less unanimous than the one that had greeted him.

Johnny didn't listen to the questions and answers. He was too busy trying to reassemble the splintered certainty of his long-held image of his father. It didn't fit this dignified, quiet, certain man. His job told him he had to stay. His feet wanted to leave. The opposing forces pulled him down huddled into his seat with his arms folded tight across his chest and his chin down. He was roused from that only when Jo, next to him, stuck up a hand and called out a loud question to Sir Michael. Johnny lifted his head.

His father was leaning forward diagonally across the table, twiddling his glasses in one hand, swinging them by one of their arms, neck stretched as if straining to hear her words. His gaze was fixed on them and Johnny's eyes crossed with his for a moment as he looked up. Sir Michael seemed suddenly to rock back into a slightly more upright stance. He pushed his glasses back on to his nose and looked hard towards them over the rows of seats that separated them from the stage. Did he recognize Jo, perhaps? It seemed to Johnny that his father's gaze was fixed not on Jo, but on him.

She came to the end of her question and nothing happened; he simply went on staring towards them, then he seemed to shake his head slightly.

'I'm terribly sorry,' he said, 'would you mind awfully just saying that again. My ears are past their best, you know.'

Jo smiled. 'I was only asking whether you thought the new criminal trespass proposals are fair?'

He sat back. 'No, I don't,' he said slowly, 'I think it's another long-standing right that we are in danger of losing without really registering the fact. Let's be clear. The first stage was bad enough. That made it a criminal offence to trespass on someone else's ground if it impeded the occupant's lawful activity there. It was aimed at hunt saboteurs, travellers and peace protesters. Now they're proposing to make it more general still so that whatever the reason, it would be a criminal offence to trespass anywhere where the occupier didn't want you.'

Councillor Percival looked sideways at his fellow-panellist and said loudly, 'Private property's private property. What's wrong with that, then?'

Sir Michael considered him. 'I think I've seen you walking up the hill above Foxdale Mire, near my house?'

'Aye, that's right. I've walked there since I were a lad. What about it?'

'Well, I own that stretch of hillside, Councillor Percival and under the new proposals if I decided I didn't like your face, I could have you arrested for it.'

There was laughter and clapping. The point was won. Percival sat back shrugging and looking discomfited. Sir Michael had a broad smile on his face to rob the words of hurt and for just a moment, Johnny found himself smiling with him. He checked himself and looked around. It was easy to see the audience approved. The voice of reason or the Lorelei? He rubbed his forehead hard to fight off the first twinges of a headache.

That was almost it. There were two more questions and the CPRE lady announced that there would be a petition for their signatures by the door. The planning man gathered up his pile of papers again and Councillor Percival tried to buttonhole Sir Michael about something but had difficulty getting his full attention as the old diplomat scanned the crowd. Johnny helped get Jo's chair down the side of the hall, through the people to a quiet corner at the back where he saw the other women waiting. The group didn't seem to include Heather and he couldn't immediately see her.

Margo turned to him. 'What did you think of that?'

Johnny shrugged. 'Interesting.'

'Pretty pointless when it comes down to it. This lot aren't

going to get too stirred up about it, not with Percival and his cronies in there. Thank God for Sir Michael.'

'Yes.'

Jo looked up at him. 'I suppose you've heard him before. Did you see *Question Time* last week?'

'No, I didn't,' said Johnny and sought to change the subject. 'By the way, you were telling me about your case. What happened when you went to serve the writ?'

'Oh that,' said Jo, 'it was a laugh a minute, that was. We went up there to the base, and you know you have to serve the writ personally? Well, we were told if we got the guard at the gate to accept them that would be good enough.'

'Some chance,' said Margo.

Jo nodded. 'Yeah, he wasn't having that. Anyway we demanded that he should call up Hayter or the Chief Inspector and he wouldn't. He got on the blower and next thing there were modplods everywhere, vans blocking us in, the whole caboodle. All kinds of threatening stuff. Elsa went for a phone and she called up the real coppers in Harrogate.'

Johnny was surprised. 'Did they take any notice?'

'Didn't they just! Elsa told them we were trying to perform our legal rights and we were in danger of assault from the modplods and ten minutes later there was a squad car up there backing us up.'

'Backing you up?' he asked in amazement. 'Against police?'

'The real coppers don't think much of the modplods. They say they don't know anything about the law. Anyway there was this weird stand-off for a bit then the coppers in the squad car went and told the modplods they'd arrest them if they interfered with us trying to serve the writ, so they were forced to accept it.'

At every turn, Johnny's certainties about normal official behaviour were being shaken. The women went on talking as the hall slowly emptied around them and he stood there, trying to imagine the scene and wondering what his next move should be. He was very much the outsider still, treated with amused tolerance; certainly in no position to start asking more probing questions about how the group had got its hands on the Rage papers.

Heather's voice from behind him broke in on his thoughts and he looked round to see her walking down the aisle, talking animatedly to her companion. She was only a few steps away, coming towards them. The man she was talking to was Sir Michael Parry. He took an involuntary step backwards and stumbled over a chair.

'Hello everybody,' she said, 'I've just been saying how much we all liked what Sir Michael had to say.'

'It's very kind of you,' he said, 'I don't think I added anything, at least nothing that will stand up against the Chamber of Commerce's symphony of ringing cash registers.'

'Well, I thought you did and it was nice to hear it,' she said and there were noises of agreement all round. 'I think you've met everybody before?'

Through the fog of semi-panic Johnny recorded that as an interesting fact but her next words pushed it far to the back of his mind: 'Oh, except Johnny, I should say. Michael, this is Johnny Kennedy . . .' and – bizarrely – he found himself shaking hands with his father, being forced to meet a pair of level, interested eyes, knowing that his own gaze was far from level and the hand he offered had turned suddenly clammy.

Handshake over, he stepped back, offering no conversation, and his father turned instead to Margo. Johnny looked at Heather.

'What are you doing now?' he said.

She looked at her watch. 'Going to work in about ten minutes.'

'Work?'

'Yes. I'm on night shift at the Hall. I told you, didn't I? Tinderley Hall? The place where you thought the boys needed a good thrashing?'

'Don't. I didn't mean it. I wasn't thinking. I'm just surprised. I mean, you've been up all day.'

'Oh, it isn't too bad. If there are no calamities I get quite a lot of sleep. What are you doing?'

'I haven't really thought. I'd like to talk to you about . . . well, all this. I'll go and find somewhere to stay.'

'There's a pub near the Hall with rooms. If you follow me, I'll take you past it.'

She said her goodbyes and they went outside. Disconcertingly, Sir Michael detached himself and came out with them. He crossed to a Rover parked next to Heather's Citroën and called to her. 'I'll follow you up there, shall I?'

'Fine. Johnny's coming too. I'm just going to take him to the King and Queen on the way.'

'The King and Queen? Why?' said Sir Michael, puzzled. 'It's closed. There was a story in the paper. The tenant did a bunk or something like that.' He turned to Johnny. 'Were you going to stay there?'

'I was hoping to. I'll find somewhere else.'

'Well, there's a place down at . . . No, look, if you just need a bed for the night, I can put you up. There's lots of space.'

Johnny tried to frame some reasonable, polite refusal but Heather quickly said, 'That's very kind of you, Sir Michael.'

'It's all right. I only need to drop in at the Hall for a few minutes. They've got some papers for me.'

'Sir Michael is chairman of our trustees,' Heather said to Johnny, then turned to look at the older man. 'You don't need to. I can drop the papers in tomorrow morning on my way home.'

'Good idea. Come and have some coffee. Now, young man. Follow me.'

Three minutes later, the Rover's tail-lights shining in front of him, Johnny could think of no way out short of simply turning abruptly and driving off. Getting lost accidentally was out of the question. Sir Michael drove with exaggerated care, signalling every turn far in advance and going slowly when Johnny got held up at a junction by other traffic. Behind him, his son had all the options that his steering wheel and accelerator laid before him to escape this approaching nemesis; but he knew that if he took them there could be no plausible re-entry into this group.

* * *

There were stone gateposts with no gates, then a long drive on a bumpy track that seemed, so far as Johnny could tell in the dark, to take them round a sweep of hillside. They pulled up in front of a house whose stone walls shone with a grey glimmer in the turning headlights as Johnny swung in beside the Rover.

When he switched his headlights off thick darkness cloaked everything and he realized that there could be no one else waiting for them inside the house. From somewhere outside, near the door, Sir Michael called to him.

'Won't take a minute. Just get some lights on.'

He heard a scrabbling of keys, the click of a latch and then a dim outside light, shrouded in tangled ivy leaves, came on to show the way. With a sense of deep foreboding, he went in to a stone-flagged hall, concentrating on the details to fill up his mind. Two torches on a side table, with secateurs, a roll of garden wire and half-used seed packets, closed up with clothes-pegs. A pair of binoculars, old but good, sticking out of an open leather case. Two pairs of wellingtons, one old, one new and they both looked the same size. Coats on a row of pegs, a Barbour, a tweed overcoat and some sort of mackintosh, all male but at the end, a paler, lightweight raincoat that looked like a woman's. There was a dog basket under a table at the end of the hall, but no sound nor sign of a dog.

The other man led the way into a big, comfortable country kitchen. A battered Aga radiated warmth in the space which a range had once filled. Old tatty armchairs were arrayed along one wall and a long refectory table filled the middle of the room. Sir Michael dumped his briefcase on the table and looked around.

'Sorry about the mess,' he said, 'Mrs Thompson comes during the week but I make do at weekends by myself.'

'You live alone?'

'Oh yes,' he said vaguely, 'my wife died two years ago next month.'

My wife. Not my second wife. My wife. Johnny had never thought of his father having a wife, not after Lady Viola.

'I'm sorry,' he said, then, because he couldn't stop himself: 'Do you have children?'

'No,' said Sir Michael, 'not really,' and he bent to open a cupboard.

'Look,' said Johnny, 'I think I'm putting you to a lot of trouble. I'll go and find a hotel. It won't be a problem.'

'Please don't,' said the old man, straightening up with a bottle in his hand and turning to look directly at him. 'There's a room made up. Mrs T. always leaves a room made up. She knows I like people to drop in.' He looked at Johnny and took two glasses from the shelf with his other hand. 'Come and have a glass of something through here.' He nodded sideways at a door in the far corner of the kitchen.

Although it was summer there was an night-time chill as they went into what was clearly Sir Michael's study, and he switched on an old-fashioned two-bar electric fire. Two walls of the room were completely filled by packed bookshelves and another, against which stood an old oak roll-top desk, was almost equally covered with pictures and photos. He poured Johnny a glass of Laphroaig.

'I'm glad to have the company,' he said, sinking into a chair and waving Johnny into the one opposite. 'It's a bit quiet round here at the moment. My old dog died last week.' He paused for a moment, clearly moved by the reawakened memory. 'Fifteen years old. Pretty good for a spaniel, but it's quiet without her.'

'I'm sorry,' said Johnny.

'These things happen. In fact they happen more and more as you get older.' It could have sounded maudlin but he said it with dignity and a wry smile. 'Now, Heather was telling me that you're a pilot.'

'Yes,' he said, and immediately felt keen guilt because he knew, uncomfortably, confusingly, that this wasn't at all like talking to a stranger. At some genetic level there was contact between them. This was, unmistakably, his father to whom he had just told the first of what looked set to be many lies.

He told the rehearsed fiction of his recent years but that wasn't enough for the man sitting opposite him. His questions sought to carry Johnny ever further back into increasingly dangerous territory, where he hadn't even begun to construct considered answers.

To distract as much as anything, he asked, 'How long have you known Heather?'

The old man wrinkled his brow. 'A year or two, I suppose.' He nodded. 'We met under somewhat unusual circumstances. I was supposed to be giving her the sack.'

'Why?'

'All this Ramsgill Stray business. It was just after the first time she was arrested. My fellow trustees at the Hall were, let's say, a somewhat conventional group of people. They didn't think it was at all right that someone who was employed to be a calming influence for delinquent boys should herself be up on a charge. I was deputed, as chairman, to back up the director and deal with her. I have to admit it took about five minutes at the outside to make me realize that you simply couldn't hope to find a more honest, impressive person of integrity than Heather Weston. Fortunately the Director agreed with me.'

'What about the other trustees?'

'We have a slightly different group now.' He chuckled. 'They know my views.'

'Jo told me you'd helped the peace group a lot.'

'Oh, I don't know about that. I've given them a bit of guidance on their court cases.' His voice took on a greater intensity. 'I mean, if they go closing off public rights of way and things like that, they simply have no right to arrest people walking across them. No right at all. The greatest mark of civilization is the preparedness to live by the laws you create, not bend them when it suits you.' He stretched out with the bottle and topped up Johnny's glass.

'What about Councillor Percival and his line? "The base is doing us all a service"?'

The old man looked down at the fire. 'In the days when I earned my daily bread representing HMG's point of view and trying to turn America's eroding sentimental affection into something a bit more tangible, I would have agreed with that. I don't know now. I've seen some things recently . . .' He seemed to stop himself. 'Things those women have shown me. I think it's a huge cuckoo in the nest and what we're doing feeding it, I simply can't imagine. Protecting that place, against our own people.'

'I know what you mean,' said Johnny, rubbing the back of his head.

'Do you? I'd be surprised if you do. I think there are very few people who have any real idea what's going on in there.'

'No, I just meant I had a close encounter with Sergeant Hayter this afternoon.'

'Yes, Heather told me. I can well understand that their tactics annoy the police. It must be dreadfully difficult to be put in the position of having to enforce unenforceable rules but those police have a heavy responsibility to control their behaviour and what they did to her was unpardonable. You do know she's facing prison, don't you?'

'Yes.'

'I simply can't imagine what it will do to that girl, and then look at what happened to Jo.'

'You believe her account?'

There was a sharp, tense silence and Sir Michael's eyebrows shot up as he looked at Johnny in surprise. 'Of course. Don't you?'

'I didn't mean to sound suspicious. It's just I only heard the story this evening.'

'Make up your mind about the person and all the rest follows. Allow a bit for over-excitement, emotional involvement and straightforward observational error and that still leaves me convinced – and that counts for both of them, Jo and Heather.'

'Isn't there anything Heather can do?'

Sir Michael got up and crossed to the desk. Its cover was rolled three-quarters open and every pigeonhole was stuffed with papers. From the top drawer he pulled out a pink cardboard folder, checked its contents and tossed it to Johnny.

'If you want some bedtime reading, it's all there. Statements, the doctor's reports, the whole lot. There's no doubt in my mind.'

'Do you think she has any chance?'

'She could have. She could have if they could find the doctor.'

'What do you mean?'

'There's a doctor who got her to hospital who's a key witness. Mysteriously enough the doctor has suddenly moved away.'

'They can't find him?'

'It's a her. No, they can't. The hospital and the BMA won't give any information at all. So far it's a dead end.'

'Maybe I could help,' said Johnny, lulled by the whisky and the warmth, not thinking.

'How?' The man's tone was curious.

'Oh, well. I've just got a bit of time on my hands. I could do some looking.'

'You like Heather, don't you?'

It wasn't hard to sound convincing. 'Yes, I do.'

'I'm very fond of Heather. She's like – well, I wouldn't know what it's like to have a daughter, but I certainly think of her as a niece.'

Johnny understood it as some sort of warning, given in a lighter tone than it deserved.

He cradled his whisky glass and a silence fell between them and when he broke it, it was with a question that maybe the moment or maybe the whisky made him ask.

'You said you didn't really have children. I wondered what you meant.'

It seemed to him that Sir Michael looked at him for a long time.

'I was married before. A long time ago and only for a year or two. We had a boy. She took him with her. That's all I meant.'

Johnny's room was simple and comfortable. He sat in the bed against fat pillows, switched on the bedside light with its tasselled floral shade and opened the pink file. He read the statements and the medical reports and a detached part of him was capable of showing surprise at the anger it stirred up in him. He made a note of the doctor's details: Caroline

Beevor, with her last address in Leeds. He put it down and switching out the light, heard an owl screech somewhere out in the night. His head was full of swirling words and sleep was not going to be easy. Making a black central shape in his mind's eye, images kept creeping in, the study, the whisky, the desk. He pushed them out, tried to suppress Sir Michael's voice but the images persisted.

I've seen some things recently . . . things those women have shown me.

It leapt into his mind as clearly spoken as if the man had been standing at the end of the bed. The image of the desk followed hard on its heels. Sir Michael rooting through the drawer for the pink folder. Sir Michael who had been advising the women. Sir Michael who would naturally, if confronted by the Rage documentation, think first of turning to the Hurst Inquiry, to people like him with a sense of honour, people who would bring it all out into the open.

They would have shown him the papers, surely they would and down there, down in that stuffed desk, who knew what might still be around.

He found a book in the bedside table, an old dog-eared Agatha Christie and started to read it. Perversely, as soon as he needed to stay awake, he began to feel extremely sleepy. He got out of bed, opened the window wide and stuck his head out into the fresh night air. To his right, at the extreme end of the house, another window glowed yellow through muffling curtains. He sat on the hard chair by the basin, reading, and in five minutes when he looked again, the other light was out. That was a Godsend. It told him Sir Michael's room was well away from the stairs down to the hall below. He looked at his watch, set the timer for an hour, lay on the bed and was instantly asleep.

When the bleep of the alarm woke him, he rubbed the sleep from his eyes, stretched and checked out of the window again. Everything was dark and quiet. He opened the door, moved quietly across the landing and down the stairs, keeping to the sides of the treads and taking up his weight gently and slowly on each foot. In the hall he took one of the torches and played the beam around the room looking for any evidence of infrared detectors or other alarms but, as he expected in this gracious, dilapidated old house, technology of that sort had never crossed its owner's mind.

He stepped softly through the kitchen into the study, shut the door behind him and considered turning on the light. The window, after all, faced the opposite way to Sir Michael's bedroom. Caution won and he stuck to the torch. On the top of the desk a framed photo caught his eye, Sir Michael, twenty years younger, a fit looking fifty-year old, with his arm round a smiling, sweet-faced woman of the same age. The second wife, clearly.

He pulled the top drawer open. At first glance it didn't look likely to be a quick job because there was so much in it, but he soon found out there was order to it. Sheaves of bills, all clipped neatly together in subject groups – a typescript of some sort, occupying a large chunk of space underneath. He passed a quick eye over it. Memoirs? No, some sort of literary critique. E. M. Forster's influence on someone or perhaps it was the other way round. It took half an hour to be sure there was nothing in the drawer of relevance and only slightly less time to perform the same check on the second drawer.

That left the pigeonholes. He leafed through credit card statements, bank letters, a proposal from a publisher, instructions for an electric hedge-cutter and an envelope of certificates: Michael George Parry, born Broadstairs, May 3rd. 1924. Elizabeth Bettina May Maxwell born Worthing, May 19th. 1928. Elizabeth Bettina May Parry, died Leeds . . . He felt suddenly intrusive, put them away and reminded himself that his job obliged him to do this. It didn't feel quite the same when you could no longer invoke the protection of the power of government behind you.

He found it in a plain, white envelope – photocopies of two sheets of paper from somewhere in the run of a multi-page document. It started halfway through a sentence.

> . . . such quantities as you may require. An instructor will accompany the first shipment to direct your men in the

calculation of the timing and size of doses. You will discover that CN512 is an extremely effective product for stimulating short-term extreme aggressive behaviour. When properly used with well-prepared troops with a clear strategic objective, results are quite exceptional. From the start of testing of the CN512 compound, its effect in suppressing normal pre-combat anxiety has been found to be virtually independent of personal characteristics. Now marketed as 'Rage' in handy disposable drink packs it is not even necessary, on first use, to tell combat troops what they are drinking. So long as strong unit identity and loyalty has been developed within the group and a readily identifiable outside threat exists, there will be a quantifiable and well-directed augmentation of the kill-capability of your unit.

It went on to give a list of prices.

Johnny saw that across the top of each page was a boxed-off section. It looked like some form of coding put on – he presumed – by the computers at Ramsgill Stray. He read '2 of 4' and '3 of 4' and a string of numbers which he carefully copied down before he replaced the papers in the envelope and put it back in the pigeonhole.

He didn't want to leave the desk without checking for anything else and so it was that ten minutes later, getting near the end of the search, he pulled out an old brown envelope and found inside it some photos. A baby in christening robes, arranged in a crib by itself, and then another with the baby being held by a slim woman who looked more determined than pleased. Lady Viola and therefore, by extension, Johnny himself, although he had never seen the photo before. He stared at it in shock but that was nothing compared to what was to come. Under them, he saw a third picture and this was newer. It showed a twelve-year-old boy, holding a cricket bat and a cup proudly. He knew exactly when it had been taken, a June Saturday when he'd captained his prep school First XI to victory against Winsham Manor. He remembered the circle of masters and parents snapping away as he held up the cup, remembered wishing his mother had bothered to come. He certainly didn't remember anyone who could have taken this photo. There were two old cuttings with it. One was from the school magazine. *John Kay led the team to a fine victory in the annual Winsham match, scoring a season's best of 86 before giving up his wicket to a marginal LBW decision.*

He'd thought his paternity was a dead issue, a fossil of a relationship, existing only briefly and a long time ago. He couldn't think that any more. This pushed the boundaries back. Twenty years ago, his fossil father had been interested enough to procure and keep a photo.

Then he turned over the other cutting and the hot breath of the much more recent past burst into his face. It was folded four ways, a quarter-page from the *Independent*, judging from the typeface, a version of the story he hadn't seen at the time.

> TOP IRA COMMANDER SHOT IN FARMHOUSE MYSTERY the headline announced. The bodies of Joe O'Hanlon, a senior figure in the IRA command structure and two of his lieutenants, Patsy Steel and Sean Rooney, were discovered at a remote farmhouse in South Armagh yesterday after soldiers responded to reports of shooting. Weapons were recovered from the scene which was cordoned off for several hours while the soldiers checked for booby-traps. An army spokesman said no details were available of the shooting but it is understood that they believe it may have been the result of a factional squabble within the IRA's command structure.'

Wineglass. That gut-wrenching, terrifying foul-up of an operation. The operation that simultaneously limited his rise and made his name in MI5, pegged him forever as a hard man, ready to break rules and heads. Wineglass.

It had followed him everywhere so far but it had no right to be here, tucked away in this old man's store of memories, implying all kinds of terrifying things. Not just implying, he corrected himself, proving rather – proving that Sir Michael Parry, far from being a forbidden name from thirty years ago, knew exactly what his lost son had lately been doing for a living.

CHAPTER ELEVEN

It took a tremendous effort to go downstairs in the morning and be natural. A photo from his schooldays was one thing, he was quite sure he was unrecognizable now: the newspaper cutting was quite another. He'd woken up to the full impact of that, getting him while he was unprepared, flooding him with anxiety that this genial old man knew so much more about his remote son than he ought to have done. And here he was, in the middle of it, having to go down and be Johnny Kennedy, a name he now kicked himself for choosing, far too close.

And yet there had been no sign of any suspicion in Sir Michael's face.

While he was shaving a car drew up outside and when he walked into the kitchen he saw Heather sitting at the long table where Sir Michael was pouring coffee. She was passing him an envelope. Yesterday's documents, he thought, our usual friend . . . that was what she'd said, our usual friend would be looking after it. Sir Michael took it, nodded and put it on the dresser.

Johnny put the pink file down on the table. 'Good morning,' he said to both of them.

Heather gave him a quick smile. She looked tired

'Good morning,' said Sir Michael, 'I do hope you slept well.' He poured a third mug of coffee, pushed it towards him and looked at the folder. 'You read it?'

'Yes, I did. It makes you think.'

'John here said he might be able to help you find this doctor person of yours,' he explained to Heather.

She gave him a questioning look. 'That would be clever of you. We've drawn a complete blank.'

'I'm not promising,' he said, 'but I'll have a bit of time on my hands this week and I enjoy a challenge.'

Five hours later he was doing his best to gloss over the whole thing to Ivor Sibley, who was looking at his report with the rapid notes he'd made of the text and headings of the Rage document. On the way back down the M1, he'd gone through a range of emotion. He'd met his father and survived the experience. The man had not reached into his mind and rearranged it. North, south, east and west were still in the same place. Looked at in a certain way, he wasn't really betraying them, Heather and Sir Michael. Their interests all lay in the same direction. Surely none of them wanted Ramsgill Stray to be able to eavesdrop against Britain's interests. It was just that he was obliged by circumstances to operate covertly. 'Operate covertly' sounded so much better than 'betray'.

He could make up any slight imbalance in the sum of actions by helping find the doctor and, strictly professionally speaking, it might prove helpful to stay in touch.

For all that he wanted more time to sort out the chaos in his head before putting his superior completely in the picture so he was hoping Ivor would be satisfied with his generalities about the precise circumstances of his finding the documents. He wasn't. When he seemed to be paying you only half his attention, that was when you most had to watch out for him.

'Good stuff, Johnny,' he said, looking up from the report and glancing over his shoulder at the cricket on the monitors behind him, 'sounds like you stumbled over the mother-lode. I haven't quite understood exactly where this came from. You were staying in someone's house last night, you say? Are you screwing one of these peace women? That would be carrying duty a little far. We'd have to pay you overtime for that, I expect.' He laughed at his own joke. Johnny was silent.

'No, go on,' he said, trying to keep a straight face, 'just

tell me the rest. Who exactly had these papers? I'm sure Sir Greville is going to ask us.'

God forbid, thought Johnny. He's the very last person I would want to know about it, or at least the second to last.

He shrugged. 'A man who's helping them out. I stayed at his house last night.'

'What man was that?'

'He's called Parry.'

'Just Parry? Barry Parry, Harry Parry, Gary Parry maybe?'

'Sir Michael Parry.'

Sibley shot a startled look at him, breathed in and gave a snort of exasperation.

'And you didn't think it was worth mentioning until now that you've been rifling the drawers of the best-known former diplomat in Britain? Or that he, of all people, just happened to have these extremely sensitive papers on him? For God's sake, Johnny, that's quite a major point to leave out.'

'Ivor, this is rather difficult for me.' It sounded lame. 'I'd better explain something you probably don't realize.'

'Fire away.'

So Johnny told him as little as he could get away with of the story of his parentage, of how he hadn't been allowed to meet, see, listen to or even read about his father since he was a baby, of how Lady Viola regarded Sir Michael Parry as evil incarnate. Sibley's gaze was fixed on him in fascination throughout.

Johnny came to the end and looked at him. 'You're seeing Sir Greville?' he asked.

'Yes, this evening.'

'Ivor, I don't think there's really any point in bringing Parry into this. He doesn't even know I'm his son.'

'I think I have to tell them.'

'I warn you, Ivor, my mother will not behave logically. She'll fly off the handle. It will just make things harder.'

'Johnny, you're a little old to be frightened of your mother.' Sibley made a face. 'On the other hand, I know what you mean. I'm ten years older than you are and she bloody terrifies me. Anyway,' he said, 'leave that to me. You've done OK. It doesn't sound like there's any need for you to go back up there again.

Take the rest of the day off. I'll have something else for you in the morning.'

Johnny didn't go home. There was too much unfinished business in Yorkshire to begin to think about closing that chapter. He went back to an almost deserted office downstairs and logged on to the computer.

The first bit was easy. Dr Caroline Beevor had the sort of record with the DSS you would expect. Addresses, everything. It was all there until five weeks ago, then it seemed she had just upped and gone. There was no record of her working anywhere else in the UK since then. The DVLC computer in Swansea revealed that she'd sold her car at the same time. It gave him a name and address for the car's new owner and he soon had a phone number to match. That was a start.

The phone rang for so long that he almost put it down but then an elderly woman's voice answered it.

'Hello?'

'Mrs Mitchell?'

'Yes, I'm so sorry, I was down the garden.'

'Sergeant Miller here, Metropolitan Police. I'm sorry to trouble you.' His voice was nasal and slightly slurred.' It's just a routine enquiry about your car.'

'Oh dear, I haven't done anything wrong have I? Metropolitan Police, that's London, isn't it. I don't go to London, I—'

'No, it's nothing like that at all. It's a Fiesta, isn't it? It's just we're looking into a crime committed two months ago using a car with the same number plates. It's ten to one they were false plates but we have to go through the motions, just to make sure.'

'Two months ago? Oh dear no, that was before I bought it. It belonged to Caroline then, not me. I'm sure she wouldn't have had anything to do with it. She's a doctor, you know.'

Caroline. Just the first name. She knows her. He felt the thrill of the bite on the hook.

'Oh, yes, I see what you mean. I'm looking at the dates. That would be Dr Beevor, the previous owner?'

'That's right. She used to live next door. Lovely girl.'

'D'you know where I could contact her?'

'She's upped and gone off to France. Married a Frenchman. Somewhere down south.'

'Do you have a phone number?'

'Oh, they're not on the phone yet. They sent me a card last week. They're doing up some tatty old place, living in a caravan. Here it is. I've got it.'

'Perhaps you could give me the address.'

'It doesn't say. I am sorry. It just says they'll send me all the details when they finally move in.'

'Do you know her husband's name?'

'Oh no. Something French I think.'

'What about parents, relations, any other way we could contact her?'

'Now let me see. I know her mother married again and she lives in Australia, or was it New Zealand? That's all I can remember.'

It seemed to be a dead end. 'Is there a postmark on the card she sent?'

There was a doubtful silence. 'It's all squodgy. I think it starts with an E. Oh hang on, there's a bit here. Shall I read it to you?'

'Please do.'

'Oh, yes, this might help. She says, "Life at La Maison Ruineuse is full of dust and dry rot. I'll be glad to get to Cherbourg." That sounds like the name of the house. Does that help?'

'I think it's probably just a joke name,' he said tactfully. 'But what was that about Cherbourg?'

'Er, where is it . . . "I'll be glad to get to Cherbourg for some fresh air. I'm going to a conference on the weekend of the twentieth. I'll gaze across the Channel and give you a wave."'

He thanked her and hung up. The twentieth was twelve days away. It took only one call to the Cherbourg Syndicat d'Initiatif to locate a hotel staging a medical conference. With three hundred delegates on their list, the hotel couldn't help him find one whose surname he didn't know. There was no Beevor so she was using her married name whatever that might be, but at least he had made some progress. He thought of phoning Heather, realized it would seem suspiciously soon and that anyway she might well be asleep after her night shift then fell into a reverie imagining a simpler world in which he could spend as much time as he wanted with whoever he wanted.

Ivor Sibley, who liked to know how his money was being spent, had a little bit of software that gave him an activity check on all the office phones as well as the computer network. A quick glance told him that someone was down in the office below, hitting the phones and a further check told him who was phoning and where.

By the time the clock reached ten, Ivor Sibley had been kept waiting for over an hour. Mossiman's Belfry was a wonderful place to spend an evening, but only if you were eating there, which Sibley had rather hoped he was going to be. Cruelly, there was a menu on the table and he'd made the mistake of looking at it when he had thought food was going to be on the agenda. Then the waiter had returned.

'Sir Greville says, will you have a drink while you wait and will you join them for coffee in a little while.'

Bastard. There wasn't much he could do. He wasn't a member, although he was increasingly inclined to think it was well worth the substantial subscription to have the advantages of private dining amongst tables protected by the discreet screening of money.

Sitting in the side room, making his second gin and tonic last, he knew he was being made to feel like a tradesman and tried to restrain his rising resentment. He had assumed Sir Greville must be dining important guests but when the waiter finally appeared with the summons to the table it was clear that he and Lady Viola had been the only ones there all along and Sibley fumed privately a little more.

'What have you got, Sibley?' demanded Lady Viola.

'Good evening,' he said with exaggerated politeness to both of them.

'Good evening, Sibley,' said Sir Greville. 'I understand young Johnny's efforts in Yorkshire have been productive?'

Lady Viola just reached out a hand in Sibley's direction and snapped her fingers. He took two copies of Johnny's report from his inside pocket and gave them one each. It was less than a page long and took them very little time to read.

'Those numbers at the top,' said Sibley. 'We were hoping they might mean something to you.'

Sir Greville peered at them with raised eyebrows and the expression of someone examining a slightly smelly oyster.

'They do,' he said, 'one of them anyway. The 4836 number, that's the secure fax in my PA's office. Don't know about the rest.'

Lady Viola was still looking at the report. 'Silly boy doesn't say where he got it. Just some tosh about "an associate" of these dreadful women.'

Because he wanted to shake her for making him wait, though afterwards he rationalized it to himself as being because she and her husband were after all paying his bill, Sibley said very slowly and deliberately, 'He got it from Sir Michael Parry.'

He couldn't have hoped for a better effect.

'From Michael?' she said. 'Don't be absurd, you stupid man. How on earth could he have got anything from Michael?' She clearly thought he had made a simple mistake.

'He did, I assure you. He stayed with Sir Michael Parry last night in Yorkshire and found out that Parry has been helping these women. It sounds as though they came to him with the papers and Parry advised them to send them to the Hurst Inquiry.'

'Michael Parry? Yorkshire?' was all she could say.

Sir Greville gave her a concerned look and leaned towards Sibley. 'But Johnny doesn't know Parry. Never met him. We've kept it that way. Bit of a family thing, you see. There's a past connection.'

'Really? Well, he's met him now. Of course, Johnny was there under a different name. Parry wouldn't have known who he was.'

Lady Viola was belatedly coming to the boil and Sibley didn't like the look in her eyes.

'All my life,' she said, 'I have done everything I could to

keep my son away from that man. Years of struggle. We employ you to do a job and you've managed to screw it up just like that.'

'I beg your pardon, Lady Viola,' Sibley said slowly, 'I had no idea the man was involved. Even if I had known, I'm afraid I had also been given no information to suggest there would be any sensitivity in that direction.'

'You should have known!' she snapped. 'What else don't you know? You're in the knowing business, for God's sake. You're paid to know.'

Her colour was rising, turning the deep tan to the colour of bloody battlefield mud. Her eyes had a glassy, wild stare in them. Sir Greville took one appalled look and changed the subject. Sibley's relief was quickly demolished when he found what the new subject was.

'This Quill character,' said Sir Greville, 'he's still around.'

'Yes, I'm afraid the first phase of our deterrent programme was nullified because he received a substantial inheritance. He turned down the job offer.'

'I know that.'

'We then took certain other steps to persuade him it would be in his interests to leave. One of my staff made the point to him in a rather direct way.'

'And?'

'He still appears obdurate. He did pay a visit to the local police to complain but we were able to pre-empt that by placing information in the system that indicated he had a somewhat unreliable personal history.'

'Which leaves us where exactly?'

'Which leaves us with the need to take a more firm approach still if you will sanction such a step.'

Sir Greville looked away and waved a dismissive hand. 'I pay you to get results, Sibley. It's no business of mine how you get them. I know you'll stay within the law, of course.'

Always careful, thought Sibley. Perhaps he thinks I'm recording him. If so, he's right.

Lady Viola hadn't been listening. She had been sitting stiffly upright, staring with her eyes open unnaturally wide at the wall, drumming her fingers on the table. Now she turned abruptly back to Sibley.

'I want to know exactly what's going on with my son,' she said. 'Who knows what may have happened in Yorkshire? He's an incredibly stupid boy and Michael Parry is a snake. Put someone on to it.'

'You want Johnny under surveillance?' asked Sibley incredulously, thinking of the organizational problems that would create.

'Well, it shouldn't be difficult, should it? Put a girl on to him or something. That girl, Maggie. She looked his sort.'

Maggie, thought Sibley hysterically. Johnny's sort? Only if he buys a whip.

'I'll see what I can do,' he said with extraordinary self control.

'Is she suitable?' asked Lady Viola. 'Does she come from a good family?'

CHAPTER TWELVE

Johnny had Matthew Quill on his mind. Sibley had teamed him up with Maggie again for a black-bag job. She seemed more friendly, even flirty, this time and he wasn't sure how to take her. They arrived outside Quill's flat in an anonymous Rover with hire company stickers.

'We've got an hour,' said Maggie. 'He's gone to the cinema. The film finishes at five past ten and it should take him eight minutes to cycle back.'

'And if he doesn't like the film?'

'We'll get a shout.' Maggie held up a mobile phone, 'Martin's outside the cinema.'

The job sounded simple enough. They were to check the house for papers, anything related to CN512 and the same name list as last time. Johnny saw Jean Davies's name again and it gave him brief pause for thought. What had happened after they reported her letter to Quill? Had she come in for so much criticism that she killed herself, or was something else going wrong in her life?

Maggie had a key and they went quietly up the stairs and into the flat.

'You take the bedroom, I'll start in the sitting-room. Whoever finishes first does the kitchen,' she instructed. She had automatically adopted the senior role.

'Where's the copier?'

'No copier this time. Anything you find, we take with us, right?'

That made no kind of sense. 'But he's going to know.'

'It doesn't matter,' she said, but he still looked hesitant. 'Special circumstances. Just do it, OK? It'll make sense later. Really.'

He stood there, irresolute, thinking it went against everything he'd ever been taught.

She took two steps closer to him, smiled and ran her fingers down his shirt to stroke the crotch of his jeans. 'Pity there's no one around to interrupt us this time,' she said, and turned away leaving him seriously confused.

The bedroom yielded nothing except several bags of new, unworn clothes, labels still attached by their plastic umbilicals. Quill had been indulging himself. Johnny checked carefully in every possible hiding place. He took equal care putting things back, though if Quill was going to know about their visit as soon as he spotted any missing papers it was hard to see the point. Maggie was still searching the desk when he went back into the living-room. There was a file and a pile of loose sheets of paper on the floor and as he walked in, she added another one to it. The kitchen never looked promising, being small, bleak and ill equipped, and he wasn't at all surprised when it yielded nothing extra.

'OK, I'm through,' she said as he came back in. She put the file and the papers in her bag and looked at her watch. 'Fifteen minutes in hand,' she said, 'not bad.'

They saw no one on the stairs on the way back to the front entrance and anyway they could have been coming from any of the flats in the block. Maggie got in the driving seat and started up.

'We might as well have a ringside seat for part two,' she said. 'Part two is when you see why taking the papers made sense.'

She drove the car no more than a hundred yards to where the main road crossed their path and they pulled in to the kerb close to the junction. She dialled a number on the phone and Johnny could hear Martin's distorted accents in the voice at the other end.

'Film's just ended,' the voice said, 'they're starting to come out.'

'We're outside,' she said and putting the phone down, looked at her watch.

'Eight minutes then,' she said and, turning to him, she shook her head so the fine, long, black hair flew around it. She reached across slowly and traced a line along his thigh with a finger nail.

'I always get horny after a job,' she said.

'You didn't last time,' he replied, disconcerted.

'Oh, that . . .' She shrugged. 'You were new. I was just keeping my options open.'

'I believed you.'

'Did you?' she said, moving towards him, and her lips stayed parted. Her arms and upper body seemed to snake in his direction around the obstacle course of the handbrake and gear lever and before he had much more time to consider his part in it all, her hair fell across his face and her mouth met his with a savage urgency that blocked out rational thought. He just had time to think that it wasn't very professional before her tongue reached in and turned off his brain.

Matthew Quill had found the film disappointing but the cycle ride back made up for it. The new bike was fast and light and the gear shift was a joy. His bank manager had changed his attitude completely when he'd seen the solicitor's latest letter about the legacy. An overdraft until the house was sold? Certainly, sir. The college was quite happy to let him go on using the labs if he was funding his own pay cheque and the new set of tests was going well. He dropped a couple of gears and stood on the pedals up the slight rise towards the junction, glanced over his shoulder and pulled into the middle of the road ready for the right turn up towards the flat. There was a car coming down the main road towards him so he waited, a car coming fast, very fast. A Ford Escort Cosworth, favoured wheels of teenage car thieves everywhere, stolen from Peckham that morning. Stolen on purpose just to be here at this junction, at this moment.

He had no time to escape and nowhere to escape to. He was trapped in the centre of the road, the bull on the dartboard, and the dart was a ton of steel doing sixty-five miles an hour. In the second and a half left, when he realized the Escort was swerving towards the centre of the road, he could have flung himself from his machine and he might have made it. Instead he tried to save the bike and himself, believing quite wrongly that the car simply hadn't seen him. In that second and a half he got no more than six feet and for the Escort's driver, the tiniest wrist movement was enough to correct his aim. The car hit the bike and Matthew's left leg at the same moment, scooping him over the bonnet. His cycle helmet made only a marginal difference as his head hit the top of the windscreen by the roof, shattering his skull. He was dead before his limp body windmilled to the ground and the Escort was out of sight before the wheels on the bike stopped spinning.

Johnny had been sitting there in a daze since Maggie abruptly disentangled herself, said, 'Here we go' and sat forward with a look of anticipation on her face. He'd only just realized that the object of her attention was the man on the bike and that this must be Quill when the scarlet Escort shot into his field of view and with a thump that carried loudly, Quill's body, spraying a bloody Catherine wheel, was sent arcing into the air. His first shocked reaction was to yank the door handle.

'Don't be an idiot,' said Maggie, grabbing his arm, 'stay inside. We're off.'

She had the car moving before he could think of an argument, reversing on full lock to swing round in the road and heading away up the hill before the first shocked passer-by could fearfully approach the bloody bundle in the road.

'That was . . . us?' he asked. 'You knew about it?'

'Why did you think we were sanitizing the house?' she said. 'I would have thought it was obvious.' She was excited, eyes glistening, breathing hard.

'Why was that necessary?' he said angrily.

'Hey, what happened to big bad Johnny Kay?' she asked, surprised. 'Wineglass Johnny, who blows away top Provos when he loses his temper? What gives?'

He bit his lip. 'Quill's not PIRA,' he said. 'Maybe someone could have told me.'

I haven't got to the bottom of him yet, Sibley had said when he'd suggested she didn't tell Johnny first. Watch his reaction, he'd said. Tell me how he takes it. She had and it hadn't been what she expected.

'What he's doing was bloody dangerous,' she said. 'You want to argue with Sibley?'

She phoned one-handed while she drove. Sibley's private number. Someone answered.

'Been there. Done that,' she said and switched off.

They said nothing on the way back. Johnny sat there, the picture of the cartwheeling body assaulting him so that he had to keep pushing it aside. It came back at him again and again, spraying its appalling, irreparable blood and he fought it, struggling to lock it away in a box with the fox hunting memories and all the rest, down there in the darkness. He blanked it all out, blanked out everything around him so that he seemed for a time to be in a trance. When all was serene again and he could afford to let his mind surface, he did what he had always done, took on the protective camouflage of those immediately around him. It had been sanctioned, he told himself, it must have been necessary. Magie seemed quite relaxed about it.

She was driving with total concentration, shifting gears and carving through the traffic as if every split second counted, then her mood seemed gradually to change. She slowed, took one hand off the wheel and began to play with Johnny's knee, stroking up the inside of his thigh. He accepted it, switched on to autopilot, looking at her feline face, and even, after a while, began to enjoy it.

She drove straight to his house, slotted quickly into a parking space, got out and locked the car. No doubt, no questions. She stood separately, demurely, as the porter came to open the door, but as soon as they climbed the stairs to Johnny's flat her hands were all over him, pushing down between his shirt and his jeans as he fiddled the key into the lock.

'Come on,' she said and he got the door open. He turned

to close it and she was past him. Inside, he turned back and she was standing there at the end of the hall, eyes glazed, breathing hard, kicking her skirt clear of her feet, pulling her blouse over her head so that for a second he couldn't see her face, just her hard, slim body in pointed leather shoes and lacy red silk knickers, breasts bobbing clear of the blouse. Then it was over her head and she was looking at him again.

'Hurry up, for Christ's sake,' she said in a thick voice. 'Are you always this slow over everything?'

Go with it, he thought, and was pulling off his clothes as he followed her into the bedroom. Her legs and her lips opened as one as she rolled backwards on the bed, each in matching, moist warmth. As he slid into her, she gasped, pulled her head away from his, arching back with her eyes closed. She seemed somewhere else entirely and, had he known, it wasn't somewhere he would have liked to be. She came before he did, crying out, then came again, shuddering with him, only – as soon as their bodies stopped moving – to pull abruptly away. He wondered at that but she lay next to him, still, exhausted and in the end they both slept.

He was deeply asleep at 2 a.m. when her eyes flicked open and she moved carefully from the bed. She did the phone first. Sibley had said this device was brand new. Johnny wouldn't recognize it even if he did happen to find it. It looked just like a BT component and it went not in the handset but in the base of the phone. For all that, she took care – slipping it into place with its adhesive pad lined up with the other capacitors so it would pass any casual inspection. The next two devices had been carefully prepared after the recce, a hollowed-out wooden block that matched the colour of the bedside table and fitted in underneath as if reinforcing the angle of one of its legs and a similar white painted piece, longer, that she stuck up inside the corner of the pelmet in the sitting room. The batteries would last two weeks. The bugs, with their own short range radio transmitters, would each feed a different tape recorder in a car parked in the street near by. If Johnny had the room swept while they were transmitting they'd show up, but not otherwise. Not otherwise, that is, except to Pacman Gerow, who would spend some time wondering about the strange interference creeping across his own tap on Johnny's phone.

She slipped back into bed and went straight back to sleep.

It was eight thirty when Johnny woke, turned over to find his face in unfamiliar hair and felt her long, smooth back warm against him. His arm went round her to cup her breast and she stirred slightly in her sleep. This morning, without her passion to lead him, it felt a little odd, distant, and as if to make up his mind for him the phone began to ring in the next room. He got carefully out of bed and went to answer.

Heather's voice disconcerted him. 'Johnny? Good morning. Have I woken you up?'

'No,' he said, and pushed the door closed with his foot feeling suddenly embarrassed, as though she could see.

'I just thought I'd catch you. I was wondering if you really thought you might get anywhere with the doctor. My lawyer says we'd have to know pretty soon to be able to use her.'

'Yes. Yes, I have,' he said, thinking how to play this, 'she's somewhere in France. It's complicated.'

'That's fantastic.'

'Up to a point,' he said, 'I haven't got an address as such. It needs a bit of discussion.'

'You can't come up, can you? Sir Michael's invited me to have supper with him on Saturday. He said he really liked you and was there any chance you could come too?'

Good God, thought Johnny. 'Saturday, I don't know if I can,' he said.

'It would be nice,' she said and he could see her face as if she stood there. Acutely conscious of the traces of Maggie on his body and suddenly certain that the one in his bed was not the woman he would have chosen to wake beside, he heard himself agreeing.

He put the phone down and turned to find Maggie, slim and naked, leaning in the now open doorway, reaching one arm up the wall to accentuate the long flow of her body.

'Good morning,' she said, 'and how are you this morning?'

* * *

The text of Johnny's brief phone conversation was delivered by Ivor Sibley's driver to Lady Viola's secretary two hours after he put the phone down. Sophia was the sort of secretary a wife might choose for her husband. Indeed that was exactly what Lady Viola had tried to do, but Sir Greville had managed to finesse his way out of trouble. It was a terrible waste of such a light, lyrical name. Sophia's parents, keen movie-goers, had been torn between honouring Sophia Loren or Claudia Cardinale when it came to baptising their daughter but Sophia grew up to be a grim, solid girl whose need to be shackled to an institution led her first to try to join the police force, which turned her down for lacking sufficient sense of humour, and then, eventually, to Lady Viola.

She devoted herself to anticipating Lady Viola's every need and she knew that her employer would want to see anything from Sibley's office at once. She sent it straight on by GKC's own messenger to an expensive gallery off Bond Street where Lady Viola was inspecting what purported to be an Alphonse Legros study of a blacksmith.

'Your Ladyship will of course know that Legros studied under Lecoq de Boisbaudran,' said the gallery owner, looking nervously at her face. Lady Viola ignored him. She seemed to him to be looking at the frame, not the picture. 'He was, of course, a leader of the Realist movement, very strong on detail and depth. You will have noticed the fine metallic effects.'

Lady Viola was peering closely at the picture. He thought she was taking in the sheen on the burnished iron of the cauldron in the corner of the canvas. She was in fact wondering whether the browns and yellows would go with the wallpaper in her morning room.

'Blacksmith looks a bit like that sod Delors,' she observed. 'Frenchman, I suppose, this fellow?' she barked, looking around.

'Well, of course, Legros was a native of France but he did work chiefly in England. He was a Slade Professor of Fine Art for nearly twenty years . . .' It seemed to be cutting little ice but in any case, he was interrupted by the arrival of the messenger.

Lady Viola ripped the envelope open, scanned the sheet of paper inside with cursory irritation which slowed through horror and then, as the meaning became clear to her, coalesced into fury. She read it again, looked about as if searching for something to kick and her gaze happened on the painting.

'I hate the bloody thing,' she said, 'French rubbish. To hell with it. Why don't you get some decent English pictures in?'

'Well of course, your Ladyship will know that, as a gallery, we specialize in nineteenth century French . . .' He was talking to himself. The door had slammed behind her and his sentence tailed off in a faltering mumble.

At GKC's headquarters, Sir Greville had given instructions that he wasn't to be disturbed. He had the text of the intercepted material that Johnny had retrieved from Sir Michael's desk and the first task was to construct a plausible set of answers for the Hurst Inquiry. That should be much simpler now he knew precisely what they had in front of them. The document which had been sent to them was incomplete. Thank Heaven for that. It could therefore be portrayed, with a bit of skill and care, as something else. Some marketing man's joke, perhaps? The subject of a bit of mistyping? Perhaps, if he could be sure this was all they had, he could produce a new beginning and end to the document which would put a much less dangerous gloss on it.

Whatever, possession of the intercept gave him the upper hand but it had suddenly dawned on him that possession also gave him a possible ace in the hole in a totally different direction and he had given himself an hour's peace to think it through.

He looked up with intense displeasure when the door opened but the white-faced secretary who stood helplessly beyond it was powerless to prevent Lady Viola in full swing going precisely where she wanted.

His wife seemed to push a bow wave of air before her like a tube train entering a station and he motioned to the secretary to shut the door behind her. He looked uneasily at Lady Viola, whose expression bordered on the manic. She threw

Sibley's transcript in front of him with an expression that implied that if he couldn't quickly spot the problem then he would be bracketed with it and he turned his gaze to it with trepidation.

He soon thought he'd found some safe ground. 'Well, I suppose we have to assume that Johnny's becoming attached to this Heather Weston,' he said.

Wrong.

'Are you being deliberately stupid, Greville?' Her voice wavered not with weakness but with the overload of hatred it was being forced to carry. 'I don't give a toss about the girl. That's . . . that's piffling.' Venom gave a bizarre quality of menace to the schoolgirl word. 'I can sort that out any time I want to. He's visiting Michael again. Don't you see? Anything could happen, anything at all. I've done everything I could to keep him from coming under that man's influence, without very much support from you, I have to say.' Her eyes seemed to bulge more and more as she paced up and down in front of his desk. 'Now he's going to have dinner with him. Johnny's not clever, you know, Greville. He's suggestible. Michael will take him and twist him like a piece of string. He'll tell him all kinds of lies about me. We can't just . . . can't just . . .' She was panting, hyperventilating. Sir Greville got up and helped her to a chair.

'But Michael Parry doesn't even know who Johnny is, does he? Johnny's report to Sibley said he went under a false name.'

'Johnny knows who *he* is. That's bad enough. Absolutely anything could happen.'

'Before we go off at the deep end, perhaps we'd better be in a position to hear just exactly what they do say to each other?' her husband suggested.

Her breathing slowed down then and her eyes narrowed, became hooded. There was a long silence. 'Yes,' she said eventually, 'we'll hear all of it, every syllable of every word.' She strode out of the office, pouring her molten anger into the cooling moulds of dangerous plans.

Her husband went back to composing what he hoped

would be the most profitable fax message of his business career.

Maggie and Johnny went to the office separately. She was called to see Sibley and disappeared for the rest of the day. He was allocated to a boring and routine analysis and on the way home found himself looking forward to a quiet evening's reading. There had been something spiritually exhausting about the past few days and the idea of two or three hours slouched comfortably in his soggy armchair with a Wilfred Owen collection had a deep appeal.

There was something odd in the porter's manner when he opened the door to let Johnny in to the flats, a touch of matey joviality which he found unsettling.

He opened his door, thumbed through the post, went into the bedroom reading a circular letter about subscriptions from his shooting club and unbuckled his belt. When he had stepped out of his trousers and was stooping down to pick them up off the floor his eyes, close to the edge of the bed, focused on Maggie, lying on the bed on her stomach. Her hair, stretching down her back, was the only thing covering her. She turned her head and smiled.

'You've been a long time,' she said.

'How did you get in?'

'Johnny, you sound quite indignant,' she said, amused. 'It wasn't difficult. The porter hadn't forgotten me, you know.'

'He let you in?'

'You forgot to give me a key.'

'I wasn't . . .' *expecting you to come back*, he had been going to say, but that sounded ungallant. '. . . sure you'd be coming.'

'You didn't think I was just using you as a one-night stand?' Her voice was arch. 'I'm not that kind of girl.'

He nodded slowly, seeing the course of his evening changing and regretting the change. Manners reasserted himself. What to do when confronted by a desirable but slightly unwelcome naked woman?

'Would you like a drink?' he asked.

She twisted over with studied grace and the full-frontal impact of her body tilted the scales a little further away from the war poets, though not as far as she might have hoped. Johnny felt like someone being offered a second Chinese Imperial banquet two hours after their last one.

He took a pair of jeans from the chair and put them on as if that was a necessary prelude to going to the kitchen. He chose a bottle of white wine from the fridge, took his time with the corkscrew, hoping she would appear from the bedroom into more neutral ground but she didn't, so, drawn back to the vortex of her whirlpool, he went slowly back into the bedroom with two glasses and sat down on the edge of the bed.

'Tell me a story, Johnny,' she said as she squirmed across the bed and settled her head into his lap.

'What story?' he asked, pouring the wine and finding his jeans suddenly tight. The war poets formed a quiet queue at the exit to his mind.

'Wineglass,' she said, 'I never heard the whole thing. Tell me the story.'

'Nothing much to tell,' he said, knowing that wouldn't do.

She just waited, moving her head gently so that he could feel every seam and stitch of the area around his zip, inserting herself into the space between his puritan mind and his animal body.

'It was somewhere outside Mullaghbane,' he said. 'I suppose, coming from Six, you've never done South Armagh?'

She didn't answer, doing something with her hand up by her head and suddenly there was cooling air around his crotch as the zip opened. He took an involuntary breath in.

'It was just a stake-out. A hole in the ground job with mikes and a camera, watching for Sean Rooney. We knew he'd used the house for meetings. I was lying there for hours from before dawn right through the day until it got dark. You get really cramped in those holes. You can't move for anything.' He remembered the stench, the pain and the numbness.

'Anyway in the end Rooney turned up, then Patsy Steel arrived, which was an added bonus. We weren't expecting anyone as big as that. Just as Steel went in the bloody mike lead came apart. It all went dead. I knew they hadn't found it, at least not on purpose. Steel leaned his bike against the woodpile and a log moved – pulled the connector apart. I could see it from where I was, right near the wall. They were inside the house so I took the risk and went out to fix it. Trouble was, right then I heard footsteps on the drive and Joe O'Hanlon showed up. That's when it all got a bit out of hand.'

He knew he'd missed out everything that mattered, hoped she'd be satisfied, hoped in vain. She was doing distracting things with her tongue, light touches that made it hard for him to talk.

'You shot them.'

He shrugged.

She moved suddenly, slid past him, pulling his jeans down with a jerk that almost had him sliding from the edge of the bed so that he was now sitting with her kneeling on the floor before him. His pants had gone with the jeans.

'You shot them. With what?'

'What does it matter? They wound up shot,' his voice was dry. He blocked out the memory. It was obviously arousing her but it threatened the opposite for him.

She rose from the floor on to his lap, as weightless as an acrobat, defying gravity for a moment before wrapping her legs round his waist and beginning to rock her pelvis against him.

'How many times?'

'Three or four.'

'Did you like it?'

He didn't answer.

'You pulled the trigger.'

He seemed unable to produce the words she wanted. She bent a little backwards, reached down and guided him into her.

'Tell me.' Her voice was rough, deeper. 'Pulling the trigger. What was it like?' She was moving harder and faster.

'I . . . don't know,' he said.

'Tell me,' she said, 'tell me,' her voice was slurred, 'did it give you a hard-on? I bet it did.' She closed her eyes.' I want to know.' She was panting, 'How . . . did . . . they . . . look?'

The images were forced on him whether he liked it or not, nibbling away at the physical power which was all there was to this synthetic passion. The secret of Wineglass, the fake mystique of macho Johnny, seemed bound up with the security of his erection. He knew there was an urgent need to shut her up.

He rocked hard back on the bed, holding on to her, squeezing her so that she came with him, rolled over on to her, covering her mouth with his and kept it there until their violent act of making something that was nothing like love beat its way to an end.

The tape recorders got none of it. She'd switched them off before going in. She had standards when it came to her own privacy.

Afterwards, when he'd withdrawn as soon as he gracefully could and Wineglass had receded to some corner of her mind, she sat up, drained her glass and said, matter-of-factly, 'What's Sir Greville like?'

'Why do you ask?'

'Well, he's our client and he is your father after all.'

'Stepfather,' corrected Johnny absently.

'Stepfather?' she said, sounding as if she had no idea. 'What happened to your real father? Is he dead?'

'No, he isn't.'

'Do you see him?'

'Not really.'

'Wouldn't you like to?'

'Maybe. I don't know,' said Johnny taking the question, quite wrongly, at face value.

'And your mother? She has quite a reputation.'

Johnny laughed. 'Even Ivor's scared of her. She's ferocious. She gets what she wants.'

'Your father, your real father . . .' she began.

Johnny knew it was a subject he really didn't want to get into and it gave him an idea.

'My mother. Good Lord. She's coming over. What time is

it? She's got some family things to discuss. Look, I think we'd better get dressed. She has a tendency just to walk in on me.'

'Always discreet,' said Maggie, getting up and reaching for her clothes, not believing a word of it. It suited her to go along with the fiction. On the way out, she went to the parked car and switched the recorders back on. Then she headed home to wash away Johnny's tedious traces and call a friend over who really understood the pleasure pain could give.

CHAPTER THIRTEEN

Tinderley Hall was a fussy building by Yorkshire moorland standards. In a county rich in graceful, practical Georgian manors, some nineteenth-century *nouveau riche* captain of industry had imposed a Victorian Gothic pile on a perfectly harmless hillside. Johnny drove up the long drive slowly, feeling his way through the minefield ahead. Tinderley was flanked on the right by a low range of temporary buildings with an industrial look about them. Down the slope to the left, into the edge of a small patch of woodland, were the ropes and scrambling nets of an assault course.

He drove into a courtyard beside the house where a sign painted institutional green said VISITORS' CAR PARK. Two youths in dirty orange overalls, their heads shaved, were bent over the open bonnet of a battered Morris Marina lacking any window glass and fortified by lengths of scaffold pole. It was crudely sprayed in many different colours, carried hand-painted racing numbers and a team name, unevenly lettered in red along the roof, *Bad Boys Bangers*.

The way in, under a glass and wrought iron canopy made gloomy by the load of old leaves it carried, was through a modern door with electronic locks and a microphone. Another sign next to it said: TINDERLEY SECURE UNIT. CONTROLLED AREA. ALL MOVEMENTS TO BE LOGGED.

Johnny pressed the bell. A voice from the speaker said something unintelligible.

'My name is Kennedy,' he said, 'I'm here to see Heather Weston.'

The door buzzed open and he went in to find himself confronted by another one, an airlock to ration access to the outside world for Tinderley's inhabitants. An old man came to the inner door and opened it for him.

'Come on in then,' he said, 'Get in 'ere and shut door quick before they all get out.' He had one eye almost closed and one wide open, giving Johnny a ferocious sideways smile. It only lacked a corncob pipe to be Popeye to a T.

'Is that a problem?' asked Johnny.

The man cackled. Even the cackle had a Yorkshire accent to it, 'Oh, aye. Don't want to be in 'ere, they don't.'

'I've come to collect Heather Weston.'

'I know you 'ave. You said so, didn't you? She'll be along in a tick. You 'old on 'ere and guard the bridge and I'll go and see.'

The old man disappeared through a door and a teenager immediately came crashing, flat-footed in Doc Martens, down the stairs at the end of the hall. He was cadaverously thin and had a dragon tattooed on one cheek, peppered painfully by acne so that side of his face seemed made up of red and blue volcanoes. It hurt to look at it.

'Oo the fuck are you?' said the apparition.

'Just a visitor.'

The youth switched his attention to the doorkeeper's desk. He leaned over and pressed buttons. Nothing happened. Johnny became acutely aware that the old man had entrusted the security of the building to him. He watched closely but the teenager looked at the door in disappointment.

'Din't 'e leave yer the key then?'

'No,' said Johnny gratefully.

The boy looked him up and down. 'Anyway, wotcher 'ere for?'

'I've come to see Heather Weston.'

The boy's demeanour changed in a flash. His face lost its surliness.

'Eth,' he said, 'Are you Eth's new bloke then?'

'No, he's not,' said a voice from the doorway, and Heather appeared in the hall. 'Hello, Johnny,' she said. 'Button it, Rodge, he's a friend of mine.'

'Rough luck, Johnny,' said Rodge jauntily in a burlesque posh accent, 'she's all right is Eth. You ought to work on it.'

Johnny, who had felt a disconcerting burst of inner electric warmth at Heather's appearance, felt oddly exposed by the boy's words.

'You fix your own love life, Rodge,' said Heather, unruffled, 'I'm quite old enough to look after mine. Anyway I notice you're still short on incentive points this week and it's after seven.'

Rodge was half way up the stairs before she finished the sentence.

'I'd like to show you round,' she said, 'but I suppose we ought to get on.' She used a key which was chained round her neck to light up the electronic lock console on the desk and the door locks buzzed.

'Do they try and get out much?' he asked as they went out to the car park.

'Try? Not just try, they succeed. There's a million ways. It's not a prison. We've got some of the wiliest little beasts you could hope to meet in a month of Sundays.' She said it with affection.

'What do you do about it?'

'We give them reasons to stay, try to save them from the prison system while we can. They're all extremely difficult, no sense of community responsibility. We try to show them how to work together.' She looked towards the two boys still deeply involved in the innards of the old Marina across the yard.

'If they build up enough points by sticking to the rules, they get to do things like that. Working under supervision, then outside by themselves on trust. We've got scrambler bikes, hot rods, all sorts. If they get to the top of the tree they even get to race them.'

'They seem to like you,' he said.

She laughed. 'They think I'm an outlaw too. It's a bit difficult in some ways. Whenever I'm up in court, I get the hero treatment from them. I have to keep explaining why I do it, that it's not in the same bracket as their sort of GBH. When the management nearly fired me I thought there was going to be a riot, then Sir Michael saved the day. I don't know about this next one, though. I don't think he can stop them this time.'

Sir Michael. The evening ahead faced Johnny like a mountain, the risk he had accepted as the price of seeing Heather again.

He opened the Mazda's door for her, took her arm quite unnecessarily to guide her into the passenger seat just for the sake of the contact.

'It's nice to see you,' he said as they drove off.

She looked at him, considering. 'It's good of you to come. It's a long way to drive for dinner.'

'I'm flattered that he invited me,' said Johnny, and Heather said nothing in reply. 'About this doctor . . .' he said to fill the gap.

'Save it for later, I'm sure Sir Michael would like to hear it too.'

'Really? Oh, well, OK.'

It wasn't far to the house and this time, in daylight, Johnny could get the measure of the place. The gateposts were weather beaten, softened by moss and lichen, and marked the entrance to a drive where the potholes would soon be in need of attention. There had once been a fine avenue of chestnuts but now the irregular gaps produced by gales and rot had degraded them into parallel lines of Morse code. Beyond the end of the trees the ground opened out into a sweeping curve, falling away to the River Wharfe below and the house nestled ahead under the shoulder of the hill, an outcrop of the old stone that spawned it.

The geography of the house had caused some problems that day. Sir Michael had been out for most of a frustrating day, called to what he regarded as a quite unnecessary meeting with the chairman of the Police Watch Committee in the morning. Then he was delayed on the way back from a long-scheduled speaking engagement at a Round Table lunch with a mysterious electrical problem somewhere inside his car which the AA took over an hour to sort out. Neither event had been a coincidence, though they had each been engineered quite separately. Sibley set up the first one, putting Lady Viola's instructions into action and calling in favours from old contacts. Pacman Gerow, extending his web of phone taps from Johnny at the centre, was listening in as the Round Table rang to confirm arrangements. He passed the information on to Ray Mackeson who had a man do some subtle tampering.

In both cases, the object was the same: to gain some safe time for their installation specialists.

Each team therefore arrived at the house separately, one in the morning and one in the afternoon. Ivor Sibley, worried enough about bringing Maggie into it, didn't want any more of his staff seeing surveillance games played on one of their own number and had contracted this one out to a rival firm. They sent two men, who found that installing the first set of mikes was no more than half an hour's work. Getting the radio links sorted out had been much more of a headache. There weren't any public roads within a convenient distance where they could park a car or a van unobtrusively as a hiding place for the gear. They were up against it on time and they put together a serviceable lash-up, mikes with short range transmitters legging the radio link to the hay loft of a barn up the hill in line of sight of the house. There was a booster there and a switch, beefing up the signal and sending it across country to the nearest available phone line. No one had been in the hay loft for a long time and they decided they'd be very unlucky indeed if the metal boxes hidden in the hay were found. The boxes would be gone within twenty four hours, after all.

The barn was such an obvious way-point that, had they been in the same technical league, the Americans would certainly have picked it as well, with unpredictable consequences. They didn't because they didn't have to. The unit their man installed in Sir Michael's roof space, hidden in dust behind a joist, took in the signals from all six of their mikes, recorded it in sequential ten second chunks, compressed each chunk to a thousandth of that length and squirted the result straight back to Ramsgill Stray. One micropulse every ten seconds, switching frequencies between pulses just in case. It was watertight technology. No one would know it was there, no one would accidentally tune into it and putting it in took no time.

Until the big surprise.

Louis, Ray Mackeson's man, was by himself – which was just as well because he'd been completely silent while he was in the house. He was taking his time, knowing Sir Michael's movements were being well monitored. He began in the study, choosing a picture in the prime spot for the acoustics and lifting it carefully off the hook. That was when he saw the best seat was already taken and a simple operation suddenly turned very wobbly. Sibley's little device taped to the back of the picture was a low-tech bug, but it was a bug for all that, right where he had planned to put his own. He put the picture back very, very quietly so as not to give away to whoever else was listening that he'd stumbled on their secret then he went outside to call Ray Mackeson on the secure link.

'You did?' said Mackeson drily, down the line. 'Well, there's a surprise.' He said it like it wasn't.

'What do I do?'

'Go right ahead and find someplace else. Mind out, though, there are gonna be more.'

There were. Whoever put these bugs in went to the same school as Louis. All the best places. He did what he could as second best.

Sir Michael came out to welcome them when he heard the car arrive, kissing Heather affectionately and shaking Johnny's hand while looking into his eyes with remarkable intensity. They had a glass of sherry in the kitchen.

'I'm so sorry,' the old man said, 'I'm a bit behind. It's been one thing and another all day today.'

They helped him with the final touches and if Johnny was wondering what a dinner with a recently widowed man would taste like he was surprised by the quality of the food Sir Michael had prepared. A chilled soup of spiced banana followed by salmon in a subtle, lemony sauce. Over the meal, they talked banalities. Sir Michael told tales of exotic postings in his long career, tales that always seemed to revolve around a central common point, that absolute truth did not exist and was decided partly by point of view. Johnny supposed that was the effect of being a diplomat for all those years but he found it easy to listen, to take him at face value, hooked by the man's easy wit and charm.

In a room at GKC's headquarters, Lady Viola, flanked by Sibley and Sir Greville, curled her lip and made disgusted little noises. At the Stray, Ray Mackeson, a tumbler of good malt whisky in his hand, sat with his feet on the desk staring into space waiting patiently.

After supper they took coffee into the study with them. Johnny looked at the desk, the scene of his breach of trust, and the desk looked reproachfully back at him.

'Now about this doctor,' Sir Michael said as he poured the coffee. 'Do tell us.'

'She's moved to France and I don't know her name or her address but I do know she's going to be in Cherbourg next week. I know the hotel and I know the date. She's attending a conference. I was thinking perhaps if someone went over they could at least talk to her.'

At the Stray, Ray Mackeson raised an eyebrow. In London it passed completely over Lady Viola's head but an irritated look crossed Ivor Sibley's face.

Heather exchanged a strange glance with Sir Michael, then he said, 'That's very good. Very good indeed. How on earth did you find out?'

'Blind luck really. The person who bought her car when she left England was a neighbour. Dr Beevor sent her a postcard about the Cherbourg conference.'

'Finding out who owned the car can't have been easy. How did you do that?'

Johnny saw a small elephant trap ahead and side-stepped it. 'I know someone who can get access to the computer,' he said.

'I would have thought that was illegal.'

'Well, yes, but the end seemed to justify the means in this case.'

'I'm very impressed,' said Sir Michael affably. 'A chap like you, comes back from being abroad all that time and can find someone with the right connections just like that.'

Johnny shrugged, pleased with his evasion, happy to take the credit. The older man put his coffee cup down, very deliberately, 'I would have thought it was more likely you'd done it through your job at this Baron, Hockley place – or have you started calling it MI7 too?'

Of the six people listening to him, only two stayed calm: Ray Mackeson at the Stray, who simply leaned towards the speaker with increased interest, and Heather, who was watching Johnny like a goalie facing a penalty. In that second, Johnny realized with acute and overwhelming dismay not just that Sir Michael knew exactly who he was but that he'd always known, right from the start and that Heather must have taken part in this set-up.

He bowed his head, exhaled as if he'd been punched in the stomach and spoke to the floor.

'Would you like me to go?' he asked in a flat tone.

'No,' said Sir Michael, 'certainly not. In fact if you try to, I will do my level best to prevent you, old as I am. I may not succeed but I shall try.' He glanced across at Heather. 'Would you mind making us some more coffee, my dear?'

She got up and went into the kitchen, closing the door carefully behind her.

Sir Michael poured two glasses of whisky and held one out to Johnny.

'I don't like playing charades,' he said, 'so I intend to speak very plainly indeed to you. You are my son and I knew it almost as soon as I saw you at the meeting.' He gave a small sad smile. 'I've kept tabs on you for years. I've got contacts too, you know.'

He leaned forward and stared intently at the younger man. 'This isn't the way I should have chosen to meet you again.'

'Nor me,' said Johnny and his tongue seemed to have an independence that surprised his brain. 'I had no idea you were involved in all this. It's all very well, isn't it?' His voice thickened suddenly with unexpected emotion, anger and a touch of self-pity. 'You're the invisible man all my life and you suddenly pop up out of the blue and put me wriggling on the end of a bloody pin. Do you think that's fair?'

In London, Lady Viola nodded slight approval through her fury.

Sir Michael shook his head. 'Not entirely. I'm sure my involvement in all this came as a great surprise to you,' he said. 'You're a pretty poor actor, Johnny. I could see quite clearly that you had no idea I'd be at the meeting. I can't really blame you for wearing false colours in your father's house. It's Heather that worries me.' His eyes tightened into a frown. 'I think a great deal of her.'

'So do I.'

The older man gave an indignant snort. 'Do you indeed? Not enough to stop you spying on her, telling her lies. God knows what you're up to now with the flying and this French business.'

Johnny got to his feet.

'Don't go,' said the old man sharply. 'I meant it. I shall try to stop you.'

'I'm not going,' he said wearily, 'I can't go. I . . . I need to talk about it. It's not like that at all.'

'Well, what is it like?'

'The reason I took Heather flying was because I wanted to see her again. The job part of it was more or less over. I didn't expect to meet you and I didn't know I'd wind up here for the night.'

Sir Michael was watching him closely. 'And that is all?'

Johnny realized he was dealing with a man who had made an entire career out of penetrating the evasions and distortions of diplomats much more used to lying than he was. He also realized that regaining Heather's respect and, inextricably it seemed, Sir Michael's, was the single most important thing in his mind at that moment. This was the moment of decision.

'No, it's not all,' he said, 'because of the job, I came down in the night and looked through your desk. For that I apologize.'

Sir Michael sat there considering him, steepling his fingers together. 'Well, I knew you had,' he said, 'I have to confess I set a bit of a trap for you there. Wanted to find out what you were after, you see. I thought I recognized you when I first saw you at the meeting. I was quite sure as soon as we got back here. I had to protect Heather. I didn't tell her anything until the day before yesterday.'

Johnny thought about that. The day before yesterday. So effectively Heather had only been playing games with him for the duration of their drive over today. It struck him that was an odd way to look at it considering the part he'd been playing. The world seemed to him to have shrunk to contain just the two of them.

In London, Lady Viola, Sir Greville and Ivor Sibley sat frozen to the spot, hanging on every syllable. At the Stray, Ray Mackeson refilled his glass.

'The job you were set to do. Would you like to tell me what it was about?'

Johnny nodded slowly. 'Yes, all right.'

'Do you mind if Heather hears this too?'

'No.'

Sir Michael went to the door and opened it. Heather was sitting quietly at the kitchen table.

'Would you like to come in now,' he said softly.

She came into the room, looking at Johnny as she had always looked at him, with open interest. It's the way she probably looks at the boys at Tinderley, he thought.

'John has volunteered to me the information that he went through my desk. He says however that he had no idea before he came up that I knew you, Heather, and he also says the job was . . . well, a peripheral consideration. I won't embarrass either of you by repeating the real reason for his trip. He has decided he wants to tell us more about the requirements of this job he's been doing.'

They both looked at Johnny.

'I suppose you both know who I used to work for?'

Sir Michael nodded. 'I do. I have done since you joined, though I regretted it, I must say. I decided Heather could be trusted with the information.'

Trusted. His father was taking his interests into account in this.

'How did you know?'

There was a sign of a smile. 'You must appreciate that a lifetime in the Foreign Office in the sort of jobs I had puts one in fairly constant contact with the Secret Intelligence Service. It wasn't really very difficult.'

MI6. Of course, Johnny realized, his father would have any number of old contacts to tip him the wink, delighted to dish the dirt on their down-market colleagues at 5. Sibley's organization was stuffed with people from 6. Look at Maggie, he thought. God, Maggie. He hoped devoutly that Sir Michael's intelligence didn't run that far.

'Anyway, when I changed jobs I was told to find out how you'd got your hands on the papers you sent to the Hurst Inquiry.' He turned his gaze to Heather. 'You see, I'm sure you didn't know it but there was a serious defence risk in doing that. This product, CN512, is very important to—'

'Johnny, just stop there for a moment,' she said in a voice that was suddenly cold. 'Don't start giving me that sort of line. Believe me, you don't know what you're talking about. CN512 is one of the most disgusting products ever dreamed up in this country. Do you know what it does? Do you?'

'Heather, perhaps you would allow me,' put in Sir Michael. He looked at his son. 'I'm sure you've been given a very partial view of this. I have been able to do a little research by speaking to a few of my old friends. Whatever you may have been told, John, there is no likely application of this stuff for our own armed forces. CN512 seems to be a sort of berserker drug. It takes away most of the inhibitions that make men human. It turns them into beasts, lethal beasts. It's absolutely no good for a high-tech army. It's for Third World countries fighting man-to-man wars. It is unspeakably dreadful and your stepfather's company is seeking to market it like toothpaste, with some awful trade name. They're calling it "Rage". Isn't that dreadful? Anyway I completely support Heather's decision to send off the papers.'

Sir Greville gave an audible groan at the extent of the man's knowledge, which went far beyond the intercepted material. He was seeing his avenues of escape from the Hurst Inquiry questions dwindling fast. Sibley looked at him nervously as his own operation was shredded before their ears, thinking furiously through his list of ex-MI6 officers, wondering who was leaking. Lady Viola got to her feet and began to pace up and down. At the Stray, Ray Mackeson drew a dollar sign on his note pad, shading it in to give a 3D effect, and waited for more.

'I think at this stage,' Sir Michael said to a mesmerized Johnny, 'we really have to ask you the question, whose side are you on?'

Six pairs of ears hung on his answer.

Sir Greville Kay looked at his wife with extreme unease, registering the fact that she'd gone an unusual colour, a shade of yellow below the tan. He wished Sibley would stop shaking his head like that. He'd been doing it solidly for the last ten minutes as the diplomat's voice, relayed with astounding clarity down the lines to their loudspeaker, had laid out the cards before Johnny, painting a damning picture of the Rage business, forcing the boy further and further into a carefully designed corner from which there was no escape.

That was an enormous problem for him and for Sibley but at least it was a finite problem with fixed constituents, a problem they could surely find some way of attacking. Apart from the partial paperwork in the hands of the Hurst Inquiry, the dangers to them were contained entirely in the knowledge in the heads of these people, these disembodied voices. Knowledge, Sir Greville knew, was a flickering, ephemeral affair, reliant on life and breath.

That was something he might be able to solve. In terms of Sir Greville's personal comfort, which relied heavily on his wife's continual, innate fury being directed at targets outside the domestic circle, the direction the far-off conversation had now taken was far harder to address.

Johnny and Sir Michael were talking to each other as if Heather simply wasn't there.

'I can't leave your mother out of this, you see, John. It always comes back to her way of looking at things. She's the power behind your stepfather, you must know that.'

'But I've never known anything else. You can't just abdicate all responsibility for the whole of my life and then expect me to be your son.'

'I didn't really have the choice,' said Sir Michael in a flat tone. 'She had all the money. She had a whole cricket team of lawyers. I was pretty junior in those days. I got hauled up in front of my Permanent Secretary, told the department wouldn't want to see anything dragged through the papers and that – how did he put it – "anything controversial in the field of custody would be fuel for the gutter Press and would significantly impede my career". Something like that, anyway.'

'So you put your career first?' There was some relief for Johnny in anger.

'Not really. She held all the cards. I didn't stand a chance of fighting it. In retrospect, I think she probably got one of her friends to put the Permanent Secretary up to it. She's always had those sorts of friends. In any case, you know, the conventional wisdom of the time was that mothers brought up children, not fathers. Don't think I haven't regretted it a million times.' The old man's urbanity had frayed edges. His eyes looked momentarily damp.

'Where does that leave me now?'

Sir Michael's head jerked up sharply and Johnny got the full benefit of his stare. 'With yourself, if you know who you are, and I suspect that perhaps you do.'

'What does that mean?'

'You seem to me to be a little unhappy with the way you perceive yourself.'

'What?' Johnny broke the gaze and turned a cross stare on the nearest picture instead.

'Please. Give me a chance. Listen to me for a minute. I wonder whether you perhaps sometimes wish it was easier to form a fixed opinion, whether you feel at a bit of a disadvantage when you're surrounded by people who seem to know exactly what they think?'

It felt to Johnny as if the man had reached into his head and put his finger at the exact centre of his brain.

'Perhaps,' he said. 'Doesn't everybody?'

'Your mother doesn't. She has very firm convictions.'

'She's . . . done a lot of things. She knows . . . well, she knows more than I do, I suppose.'

'She was always like that, believe me, long before she knew anything. I would have said that kind of certainty got in the way of knowledge not that it results from it. '

In London a cut glass vase splintered into shards as Lady Viola hurled it against a wall.

'So what are you saying?'

'I'm saying that you've been a square peg in a—' Sir Michael stopped himself. 'No, better, a round peg in a square hole all your life. We're not made of square, straight-line certainties, you and I, we're more blurred, aren't we? Round suits us better.'

Johnny said nothing. His father sighed and tried again.

'You've been brought up to think that being open-minded is being weak. You've been forced to take up positions you don't really believe in. You've covered yourself in layers of camouflage, but I can see you under there.'

Johnny found himself blinking a tear angrily away. 'You're guessing,' he said bitterly. 'This is stupid.'

'I'm not guessing. I know you because I know myself.'

'God Almighty.'

'Am I not right? Do you really enjoy the sort of company you keep, the sort of things you do? Hasn't it ever seemed hollow to you?'

Always, thought Johnny. 'I don't know where this takes us,' he said.

'Back to my question. Which side are you on? I think you probably have to choose.'

'That's an odd question, coming from you, isn't it?' Johnny said. 'You've set yourself up as the great freethinker, able to see all sides. How can you suddenly divide it up like that?'

'I never said there weren't things I'm against,' said Sir Michael firmly. 'I'm against people who pervert the truth to sell filthy chemical weapons. I don't need to be open-minded about that. I'm against the Americans abusing their status as our old allies to sit on our doorstep and listen in on our conversations, though that's our government's fault for being so entirely lily-livered about it. I've considered the other point of view in both those cases and rejected it utterly. Considering doesn't mean agreeing, you know.'

'Hang on. That really is having it both ways. You wouldn't have known anything about Rage if the Americans hadn't been bugging that fax.'

'It's perfectly true that the Rage material came from Ramsgill Stray but two wrongs don't make a right.'

'But you were an ambassador. You knew what Six got up to. You must have used signals intelligence. Everybody does it.'

'All right. That's a good question. Heather asked me the same question. I'll give you the same answer.'

The mention of her name made Johnny suddenly aware of her presence in the corner of the room. He looked at her and she met his gaze neutrally. Sir Michael went on.

'On one level, there's the game all the big boys play. We've all got dishes. We can all try and listen to the stuff that's whizzing about in the ether. As you say, everybody does it. I don't know about the ethics of it but I do know that no one in their right mind expects an international phone call to be secure and as for diplomatic traffic, we break their codes and we always have to assume they're breaking ours. It's the law of the jungle and it always has been. But I do draw a line. I think there are times – a *few* times – when our own government should be able to listen in on our private phones – subject to proper checks and balances, which are, I'm quite sure, often abused. I draw my line when it comes to another government tapping into our domestic system. In my book, that's simply not on.'

'How can you be sure of that?'

Sir Michael just looked at him. Heather answered, 'You know what we've got, Johnny. I've already talked to Maurice Cannon. He agrees. BTRS on that plan has to mean British Telecom Raven Stones. He says the details show clearly it's a hook-in to our phone system. There's no doubt. We found the smoking gun.'

Ray Mackeson broke his silence for the first time since he'd started listening to the conversation. He crumpled up his sheet of doodles and lobbed it into the waste bin. 'Shit,' he said.

'The plan doesn't prove there's a line there. Maybe it was just an idea.'

'No, it wasn't. There isn't any doubt, thanks to our flight. I don't think you saw it, but when we passed the Raven Stones tower there were some men working with a little digger, right in the middle of the moor.'

'They could have been doing anything.'

'Out there? Exactly in line between the tower and the Stray? No they couldn't. Whatever they were doing, maintenance, modification, I don't know, it was right where the line must run.'

'So what are you going to do?'

'We'll keep the papers safe. We're not stealing them because we'll give them back when we're ready, though of course, we'll copy them before we do that. When the court case is over, Margo and Jo will call a press conference to display them.'

'You'll be there too.'

She just smiled.

You can't let go of a lifetime all at once. Johnny was playing for time, asking his stalling questions about the marginal points because a seismic disturbance was running through his soul. But he already knew that his deepest unhappiness, the uncertainty that had blinkered and hobbled him, made him an awkward counterfeit of a man for all his adult life so far, was in the course of being unpicked. The man in front of him, the man he had been brought up to fear and loathe with a pathological mistrust, stood revealed as the one who was, in every way that mattered, closest to him.

'I think I'm ready to answer your question now,' he said, 'I'm on your side. I suppose I always was really.'

No one listening to him could have doubted his sincerity and Lady Viola, looking like a day old corpse that had been painted with thin brown varnish, sat down and became extremely still.

'Welcome,' said Heather. 'Now, tell us about France.'

'There's nothing else to tell really. That's where your doctor is going to be. It's just a case of going and grabbing her.' Then because he wanted to make some extra act of atonement he said, 'Why don't I fly you over there?'

'You don't have to do that.'

'I'd like to.'

'What in? You'd have to hire a plane.'

'No, I wouldn't. I have a share in a Cessna. It's a 172, just like the one we flew up here. It's at a little airfield just the other side of Basingstoke, a place called Popham. We'd clear customs at Hurn. It can't be more than eighty or ninety miles across from there. I've done it before.'

'We'd need to take Jo,' said Heather, considering. 'She's the one who'd recognize Dr Beevor. It's got four seats, hasn't it?'

'Could I come too?' said Sir Michael, 'It sounds interesting.'

Johnny added up rough weights and fuel loads in his head. 'I think so,' he said, 'I'll have to check.'

They made their plans for the trip then Sir Michael told them stories of his time at the Paris Embassy. Johnny sat back and listened to him, letting the words wash over him, easing away the tension. In its place he felt an enormous weariness creeping up on him, the toll exacted by the emotional stress of the evening. It dawned on him that he had nowhere to stay.

'Well, if you'll excuse me,' said Sir Michael suddenly, seeming to read his thoughts, 'I think I'll be getting to bed. Your bed's made up, John, the same room as before. Heather, you know your way around by now.'

'Goodnight,' said Johnny and on impulse added, 'Dad.' Father sounded too formal. Dad was a sort of joke.

'Dreadful word,' said Sir Michael but he looked pleased for all that.

Left to themselves, Johnny felt a moment of awkwardness. 'I wouldn't blame you if you didn't believe anything I ever said again,' he said.

'I do believe you. When you told me that story about your name, after the flying, you said you didn't like calling yourself Kay because that was your stepfather's name and he was a smooth, rich shit. You said your mother was off her trolley and you preferred using your father's real name . . . The thing is, I believed you.'

'I'm sorry.'

'No, that's not what I mean. I think I was right to believe you. Swap Parry for Kennedy and I think it was pretty close to the truth, wasn't it?'

'If it was, I didn't know it at the time.'

'But you do now?'

'Yes,' he said, 'I think I do.'

That was the final straw. Lady Viola didn't want to listen any more.

'Turn the bloody thing off,' she said to Sibley in an unsteady voice. 'This has been a terrible, terrible experience.'

She turned on Sir Greville. 'Michael's got him,' she said, 'That's the end of it. The little sod's taken it all in, every word of it.'

'Look, Viola,' said Sir Greville uneasily, 'I quite understand how you feel, but we do now have a wider problem. Parry's going to let the cat right out of the bag on Rage, that's clear. If he knows about the field tests too, we're in a lot of trouble. Sibley here's going to have his work cut out to pull the chestnuts out of the fire this time.'

Lady Viola swung round on the other man, 'So what do *you* suggest we do about it, Sibley?'

He paused judiciously before replying. 'I'm afraid most of the obvious options are rather ruled out by the fact that Johnny is your son, Lady Viola.'

'He cannot be both my son and Michael Parry's son,' she said slowly and clearly. 'He's made his choice. As far as I'm concerned, he's not my son, not any more.'

CHAPTER FOURTEEN

The first thing that came into Johnny's mind when he woke up to a morning of sunshine and birdsong was not the momentous unburdening he had been through the evening before but the finale, the last few minutes before he went to bed.

'I'd forgotten,' he'd said, when they were by themselves, 'You need a lift back.'

'No, not tonight. I'll stay here too. I often do. I like to keep him company when I can.'

They stood there at the study door, looking at each other.

'I want you to know something,' she said, 'I'm very glad you said all the things you did this evening.'

'So am I. It is true, you know, once I'd met you the first time, you really were the only reason I came back. The rest, staying here and everything, was just an accident.'

'There's a good person in you,' she said softly. 'Sleep well, you deserve to.'

He moved towards her, took her hand, went to kiss her but she turned her head just slightly aside and he kissed her cheek instead. She squeezed his hand.

'I've only just met the real you,' she said, 'Go slowly or I can't keep up. Goodnight.'

He joined them for breakfast, welcomed by smiles, and it felt almost like a familiar domestic routine.

Over the coffee, toast and eggs, Sir Michael studied him for a while, then said, 'I suppose you've got a bit of a decision to take. Over the job, I mean.'

'I've taken it. I'm going to resign. I thought about it last night. It's the only thing I can do really. I'm not even going back in the office. They can whistle.'

'What will you do instead?' asked Heather.

'I haven't a clue. Maybe I'll go for my commercial licence and become a proper pilot after all.'

She laughed, 'But not in Australia, I hope,' she said.

Sir Michael wrinkled his nose, unsure what she meant, 'If you resign, how does that leave you, er . . . financially?' he said a little diffidently. 'I could help, you know.'

It felt odd, being offered money by this ex-stranger. He wasn't used to the idea of having a father yet.

'Thank you,' he said, 'I'm all right for a while.'

A fleeting look of something that could even have been disappointment crossed his father's face.

'Can I contact you if there's a problem?' he added quickly.

Heather looked at her watch. 'I'm sorry, I mustn't be late. I don't want to hurry you, Johnny.'

Hopes of a day together shattered. 'Late? Are you working?'

'Yes. Oh I'm sorry, didn't I tell you? Today and tomorrow. I do one weekend in four.'

'Oh . . . right. I suppose I'd better get back to London, then. I'll drop you and go on from there.' He turned to Sir Michael. 'I'll see you at the weekend.'

'You can stay if you like. We've got a lot of catching up to do.'

'That's true. I'm looking forward to it, but I think I've got to let it all sink in for a few days first.'

'What will you say to Viola?'

'I haven't a clue. She'll be round like a flash when Sibley reads my letter.'

'Rather you than me,' said Sir Michael, and he patted him on the back.

The old man stood there waving as they drove off, roof down, each glancing back at the house from time to time until it dwindled out of sight round the curve of the drive.

'You're very lucky,' Heather said, 'not just finding a father, but finding one like that. He's a real dear.'

'It's a shame you've got to work.'

'No it's not. It's a very good thing,' said Heather practically. 'I can tell you're a great one for rushing in to things.'

'I'm not sure that's right. I feel like I've just taken off a great big blindfold,' he said. 'Which way?'

'Right then first left. Are you regretting anything you said last night?'

'No.' He said it with a new tone of certainty in his voice.

She glanced at him surreptitiously. It had to be her imagination but the profile of his face seemed sharper, firmer, as though in the course of evading himself for so long he had blurred not just the emotional side of him but the physical side too. She was very fond of the father. It was easy to feel fond of the prodigal son.

Heather's home was a small stone cottage on the edge of a village, hanging baskets of bright flowers livening up its porch and tomato plants climbing out of pots up the side wall in the sunshine. Her little Citroën was parked outside.

'I hope it starts,' she said, 'it's usually all right in the summer. I don't know why it's being so difficult.'

Happy for an excuse to prolong their time together, he opened the bonnet and looked at the tiny flat twin engine tucked away low down inside. 'Have you got a rag?'

He cleaned the plug leads, wiped the oily dirt from all the exposed electrics and made sure the contacts were good. 'Try it now,' he said. 'If it doesn't go, I'll take the plugs out.'

Much to his regret it started first time. 'Thursday evening, then,' he said, 'I'll ring you with the details. I should be able to meet you all at King's Cross.'

'Thank you,' she said, 'I must go,' then she bent towards him, kissed him on the lips and was in to the car before he could react, leaving only a sweet taste and a haze of exhaust fumes as the Citroën buzzed away, swaying down the road. As he watched, its brakes went on hard and, gears whining, it reversed back to him. The lower half of the window shot up, latching in place with a crash, and Heather bent her head out.

'I didn't tell you which way to go,' she said. 'Turn left at the end. Follow the Harrogate signs.'

He waved her away. 'Don't worry,' he said, 'I'm not in a rush. I'll find it.'

She looked at him for a few moments longer than was necessary, nodded and blew him a kiss and he stood watching long after the car had disappeared around the corner, until its bumble-bee buzz had faded from his ears.

He didn't go to London, he drove west towards the Pennines, took the road to Malham again and walked up to the high rocks above Malham Cove, sitting in the sun where he'd sat as he'd watched Heather and Margo climb the slope that day.

For the first time in his entire life, he opened the trap door to the deepest, darkest oubliettes of his soul, letting out the pallid imprisoned thoughts that he had been forcing down into them through all the years of his upbringing. In the clear upland air, it was no longer seditious to question the guiding principles of his childhood. He felt happy, strong and certain and, looking down the hill, remembering the contorted contradictions of duty and impulse which had fought in his head last time he had been here, he knew that the two most important people in his life were the two he had left that morning. Fulfilment seemed just within his grasp.

•

In a backstreet that was little more than an alleyway near the walls of the Portsmouth naval base, where the wind off the harbour carried with it a mixed smell of salt, paint and diesel fuel, an unmarked blue door in a high brick wall led into the protected world of a man known to his customers almost universally as the Magazine Man.

The first door was monitored by a discreet camera and led, in any case, only to a second door from where the Magazine Man, who had no other staff, could see his visitors for himself through a smoked glass panel. The precautions were to reassure his customers of their privacy, rather than for his own sake. Nothing that happened here was, by itself, illegal. Teddy Goodman's books were above board. VAT inspectors came to his door only for their routine inspections. He paid tax, a lot of tax, but then he also made a lot of profit.

The Magazine Man's main business expenditure, apart from

the goods he bought in to resell to his customers, was on information. He subscribed to every obscure technical and industrial journal that he could, from every technologically advanced country. Language was the only limitation and to spread his net wider he studied a new one every year. He wasn't fluent in any of them but his German, French, Dutch, Danish, Norwegian, Spanish and Italian were already good enough to alert him to the need for more expert translation when he stumbled over something promising.

The roots of his operation lay in the fact that as industrial processes became ever more complex, so the problems they raised demanded increasingly sophisticated solutions. Usually the devices and products that made up those solutions got very little airing outside the industry for which they were intended, but in many cases, he had found, a bit of lateral thinking could find other applications in completely different areas. He liked the industries where the pay-offs were high and the battle for profit produced a war-time mentality of no holds barred, no corners cut inventiveness. The offshore oil business, Formula One motor-racing, aerospace, they were all grist to his mill. The collapse of the Soviet Union had opened up new areas of defence know-how to anyone with the cash to pay. He'd had to take on a local Russian partner to get the best out of that. His great skill lay in knowing about every new idea, making the links to those other applications and supplying needs that his customers didn't even know they had until he called them.

Over the years he had found that some of his keenest, most generous customers came from organizations which preferred to remain anonymous. He didn't ask whether they had legal or illegal purposes in mind and he certainly didn't want to know the details. Teddy's rules were that they just defined a technical need to him in technical terms. If, often, his inventive mind could easily put two and two together, he chose to ignore the answer. The rules were that if they didn't tell him, then it was all right. Business came first and spook money was the best of the lot, so when he scanned the magazines and catalogues, applications in the spook trade were always high in his mind.

Similarly, his phone number appeared in a lot of strange notebooks.

The man who came to see him this time was a stranger to him but carried a note of introduction from someone with whom he'd done business on several occasions, someone whose requests were always at the peculiar end of the spectrum, someone who answered his questions very obliquely indeed.

They sat there in Teddy's office, the two of them, an indoor man and an outdoor man. The Magazine Man was overweight, pale faced with a small mouth and pouchy cheeks. He wore reading glasses. He had good distance vision but he never needed to look at anything further away than the computer screen or the printed page. The customer looked to him like a football referee, as fit as he needed to be, his authority kept tucked in his back pocket, there when it served his purpose, someone who would disappear in a crowd or run up a mountain, whatever you needed.

'Hang on,' said the Magazine Man over the coffee, 'I don't want to know any of that,' cutting him off abruptly as the customer started to go into far too much detail about his needs. 'I'm sure you recognize that from my point of view all I need is the tech specs. That's where my interest begins and ends. What you want it for is none of my business, right?'

'Right. OK, then. It's got to be soluble in petrol.'

'How long?'

'I don't know. Depends on the width.'

'No. How long to dissolve, I meant.'

'A few hours certainly. Be nice to have a choice, but the timing has to be consistently accurate.'

'And the shape?'

'Long and thin's better than short and thick. Maximum outside diameter of about two inches.'

'Sit tight, then.'

The supplier swung round on his swivel chair, knowing he'd seen it somewhere, just the thing, thinking. He called up a database on the Apple Mac, skimmed it, clicked to a subsection, sucked his teeth and jotted down a reference note.

He got up and went down the passage to one of the eighteen

rooms that made up his reference library, the backbone of his organization. The note told him the catalogue he wanted was in a box file on the very top shelf of the fifteenth shelf unit. He had to climb a ladder to get to it. The date sticker on the catalogue was three years old which worried him a little. He put it in a plain folder before he went back to the customer. No sense in losing the business because some smart ass saw the name on the cover and thought he might cut out the middle man.

'All right,' he said, 'I think you're in luck. There's just the thing. Made of stuff called PIB. Comes in thirty different sizes and each one has twenty different possible wall thicknesses for release times between five minutes and twelve hours. Hang on, there's a note.' He read it carefully to himself. 'Oh yeah, the exact time depends on the level of fraction of the distillate it's in.'

The customer looked blank.

'I mean,' he said patiently, 'if you stick it in crude oil, it might take ten hours to dissolve. If you stick it in aviation spirit, it might be ten minutes.'

'Got it,' said the customer. 'This'll be quick acting. I still need a choice, though. What are they for really?'

'Refineries,' said the supplier, figuring it didn't matter him knowing that, 'refineries and oil platforms, anywhere you might have to get some special liquid a long way inside the pipe work before you release it. Cleaning, neutralizing, that sort of thing.'

The customer nodded. 'How long's it going to take to get them?'

The supplier breathed easier. He liked it when they asked that first, before the 'What'll it cost?' question.

'Tell you in a minute,' he said. 'Give me the size and the time specs and I'll find out right away.'

Armed with the details, he went to a different room to phone. It was lucky there was an Aberdeen agent. The manufacturers were in Norway and that could take a bit of sorting.

The agent was on the ball, had almost all the sizes he wanted right there on the shelf and could get the remaining ones in two days. Four hundred quid would cover it all, Red Star on British Rail.

He went back to the customer. 'I can do it,' he said. 'It's a special order and the transport's tricky. Two grand should just about do it. I'll need half the cash up front. You can collect them here with the other half.'

'Do it,' said the man, reaching for his briefcase, as the supplier had known he would.

Johnny got back to the flat at 8 p.m. The porter was looking at him in that knowing way again.

Johnny squared his shoulders and unlocked his front door. 'Maggie?' he called.

'I'm in here,' came her voice from the bedroom.

'I'll be along in a minute,' he said. He went to his desk in the corner of the sitting room, found the writing paper and wrote a short note which he tucked into an envelope. He took a deep breath and pushed the bedroom door open.

There was a low buzzing noise. Maggie lay sprawled diagonally across the bed, one hand artfully arranged under her head, the other holding a vibrator with which she was tracing lines up and down the centre of her pubic hair. Her eyes were half closed and she was rolling her head back and around, slowly. She brought one foot up as he came in and dipped the vibrator deeper.

'Just in time,' she said in a voice intended to convey deep arousal. 'Come on, Johnny, I'd rather have the real thing.' It sounded unutterably fake to him.

He stood over her, looking down for a moment, reached down and took the buzzing vibrator from her hand, switched it off and dropped it on the floor. She misunderstood him, smiled and tried to pull him down towards her but he stepped back.

'No thanks, Maggie. I want you to go,' he said, 'it was never a very good idea. I've decided you're not my type.'

That startled her. 'What are you on about, Johnny? Come on. I've been waiting for you.'

'Maggie. I mean it. Really. I've thought about it and I'd like you to go.'

'Have you got someone else?' Her question sounded impersonal to Johnny, more like an interrogator's than a lover's.

'That's neither here nor there. I don't like you wandering in and out of my flat, OK? I didn't ask you to come.'

'Have you had a bad day?'

'No,' he said, 'on the contrary. I've had a great day. Let's say I've come to my senses.'

'Wham, bam, thank you ma'am and bye bye, is that it?'

'It seems to me, Maggie, that most of the wham, bam was your idea.'

'Who's been pulling your strings, Johnny? Darling Mummy?' She knew it couldn't be but she was curious.

That really got to him. 'Out,' he said, 'right now. I promise you I do mean it. Up and get dressed or I'll put you out of the door as you are.'

He picked her clothes up from the chair and threw them at her. She jumped out of bed on the other side reached for a pair of lace knickers and stood flaunting herself at him.

'Why don't you come and try it?'

'Forget it, Maggie. Just go, please.'

'You could try and make me. I passed out top of my intake on the mats.'

He felt weary, disgusted by her and it dawned on him that she really wasn't going to go.

'There's something I'd like you to take to Sibley,' he said.

'What is it?' There was that interrogator tone again in her voice.

'Come with me, I'll give it to you.'

She followed him out to the hall, dangling the knickers from her finger. He gave her the envelope.

'It's my resignation,' he said and she stared at him. 'It's open, you can read it if you like.'

She took it out of the envelope, unfolded it and began to read. While she was distracted, he quietly opened the front door, took her wrist, yanked her, suddenly off-balance, through it and slammed it after her.

There was a shout from outside of 'You bastard!'

He looked through the spy hole. She pulled on the knickers,

crossed her arms over her breasts and looked nervously at the door of the other flat across the hall. Johnny went back into the bedroom, feeling a little ungentlemanly, picked her clothes up off the bed, returned to the front door and opened it for just long enough to throw them out into the hall.

As soon as she had dressed, she began hammering on the door and shouting at him. He picked up the phone and called the porter's desk.

'Mr Webley,' he said, 'there's a woman banging on my door. I don't want her here. You let her in. Could you please get her out?'

CHAPTER FIFTEEN

Sir Greville Kay put the finishing touches to his work, read it through a final time to make absolutely sure, walked out into the ante-room of his office and fed it into the fax machine himself. His secretary pretended to ignore the action but felt secretly slighted as she always did when he treated her as if he couldn't trust her. He waited for it to feed through, took it from the machine and pushed it into the shredder.

He caught sight of her expression as he turned back to the inner office, checked himself and crossed the room to her desk. She was pretty, this one. He knew it wouldn't be much longer before Viola found a pretence for getting rid of her.

'Do you know where my wife is, Mandy?'

'She'll be back at three, Sir Greville. She's gone to the City for lunch.'

His hand dropped to her shoulder. 'Well, would you like to come in and do some special dictation, if we're sure we're not going to be disturbed.'

She choked off an involuntary sigh. He was feeling pleased with himself. Always seemed to want a bit when he thought he'd done something smart. Still, the bonuses were good. She let her hand waft lightly across his groin as she got up. Nothing yet. This was going to be hard work.

Sir Greville's fax message bounced across the surface of the Earth like a yo-yo. It went straight on to hard disk at GCHQ Cheltenham with all the rest of the international fax traffic, but there was nothing in it that matched entries in GCHQ's computer, so it sat there with all the millions of others against the remote possibility of a far-off day when someone might seek it out.

It also took its intended route, direct to a large private house in Germany's Eifel mountains where a man with whom Sir Greville had done business in the past took it from the machine, read it carefully in the light of the earlier message he'd received by quite a different route and chuckled to himself.

It went a third way too, plucked out of the air at Ramsgill Stray, ringing all the bells on Pacman Gerow's watch set-up. He read it off the screen, printed it for Ray Mackeson, copied it to Grosvenor Square then packed it off with a few keystrokes up to a satellite stationed over the Atlantic. It downlegged straight from there into the big dishes at Fort Meade, blinked into their computer system and was passed up the chain of command all the way to the Deputy Director before Sir Greville's secretary had finished beating him behind his locked office door. The Deputy Director called his boss.

'We'd better meet,' he said, 'GKC and this Rage thing. It's moving.'

'Come right now.'

The Deputy Director didn't have to walk far. The executive offices, on the ninth floor of the Tower building, were on a corridor known as Mahogany Row. Room 9A197 had a bright blue door, set in an equally bright blue wall, decorated with the NSA seal. The man inside was known throughout the Agency by his job title, DIRNSA – they said it like 'Durnser'. He was waiting.

'What's the hurry, Clay?' said the Director as the Deputy entered the room.

'The Rage business. Kay's gonna sell. The whole thing.' The Deputy Director was Eastern European by origin, thin and white – a sufferer. Normally a dry and methodical man, when he got like this the Director knew something was popping.

'It's that guy Arntsen in Germany, the one near Bonn? Kay's offered him the whole division, the group that makes Rage. Says he's got all the bugs out and it's ready to market. Message says he feels the heat's on in Britain. He says Arntsen gets five per cent of the price if he finds a buyer at two hundred and fifty million.'

'That's dollars?'

'Pounds.'

'So what's the problem?'

The Deputy Director, like Deputies everywhere, knew it was really him who ran the show. Sometimes he wondered whether the Director ever retained any important information at all.

'The problem is,' he said, 'that Arntsen sells to the chaos jockeys. Iraq, Qaddaffi in Libya, Syria, whoever. Highest bidder. They got the cash, he ain't picky. You wanna see CN512 go that way?'

The Director was younger, bigger, funnier than his deputy. He'd only asked the question to give himself thinking time and to see how the man in front of him would lay it out.

'So? Time to call Langley back again. Tell the CIA we've given it to them on a plate like we always do, see what they come up with.'

'What about Mackeson? What about Kay's stepson? I thought we were running this one on account of all the angles.'

'I'll talk to Langley,' said the Director, 'I've got an idea. They hate having to listen to my ideas.' He grinned. 'This time they won't have too much choice. We can cover our end separately. Tell Mackeson what's happening. I want a secure three-way with him and Curtis Walsh in an hour's time.'

Johnny made his plans for France, plans he'd made several times before, but then it had been for debauched weekends of peculiar upper-crust fun at the French race-tracks. He called Popham, asked Frank to give the Cessna a special check and rang round the partners in the plane to book his three days. It went down badly with one of them, but each partner had the right, once a year, to take the plane against all objections for up to three days. Johnny had always been far too diffident to use the right before. Now he put his foot down.

He did some reckoning. They could all be at Popham by eight o'clock with an early start. Hurn at nine, stop there for fuel and customs. That meant they could leave by ten and be in Cherbourg in time for a decent lunch. Hurn was a PPR airport, which meant prior permission was required for their visit. He rang Bournemouth and got put through to Hurn's Air Traffic Control.

'I'm coming in Friday morning,' he said, 'Cessna 172 *en route* Cherbourg. I'll want fuel and customs.'

'What time?'

'I want to leave you at ten a.m.,' he said, 'so let's say nine?'

'Let's make that nine oh five,' said the man, 'then you won't have to stooge round waiting for a runway. I've got one scheduled and two charters leaving around then. You'll definitely be out again by ten? It's busy again after that.'

'No problem.'

Johnny spent much of the week in a fine state of anticipation, sure that at any moment his mother would ring or come crashing through the door. He replayed the likely scene with all its possible variations in his head a hundred times in the next few days, determined that he wouldn't give an inch, but the moment never came. He'd posted a second letter to Sibley in case Maggie had failed to pass on the first. No word came from MI7 about his failure to appear there, but then an envelope arrived with a cheque for the balance of his pay and a P45. No note, nothing else.

Nick Mankovitz, in the flat across the hall, was delighted to swap cars for the long weekend, his Volvo estate for Johnny's sports car. The next question was where to put his guests for the night. A twenty-pound note to Webley secured the key for the unlet furnished flat on the next floor up and he was ready.

He was at King's Cross absurdly early for the train and when it finally arrived he thought at first they must have missed it until he remembered they'd have Jo's wheelchair to deal with. He set off up the platform through the dwindling crowd and spotted them getting out of a carriage a long way down the train.

He went to shake Sir Michael's hand but ended up in a bear hug. Heather kissed him warmly and stayed close to him as he turned to welcome Jo, who looked like a child on a school outing she wasn't quite sure she was going to enjoy.

'I've got the car over there,' he said.

'How are you going to fit us all in?' asked Heather.

'I thought we could tow Jo along behind us.'

There was an indignant squawk, but then Jo saw which car he was making for and subsided.

The Magazine Man had already received and passed on his goods by then and picked up his second thousand pounds from the football referee. The goods in question were still inside their protective plastic wrappers in the back of a Peugeot 309GTI parked outside a small guest-house in Winchester. The man who'd bought them was poring over the instructions that came with them, cross-checking with the details gleaned from the telephone intercept, playing with margins of error. Later on, well away from the public view in the back of a derelict garage, he conducted an experiment with a can of petrol and a stopwatch using one of the spares and then made a small correction to the calculations in front of him.

He went to bed early, paid his bill in cash before he did so, telling the landlady he'd have to be off well before she was up. That was certainly true. It was 5 a.m. when he went quietly downstairs and started the car. Before 5.30 he was nosing the car off the main road again, down the bumpy access track, past the warning signs. It was dawn and the glow of the sun hanging over the end of the grass runway to the east glinted on the long row of small aircraft.

He drove along the back of the sheds and the hangars, right to the far end, parked and got out, watching and listening. There should be no one around, and fortunately that seemed to be the case. He was a very methodical man and he'd done a recce the day before. Nothing had changed. The Cessna, white with its blue stripe, was still in the same place, right outside the hangar where the mechanic had left it after the check he'd seen being done. So much the better. As soon as he got out of the car he realized how windy it was. Windy enough to stop them flying? He hoped not.

Even though he knew it was the right plane, he still took out the piece of paper, unfolded it and checked the registration letters. Attention to detail had always been his strong point. Straying into the realm of obsession, he'd even gone all the way up and down the line the day before in case there was another Cessna with similar letters which he might mistake in dawn's light. There wasn't.

He fetched the small scaffold tower on wheels which stood outside the hangar, an improvised inspection platform, and pushed it across to the plane, noticing the marks it left in the dewy grass and reminding himself to do something about them. Climbing up on to the platform, he could reach the top wing and he leant across to unscrew one fuel cap. He checked his watch. Too early. He climbed down, moved the platform away from the plane just in case anyone should pass by and used up five minutes pacing up and down, keeping on the alert for anyone, anything, turning up unexpectedly to interrupt him. No one came. It was far too early for the sort of people who flew Cessnas.

At exactly five forty-four, he put the platform in place again, climbed up it, took one of the two objects he'd prepared out of its bag and fed it carefully in through the fuel cap. It was a long, thin sausage – provided empty by the Magazine Man but now full. It went all the way in and he pushed it out of sight, into a corner of the tank with a thin stick. He checked it from all angles, craning his head around to ensure it couldn't be seen, then he screwed the cap back on. It took barely more than a minute to move the platform round to the other side and repeat the process on the second tank. After that, he turned his attention to the interior of the plane. He'd researched Cessna access panels and their fastenings thoroughly and he knew exactly where to put the sticky lump which he unwrapped carefully, using rubber gloves to mould it into place.

Once he'd pushed the platform back to where it came from, he broke a leafy branch from a nearby tree and ran it back and forth over the dewy grass to confuse the marks. The dew would certainly be gone by the time anyone came and in any case they probably wouldn't notice anything amiss, but he had his reputation to consider. He drove out of the airfield to a spot he'd found the day before, a little clearing down a farm track where someone had been dumping broken tiles and bits of concrete block. Through the trees he could see the Cessna a couple of hundred yards away. He got a Frederick Forsyth paperback out of the glove compartment and began to read.

There was a holiday mood about the party in the borrowed Volvo all the way down the M3. Except for Jo. She was nervous about the flight.

'It's only got the one engine, hasn't it? What happens if it stops?'

It was meant to sound a bit like a joke, but Johnny knew it wasn't really. 'They're very reliable, and just to make sure I've had a quick check-up done yesterday. It had a full service very recently. It will be all right, I promise.'

'You'll love it, Jo, when we get up there,' said Heather, 'Johnny let me fly it last time.'

'You're not going to this time, are you?' she said in alarm. 'I'd rather you flew it, Johnny. Here,' she said in sudden alarm as a gust of wind buffeted the Volvo, 'there's a gale blowing. We can't go if there's a gale blowing, can we?'

'We'll get a forecast before we go. It's a westerly so there's no problem taking off. The airfield runs east-west.'

'What about landing?' said Jo, and her voice didn't sound at all jokey this time.

Sir Michael picked it up and moved in. 'I'll never forget once,' he said, 'I was on some dreadful Aeroflot flight and the stewardess . . .'

The story meandered amusingly through the vagaries of Russian airline food and by the time it and the substories it spawned were over Jo had forgotten her objections. 'I hope I remembered to put my passport in,' she said.

'You did,' replied Heather calmly, 'I saw it.'

Popham was a curious looking airfield, right alongside the A303 just a mile or two after they left the M3. It was a long thin ribbon of a field with quite a pronounced slope and a row of small aircraft lined up all down the far side. As they drew up by the hangar, a man came out. He looked blankly at the car until Johnny climbed out then he gave a welcoming shout.

'What you doin' in this bloody barge, Johnny. Where's the old sporty job, then?'

'Too many passengers, Frankie. We're all going. Is she ready?'

'Right, tight and ready for flight. No probs. Changed a bulb for you, topped up the oil. That was it. You in a rush?'

'Hurn want us there in forty minutes. We're going to France. I'll do the pre-flight right now.'

He did it even more carefully than usual, checking everything on the plane that could be checked, and Frankie came round it with him. He drew off a fuel sample, looked carefully for telltale globules of water, but there were none. He used the inspection platform to look in the wing tanks. They were half full but he planned to get more at Hurn in any case.

Getting the passengers in took longer. Jo flatly refused to go in the front seat.

'What happens if my legs twitch?' she said. 'I might do something dreadful. There's all these knobs and things all over. Anyway if something happens, I don't want to see it coming.'

'Nothing's going to happen.'

'I'd still rather go in the back.'

It was difficult getting her in there but with some pushing and shoving they managed it. Minimum luggage, Johnny had said. It's the light-plane flyer's prerogative to look rumpled. He stowed their bags in the luggage compartment behind the seats but the wheelchair, although it was a lightweight one and folded up surprisingly well, still had to be wedged across Jo's knees.

'It's a question of the centre of gravity,' he explained, 'I need the weight as far forward as possible.'

It was just as well none of them were too heavy. Adding up their weights and the chair gave him 125 lbs weight for fuel – just over two hours' flying time. It was enough. Heather went in the other back seat, wrapping herself round the wheelchair, insisting that Sir Michael, with his longer legs, should sit next to Johnny.

'I'll sit there on the way back,' she suggested, 'then maybe Jo won't mind me having another go.'

So Johnny climbed in the left-hand seat, the commander's seat, and Sir Michael got in on the right.

'Everybody ready?' asked Johnny when they were all strapped in.

Jo gulped. The others nodded. He started up, letting the engine warm while he went through the rest of the check-list. When it was all done, he set the radio and taxied out, wings swaying over the bumps, heading for the downwind end of the strip. The plane, as usual, felt noisy, flimsy and gawkish on the ground – its undercarriage creaking over the bumps like a rusty gate – but when he pointed it down the strip, opened up fully and felt the wheels clear the ground, its true nature began to return.

The man in the parked Peugeot watched it go and checked his watch. He was pleased and relieved to see that Johnny was turning out to be extremely punctual. That had been his main concern, the part of the plan that was outside his control, and he didn't like any part of his plans to be vulnerable to the sloppiness of others. He started the car and headed for Bournemouth to watch the next bit of the action.

In the morning sunlight and with time in hand, Johnny flew them west to start with, until Salisbury Plain opened up ahead of them and Stonehenge stood, tiny but distinct in the light, on the rising ground in front. Once he was clear of the Boscombe Down flying area, he swung south down the valley of the Avon. Ahead and to the left, the spire of Salisbury Cathedral defied the intimidating perspective their height gave them and still managed to impress itself on the landscape even from fifteen hundred feet up. Jo had gone through five minutes of silence for the take-off and the climb but now that they were in an easy and quieter cruise she got used to it, became much more animated and, leaning forward to shout in his ear, wanted to know exactly where they were and what they could see. He had to lift one side of the headset to hear her and it wasn't easy to make her understand his replies.

Sir Michael had the advantage of the second headset and Johnny could talk to him without difficulty through the mike.

'Are you enjoying it?' he asked.

'Rather. Haven't been in one this size for ten years or more.'

'Would you like to have a go?'

'Don't let Jo hear you.'

'She won't notice. Go on.'

'Well, thank you for the thought, but I've always believed in leaving it to the experts.'

Expert. It felt good.

South of Salisbury with Wimborne and the spreading blot of Bournemouth ahead, he called up Hurn Air Traffic Control and identified himself. They were expecting him but they asked him to waste a few minutes on the way in to let the late traffic clear, so he flew some circles around Ringwood, looking out to the glinting Channel ahead.

Despite the delay, within ten minutes they were on the ground at Hurn, Johnny taking enormous care to pull off a smooth-as-silk slightly cross-wind touchdown to make sure Jo stayed happy. The man he was expecting was waiting there for him on the apron with a van.

'Mr Kay?'

'That's right.'

'I'm Bill from Aviation Services. I've got your life-raft for you.'

Johnny signed the paperwork for the hire, gave the man a deposit cheque and then had to rearrange the baggage compartment to fit the bulky raft in through the side access hatch. It was a four man model, packed away in a rigid plastic case from which one tug of a lanyard would release it to swell explosively into shape.

He took on a carefully calculated quantity of fuel, got back in the plane to taxi over to deal with the air traffic and customs formalities and Jo started grilling him.

'What was that thing, then?'

'Oh, just a life raft.'

'Life-raft?' she said in tones of pure horror. 'Why do we need a life-raft? I thought you said it was safe.'

'Well, safety comes from being prepared for anything,' said Johnny. 'If you're crossing water, it's always a good idea to have a life raft on board. That's all.'

'Doesn't the plane float?'

'For a while. Long enough to get a raft out.'

'Oh, look, I'm not sure about this,' she said, 'no one said anything about life rafts.'

'Jo, I've been across lots of times. I always take one but I've never needed it. Surely you wouldn't feel happier without it?'

They had to help her out of the back seat again for customs and emigration. Johnny filed his flight plan at the tower and picked up the latest weather. There was a stiff wind from the sou'sou'west, blowing twenty-five knots. It was expected to stay that way for a couple of hours before strengthening a little more. He sat in a corner of the office and did the sums all over again, realizing it would make the journey a little slower, require more fuel. The margin was still just about comfortable. Heather came in and set down next to him and he looked at her appreciatively. It seemed to be the first moment he'd been alone with her since King's Cross.

'Where are the others?'

'Your father's pushing Jo round the flower beds, talking nineteen to the dozen about the strange habits of exotic flowers. He's keeping her attention firmly on the ground until the last moment.'

'Good for him. We ought to get going, I suppose. Don't want to be late for lunch. I know a nice place.'

'I thought this was meant to be business, not pleasure.'

'I hope there'll be time for both,' he said, 'I've hardly had a chance to talk to you.'

'There'll be lots of opportunity for that,' she said in her calm way.

When he'd finished the paperwork, he got them all back out to the Cessna.

'Jo,' he said tentatively. 'I think you really would be a lot more comfortable in the front.'

'No way,' she said. 'I don't like it. It looks scary. Anyway there's your centre of whatsit to think about. Sir Michael's heavier than I am. I'm staying in the back.'

He wanted to say what was in his mind, prompted by her reaction to the life-raft, that if anything did go wrong, it would be a whole lot easier to get her out of the front seat; but he couldn't think of a way of persuading her that didn't imply there really was a danger, and rather than risk total panic he let it go.

They took off at exactly ten o'clock and the man in the Peugeot, who'd arrived a quarter of an hour earlier, allowed himself a smile of satisfaction.

The Cessna climbed out over Christchurch and Hengistbury Head, labouring up over the mouth of the Solent, thick with the sails of yachts making the most of the wind. There were white caps all the way to the Needles to their left and Johnny could see by looking down at the boats that there was a big sea running. It was one of those fine, blustery summer days when the wind is warm and the sea makes an even better sporting arena than the air.

He levelled off at four thousand feet and set a course that allowed for the drift. The sea looked rougher than he expected and the yachts below, though they were thinning out as they drew further away from the coast, seemed to be making heavy weather of it. He'd checked Cherbourg weather just before leaving but he resolved to try again in mid-Channel while there was still plenty of room for changing his mind. He wasn't bothered about his ability to land the plane so much as the effect on Jo of a bumpy arrival. There was a coaster ahead and he could see it dipping its bow into the waves.

He checked the instruments. All was well. The fuel gauges hadn't yet moved from where they were at the start. He had enough petrol on board to get across the Channel and most of the way back again. It really wasn't a problem. He looked again at the coaster, used it to check his drift. The wind had to be more than twenty-five knots now. He eased a few degrees more to the west to make up for it.

Sir Michael's voice sounded metallic in his headset. 'Everything all right?'

'Yes. I was just keeping an eye on the wind. It's stronger than the forecast said.'

'They can't hear us in the back, can they?'

'Not if you keep your voice down, no. Not over all this racket.'

'Do you mind if I talk, then? There's some things I've been wanting to say to you.'

'No. I'd like it.'

Inside the fuel tanks, the coiled plastic sausages were doing their job. The petrol surrounding them had now been eating away at the outer skin for four and a half hours. As the plastic dissolved into the high octane petrol, it left its mark on the engine, not enough to cause a misfire or move any of the instruments far enough from their normal position to notice, but certainly enough to cause a lot of problems at the next strip-down as a thin black layer began, like burnt varnish, to coat the valves and the piston crown.

'Your mother and me. What I said to you before . . .'

'Yes?'

'I should have tried harder to make sure I had access to you.'

'How could you have done? You were by yourself, weren't you? Based abroad. Anyway, as you said, she had all the cards.'

'The circumstances were so odd, you see. It was all very extreme.'

'What happened? At the end, I mean.'

Even through the headphones' distortion he could hear the fine nuances of his father's hesitation.

'One of those interminable receptions. Somewhere ghastly where the electricity kept going off and all they served was warm Sauternes. I think it might have been Kano or somewhere like that. I always had trouble with Viola when it came to diplomacy. I had to deliver some carefully chosen words on the progress towards independence of HMG's remaining colonial possessions or somesuch. Viola disagreed totally with the whole thing. You know what she's like, thought the blacks were only truly happy with a white man's foot on their neck, that sort of thing. She'd had a few drinks beforehand and she decided to start heckling.'

'Heckling your speech?'

'Too right. It might have been funny if it hadn't been so bloody serious. Everything I said, she'd just shout "nonsense" or "rubbish" or something like that.'

'What did you do?'

'Only thing I could do. Stopped the speech, had her quietly taken out. Well, it should have been quietly. She started kicking up a hell of a fuss. Then I had to go back and apologize and start all over again. By the time I left the reception she'd gone. Taken you with her. Just left me a note saying I'd humiliated her. *Me*, humiliated *her*?'

'So that was it?'

'We'd always disagreed, you see? On politics. But we'd steered clear of that in private. From then on she hated me. It wasn't like a divorce, it was more of an extermination. I didn't seem to have the means to fight her.'

'She wouldn't even let your name be mentioned in the house,' said Johnny. 'When I was a teenager she used to tear out articles from the newspaper that mentioned your name in case I read them. I wondered why our papers looked like Swiss cheese for years.'

'When did you see her last?'

'About two weeks ago. She was taking a close interest in this Rage stuff.'

'Was she now?' He seemed to think about that for a while. 'You know, what worried me more than anything else was that you'd turn out to be like her. It seemed . . . well, it seemed to me that maybe you were going that way, once I found out what you were doing with your life. I jumped to the wrong conclusion.'

Johnny remembered the night he'd gone through his father's desk and knew exactly what he was talking about. He felt a sudden need to clear the air. 'I think you know a bit about Wineglass, don't you?'

'Wineglass? What's that?'

'Sorry. That was what the office called it. It was the name of an Irish operation. It went wrong. I saw you had the cutting.'

He got a wry, appraising look in return. 'I know the stories that went round your office. They made out you were some sort of Rambo executioner, that you were meant to be sitting quietly in a hole in the ground listening and instead you climbed out and shot most of the IRA High Command.'

Johnny made a face. 'It wasn't like that at all. Everyone jumped to the wrong conclusions.'

'What did happen?'

'I was in a hidey-hole in South Armagh, watching a house. I had a mike and a tape recorder. Sean Rooney was inside. He was the target. He was quite important in the area and we thought he was meeting some of the younger lads. Anyway, the first person who showed up was a man called Steel who was joint number two with Rooney. The trouble was, by a complete accident, he managed to pull the mike lead apart on his way in, didn't even know he'd done it.'

'So you couldn't hear anything?'

'That's right. The thing is, I'd had a couple of screw-ups before on that sort of job. Not really my fault, just the kind of thing that happens. In the normal run I would have stayed put. That would have been doing it by the book, but I thought this time, I'd better take the risk.'

'You got out of the hole?'

'Yes.' Johnny remembered, trying to get a sense of the overwhelming fear as he'd broken cover, crawled up out of the hole, knowing he was burning his boats and he couldn't hope to conceal himself as well when he got back there. He'd crawled all the way to the wall of the house. He could still feel the heavy mud slicking his trousers.

'I got right up to the house and I had to stand up to reach

the wire. It was behind a log pile. I had cramp from lying in the same position for so long and my leg just gave way under me.'

'Good God.'

'I brought half the log pile down with me. Rooney and Steel came charging out through the door. I really thought that was it.'

'But you had your gun.'

'Well, I did, yes. I had a gun but it was in my pocket, the side I'd fallen on. I couldn't seem to get my hand on it.'

Sir Michael looked perplexed, waited.

'Just as they came out of the door, another man came running round the corner of the house from the path. I could see it all happening but I seemed to be frozen to the spot. You have to understand it was very dark. There was a hell of a bang. I think it was Steel who fired. He was in front and he must have just reacted on instinct when the other man appeared. The man grunted and went down. He rolled over and opened up with an automatic weapon. Turned out afterwards it was one of those vicious little MAC things the drug dealers use in the States. Steel and Rooney just seemed to come apart. It was horrific. Anyway the shooting stopped and I lay there, trying to get the gun out of my pocket without alerting him. He was lying quite still on the ground only ten or twelve feet away. I thought he was watching out to see if anyone else came. I stayed there for what seemed a hell of a long time and he didn't stir a muscle so eventually I took my courage in both hands and started to crawl towards him. I had my gun out in front of me and I would have shot him if he'd so much as twitched.

He didn't, though. He was as dead as a doornail, shot just above the heart. From the blood it must have got an artery. He must have lived just long enough to shoot.'

'You got away?'

'You bet. I grabbed all the gear and ran for it. The army came in the end. By that time I was well away.'

'Why did everyone in MI5 think it was you?'

'You probably remember, the Press assumed it was a factional squabble. I'm sure there was a bit of disinformation going on to push that idea. Anything that helped sow discord in the PIRA High Command seemed like a good plan. I got it in the neck when I was debriefed, then I was told to say nothing at all in the office. I went on leave for a fortnight and when I came back I discovered the office rumour mill had rejected the squabble theory and turned me into Rambo. Everyone thought I'd had a rush of blood to the head and decided to take the opportunity for a spot of freelance execution.'

'Yes, that was what I heard. How did you feel about that?'

Johnny was slow in answering. 'I didn't discourage it. Couldn't. I'd been told to keep quiet and it meant no one pushed in front of me in the lunch queue.'

'I'm glad to know it wasn't true. I thought it was until I got to know you. That made me rather worried about Heather to start with, you see.'

'Heather? You didn't think I'd harm Heather, did you?'

'I know you wouldn't now.'

To change the subject, Johnny looked at his watch. 'Coming up to half way. I'll just call for the Cherbourg weather.'

He had trouble getting a response. They came through in the end – crackly.

Gusting thirty knots was all they were saying. That would do. The seas below looked even larger. Jo tapped him on the shoulder and he pushed back the headset and turned to her.

'How far?' she shouted.

'We're half way. We'll be over the coast in another twenty-five minutes.'

She nodded and Heather smiled at him. She leaned forward again, as he put the headphones back over his ears.

'What did you say?' he called.

'I said, can you see Fr—'

She broke off just as he was thinking how much better he could hear her suddenly and then it dawned on him that the reason he could hear her so well, and the reason she'd stopped talking and was now sitting there with her mouth open, was that the engine had stopped.

CHAPTER SIXTEEN

In the starboard wing tank the corrosive aviation spirit had finished the job, dissolving the long sausage more or less evenly until the thinnest part ruptured. Three pints of water contained in it rushed out to mingle with the petrol around it. The tank was gravity fed and the water, heavier than petrol, swirled down in a fairly uniform mass to the lowest point of the tank, through the outlet pipe to the selector valve and on through the fuel strainer to the carburettor. There it filled the float chamber, was drawn through the jets and vaporized into a fine spray and was sucked into the engine's cylinders by the vacuum of descending pistons. It was only when the pistons rose again to compress it and the spark plugs flashed that it made its presence felt. Water doesn't burn. The engine could have coped with a few drops, spluttering for a while and kicking it out of the exhaust as extra steam, but three pints was far too much.

The whole process, from the sausage rupturing to the engine stopping, took less than a minute.

Johnny shot one horrified look at the fuel gauge, seeing it still showed plenty. Training took over. He pulled back on the yoke, climbing to convert his surplus speed into vital, life-extending height. He checked the primer was locked, felt the mixture control. No clues there, it wasn't either of those. He switched to the other tank. Inside it, the second sausage had lasted an extra minute and a half but the fuel lines were already full of water and soon that was joined by a further three pints. He pulled carburettor heat in case it was icing in the humid air, tried cycling the magnetos. Nothing worked. In desperation he tried the starter again, but the engine stayed dead, the propeller windmilling in front of them.

From a far place he heard Heather's voice. 'Do you know what's wrong?'

'No. It's like there's no fuel but I know there's plenty. Everything else seems fine. I'm working on it.' He was going through every possible procedure for a second time as he talked.

'I'm glad you brought the life-raft,' said Jo, calm, almost cheerful now that there was a real problem to face. He could have hugged her.

He watched the air speed, settled it at seventy knots and trimmed the plane so it stayed naturally in a shallow dive at that speed.

'How far can we get?' said his father.

'From four thousand feet? Maybe six miles.'

'How far's land?'

'France is nearest. Thirty miles, maybe thirty-five.'

'Oh dear.'

Johnny turned the radio selector to 121.5 megahertz and pressed the button to transmit. 'Mayday, mayday. Cessna Lima Tango Kilo, engine failure thirty miles north of Cherbourg.'

Nothing happened. The radio sounded completely dead. He frowned and tried again.

'Mayday, mayday. Cessna Lima Tango Kilo, engine failure thirty miles north of Cherbourg. Descending from four thousand feet. Intend to ditch. Four POB, including one disabled. Please respond.'

Still nothing. Had he been able to see the cable to the antenna, he would have seen that a two inch section of it had turned into a soggy blackened mess, where the acid soaked putty had done its slow job.

'You fly it,' said his father, 'I can do that.'

'Good. Just keep trying. You're calling Distress and Diversion at West Drayton. They must be able to hear. Keep calling Mayday, don't bother about the details until someone responds. Just say we're a Cessna in trouble thirty miles north of Cherbourg. Someone will be hearing it even if we can't hear them. They've got satellite gear that can spot a gnat in a sandstorm. They'll find us.'

He spoke with more conviction than he felt. The engine *and* the radio? That was starting to feel uncomfortably deliberate. He looked down at the inevitable sea. From this height, he could just make out the French coast on the impossibly far-off horizon. No comfort there. It would have to be a ditching as near a ship as possible. He could see three, one that looked like a tanker a long way ahead, a Channel ferry to the south-west, upwind, and a big freighter of some sort to the east. A minute had gone by since the engine had stopped. They were down to three thousand two hundred feet.

He swore at himself. He'd forgotten the transponder. He fiddled the dials to the right setting and switched it to transmit. That would send out an automatic distress signal. If it was working. He pushed the uncomfortable thought away, turned to Heather and Jo behind.

'If it won't restart, we're going to ditch right next to a ship. Sit tight. I'm sorry about this but we'll be OK.'

Heather nodded, looking serious. Jo gave him a tight grin.

He turned back to the task in hand, went on sliding the throttle knob in and out, trying carb heat, magnetos, everything, hoping for a response from the engine. None came. He kept one eye on the air-speed indicator, reminding himself not to try to stretch the glide too far. Stalling would lose far more than he stood to gain. It felt like he was just prolonging the agony. In three or four minutes gravity would have its way whatever he did. The plane would reach sea level and he would have to do something he had never done before, something they couldn't teach you at flying school, not by practice anyway, something on which three other people's lives now depended. He strove to remember the theory. Next to him, his father was still calling 'Mayday, mayday' into a silent radio.

Johnny had a good memory. Unlatch the cabin doors before ditching, he remembered that from the Cessna manual. Jettison heavy objects. Jo's wheelchair? The thought struck a chill into him. Ditching, then getting Jo out of the back seat? It had been hard enough on land. What chance did they have in the water even if he managed to pull off a gentle ditching? They were stuck with it anyway. It was out of the question to get it out of the back and through the door until they were down. The approach – did you use flaps? Yes. Ten degrees of flap and sixty knots. Sixty was going to seem bloody fast, he knew. On a calm sea it would be bad enough. This sea wasn't calm.

Another minute had passed, down to two thousand four hundred feet now. Decision time. He thought hard and picked the freighter. It was downwind, that was one thing, also it seemed somehow less frivolous than the ferry, more likely to have good seamen on board. Was that right? How he could tell? Any decision seemed better than none so he banked into a gentle curve towards it.

It was so quiet now, just the swish of air past them and Sir Michael's low insistent voice. He turned his head to the women in the back.

'I'll tell you when we're about to touch down. Just to be on the safe side, I want you bending forward, put your head down on your crossed arms in your lap. Use your jackets to pad your face. Try to wedge the wheelchair so it doesn't fly around.'

They nodded. He pulled the handle and pushed his door open so that the slipstream held it against the latch, then he told his father to do the same. Another minute – down to one and a half thousand feet and the freighter was close. He'd have to ditch ahead so the ship would stop as near as possible. He worried in case they weren't keeping a good look-out but then he saw a flash of reflected sun from the bridge. Binoculars? He hoped so.

It was a big ship, fully laden with containers almost up to its bridge level. Johnny switched his gaze away and studied the sea. My God, he thought, those waves are big. Into the wind and across the waves, that was how they told you to land. These waves were going the same way as the wind. As he studied the waves he realized with complete and sickening certainty that there was absolutely no hope of pulling off a controlled textbook ditching in that heaving sea and that even if he got out, the chances of getting Jo and Heather, trapped in the back by the wheelchair, safely into the life-raft were very low indeed.

Sir Michael, who'd been staring down at the sea, shot him a worried look. Johnny grimaced. A thousand feet. Another minute, that's all they had.

'Not long now, get into position,' he said. 'I'm . . . I'm very sorry about this.'

'Good luck, Johnny,' said Heather.

'Yeah, go for it,' said Jo.

He started to turn into wind, taking a good look at the ship's position, hammering towards them, down to the east, straight into the teeth of the wind.

On a calm sea it might be possible, bringing it in just over stalling speed, levelling off to flop into the water. In this sea, the chances of staying upright were zero. It was fifty-fifty for the two of them in the front seat. For Heather and Jo, survival was a long shot. He'd left the throttle wide open and the windmilling propeller, turning the engine slowly over, was – had he but known it – sucking the water slowly through the system. One pint out of the six pints queuing up in the pipes had already gone. If they'd had thirty thousand feet of height to play with the engine might in the end have laboured its way through the water back to petrol again, but they didn't have thirty thousand feet. They had little more than five hundred feet left.

It was the reduction in their height that allowed Johnny to see what he hadn't seen before. Glancing diagonally back at the freighter, where he could now clearly see someone on the wing of the bridge staring in their direction, he also noticed how clean cut the profile of the ship looked from this height. Every last available space had been used in the stack of containers which rose high off the deck. It looked like an aircraft carrier.

It was one wild chance. Should he take it? He glanced back at Jo and Heather and knew it was their only chance. Simple choice, evens for his father and himself only if they ditched against what? Maybe one chance in three for all four of them if he could do it.

He looked at Sir Michael. 'I'm going to try putting it down on the ship. Are you game?'

There was a short silence then he said. 'I'm happy with

whatever you decide. If you think there's a better chance that way, take it.'

Every foot of height was precious now. He banked cautiously, paralleled the ship going the opposite way, sinking all the time. When he was behind it he banked again, levelled out in line with the stern, sinking, sinking. He was into wind now, the stern of the ship dead ahead, staring down at what looked a very, very short space from this angle.

He reached over in front of his father and tapped the flap control down to the first detent position for ten degrees and felt the plane lift a little, slowing. They seemed barely to be gaining on the ship and he feared suddenly that he might not have enough height to reach it. He did frantic sums. The ship was doing maybe fifteen knots into a head wind of something like twenty-five knots. If he was doing sixty-five, he was closing on it at only twenty-five knots.

If he could just get there, they were in with a chance.

They were committed now. He switched everything off except the electrical master switch – knowing he'd still need that for the flaps.

The ship's bridge stuck up ahead, in his way though it was only maybe ten feet higher than the top surface of the containers beyond it. He'd have to come down hard once he was over it.

Then he saw the derricks.

Closer up, the top surface of the containers wasn't so even. There were small gaps between them. More worryingly, two thick loading derricks protruded half way down the ship, side by side maybe fifteen feet apart.

The stern of the ship was just a hundred feet ahead now and men were pouring out of the bridge, out of hatches, everywhere, staring back towards him.

Time slowed right down for him. There seemed an age to make every tiny correction. He pushed the nose down for a fraction more speed until he was almost on the ship, below the level of the top of the bridge then pulled the nose up, just cleared the bridge in an ungainly hurdle and in the same moment selected full flap. The plane slowed abruptly. Its nose lifted sharply into the air and he fought it, seeing only sky ahead. Then it dropped hard so that the windscreen was full of containers rushing up at him, and he put both hands on the yoke and pulled for his life. The nose was starting to lift, the plane squashing down in the air as they hit, then it was all in the lap of the gods. The landing gear disintegrated in a rattling, tearing screech of metal and an impact that rocked the belly of the plane down, knocking the breath out of him.

He could see forwards now.

They were sliding, crabwise, bumping diagonally across their precarious landing-strip at what felt a terrifying speed towards the edge.

The noise, that was the startling thing – the noise you get when you tear up an aeroplane. Rending metal filled Johnny's ears and stopped him thinking anything except for one, dominant thought – they were going over the edge and there was nothing he could do to stop them, going over the edge to plunge down the side of the ship and be minced up by its propellers. His foot was trying to press the rudder pedal through the bulkhead in a futile attempt to swing the sliding, bucking plane back towards the centre line. It was to no avail.

In the last second before the nose had lifted and he lost sight of the deck he had tried to keep the plane straight. The pair of loading derricks stuck out halfway down the container runway. If you had to land in trees, you aimed the nose between two, so they'd take the wings off and slow you down. That was what the textbook said and Johnny had tried to apply the same theory now but that's where the textbook stopped. The ship was rising on a wave when they hit, the undercarriage buckled unevenly and a line of ring bolts on the top of one container, ripping into the Cessna's belly, served to skew them further to the left. The makeshift runway looked very narrow.

Bouncing and skidding, their oblique course was set for the edge and the edge, Johnny knew, offered only death.

It was, after all, a derrick that stopped them, but not as Johnny had intended by serving as one of the goalposts for their shot into the net. The left hand derrick of the pair, sticking up between the containers, sliced into the right wing a couple of feet out from the wing root while the plane was still sliding fast, a mass of metal, skidding along at the speed of an Olympic sprinter. Each derrick had two legs, one in front of the other. As the wing folded up around the rear leg, the impact swung the plane hard right, away from the drop. The derrick's second leg, built massively out of steel, bit brutally into the fuselage right by the wing root, into the front passenger area.

The windscreen popped out and Johnny, on the opposite side, jackknifed forward against his straps, and as the instrument panel seemed to jump to meet him there was a loud grunt from his father.

After that nothing seemed to make sense. He was trying to fly the plane but it was rising and falling, rising and falling. He wanted to control the motion with his arms and legs but they didn't respond properly. As the plane moved up and down it seemed to shift slightly sideways to small sounds of stressed metal. There were voices, voices behind him and voices outside the plane. How could there be voices outside when they were flying? He kept thinking his eyes were open but he knew they were shut and the clouds through which he was swooping in this uncomfortable slow switchback were just dream vision.

There were more shouts and a lurch and then cold air poured over him as the door beside him was torn off. Hands took him, unstrapped him, lifted him out and laid him on a wet, hard surface that was still lifting and falling under him. The air was thick with the smell of petrol. Time to wake up now, he thought. Time to get those eyes open. There was a hand on his face and a voice calling.

'Johnny? Johnny? Can you hear me?'

He got his eyes open with a huge effort for just a moment. Bright sky seared the back of them. A face, dark against the sky, blotted out part of it. He knew from the voice that it was Heather.

'You're all right?' he said.

'I'm all right. So's Jo. How about you?'

'Banged my head.'

'I know. Can you see all right?' Jo, he thought. Why had she only mentioned Jo?

'Where's my father?'

'They're just getting him out now.'

He lurched up, got to his feet then found himself somehow, painfully, down on his knees, vomiting violently. The sight that greeted him was a shock. They were up on top of the containers. The Cessna was on its belly ahead of him, leaning over so the tip of its intact left wing hung down over the edge. The right wing was reared up in the air, buckled and waving in the wind and half a dozen men were swarming in and around the cockpit. Ropes were roughly lashed around the fuselage, tied to the derrick, making sure the remains of the plane didn't slide over the side in the motion of the sea.

Johnny tried to stand again, fighting off her restraining arm and made it upright, his head swinging dizzily. He lurched across to the plane, pushed a seaman aside to look in. His father was in the crumpled mess that had been the right hand side of the Cessna's cockpit. His eyes were closed and his face was white. The derrick that had saved them had turned him into the padding for that last split second of deceleration.

Johnny felt a terrible fear.

'Is he breathing?' he said.

The nearest seaman was Asian, Korean maybe, and looked at him uncomprehendingly.

'Yes,' came a voice beside him, 'he is breathing. You go down below. We get him out.' It was an officer, big, fair haired, with an accent that sounded Dutch. Johnny's legs gave way again and the man caught him as he fell.

He didn't resist then as they strapped him to a stretcher, lowered him down to the deck and took him below to a sickbay. Heather came with him. Jo was already there, looking pale but unhurt.

'Heather,' she said, 'can you tell this guy there's nothing wrong with me? I can't make him understand.'

'She not all right.' The sickbay attendant was small, elderly, also Asian. 'She shocky. Legs not working.'

'No,' said Heather, 'her legs didn't work before.' He frowned. 'Wheelchair,' said Heather, 'she uses a wheelchair.'

The door opened and the room was suddenly filled with bustling men, lifting Sir Michael, inert on a stretcher, carefully in.

Heather and the attendant bent over him. Johnny levered himself up. He felt less dizzy now. The attendant was cutting his father's jacket off him, probing his right side with what seemed to Johnny to be rough fingers.

'Ribs' he said, 'ribs bust. Maybe pelvis too.'

Johnny felt numb panic crawling up him. His father looked frail and broken. Where would skilled help come from? A few minutes earlier he had been facing the high chance that all of them would soon be dead. Now there were three people safe on the ship but contained in the motionless form of the fourth was a shadow large enough to eclipse any joy he might have been able to feel at that achievement.

The door opened again and a big man came in. He had a pot belly, a fleshy, damp face with a purple network of broken veins across his nose and cheeks and very little hair except for a grey spade beard.

He looked around him. 'What's the news, Sammy?' he said to the attendant and his voice was a guttural growl.

'Broke bones,' said Sammy, 'ribs, maybe pelvis, maybe leg. Life signs so-so. Maybe bleeding inside. He need hospital, Captain.'

'Do you have a doctor?' Johnny demanded.

'Course we don't. We'll call a chopper.' He didn't look too friendly. 'Are the rest of you all right?' he said.

'We seem to be, thanks,' said Johnny.

'You sure?' said the Captain. 'Looks like your head put a dent in my ship.'

They made him sit down until Sammy had done what he could with Sir Michael and had time to peer into Johnny's eyes and ears.

'He'll do,' said Sammy cursorily and went back to Sir Michael.

'I'm Captain Lammers. Your names are?'

'Johnny Kay, Heather Weston, Jo er . . .' Johnny's mind went blank.

'Howitt,' said Jo.

'And the injured man?' asked the Captain, writing it all down.

'Sir Michael Parry.'

'Oh yes?' said the Captain and stopped writing to look at him in surprise. 'That one? The famous Sir Parry?'

'You know about him?.'

'Even in Holland, yes.' A little drop of sweat splashed off the Captain's nose.

'Get your breath. I go to call up the chopper,' he said. 'There's tea coming. Then I wish to talk to you on the bridge.'

'He's not too pleased,' said Heather when he'd gone.

'Nor would I be if someone had just dropped an aeroplane on my ship. He probably thinks I've been highly irresponsible.'

'But you haven't been.'

'No,' said Johnny, 'I really haven't.' He catalogued it, as much for his own sake as for hers. 'I had Frankie check the plane over. He's brilliant, Frankie, used to be in the Czech Air Force. He's the best aircraft mechanic I know. I did the pre-flight properly. Well, you saw. He did most of it with me. There just wasn't anything wrong. Then the engine *and* the radio, I mean to say.'

'There is another possibility.'

'What?'

'That it was done on purpose.'

'Someone fixed the plane, you mean?'

'Is that possible?'

His face took on a grim aspect as he considered it. A steward brought tea and they swallowed it down, thick with sugar.

'Who?' he said.

'The Americans, the Ramsgill Stray lot.'

'Surely they wouldn't do that. What have we got that's so important to them?'

Jo chipped in. 'They'd love to have Heather out of the way. Her case is a big embarrassment to them. So's mine, and your father's their biggest problem with their planning applications.'

Johnny was shaking his head.

'No, of course,' Heather said, 'stupid of me. It's not that at all, is it? That's all old hat. It's something new. It has to be. They know we've got the cable diagram for the link into BT. The Raven Stones tower link. You said yourself it was the smoking gun.'

He looked at her hard, then he shook his head again but this time it was different. It was a gesture of hopelessness rather than denial.

'You want to come with me to face the Captain?' he said.

There was no change in Sir Michael's condition so they left Jo there with Sammy to call them if necessary.

The door from the sickbay led to a covered passage with a companionway at the far end leading to the bridge. Heather took Johnny's arm, steered him away from it out on to the side deck where the wind took his breath away. She led him to a sheltered corner.

'I just want to know something,' she said. 'Why did you decide not to land in the sea?'

'We might have got out,' he said, 'you wouldn't have – probably not you and certainly not Jo, wedged in by the wheelchair, with only one door.'

'Thank you,' she said, 'I thought that was it. Thank you from both of us. You did brilliantly.'

'No I didn't,' he said miserably, 'look what I've done to my father.'

She put her arms round him and held him tight. 'Not what *you've* done to him. He's alive, Johnny. There'll be a helicopter coming as fast as it can. Four people are still alive thanks to you.'

'I simply couldn't bear it if he died now.'

She was silent.

'Heather,' he said, 'all the way down in the plane I thought you were going to die too. I couldn't see any way of being sure I could get you out if we tipped over. When I decided to land on the ship I did it because of you.'

'Me and Jo.'

'No. You.'

She sighed. 'Come on. Let's go and see the Captain.'

On the bridge a plate proclaimed the name of the ship, the *Waspik Trader*. The Captain nodded at them and gestured ahead through the glass to where the plane lay, crooked in their line of vision.

'Chopper's coming, ' he said, 'half an hour they say. I tell them who it was and they say they hurry.'

'Oh good,' said Johnny, 'that's a relief.'

'I thought you had gone crazy,' said the Captain. 'We were watching you come down. We thought maybe you wanted to see the ship, then you came in so low and slow behind us. My first mate, he said your engine was stopped so I send him to get a boat ready then bang.'

'My engine stopped at four thousand feet,' said Johnny.

'You know why?'

'I haven't a clue.'

'You don't take care of it maybe?'

'Oh yes I do.'

'You have a radio?'

'Yes.'

'But you didn't call?'

'We were calling. It stopped working some time after we left England too.'

The Captain snorted in a way that suggested he wouldn't like to have Johnny as an engineer on *his* ship.

'Do you know what could have happened? You could have hit the bridge. You could have gone over the side. You could have gone over the bow and we would have run you down. You could have set my ship on fire. Your petrol has gone everywhere. All down into the containers. It is very lucky it didn't blow.'

'Captain Lammers, I am very sorry if you feel I put your ship in any kind of danger. It was our only hope of saving lives, particularly with a disabled passenger in the back.'

'Your lives against my ship? That makes it OK, you think?'

'There wasn't much time to think. I suppose I didn't think we could do much damage to the containers.'

The Captain snorted.

'Look, Captain, we think there's just a possibility that someone might have interfered with the plane.'

'Oh, I see. That is a good excuse.'

'We took good care, I promise. Anyway at some point the authorities will want to inspect it. Can it stay there until you get to port?'

'Is there a choice? What can I do, push it over the side?'

'Where is your next stop.'

'Mobile.'

'Mobile, Alabama?'

'That's right.'

Oh shit, thought Johnny, couldn't it have been Ireland or France or somewhere simple? Mundane complications began to multiply in front of him, telling the insurers, telling his co-owners. Having the plane sail off to America was not an easy way to start the process.

'That's a long way,' he said. 'Our Civil Aviation Authority will want to look at it.'

'You want my engineer looks now. Sees if you're trying to get out of the blaming?'

The CAA might not like it, Johnny thought. On the other hand who's to say whether there'd be anything left to find if or when the Cessna reached Alabama?

'Thank you. That would be very helpful.'

That was when the radio operator butted in.

In Hastings, Jeremy Randall, housebound with acute arthritis, passed the long days in his Victorian terraced house up on the town's highest ground by scanning the wavebands on his expensive receivers, logging and passing on to the news agencies anything interesting he picked up. The agencies paid him a tiny tip-off fee but it kept him in cigarettes and just once in a while, when he gave them a big one, they'd be more generous. When he heard the ship's call he knew this was just such a one. When he heard Sir Michael Parry's name, he couldn't believe his luck. He started dialling.

The first call came through on the ship's RT five minutes later. It was the Press Association and it was only then that it occurred to Johnny that this was going to be the stuff of headlines.

'Chopper's ten minutes out,' said the Captain, 'I'm ringing slow engines. He says he'll pick up Sir Parry first. Doctor is on board. You want to talk to these Press guys?'

'No, I don't, thanks.'

'So I talk, yeah?'

'If you like.'

The Captain retired to the back of the bridge and seemed to be getting quite a lot of mileage out of the interview that followed.

Anxiety dragged Johnny back down to the sickbay. Jo looked up as he came in. 'He's been groaning a lot. Hasn't said anything. I hope they're not going to be long?'

'Just a few minutes now,' he said, trying to sound reassuring. Sammy was taking Sir Michael's pulse.

'Not good,' he said.

To give himself something to think about and – if the truth were known, to get away from that dreadful, still, white face – he went to get their bags and Jo's chair out of the Cessna. There was a metal stair rigged, fore and aft, angling up the side of the containers. On top, a man in overalls had forced the buckled engine cowling back and was deep in the innards of the machinery. The folded wheelchair had been stuffed back in the front of the plane by their rescuers. He pulled it out then had trouble opening the hatch to the baggage compartment which had been crushed in from the bottom by the impact.

He took their four small bags out, finding he could easily fit the other three inside his own, then he saw the life-raft and, thinking about his deposit, considered for a moment taking that too. He went to pick it up, remembered how heavy it was and decided it could stay there as another problem for the insurers to sort out. That was when he noticed that the serial number painted on the top of the raft's casing seemed to be melting and trickling down the case, leaving a messy, smeared black waterfall behind it. He bent to investigate, saw a blob of some sticky substance which had dripped down on to the paint. He wiped it off with a finger and poked his head in to investigate where it had come from. Just as he registered the corroded remains of the radio antenna, eaten through into two rough stumps where it should have run evenly along the side of the compartment, the acid jelly on his finger bit into his nerve endings like a score of razor cuts.

He yelled, wiped it off as best he could but it still hurt like hell. The engineer working on the engine straightened up. 'What is wrong?' he said. Another Dutchman.

'Acid,' said Johnny, 'acid on my finger.'

The man had the fuel hose off the carburettor. He held up a metal can.

'Stick it in this. Quick.'

'In petrol?'

'This is water. Go on.'

He did and felt the pain start to ease as he rubbed the diluted jelly off his skin. There was a red, raw area already blistering.

'You are right, though. It should have been petrol,' said the man, 'but it really is water. It all came from your carburettor and your fuel lines.'

'How could that be?'

'Bad petrol?'

'I checked. Anyway it couldn't have run for all that distance first. How much did you take out?'

'Two litres, maybe. There is still more there, I think.'

'Good God. Please, keep some in a clean jar. The investigators will want to see that.'

He showed the engineer the remains of the antenna and the man whistled.

'Could you put some of that jelly in a glass jar too, for the investigation?'

'Sure. You want I take photos?'

'Please.'

Heather was right. Sabotage was now the only possible conclusion. Johnny got the chair and the bags down on deck and went up to the bridge.

'Your engineer has found a lot of water in the fuel, several litres.'

'Bad fuel, huh?'

'No. Not as simple as that. The plane couldn't have got this far with so much of it in the tanks.'

'So?'

'So, I don't know, but someone used acid to put the radio out of action.'

'You have enemies?'

'Perhaps I do.'

'Ach, well,' the Captain said gruffly, 'I am glad for you my ship was here. It was good flying and I can tell the story to my grandchildren.'

He was called to the radio again, said a few words and then waved a hand at him.

'I'm talking to the chopper now,' he said and listened for a long time.

Johnny considered what they should do. Get his father to the hospital and see what they had to say. Presumably it would be Portsmouth or Southampton. They'd have to weigh it up. If things were under control there would still be time to jump on a ferry, get Heather and Jo to Cherbourg before the end of the conference even if he had to stay behind with his father.

'Understood,' said the Captain, 'we will maintain steerage-way into wind. Handling party will take the stretcher to the top of the containers.' He looked at Johnny then away. 'Other three are OK. Bruises, that's all.' Another silence as he listened. 'OK, I tell them.'

He put the mike down. 'The chopper will only take Parry,' he said. 'It's not one of the bigger ones and it has a medical team on board for your VIP.'

Visions of Cherbourg, their precious witness, Heather's continued freedom dwindled.

'So what about us?'

'You like Alabama?' said the Captain, and he chuckled.

It was Sunday, so the 10.15 a.m. train from Plymouth to London was full of holiday-makers returning home, children racing up and down the aisle and depressed parents queuing in the buffet for crisps, lager and British Rail bacon-and-tomato rolls, whose salty smell had spread through their carriage.

Captain Lammers had let his joke stand for an hour, enjoying their discomfiture before letting them in on the plan. They were to be transferred to a suitable ship heading for a UK port as soon as it could be arranged. The navy came to their rescue in the late afternoon, by which time the *Waspik Trader* was a hundred miles further west. Captain Lammers wasn't going to screw up his schedule any more than was strictly necessary. There had been several more interviews over the RT during the afternoon. Johnny had turned down every request to talk but the Captain seemed to like temporary celebrity status and accepted them all.

The wind had dropped by then and the sea was much calmer. They met HMS *Brilliant* forty miles off Lyme Regis and the frigate's seamen came across to collect them in one of her boats. Heather had been quiet and withdrawn for most of the afternoon. Johnny didn't know how to reach her through his own haze of after-shock. Jo had reacted in the opposite way, bubbling with humour, interested in everything around her. 'Whoops, here we go again,' she said as they lifted her into a breeches buoy for the transfer to *Brilliant's* boat.

'Are you all right?' said Johnny.

'All right?' she said. 'If it wasn't for your poor dad, I'd be having the time of my life. I haven't had so much excitement since I've been in the chair. It's better than a day at Alton Towers.'

Heather and Johnny said grateful farewells to Captain Lammers. 'We look after your toy for you,' he said gruffly as they looked forward at the plane. 'Don't know how you get it back, though.'

Johnny studied the remains through the bridge windows. 'I think it's for the scrap heap. Anyway I'm not too sure I want to do any more flying for a while.'

The messages from the hospital were noncommittal. Sir Michael was conscious but his condition was giving cause for some concern. He was running a fever. The word 'comfortable' was singularly lacking from the bulletins they were given.

Devonport dockyard found them beds for the night within the base where the medical officer checked them over carefully and decided Johnny's bruised face would mend by itself. He'd called the hospital again as soon as they were ashore. There was no improvement.

On Sunday morning they had had to run the gauntlet of a pack of photographers at the dockyard gates but the naval driver, lending himself enthusiastically to the job, got them to the station by some high-speed driving through the backstreets without any of the press following. They wheeled Jo rapidly through the station and just caught the 10.15 to London. The *Sunday Mirror*, the *News of the World* and the *Mail on Sunday* were very much in evidence around them. They had gone to town on the story. Each of them carried banner headlines with variations on the 'Diplomat in mid-Channel air drama' theme. There were photos of Sir Michael and imaginative diagrams of how they'd landed the plane.

No one was taking any notice of them and Johnny hoped that meant their own faces didn't feature in any of the other papers. He felt utterly weary, aching where his body was dealing with the damage caused by the force of the crash. He borrowed an *Observer* and the three of them pored over it. It described Sir Michael's condition as 'critical', which came as a shock until they reassured themselves that they had spoken to the hospital much more recently than the paper could possibly have done.

The papers didn't know Johnny was Sir Michael's son. All they had was his name and that he lived in London, but they did know he was a hero. That was the nub of it and Captain Lammers, for all his apparent anger at the time, was the main witness to that. He was quoted as saying he would not have thought the landing was possible and that Johnny was a skilful and daring young pilot.

The train was completely full and there was an over-friendly man in the other seat at their table, with the rest of his family across the aisle. He saw them looking at the story and decided to share his thoughts with them. 'Bloody smart, eh?' he said. 'Incredible, really. I mean that bloke saved their lives, didn't he? Bloody quick thinking, that. Must be Superman, that bloke must.' He went on in the same vein for a couple of minutes or more without adding greatly to the store of original thought on the matter.

Heather, sitting next to Johnny, reached for his hand, out of sight under the table and squeezed it. She didn't let it go.

They couldn't talk about it, not with their companion opposite certain to hear, but it was all they wanted to talk about. Johnny leaned back, acutely conscious of the tiny movements of Heather's fingers in his hand, aware that she was as worn-out as he. Jo on the other hand, was still on some sort of high, revitalized by the whole experience. She started humming and winked at them. It was a familiar tune but in his worn-out state, it took a while for Johnny to put words to it. He got it suddenly, 'Trains and boats and planes . . .' and despite himself, he nearly laughed. Something showed on Heather's face too and the man opposite looked slightly uncomfortable as though he thought he might be the butt of this private joke.

Jo broke the spell, looking through the rest of the paper and saying suddenly, 'Here. Look at this.' She pushed it over, stabbing at one of the articles with her finger. It was an account of the previous week's events at the Hurst Inquiry, centring on the admission by a former Conservative junior minister that he'd approved export permits for a variety of dubious weaponry. At the end of the article, it listed the attractions coming up at the Inquiry in the week ahead. Monday, it said, 11 a.m. Sir Greville Kay, GKC Chemicals.

A taxi from Reading reunited them with the Volvo at the airfield. Frankie was nowhere in sight and Johnny had no wish to talk to anyone else so they drove off as quickly as possible. It was the first time the three of them had really been completely by themselves since the crash and Johnny couldn't sidetrack the worry in the forefront of his mind.

'This Dr Beevor,' he said, 'tell me the whole thing in detail. 'How exactly does her evidence come into it?'

'She would have been the independent witness to Hayter's assault. I've only heard it second hand. Jo, you tell him.'

'Heather was unconscious, you see,' said Jo. 'I was in the car, out on the side road, because of the wheelchair, waiting for her. She and Rachel – you won't have met Rachel yet – climbed in. I suppose I waited about half an hour then Rachel came tearing up the road, told me Heather had been knocked out.'

'She saw it happen?'

'No, she didn't,' Heather said. 'I was in the foyer of one of the bunkers. She was outside by the domes, but she saw me being carried out and she could see it looked pretty bad, so she ran to get help.'

'Anyway,' said Jo, 'we wanted to go and phone for help but we were in Heather's car and she had the keys you see, so Rachel got me out into the chair and we flagged down a car. The first one was a farmer in a Land Rover and he just didn't want to know. He drove off but the second one was a little Ford with a woman in it, which was a bit more hopeful. We told her there was someone hurt in the base and she said, "well you're in luck 'cos I'm a doctor."'

'That *was* lucky.'

'And how. She wasn't just a doctor, she was sympathetic too. Rachel told her what she'd seen and she got us both into her car and she went storming off to the main gate. It was bloody incredible, I tell you. She just forced her way in. She told the plod on the gate that there was a medical emergency inside and she forced him to call Chief Inspector Reed, then she told Reed she'd hold him personally responsible unless she was taken to Heather straight away. They wouldn't let *us* in, of course.'

'What did you do?'

'We stayed in the car, outside the gate, biting our fingernails. About half an hour later an ambulance arrived and she came back out with it. She told us Heather was unconscious still and was going to hospital and we drove along behind it all the way.'

Johnny glanced at Heather. 'What happened to you?'

'Concussion. Lacerations to the scalp, bruising.'

His skin crawled in sympathy. 'From Sergeant Hayter?'

'That's right. He threw me against a wall. He'd tried it the time before, in a van, but one of his lads came back. This time there was no one to stop him.'

'No one saw?'

'No one except a security camera, which they say, very conveniently, failed to record.'

'So . . .' He paused and watched as a plane took off. 'Why is this Dr Beevor so important?'

'Well, half an hour after I got to hospital, Hayter turned up there too, driven by one of the other plods. He had a broken nose and a great gash across his forehead.'

'He'd had it done on purpose?'

'He said I hit him with a lump of wood and the only reason I only got injured was because he was trying to defend himself. That's why I'm charged with grievous bodily harm.'

Jo chipped in. 'Dr Beevor was the only one who could say it didn't happen that way because when she was treating Heather outside the bunker, there were a whole lot of modplods there and she heard one of them being called "Hayter".'

'And?'

'And there wasn't a mark on him. He knew he was in a lot of trouble so he got one of his mates to clobber him. It must have been the only way out he could think of.'

'You've got to have her,' he said, 'she's crucial. Listen, Heather, there might still be time to get to Cherbourg.'

'I don't think so,' she said. 'When does the conference end?'

Johnny tried to remember what the hotel had told him. 'Five o'clock, I think.'

'That's four o'clock here then. It's quarter to three now. We can't possibly.'

'She might be staying the night there. She lives somewhere down in the south. It would make sense.'

'You're clutching at straws, Johnny. You tried your best. Leave it be.'

'Look' – he wanted to punch the steering wheel in his frustration – 'what's the alternative? You'll have no evidence except what you yourself say happened. They'll find you guilty.'

'I just have to trust in the jury, Johnny. They'll have to believe me.'

'Pigs might fly,' said Jo from the back seat. 'Maybe a London jury would, but York? You've seen it all before, Heather, love.'

'What do you mean?' asked Johnny.

'Let's just say they manage to select very conservative juries when one of us is up at York,' said Jo. 'It's an amazing coincidence really.' She laughed darkly. 'Then the prosecution tells them how Ramsgill is top secret but it's crucial to the defence of the free world and Heather's a mad woman who's totally obsessed by it and that's that.'

'I'm going to tell them, Jo,' said Heather defiantly. 'I'll just have to make them listen.'

'We've got to do something,' said Johnny. 'There's so little time. I don't want you disappearing inside just when I'm starting to get to know you.'

They stared at each other then until Jo broke into their private silence from the back seat. 'Two points,' she said. 'One, I know you're a red hot pilot, but I'd rather you looked at the road while you're driving. Two, if my presence is in your way, you can always tie my wheelchair on the roof.'

They all laughed, but for the two in the front it was the laughter of the gallows.

CHAPTER SEVENTEEN

They were in Southampton in under half an hour. They pushed Jo up to the hospital reception desk.

'I don't like coming in these places,' she said, 'I always feel they're going to take one look at the chair and stop me leaving again.'

'We want to see Sir Michael Parry,' said Johnny to the woman when his turn came, but the look she gave him in reply, filled with a sudden stern blankness sent clutching fingers of dreadful foreboding into his stomach.

'Please wait there,' she said, 'someone will be down.'

'Is he . . . ? I mean how is he?' he asked in alarm.

'Someone will be down,' said the woman firmly. 'Please take a seat.'

Two or three minutes passed like two or three hours. They saw a middle-aged man in a suit come out of a lift and then be directed towards them by the woman.

'You are?' said the man in a rather peremptory way.

'I'm Sir Michael's son, John. These are two of his friends.'

'Do you have any form of identification, Mr Parry?'

Johnny was reaching for his driving licence when the words sank in.

'My name's not actually Parry,' he said, 'it's Kay.'

'So you're not his son.'

'Yes, I am, as a matter of fact. Look, please, how is he?' He knew he should ask it outright. Has he died? But his mouth seemed to have trouble framing the words.

'We've had some problems with the Press. I'll have to go and ask him.'

'Go and ask him? He's all right, then? He's awake?'

'He's awake. John Kay, you said.'

'Yes.'

'Good Lord, weren't you the pilot?'

Johnny looked round nervously. 'Yes, but not so loud.'

'And you're his son? No one told me that.' He looked affronted.

'Does it make a difference?'

'I act as Press spokesman here, you see.'

'Well, actually, I'd prefer you to keep that to yourself, please.'

The man made a phone call upstairs and when he put the receiver down the suspicion in his face had disappeared. In no time they were being ushered into a room where Sir Michael lay, strapped up and monitored, still white faced but with his eyes open and able to smile when he saw them come through the door.

They weren't allowed to stay long, just long enough to exchange experiences and for Johnny to explain the sequence of events when he realized the accident had left some gaps in his father's memory of the preceding minutes.

'It really does look like it was sabotage,' he said, and he explained about the water and the acid.

Sir Michael looked grave but got no chance to reply before the sister came back in to check his temperature and tell them it was time to go.

On Monday morning, well before eleven, they were waiting in the queue at the Department of Trade and Industry in Victoria Street for the Hurst Inquiry. The evening before had been a nightmare. They'd driven from Southampton straight to Johnny's flat but his hopes that the Press might be losing interest in their story disappeared when he saw the crowd waiting at the entrance. The photographers homed in on Jo and Heather. The wheelchair was clearly a big angle. The pack of them was physically in the way of the door with Webley, on the far side, giving palms-up gestures of helplessness.

'Hold on!' Johnny shouted. 'You've got enough pictures, for Heaven's sake.' There were shouts of dissent. 'All right. We'll pose properly for one, then if you let these two go inside straight afterwards, I'll answer questions but only if you all agree you'll go away when I say I've had enough, OK?'

There were nods which didn't inspire trust in him, but it was worth a try. They stood either side of Jo's chair while the cameras clicked, then, left alone with the crowd, he did the best he could. Yes, it was a difficult landing. No, he'd never done anything like it before. Did he think they'd die? He was always an optimist. What would he have done if the ship hadn't been there? Died probably. What did he do for a living? Nothing at the moment. Was Heather his girlfriend? Er, no. How did he know Sir Michael? Through Heather, he said, which was sort of true. They would have gone on all night, but he refused to answer anything more and slipped in through the door as Webley eased it open and shut it rapidly behind him.

The tape in his answering machine was full of messages, from Frankie, from the co-owners of the Cessna in states of mind which varied from alarmed concern on the most part to tight anger from the dentist who'd wanted to use it that weekend. Friends, acquaintances, it seemed that anyone who'd ever had his number had rung. Except his mother. He could just imagine the effect it would have had on her first to hear the news then to discover who his front seat passenger had been.

When they reached Victoria Street, it was clear there was little interest in Sir Greville Kay from the public and the Press. According to the doorman, for some sessions, when key figures were due to appear before the inquiry, the queue had stretched around the block but today was reckoned to be a very second-rate show.

They were conspicuously almost alone on the public benches. Sir Roger Hurst, the judge presiding over the inquiry, and Peter Judd, the sharp young barrister who was trying, with limited success, to emulate Presiley Baxendale's style in the recent Scott

Inquiry, arrived to conclude some left over business with a civil servant from the Defence Export Sales Organization, then – a few minutes late – they called for Sir Greville Kay.

Johnny had half expected his mother to be there too, but Sir Greville came in accompanied only by his lawyer. His attention was fixed on the judge as he walked in from the side and he sat down with his back to the three of them, without noticing their presence.

Hurst and the barrister went through some preliminary niceties then Judd launched straight in. 'Sir Greville, the principal reason you have been asked to attend this inquiry is in connection with a product apparently marketed by you by the name of "Rage".'

Sir Greville cleared his throat. 'May I?'

Judd looked irritated but paused and Sir Greville continued. 'Thank you. I don't mean to stop you in midflow but in point of fact we don't have any product called 'Rage' in our current product line.'

Judd looked down at his notes and his expression showed that he thought Sir Greville was walking out a long way on a very rickety plank.

'You may not recognize that name perhaps, but you, or rather your staff would know it as CN512, Sir Greville. It is manufactured, I believe, by your Chempropa Division at Westrop?'

Got him, thought Johnny. They've done some homework. He wished he could see his stepfather's face from where he sat, but the reply came in a voice that sounded surprisingly unflustered and urbane.

'I'm afraid you're misinformed, Mr Judd. GKC does not have a division called Chempropa.'

Judd whirled round to his table and picked up a document. 'This is a copy of an entry in the file at Companies House, Sir Greville. You must presumably be familiar with it. It shows that Chempropa, based at Westrop, is a wholly owned subsidiary of your company GKC.'

'My reply stands, Mr Judd.'

Hurst himself broke in at this point. 'Are you saying, Sir

Greville, that you have lodged misleading information with Companies House?'

'No m'lud, rather that Companies House take some time to up date its files.'

'You are saying, then, that Chempropa was a subsidiary, but that is no longer the case?'

'That is correct.'

Hurst's tone showed signs of exasperation. 'Sir Greville, could I ask you perhaps simply to spell out the situation without beating around the bush quite so much?'

'I'm quite happy to answer. The situation is that GKC has sold the entire Chempropa Division to another company.'

'And the name of this other company?'

'Pearce Loretta.'

'Not a company I have heard of, I'm afraid, Sir Greville. Could you tell us where it is based?'

'South Carolina, m'lud.'

Hurst raised his eyebrows at Judd indicating, it seemed to Johnny, that now the barrister had been given a few moments to think it was time for him to pick up the baton again. Judd did his best.

'Pearce Loretta, Sir Greville. Are they planning to continue Chempropa's activities at Westrop?'

Sir Greville turned and held a whispered conversation with his lawyer which went on for some time. The barrister was looking increasingly frustrated.

'Mr Judd,' said Sir Greville eventually, 'I am advised that what we know of Pearce Loretta's plans is covered by commercial confidentiality stipulations and we believe in any case that detailed questions on their activities would be better addressed to them. I can however tell you that you will find in the *Financial Times* this morning a report to the effect that the manufacturing activities currently carried out at Westrop are being transferred to the United States.'

'And that would include the manufacture of this Rage or CN512?'

There was another whispered conversation. 'I think we are free to inform you, Mr Judd,' said Sir Greville and his voice oozed urbane helpfulness, 'that CN512 had proved to be an unsuccessful experiment and that work upon it had already been discontinued before the sale.'

That left Judd nowhere to go. There was a question he could have asked, but he'd had enough of breaking the barrister's golden rule by asking questions to which he didn't already know the answer. In this case it had only served to push him further and further up a blind alley.

Sir Greville was extremely glad he hadn't been asked it. The question he had been dreading was, "When did this takeover happen?" and the truthful answer would have been: "Three days ago."

'May I just point out, Mr Judd,' he said as he got up to go, 'that had you told us something of the nature of your intended questions, we could perhaps have saved you a lot of time and trouble.'

He turned to leave, saw Johnny sitting there staring at him from the benches at the back and, trying to rescue himself from an involuntary expression of shock, gave him a curt nod before he strode out, giving the women each side of his stepson a hard stare.

CHAPTER EIGHTEEN

'That's it, then, is it?' said Johnny. 'The Americans have knocked Rage on the head. Best thing for it, I think, and it wouldn't have happened without you.'

'What's it like being one day old and six feet tall?' asked Jo as they wheeled her out of the building.

'What do you mean?'

'Well, you must have been born yesterday if you take that steaming load of horse crap at face value.'

A civil servant coming out behind them flinched visibly.

Heather looked distracted. 'We'd better head for the station,' she said. 'It's past noon.'

'What's the hurry? I was going to offer you lunch,' said Johnny.

'I'm on shift tonight at the Hall.'

'On shift? You're working all night then going into court tomorrow?'

'It's not so bad. I'm number two. I'll get plenty of sleep if there aren't any problems. Where's the nearest tube?'

'No tube. I'm driving you.'

'To Yorkshire? No, come on, Johnny. You don't look too good. You go back and get some rest.'

She wasn't exaggerating. The parts of his face that weren't black and blue were doubly pale in comparison but he wasn't about to argue.

'I'm coming up anyway,' he said, 'I'm going to be in court, so of course I'll drive you.'

They rang Mrs Thompson from a pay-phone at Toddington

Services. Sir Michael's cleaner was at the house, beside herself with anxiety, occupying herself with unnecessary dusting and desperate for news.

'He's much better,' Heather assured her over the roar of truck diesels behind her. 'His temperature's down. We talked to the hospital an hour ago. He's much more cheerful.'

'Are you all right, dear?'

'Yes, fine, thank you. So's Johnny. That's why I'm calling. He's driving us up. I'm sure Sir Michael won't mind him using the guest room.'

Johnny could hear a burst of excitement from the other end rising above the hubbub around them. Heather listened, smiling, tried a few times to get a word in edgeways, glanced at her watch eventually and said, 'Eight o'clock or so. I've got to be at the Hall by nine.'

She turned to Johnny as she hung up. 'She knows all about you.'

'Surely not all?'

'No, you're right. Just the simple bits. She knows Sir Michael's found his long-lost son. He's probably been talking nonstop about that and she knows you saved our lives because she read it in the *Mirror*. She says she's dying to meet you. She's leaving a key under the plant pot by the back door.'

Back on the road, Johnny glanced back at Jo, who seemed to be nodding off in the back seat, and pitched his voice low.

'How's your barrister going to play it tomorrow?'

'It's my word against Hayter's,' said Heather. 'We've just got to get them to believe me.'

'Maybe I could help.'

'How?'

'Supposing I got up as an expert witness, told them my background and said we had evidence that the NSA was tapping British domestic phones.'

'What background?' said Jo from the back. Her eyes were still shut.

'Long story,' said Heather, 'Johnny's got a bit of a past. He'll tell you some time. Anyway,' she said turning to Johnny, 'how would that help?'

'It might help to justify your going in to the base. At least in the juror's minds.'

'Oh, I don't know,' she said and there was a bleak hopelessness in her voice that he hadn't heard before. 'Anyway, wouldn't you get locked up? Breaking the Official Secrets Act or something?'

'Well, at least think about it,' he said.

Ray Mackeson was thinking about it too. There was a war cabinet in session at the Stray. Americans only – modplods keep out. Curtis Walsh was up from Grosvenor Square. The Base Commander made it three.

'They could call him into the witness-box,' said Mackeson. 'He could stand up and say anything he damn well pleases. He could say he'd seen the plans.'

'The judge would let him?'

'Sure the judge would let him. Couldn't stop him. If Kay swears on oath he's ex-MI5, it's down to us to disprove it. He's got credibility on Rage. He's got credibility on that cable diagram that he should never have been allowed to carry out of here. If he starts waving that plan around . . .'

He left the thought hanging and if none of them showed any emotion it was only because years of covert service had double-glazed their eyes.

'Well, then, let's go over the options,' said Curtis Walsh. 'And I think I might be allowed an opening opinion. Letting Kay blow us out of the water is not among them.'

'You gotta know what Kay's about,' said Mackeson. 'He's been marinaded in British ruling-class values for three decades. Women and children first. Brought up to help the good guys beat the bad guys.'

'So aren't we the good guys?' asked the Base Commander drily.

Mackeson looked at him through narrowed eyes. 'Guess the Brits didn't hear about the Nineties. Forget the adjectives. We're the *only* guys. Masters of the Universe. What more does anyone need to know?'

Curtis Walsh raised an eyebrow. 'Kay don't seem to see it that way.'

'His problem.'

'Ours too?'

'It's my job to make him see. All I need to know from you,' said Mackeson, 'is just how far to go in the process.'

Walsh looked into Mackeson's flat yellow eyes and doubted that anything he said would make any difference. He knew Mackeson had a direct line to higher authority than him and suspected the question had been phrased strictly for the record.

'There are two projects riding on this,' he answered. 'You don't need me to tell you your job.'

The phone buzzed. The Base Commander picked it up, listened, passed it to Mackeson. 'Gerow,' he said.

Mackeson gave a slow grin and glued his ear to it.

'Yeah?' He listened. 'I got it. Good going, Pacman.'

He put it down, smiled some more and drummed on the desk. 'Our boy and his friends still use telephones. He don't learn. We got him just where we want him.'

'Where?'

'In a tailor-made trap. Down the longest dead end you ever saw. A million miles from help. Remember that movie? In space, no one can hear you scream. My man Pacman's earned himself a prize.'

It was around 9 p.m. by the time Johnny had taken Jo home, reunited Heather with her car and seen her safely off to the Hall again. It would have been earlier but when they got to her cottage, he'd said, 'Can I come in for a minute?'

'Of course. Would you like some food?'

'Coffee would be nice.'

She was measuring coffee granules into mugs, her back turned to him at the kitchen table, when he gave way to an impulse he could simply resist no longer and moving towards her put his arms round her. She stopped what she was doing, stood stock-still for three loud heartbeats, then put the spoon down and turned round in his arms very slowly. Her eyes were shut. He kissed her cheek then moved his mouth towards hers but she lifted up a finger and put it on his lips.

'Stop,' she said.

He relaxed the pressure of his arms just slightly, but she made no move away.

'All my strength has to come from me tomorrow,' she said. 'I've been in the dock before. It's . . . not like anything else. All I will have is myself.'

'I'll be there.'

'Good. I'm glad, but it doesn't change things. I have to know that they can't touch me, that they can put me in prison for a year or for two years and that it doesn't matter because I know I'm right. You see? No, you don't see.'

'I don't want you to be in prison. Surely you know that by now? I want to be with you.'

'Don't tell me that,' she said sharply, ' I don't want that in my mind tomorrow. That gives me something to lose. I don't want them to see they can hurt me.'

He let his arms drop, kissed her once more, chastely on the forehead, nodded and became deliberately businesslike.

'Right. I do see. OK, then. Tell your barrister that I'm prepared to testify. Do you want me to take you there?'

'No . . . thank you. Margo's going to take me. She's been through it lots of times herself. She knows what it's like.'

'I'll be there early in case the barrister wants to talk to me.'

'You'd really go through with that?'

'Of course I would.'

'There's no of course about it. Courts are horrible. They'd be sure to try to stop you giving evidence. It might get very nasty.'

'I'll do it.'

After that she had made the coffee, taken him into the back garden, sat next to him on a bench and explained her life to him, that whatever happened in court, this wasn't going to be a final victory or a final defeat – that the Stray would still be there and she would still feel just as bound to go on showing that she objected. It would be hard, she explained, for anyone else to share that life with her unless they, at some deep level, felt the same. They couldn't choose to share it just for the sake of her. That would only come between them. He listened mostly in silence, taking in what she said, determined all the more, by testifying, to put himself through some ordeal of purification for her.

Going in to his father's house this time was so different. There was no temptation now to look in drawers however much he wanted eventually to know all there was to know of the missing years. Mrs Thompson had left cheese, eggs, milk and bacon in the kitchen for him with a note. She must have made a special trip to the shop after they phoned. He was touched and knew that it was a sign of her regard for Sir Michael.

He made an omelette and ate it outside on a stone-paved patio watching the last of the sun over the edge of the moor. He phoned his answering machine at the flat and used the tone codes to record a new message, giving Sir Michael's number just in case, then he went into the study and sat down to get to know his father at second hand by dipping into his books. He was still there when midnight struck resonantly on the long-case clock and sleep called.

Mrs Thompson had prepared the same bed he'd used before. He threw the window open and leaned out, breathing in the scent of the high ground. The waning moon made the thinnest of crescents. The window looked down the long curving length of the drive and far away, through the trees at the end of it, he saw headlights.

They seemed to be stationary, right down there by the stone gateposts at the entrance from the road, a good half mile away. He watched them for a few seconds wondering idly what they could be doing, then stiffened as he saw the beams swing slightly, unmistakably, into the driveway. The next second, the lights blinked off leaving only spots of their after-image dancing, violet, in his eyes.

He leaned out, staring hard into the darkness, scanning his

eyes from side to side to make the most of his night vision. Then he heard it on the very fringe of his ears' range, but without any doubt – an engine, turning over slowly and the crunch of a wheel into a pothole. Whoever they were, they were coming up the drive with their lights off.

He went quickly downstairs and picked up the phone, unsure who to ring. The police? Heather at the Hall? It didn't matter. As soon as he picked it up he could hear an engaged tone, even before he'd tried to dial. That meant they had to be professionals and they must surely mean him harm. He pulled on a jacket and took a torch then he went outside into the yard, looking for a place where he could see them but they couldn't see him. He could hear engines clearly now and from where he was, unable to see the drive without risking silhouetting himself against the house in faint moonlight, he had no sense of how far off they were.

There were outbuildings across the yard. He opened a door, smelt cut wood and stumbled on the edge of the pile of split logs. Pulling the door almost closed behind him, he peered through the narrow gap.

A big vehicle, some kind of Japanese four-wheel-drive, crept quietly into the yard. The doors opened and men climbed out almost silently. Five of them. They split, fanning out around the house, and he shivered at the efficient look of it all. Two men stood by the door, waiting, giving time for the rest to get into position, then they opened it and one went inside.

He knew they would soon be back and would certainly check the sheds. He grabbed his chance while the man at the door was concentrating on what was going on inside the house. He pushed the door carefully open, trying to move it as slowly as he possibly could to keep the rusty hinges quiet. There was gravel outside. He moved sideways along the front wall of the shed, away from the house towards the bushes. His foot just tipped a larger stone – a tiny noise but it was enough. He saw the man at the door turn his head and abandoned caution, leaping forward to sprint across the lawn in front of him and hurdle the fence.

A voice behind him shouted, 'Down here! He's running for it!' and the accent was unmistakably American.

Beyond the fence was a descending stretch of meadow, the long grass getting in his way, threatening to trip him as he leapt through it. He shot a hurried glance over his shoulder as he ran, saw figures come running back to the car, heard the engine start. He angled to the right, to get as far from the drive as possible, searching his memory for any record of gateways, any clue as to whether or where they could get in to the field. They were trying, using their headlights now. The vehicle tore down the drive, turned halfway, lurched down a slope a few hundred yards away and into a field but in the lights he could see it was a separate field with a long fence cutting them off.

He veered more to the right, running for all he was worth, the bruising on his face starting to pulse. A crash of splintering wood came from behind and he knew they must have driven straight through the fence. Something dark loomed up ahead and a branch whipped painfully across his cheek. He slowed to a walk, feeling more branches and knew he was in a copse of trees. A wooded slope fell away to the right and he followed it down, knowing it was taking him further and further out of their sight. At the bottom, he jumped a stream, ran into a stone wall in the darkness and hurdled it to find himself in a rough track.

He ran again, blessing his fitness, putting the yards behind him with every second, pounding at the track with his feet as if he were running on the spot and slow, heavy danger could be moved a tiny bit further away with each impact. Three minutes and half a mile later, he ran out on to a tarmac lane, looked all around for signs of pursuit and turned in the direction that felt as though it should take him away from the house. A mile or so further on, he came to a church, dark against the sky and at first seeming to stand all by itself. When he got to it, he could see ahead, some way further down the road, the loom of a small cluster of houses. There was no sign of life in any of them but next to the church, in a lay-by, stood a telephone box.

Directory Enquiries took an age to answer but when they did, he asked for Tinderley Hall and memorized the number that the robot voice repeated for him. All he had in his pocket was a pound coin so he put it in the slot and dialled.

It rang for a long time before a man's voice answered and the voice was sleepy. 'Hello?'

'Tinderley Hall?'

'Yes?'

'I'm very sorry. Would you mind getting Heather Weston for me. It's an emergency.'

'She's asleep.'

'I know she is. I said it's an emergency.'

'Who is it?'

'Just tell her it's Johnny.'

It took a couple of minutes and she sounded shocked and a little muddled.

'Johnny? What on earth's wrong?'

'Listen. A bunch of guys arrived at the house. Americans. I got out. I've been running over the fields and—'

'OK, OK. Stop. Where are you?'

'Hang on.' He peered at the notice on the box. 'I can hardly see. There's no light in here. It looks like . . . Red something? Red Gate?'

'Red Gill?'

'Yes.'

'Are you by a church?'

'That's it.'

'OK, I know it. I'll be a few minutes.'

'Great.'

'I'll come in the van, the Hall's van, OK?'

He stood in the graveyard, out of sight behind the church wall, and waited. It didn't take her very long at all. It was barely five minutes before he heard the van coming. It drove round the corner and slowed to a stop with its headlights on him and he walked into the dazzle with relief, up to the driver's door, heard the other door open and realized far too late as his eyes adjusted that this was no van. This was a Mitsubishi Shogun, the same four-wheel-drive that he had last seen plunging into the field in pursuit of him. By that time, though, there was nowhere to go and the men who'd come round from the other side had his arm clamped up behind his back. The driver's window, close to his face, whirred down and a deep American voice said, 'Mr Kay. Please. Let us give you a ride.'

CHAPTER NINETEEN

'You're a hard man to help, Mr Kay.'

Johnny was in the back, between two large, silent men. The older man with the stubble hair and the deep voice had moved across to the front passenger seat and was leaning back, head turned, to talk to him.

'Helping seems a funny definition of what you've done so far.'

'You must have the wrong idea about us.'

'I've got a bent Cessna stuck on top of a ship that says your motives weren't strictly charitable.'

'You think that was us? Let me tell you 'bout that, seeing as I know the *real* story. Man called Clapham, Andy Clapham, bought some trick oil-industry containers from a guy named Tracey, down Portsmouth way last week. They call Tracey the Magazine Man.'

The man's voice was calm, almost amused. Johnny was impressed despite himself. 'And?'

'My guess is they put those containers in your tanks, full of water. You want proof then tell your CAA to look for traces of PIB dissolved in the fuel. PIB is Polyisobutylene. Dissolves slowly in petrol. That's what the containers are made from.'

'You seem to know a lot about it.'

'I've been back-tracking,' said the man coolly, 'I like to know what goes on.'

'Are you telling me you didn't do it?'

'You want to know who paid the bill for that gear?'

'Who?'

'Man called Sibley. Ivor Sibley. I guess you know him.'

They were bumping up a track on to open moorland and suddenly Johnny didn't like that one bit. This was the way he'd been taught to do it. Keep the subject co-operative, docile – until you're ready for the crunch.

'How could that be?'

'You don't know who your enemies are, do you, Johnny boy?'

The Shogun stopped. The man switched on the interior light. He was gaunt, with leathery-looking skin.

'Lend me your ears,' he said, and he pushed a cassette into the tape player.

Voices. Two voices trying to talk at once, then a woman's dominant voice cutting through.

'*I don't want bloody excuses. You screwed the whole thing up and that's the end of it.*'

'*He was incredibly lucky. If that ship hadn't been there, they wouldn't have stood a chance.*'

'*You're out of a job. I'm going to ring Calstock. I told you exactly what I wanted. Do you think it's been an easy decision for me? Do you? I told you I wanted a clean end to them, Michael and . . . and his son. That's the only thing you had to do.*'

His mother. His mother and Ivor Sibley. No doubt at all. He couldn't find any words to say.

The man looked almost sympathetic. It was impossible not to believe it. He remembered the look on his stepfather's face at the inquiry. That explains everything, he thought, even Maggie.

'You're not telling me this out of the kindness of your heart,' he said in a voice that came through an aching throat.

'You're quick. I'm not.'

'What then?'

'I got something you need and you got something I need. That could add up to a handy situation for both of us.'

'What have I got?' he asked, although he thought he knew the answer.

'Let me tell you first what I've got, Johnny. I've got the

means to spring your girl friend out of court tomorrow, to get her off scot-free.'

'You can get them to drop the charges?'

'I can do it.'

Johnny's heart lifted. 'And the price?'

The man's growl dropped even lower. 'Your eternal soul.' He laughed. 'No. Not that, just a little piece of paper.'

'What piece?'

'A piece that belongs to us. A piece you guys lifted. Kinda nice of me, don't you think? I mean I could be getting warrants and I'm offering you trades.'

'The details of the link to the BT tower.'

'What link?' The man laughed. 'Pure fantasy, Johnny.'

'BTRS. It said BTRS. British Telecom Raven Stones.'

'No. By-pass Trunking for Routine Servicing, that's what it means.'

'Come on. We flew over your digger on the moor.'

Mackeson's laugh sounded genuine. 'Anyone digging a hole on the moor, that's their business. Nothing down any hole out there belongs to us, that I can promise.'

'We've had an expert look at that plan. We know what it means.'

'Bullshit. Maybe an engineer was doodling, you know, day-dreaming. We don't have links like that. The piece of paper's liable to be misunderstood, I guess. That's why we want it back.'

'It's not mine to give.'

'It's not yours to keep.' The voice had a very harsh edge when the man wanted it to. 'You take the trade, your girlfriend walks. You say no, there's a dozen of the MOD's finest pinning you against a wall with a search warrant soon as you walk back in the house. You telling me it's not somewhere in your old man's house? Maybe in that desk of his? And all for a fantasy.'

'Some fantasy,' Johnny said. 'If it's a fantasy, how did you get that tape? How did you know where I was just now?'

'Hell, Johnny, don't be neolithic,' said the man lightly. 'Get your mind off buried cables and wire-taps. We got technology you would not believe.'

'How can I trust you?'

'Beauty of it is, you don't have to. I'll trust you. Bring it with you tomorrow. When she walks, you hand it over. OK? Only condition is, we never met. Ever. '

Johnny thought about it for a long time. He thought of his own bruising failure to arrange the deliverance he had prayed for. He knew Heather would not approve but he also knew it was the only thing in his power to do, and in the end he could see no other way. He nodded shortly. The man next to him seemed to ease down to a lower state of watchfulness and Johnny never knew how much worse it would have got if he'd chosen to shake his head instead.

'Spoken with the full-hearted eloquent grace of a gentleman, young Johnny.' The man turned to the driver. 'Home, James.'

They drove back in silence, Johnny going over and over it in his mind, but every time he tried to think about the deal, his mother's voice seemed to get in the way. *'I wanted a clean end to them . . .'*

The first thing he knew of the attack was when the Shogun's brakes came on hard as they turned into the end of his father's drive. A big vehicle had pulled across their bows. The doors were torn open, the two men in the front and the men either side of Johnny were yanked out into the dark. Johnny heard thuds, gasps. He sat there by himself in the dark not knowing which way to move.

Sibley? The final act? Propelled by that thought, he squirmed between the front seats, got in behind the steering wheel, started up and reached out to pull the door closed. A hand grabbed his arm from outside and he wrenched it away then Heather's voice shouted. 'Stop, Johnny. It's us. It's OK.'

He let out pent-up breath, 'For God's sake,' he said, 'what's happening?'

'It's OK now,' she repeated. 'We've got them.'

He saw in the headlights four bodies lying on the ground with people kneeling on them. Boys in overalls, some with shaven heads, some with earrings. He got down and Heather rushed to him, hugged him.

'What did they do to you?' she said. 'We couldn't find you so we came back here.'

'No, you've got it wrong,' he replied faintly. 'They're trying to help.'

'But aren't these people NSA?'

'Yes. Look, really, let them up.'

'I don't understand.'

'The plane, Heather. It wasn't them. It was my bloody mother and Ivor Sibley's lot. I've heard a tape of my mother discussing it. There's no doubt, I promise.'

Reluctantly, at her command, the boys let the battered Americans get up.

'Jeezus,' said the leather-faced man as he brushed himself off, 'who are these guys, the SAS Cub Scouts?'

'Young people at risk,' said Heather distractedly.

'*They're* at risk,' he said 'you sure you got that right?'

'Just go,' she said.

'Yes ma'am. I'll say goodnight.'

When the Shogun had left, Heather rounded up the boys and got them in the van.

'It was all I could think of doing,' she said, 'I thought they might have killed you.'

'You were amazing. Thank you. Those boys are quite something.'

'I'll get in terrible trouble if anyone finds out,' she said. 'I chose the toughest nuts we've got.'

'Do you need any help to get them back?'

'No,' she said, 'it's better if it's just me. They'll do what I ask them. They were dead keen to help out.'

He kissed her but there was a chorus of cheers from the van and they stepped apart again.

'There's just no time,' she said, 'I must get them back, but I have to know what it's all about.'

'It can wait until tomorrow,' he said, 'I'll tell you tomorrow.'

CHAPTER TWENTY

It was a request from the Base Commander, a good-luck breakfast, he called it, for Chief Inspector Reed and Sergeant Hayter. Reed was suspicious. It wasn't at all the sort of thing the Americans usually did. When the Commander asked him to come ten minutes before Hayter, he smelt a rat. When he found Ray Mackeson there as well, the rat turned fetid.

'Mr Reed,' said the Commander, 'I know it's late in the day to say this, but we've done a re-evaluation of the parameters of this case and frankly, our opinion is heading south on this one.'

Reed raised his eyebrows to cover the fact he had not the slightest clue what the Commander meant.

'We don't feel that the er . . . the risks inherent in this hearing justify proceeding.'

'I'm not sure I follow you.'

'Well, come on now, Commander. I don't want to get into policy issues with you, but you gotta know we have some major planning hoops to jump through with the local population here. We don't think that a prosecution right now is going to help with that.'

Reed felt a red flush start to suffuse his cheeks. Steady, he thought to himself, hold on there.

'It's a little bit late for that,' he said.

'Things change. You gotta be flexible.'

'Sergeant Hayter was the subject of a serious assault,' said Reed, who had come to the scene after the event and had no reason to suspect otherwise. 'If the Weston woman wins this case, he is liable to be prosecuted himself.'

'That's a separate issue.'

Reed was on his feet before the cautious part of him could lasso the raging bull. His fist slammed on the Commander's desk. The Commander flinched. Mackeson merely gave a sardonic smile.

'This is not in your jurisdiction,' Reed said. 'This is a case brought by the Crown Prosecution Service, the *British* Crown Prosecution Service, on behalf of us, the *British* Ministry of Defence Police, who are charged with the difficult job of protecting you. You have no say in the matter. *I* have my men's future safety to consider.'

There was a silence.

'Mr Reed,' the Commander said, 'we could go through channels on this one but the case starts in three hours and I guess I thought you could . . .'

'I can't.'

Mackeson and the Commander looked at each other.

'OK,' the Commander said, 'get Hayter in here. Let's eat some breakfast.'

By the time Hayter walked in, the Americans were all smiles.

'Big day, Sergeant Hayter,' said the Commander.

'Normal line of duty, sir,' said Hayter in what Reed always thought of as his sergeant major's voice. 'Open and shut, I'd say. It'll be good to see that . . . er, that woman locked up.'

'You better get your strength up. We got sausage, eggs, hotcakes. You want coffee? OJ? We got tea in case?'

Johnny sat high up in the public gallery, waiting, fretting while the court below slowly filled up with the drab-clothed servants of justice. They all seemed to have urgent reasons to talk in little knots among the ranks of light oak benches but their conversations were broken by smiles which seemed, unnervingly, to imply that there was a social life which was more important to them than the temporary business they were here to transact. Heather's barrister, Lisa Gardiner, came in clutching a large pile of files.

* * *

He'd parked in the big car park under the mound of Clifford's Tower at nine o' clock and walked across the wide, open square to York Crown Court. There'd been a camera crew at the bottom of the steps and he'd made sure his face was averted out of sheer habit.

Jo, Margo and three other women were just inside the doors by the security desk.

Jo saw him first. 'Johnny! Morning, Superman.'

The other women turned, breaking into smiles. Margo gave him a round of applause. He smiled back and shrugged.

'Where's Heather?'

'Through the doorway, right then left. She's in the waiting room with her brief.'

He'd gone in, seen them sitting, drinking coffee, talking earnestly. He'd stood there until Heather noticed him and introduced him.

'Have you thought about what I said?'

Heather smiled, distracted. 'About what?'

'About my going into the witness box.'

'Oh.'

'Well?'

The barrister answered, 'I don't think it would work, Mr Kay.'

'I'm Johnny.'

'Johnny. Even if we could get you into the box – and I think there'd be massive objections as soon as we tried it, I don't think we could use you.'

'I don't see why not.'

She looked at him, summing him up. 'Let's have a go, then. I'm the prosecuting barrister, OK?'

'OK.'

She spoke very quietly. 'Mr Kay, in your previous employment, did you have any direct experience of the Ramsgill Stray base?'

'No, but I did with Chelten—'

'Please just answer the question. Before you recently trespassed into the base with the accused, had you ever been there?'

'No.'

'Have you ever, during your alleged time with the Security Service, been given any briefing on the activities carried out at Ramsgill Stray?'

'No.'

'Mr Kay, are you by any chance in love with the defendant, Miss Weston?'

His jaw dropped. Heather's head lifted sharply to look with an odd expression at Lisa Gardiner. He and Heather avoided looking at each other.

The silence hung there, crackling.

'You see what I mean?' said the barrister, and she smiled sadly.

Now he looked down at the court, wondering what unforeseeable events were about to unfold. The document from the Stray had been where he had known it would be, in the roll-top desk in his father's study. This time he thought his father wouldn't have minded the search. Now it was inside the lining of his jacket, where it had been before – a tiny and probably hopeless precaution against a double cross. He'd been very much on the alert all the way to court, looping around in big detours to avoid the obvious direct route, watching every other car for signs of possible interception, half expecting to find himself arrested at the court itself where they knew he would have the document on him. Nothing happened. Whatever game the Americans were playing, it wasn't that one.

Judge Belmont-Adams seemed exotically dressed, dark blue robes, violet sleeves, a red sash and a white cravat. He had a simple fuzzy wig. Johnny was looking steeply down on him from the public gallery, up to one side. It was a perspective that slightly diminished the grandeur of the court. The top of the canopy projecting over the judge's head was in the course of reconstruction. Rough, unfinished boarding was visible only from above and on top of it some workman had left a crumpled cigarette packet.

Johnny had a moment to look around as the judge brought out a brown leather pencil case from which he took a wooden ruler and a bottle of Quink. He began to rule columns in a green book. Johnny wondered what they were, 'For' and 'Against' perhaps.

Wigs were everywhere below. Some of them looked infinitely old and dusty as though millennia of bookworms might be nesting in them.

Lisa Gardiner was not the only woman. There was a junior on the prosecution side, got up in that odd way that judges have been able to impose on the females of the law – dark make-up, strapped in, severe drawn-back hair. The sexiness of the high-class dominatrix – the price of being allowed to play the legal game.

The clerk of the court, in front of and some way below the judge's bench, stood up, climbed on to his chair and turned to have a whispered conversation with him.

Then, suddenly and sickeningly, 'Call Heather Weston.'

It came as a shock to see Heather brought into the dock, flanked by guards from Group 4. Johnny thought how disconcertingly different she looked, that attractive, generous face now focused and intent as if an alternative set of muscles had been brought into play. She glanced up at the gallery, waved at Margo and the group of her supporters gathered at one end. She went on looking at them, searching and then her gaze found Johnny, separately, off to one side. She gave him a little nod and he put his thumb up. She looked sad suddenly and turned her face away.

There was no jury yet. Johnny believed he would at any moment hear the prosecution dramatically announce they were not proceeding but instead an argument started between the barristers and the judge about the evidence. Dr Beevor's statement lay at the heart of it. Lisa Gardiner explained the background of their inability to bring Dr Beevor to court, even bringing in the plane crash. The prosecuting barrister, Alan Reynolds, refused to accept the documents without the opportunity to cross-examine Dr Beevor. The judge agreed with him, looked at his watch, scribbled a note and said, 'Let the jury panel be brought in.'

A line of men and women filed in to the benches at the back

of the court and were called by name, one at a time, into the witness box.

Johnny looked at them and his heart sank further. They all looked like pillars of society. Two of the women could just have had mild Liberal tendencies on a good day. The others looked like *Sun*-reading Tories. There were three large short-haired middle-aged men, all in leather jackets.

Why let it go this far, thought Johnny? If they're dropping it, why let the jury in? He looked all around hoping for he knew not what. A glimpse of the American? A clue to coming salvation? There was no sign of anything to interrupt the slow juggernaut of the law. All he could see was Jo in her chair, tucked away in a corner of the main court down below – a privilege allowed because of the lack of wheelchair access to the gallery.

He became aware of the words now being spoken, the dry legal bullets aimed one by one at Heather's body down in the dock.

'. . . that on that date, at Ramsgill Stray Station, she did assault George Arthur Hayter, thereby occasioning grievous bodily harm. Prisoner in the dock, how do you plead?'

'Not guilty.' Heather's voice sounded strong.

Johnny's heart went out to her. One of the leather-jacketed men in the jury sniffed loudly.

The prosecution opened. The barrister injected just sufficient righteous contempt into his voice that Johnny, even though he knew it was simply a professional trick, felt a strong urge to go down and warn him to watch the way he spoke.

'. . . contrary to Section 47 of the Offences Against the Person Act 1861, she did on that day violently strike Sergeant George Hayter, a long-serving and loyal member of the Ministry of Defence Police, with a weapon, namely a section of timber . . .'

He droned on, laying out the bones of the prosecution case. Johnny felt despair rise. He'd been tricked, he knew that now with complete certainty. Heather would go to prison. He would be stopped on leaving the court, stopped when they knew he must have the papers on him. They'd be sure to find them.

He felt the papers, stiff through the lining of his jacket. What could he do? Give them to one of the other women? Would that help? They might all be searched.

'. . . the incident took place at the Ministry of Defence's base at Ramsgill Stray . . .'

The Ministry of Defence? Who was this man trying to kid?

'. . . a base whose work is covered by the strictures of the Official Secrets Act but whose function is absolutely central to our national security. Miss Weston is no stranger to the base. On at least one hundred and twenty-three occasions, she has gained access to it in order to . . .'

Johnny looked away and scanned the court again. There was nothing anywhere to suggest the slightest hope. The air was thick and hot up in the gallery. He yawned, mused, fell into a muggy day-dream of being loved.

It was Sergeant Hayter's arrival in the witness box that brought him snapping back to the horrid reality of a present in which one of his dearest was in hospital and the other was in the dock.

He looked at Hayter, fascinated, as the policeman took the oath and confirmed his identity. The man was red in the face but he looked horribly calm and composed.

Reynolds led him through the events of that day.

'Where were you at ten o'clock that morning?'

'I was in the office.'

'That would be the MOD Police office inside the main gate of Ramsgill Stray?'

'That's correct.'

'Were you called on the radio?'

'Yes. At ten oh five I received a call advising me that Miss Weston had been spotted at the entrance to bunker nine and requesting me to attend urgently.'

'What did you do?'

'I got in a van with PC Hoskin and drove straight there.'

'And at what time did you arrive?'

'Within two or three minutes of the call.'

'On arrival, what did you observe?'

'I saw the accused standing in the foyer to the bunker.'

'Was she known to you?'

Sergeant Hayter snorted and looked at the jury, who seemed to be hanging on his every word. 'I have had occasion to remove Miss Weston from the base on many, many occasions. She breaks in all the time. If you ask me, she's obsessed by—'

'Objection,' said Lisa Gardiner.

'Would you confine yourself to fact rather than conjecture, Sergeant Hayter,' said the judge mildly.

'What action did you then take, Sergeant?'

'I sent PC Hoskin off to make sure there were none of the other women in the vicinity.'

'This left you and Miss Weston alone?'

'Yes.'

'And what happened then?'

'I turned away for a moment and when I turned back she had a large piece of timber in her hands and was swinging it at my head. It hit me across the nose.'

'Breaking your nose and causing considerable bruising to your left eye?'

Hayter suddenly seemed under strain. His face grew redder. There was a sheen of sweat on his brow.

'Yes. I staggered back, saying something like, "Now then, there's no need for that, Miss Weston," and she swung it at me again. I had blood in my eyes and I couldn't see very well. I tried to protect myself. I was flailing around with my arms. I think I must have contacted Miss Weston as she was lunging at me again because she seemed to trip and—' Hayter broke off and stared at Heather for some time. Johnny wondered whether he could possibly be feeling any embarrassment. It seemed unlikely.

The barrister prompted him gently. 'Yes?'

Hayter's voice sounded thicker. 'And she went back against the wall, didn't she? Hit her head on it.'

'She accidentally hit her head?'

There was another odd silence.

'Serve her bloody right, I say,' Hayter declared loudly.

The judge's eyebrows went up to meet the fringe of his wig,

putting lines in his forehead that made him look exactly like a Hogarth print. The prosecuting barrister jumped in.

'Sergeant Hayter, we all understand, I'm sure, that you were very shocked by this attack and in considerable pain, but you bore no personal animosity towards the accused, did you?'

'Animosity?' Hayter seemed to have trouble with the word. His head was hanging low and he was shaking it slowly from side to side, looking at Heather from under his lowered brow. He spoke slowly in a fuddled voice, 'I hate the fucking bitch.'

There was a buzz in the court-room. Some of the jurors looked shocked. The judge banged his gavel.

'SERGEANT HAYTER. I would remind you to keep your language clean in my court room.'

'Fuck you, four-eyes,' said the Sergeant, getting to his feet swaying, 'I'm going to sort that tart out once and for all.'

'Sergeant Hayter, please sit down and compose yourself,' said the barrister desperately, but to no effect. The Sergeant turned and got up out of the witness-box. The usher, an old man with grey hair, went valiantly to stop him. Hayter shook off his restraining arm and swung a fist, sending the usher collapsing backwards over the jury bench with a horrid cracking sound.

The judge was bellowing. Two of the jurors stood up. The prosecuting barrister had his arms up, flapping at the oncoming policeman, and took another fist full in the face. Sweat was pouring off Hayter. Johnny looked at the expression of fear on Heather's face and realized there was no one left between her and Hayter who could be relied on to stop him. There was pandemonium right through the court.

He swung himself over the rail of the public gallery, hung by his fingers for a second above the long drop then let himself fall to land hard on the floor below, rolling with the impact.

He reached Hayter as he got to the dock. He was yelling incoherently now, clearing people out of his way with wild haymakers: One Group 4 guard was sent crashing backwards. Heather, white faced, was trying to get past the other one, who stood dithering, caught between preventing his prisoner leaving and getting out of the way of the oncoming madman.

Johnny jumped on Hayter's back, got an arm round his throat and tried to bring him down. Hayter twisted and bucked like a fairground ride, banging him backwards into the stout woodwork at the edge of the dock so that his ribs flared with sharp pain.

That was when the jury finally came into its own. The three men in leather jackets decided they'd seen enough to make up their minds. One of them cut Hayter's feet out from under him and he fell with Johnny still on his back. The others piled on top so Johnny found himself crushed and struggling for breath until a policeman, summoned from outside, got handcuffs on. Even then it took them all to force Hayter, struggling every inch of the way, down the steps to the cells.

It took five minutes to get the court back into some sort of order again. The prosecuting barrister had a bloody nose and a cut lip, the usher had been taken away for attention, one Group 4 guard had a swollen eye and the judge was looking very pale and breathing extremely rapidly. The jurors in the leather jackets sat there looking smug as if they'd had Hayter's measure all along, pleased to be the heroes of the hour. Johnny had gone back up to the gallery, nursing his ribs. Heather looked dazed.

The judge sounded as though he was advancing into new and uncertain territory.

'Mr Reynolds,' he said, 'I think it best if I give the jury the opportunity at this stage to consider whether they wish to hear any more of this case. I take it you have no objection?'

The barrister, leaning on the table in front of him for support, merely waved a weak hand in assent.

'Members of the jury,' said the judge, 'you have witnessed a most unusual and shocking scene. Some of you indeed have played a valiant part in restraining the witness. It would seem that you have been given the most direct evidence conceivable that Sergeant Hayter is a man prone to violent and uncontrollable temper and that it is not possible for you now to take his evidence in this case seriously. Will you now go to the jury-room and consider whether you wish to hear any more evidence in this case or whether you are now in a position to find the accused not guilty?'

It took them under two minutes and the women in the gallery broke into cheers that the judge seemed unable to bring himself to halt. Heather walked from the dock, looking up at them and then at Johnny and only then did he start to understand.

He went down the steps from the gallery and out to the front of the court. Diagonally across the square stood a big four-wheel-drive – the Shogun. He looked towards it and an arm waved out of the open window.

Unsuccessful experiments, Sir Greville had told the inquiry. Rage had been discontinued, he'd said. The Americans had bought Chempropa.

He walked up to the vehicle and looked in at Ray Mackeson, alone in the driver's seat.

'How was the show?' said the American.

'Violent.'

'Your girl friend got off?'

'Yes.'

'Guess you got something for me, then?'

'It was you?'

'Hell, I just made sure the guy had a good breakfast.'

'Rage? You gave him Rage?'

'I gave him orange juice. You complaining?'

Johnny reached into the lining of his jacket, brought out the papers and handed them over.

Mackeson looked at them. 'No copies?'

'No copies.'

'Don't sound like that. It's simpler this way.'

'You're going to sell that horrible stuff?'

'Not me, son. Anyways, your stepdaddy was a little free with the truth there. That stuff has side effects like you wouldn't believe. You want some fun? Go back and see what the Sergeant's doing now.' Mackeson broke off and looked past Johnny. 'Uh oh,' he said, 'your girl friend's coming looking for you. Time I was gone.'

Johnny turned as Mackeson sped away. Heather was walking towards him.

He ran to meet her, stopped, held his hands out smiling, but she stepped back, staring at him with an expression he didn't like at all.

'That was the American. The one from last night.'

'Yes.'

'You gave him something. What did you give him, Johnny?'

'I did it for you, Heather. They had us over a barrel. It was the only thing I could do.'

'You did it for *me*? I don't remember you asking me.'

'There was no chance.'

'There was this morning.'

'I had to say yes or no last night.'

'Yes or no to what, Johnny? What did they do?' Then she too got it. 'So that wasn't just Hayter blowing his cool.'

'I think they must have helped him.'

'Rage?'

He nodded.

'Oh, God,' she said, 'and you gave that man the plans we found?'

'There wasn't any other way. It was the only way I could stop you being put in prison. It was worth it, Heather.'

Her voice was very cold. 'No, it was not,' she said, 'that was your decision, not mine. That piece of paper gave us the chance to prove what Ramsgill Stray is doing for the first time ever and you gave it away.'

'For you.'

'No, not for me, for you. Because you think you want to be with me. Don't you see, you stupid spy? I would happily have served two years for those plans and what we could have done with them. You didn't have the courage, damn you, so you decided for me.'

She turned on her heel and began to walk off and he found himself speaking in a new voice.

'Wait,' he said, 'come with me. We'll settle this right now.'

She stopped and looked back at him, startled. 'What do you mean?'

'I mean I gave away your plan. That was just a piece of paper, Heather. I'm going to put that right – put it beyond all doubt. I want you to meet me on the moor in . . . let's see, what's the time now?'

It took him two hours with Yellow Pages, a street map and a credit card but at the end of that time a pick-up truck carrying a heavy load hidden under a tarpaulin was bumping along a rough track on Blubberhouses Moor. Every lurch sent little jabs of pain through Johnny's chest as he squinted out of the windscreen at the bulk of the Raven Stones tower. He saw Heather's little Citroën ahead and pulled up next to it.

'Here?' he said, winding down the window.

She looked in and it was like a stranger's gaze – the curiosity there but still swamped by the anger. 'Fifty yards ahead.'

He drove on a little further and she followed on foot.

He got out, looked at the ground in front and squinted back the way he'd come then he knelt, inspected the marks on the mossy grass and nodded.

Heather walked up behind and stood silently.

'This is it,' he said, 'I'll unload.'

He went round to the back of the truck, undid the ties and took the cover off the little Kubota excavator sitting in the back on its miniature tracks. Letting down the tailboard, he pulled heavy metal ramps out and set them in position, then swung himself up and sat in the driving seat with more assurance than he felt and pressed the starter.

The digger inched its way down the ramp. The instructions he'd been given at the hire centre had been basic and it took him a few minutes to get the hang of the hydraulic controls. All the time, he kept one eye on the track behind them and the loom of the Stray's domes in the distance, expecting at any moment to see a line of police vans, blue lights flashing, coming to stop him. His ribs were hurting like hell.

He was now beyond all reason. He wanted to settle the matter for its own sake. What Heather thought of it all became almost irrelevant. He tugged the lever and the shovel bit down into the turf. He registered in a detached way that there were no surveillance cameras on the tower. Come to that there was no official reason for the Americans to be interested in the tower and if they turned up out of the blue it would be a bit of a give-away.

In fifteen minutes, he had dug a ragged cross trench stretching twenty yards at right angles to the invisible line connecting the tower and the Stray, as near as they could judge to the spot where Heather had first seen the other digger. It was, for the most part, about a yard wide and four feet deep. He couldn't go any deeper than that – the bucket of the digger was scraping on solid rock.

He switched off and the clatter of the Kubota's engine was replaced by the singing of a lark.

'There's nothing there,' he said, 'after all that, there's bloody well nothing there.' He climbed out and his ribs grated so that he gasped for breath. 'It was just some bloody fantasy, wasn't it?' He realized he was shouting.

'Stop it,' said Heather.

'There's no cable,' he went on. 'BTRS? By-pass bloody Trunk Reserve or whatever the man said. Just bloody fantasy.' His chest hurt so badly that he sank down to his knees, almost pitching forward into the trench. His head was down, close to the edge of the ditch. She said something else but it was just a vague far-off backdrop to the hammering in his head and the pain in his chest.

Then he saw it.

In the exposed side of the ditch was a square patch of a different colour, measuring about three feet by three feet. He reached in and pulled at it. It was looser and there were bits of root and stalk all torn up and mixed into it. It was the cross section of another trench, a trench that had been filled-in.

'Heather,' he said, 'look.'

There was no answer.

He clambered to his feet, looked round, all too slowly, just in time to see, fifty yards off, the door of her Citroën close and a blue haze curl up from the exhaust as she started the engine.

'Heather!' he yelled but it was too late. The car was bumping and swaying off down the track.

Driven by fury and despair, he started the digger again and went back to work at right angles to his first effort. It was easier. This time there were no tough roots to snare the bucket. In a quarter of an hour, he'd dug fifteen yards, making a giant cross on the moor, scooping out the loose in-fill of this earlier trench.

When he finished he looked along its rifle barrel length, pointing straight at the white domes of the Stray. Turning to look the other way, he saw it line up perfectly on the base of the tower.

'It *was* here,' he said aloud but there was no one but the larks to hear him. 'They must have been taking it out.'

The plan. They'd wanted it back so it must have meant something. There had been a link. There must still be a link but it wasn't one you could dig up.

Mackeson's voice came back to him. 'Don't be neolithic,' he said, 'we got technology you wouldn't believe.'

CHAPTER TWENTY-ONE

He left the open trench to mark the spot – and painfully, he took the digger back. Then he drove south because there was nowhere else to drive to. The old man in Southampton Hospital was all he had left from the wreckage of his old life and the frost-nipped bud of the new one.

He drove badly, impeded by grief and by the physical pain in his chest, which in the end forced him to stop at an anonymous Traveller's Lodge Motel, gulp aspirin and lie miserably in bed until low-grade hot-headed sleep crept up on him.

In the morning his chest was stiff and red all down one side and he felt as woebegone as he could ever remember, looking ahead at darkness where a bright future had seemed to beckon. He drove on slowly, uncomfortable even when he changed gear. The M1 seemed rougher than usual. The M25 was a tedious nightmare and in his mind, many hours clocked up before he was on the M3.

At Southampton Hospital, they looked at him as if he was a candidate for the emergency room.

'I've come to see Sir Michael Parry,' he said, leaning on the desk.

'Are you all right?' said the woman facing him, concerned.

'Oh . . . yes.'

She phoned, spoke then put her hand over the receiver and turned to him. 'Who shall I say it is?'

'I'm his son.'

'You can go up.'

His father looked much better, smiling at him as he went in and then showing a sudden expression of deep concern.

'John! You're as white as a sheet.'

He sat down in the chair next to the bed. 'I'm OK. I got a few bruises yesterday in court. I don't know if you heard?'

'The whole thing. It's been on all the news and in the papers. Isn't it marvellous?'

'Well, up to a point.'

Sir Michael looked at him understandingly. 'Tell me.'

'Heather.'

'Go on.'

'She's . . . she won't have anything to do with me. I fixed it with the Americans. I didn't have a choice. There wasn't any other way of getting her off. I thought they'd just drop charges but they gave Hayter that Rage stuff. That's why he did what he did.'

'I know. I had a call or two about it.'

'The stuff works, for God's sake. All we've succeeded in doing is helping Sir Greville sell it to the Americans.'

'Up to a point.' He seemed to be suppressing a laugh.

'What do you mean?'

'Sergeant Hayter spent the rest of the afternoon listing every single wrong-doing of his long and nasty life. That's the effect it has. The York police have a very, very long statement, I gather. Anyway, I've made sure the right people know what's going on. I think there'll be a lot of pressure coming the way of GKC, and the Americans, for that matter.'

'Oh . . .'

'So tell me, what was your side of the deal?'

'I gave the Americans some documents about Ramsgill Stray that they wanted back.'

'Oh, dear; and Heather didn't want that.'

'No. I can understand. I should have asked her but there wasn't a chance.'

'Poor Johnny. She's very important to you, isn't she?'

'Oh, yes.'

'You have to see it from her point of view. She's known

you as Johnny Kennedy the pilot, then Johnny Kay the spy. It can't have been easy.'

'I'd like to try something else now,' he said, 'if it's all right with you. I'd like to try being John Parry, the person.'

'That sounds well worth trying,' said a voice behind him and he turned as Heather stepped out of the bathroom.

'Let's forget that Johnny Kay and the things he did,' she said. 'John Parry sounds a much nicer person.'

He got up with difficulty. 'I found where the cables were,' he said. 'They've taken them away.'

'Later,' she said.

Their arms went round each other and she squeezed him hard before she had time to take in his white face. The pain of his broken ribs flared white hot and he sagged unconscious to the floor.

EPILOGUE

There was a sequel . . .

Lanie Gerow was happier. So maybe Puritan Bluff, Idaho, wasn't Philly or Baltimore but it wasn't Ramsgill Stray either and above all it wasn't an Agency town. Lanie and Pacman had what felt like their final showdown back in England. He accused her of violating trust, of risking his position. She said she wasn't going to go on being no goddam stooge for no goddam spook like Mackeson. She said she was up to here with the Agency and she was leaving and she'd meant it. Pacman went all quiet on her then and she felt a little bit sorry for him but she wasn't about to back down. Whichever way it was, her message got through. The next day he came back grinning from ear to ear. She didn't make it easy for him.

'You wanna know something?'

'No.'

'Go on, baby. I got something to tell you.'

'Only thing I want to know is when we're flying out.' She sniffed.

'Thursday week.'

'Don't mess me around, Pacman.'

'I ain't.'

'So where is it? Alaska?'

With a big smirk, he said 'Idaho'.

She just stared at him. Couldn't stop herself.

'I said Idaho, doll. You hear me?'

'I never heard of no Agency postings in Idaho.'

'This ain't Agency, baby.'

'You leaving, Pacman? Leaving the Agency?' She didn't dare hope it.

'Yeah, well, not quite. Got me a secondment. You and me, baby, we're gonna be civilians for a while, maybe a long while.'

And so it was. He didn't talk about the job at the Facility and she didn't ask. It was enough to know he was out of it, away from the bugs, away from Ray Mackeson.

Had she known, only half of that was right.

Lanie was out doing the shopping in downtown Puritan Bluff, looking up at the Salmon River Mountains looming behind the Safeway parking lot. It was her dance class night and she'd found a Lycra one-piece at Twinkletoes which did all the right things for her. The clouds were blowing away from the mountains. Maybe they'd go to the lake for the weekend after all. Pacman was so relaxed these days, getting on with Billy, showing him how to fly-fish. He'd even grown his hair longer. It was different in Idaho with no Agency.

Pacman wasn't thinking about fishing or anything like it. Pacman was glued to a phone and trying to stop himself climbing the wall. Ray Mackeson, now back at Fort Meade, Maryland, was on the other end and Pacman was giving him some of the worst news of his life.

'He's out there now, Ray. I mean, what the hell we gonna do? Goddam company's screwed up on security. I told 'em. You know I told 'em. What did they think? This was some kind of cold cure? I told them, these guinea pigs gonna turn into grizzly bears. You gotta build a strong enough cage to hold 'em in.'

Mackeson, safely away from it, was annoyingly calm. 'Pacman. Calm down. No one's blaming you. One man's out, that's all. You got the National Guard coming and the Feds. They'll fix it and I'll tell you what they're going to be saying after.'

Lanie was opening the trunk when the white Chevy Malibu came into the parking lot and she stopped to look at it because of the way the tyres were squealing with the speed.

Puritan Bluff was a pretty safe town normally. Drivers who drove like that should be ashamed of themselves with kids around. As if to make the point a family came out the door of the Ribs Shack. Three kids, Mom, Pop, Grandma, the kids unhooking one of them shaggy English sheepdogs from where it had been patiently waiting, a picture of small-town American domesticity. That should show the Chevy driver this ain't the place for screaming tyres, she thought.

The Malibu driver saw them all right. He swung the wheel hard over, put his foot on the gas and went into the middle of them like a giant bowling ball.

Lanie stared, rooted to the spot. Pop, Grandma and two of the kids took the impact, hurled apart in a human shell-burst. The dog went under one wheel and came out with a red woolly puddle where its head had been. Mom and the remaining kid, a teenage boy in a Nintendo T-shirt, stood there untouched, one each side – the goal posts – and they each began to scream. The Malibu slewed to a halt. The driver got out, a fit looking man of forty or so but for the veins standing out in his neck and the high-blood-pressure flush. He reached into the car, brought out a stubby-looking weapon and more or less cut them in two with a shrill, crashing burst of fire.

Then he looked across at Lanie.

Her knees lost all their strength as the gun came round towards her and she sank down behind the open trunk lid, knowing there was no protection, that he had only to take a few paces to the side to have her in full view again, but her body could do nothing.

The first police car crew saved her, but not themselves. They'd been chasing the Malibu driver half across town from the Facility, past five other similar scenes of savage annihilation. The first police car took forty rounds of nine-millimetre through the windscreen and neither the driver nor his passenger played any further part in it. The second car was unmarked, came in through the back way but did little better. The driver took a throat wound and slammed left into a delivery truck. The passenger bounced his head off the windshield and slumped down below the dash.

By then cars were coming in from all directions but it was the chopper that got him, spraying the Malibu with such a lethal concentration of fire that the ricochets injured three policemen and the manager of the garden store, who'd unwisely come to see what was happening. That was considered at the time a low price for making sure that Wayne Spargo, the Malibu driver, was well and truly dead.

Lanie Gerow didn't get her weekend trip to the lake. She was in shock at the hospital, among the few other victims left alive by Spargo's efficient trail of destruction. Pacman was at her side more or less constantly.

'Why did he do it?' she kept asking.

'Who knows, baby?' he said. 'The news says he was an airman, on leave or something like that. Went crazy. Says they were considering dismissing him on medical grounds before that.'

It was just what Mackeson had told him they'd be saying. From the point of view of his liaison job at the Facility, he was heartily pleased there was no mention of any involvement by Wayne Spargo in the Facility's research programme. Only thing was, with Spargo dead, who knew whether it still had the side-effects?

AUTHOR'S NOTE

National Security Agency Field Station Ramsgill Stray does not exist. However any reader interested enough to head for its supposed location may pass on the way, a few miles to the west of Harrogate on the A59 to Skipton, a large array of white golf balls marked on the maps only as 'Menwith Hill Camp'. This is NSA Field Station F83, the largest of nine or ten similar American installations in Britain. Whenever it has to be referred to (usually when one of a group of remarkable women peace protesters has made another trip inside and been arrested for their pains) Menwith Hill is described vaguely as a NATO or MOD installation. It is not. Its purpose is to bug communications and although MOD Police really do guard the large number of American personnel there, its agenda is entirely American. It can certainly listen to our international phone calls, faxes and domestic mobile phones. Duncan Campbell and Linda Melvern alleged in a *New Statesman* article that Menwith Hill did have a covert link into the BT system enabling it to listen in on our domestic phones.

The late Bob Cryer, Labour MP for Bradford South, devoted a lot of time to trying to get the status of Menwith Hill discussed in the House. In his last speech on the subject in the Commons, he said: 'The fact that domestic intrusion exists at Menwith Hill Station is surely shown by the fact that British Telecom has a thirty-two-thousand telephone line capacity from Hunter's Stone Post Office tower along the B6451 to Otley. There cannot be thirty-two-thousand telephones on the base in simultaneous use; that defies credibility. The Hunter's

Stone Post Office tower happens to be a pivotal point of more than one million route miles of microwave connections installed in Britain. The cable from Hunter's Stone Post Office tower runs directly to Menwith Hill. There has never been any parliamentary authority to allow this serious and unwarranted intrusion into our telephone network.'

Sadly Bob Cryer was killed in a car accident in spring, 1994.

Lindis Percy, Annie Rainbow and other campaigners have been arrested on many occasions at Menwith Hill, succeeding in the High Court in establishing that by-laws used to arrest them were illegal.

Even in America, the NSA (the largest of the American security organizations) is little known to the public. I am indebted to the writer James Bamford, whose excellent book on the NSA, *The Puzzle Palace* is published by Penguin. For some incomprehensible reason, however, it is at the moment only available on the American market.

I am also indebted to Mike Briggs at Leeds/Bradford airport and to Mike Sullivan for painstaking care in helping me get the flying details right and in Mike Brigg's case for a memorable flight.

Chemists at Shell and BP helped me with details of PIBs. In case anyone gets the urge to sabotage a plane, I have left out one important detail.

Finally there is Rage. This is an extrapolation from two starting points. Some researchers believe one or two food additives may be responsible for much more severe behavioral disorders than is currently officially accepted. At the same time a great deal of research effort is going into what is euphemistically called 'non-lethal weaponry'. This extends from lasers that blind troops to chemicals that can affect the behaviour of fighting forces.